I0630401

BARRIE HILL REUNION

LISETTE BRODEY

SABERLEE BOOKS

Published by:

SABERLEE BOOKS

Los Angeles, CA
United States of America

Copyright @2017, Lisette Brodey
Published: October 2017

All rights reserved. In accordance with the U.S. Copyright Law of 1976, the scanning, uploading, or electronic sharing of any parts of this book without the permission of the publisher is unlawful piracy and theft of the author's intellectual property. If you would like any additional information regarding this book, please contact the publisher at saberleebooks@yahoo.com.

Copy Editing: Laura J. Daly, D. L. Savvides
Cover design & illustration: Charles M. Roth

ISBN-13: 978-0-9909606-5-2 (e-book)
ISBN-13: 978-0-9909606-6-9 (paperback)

To my brother, Kenneth Brodey,
for believing in this story for all these many years ...
for your tireless support, enthusiasm, and love.

The pain of parting is nothing to the joy of meeting again.
— *Charles Dickens*

One's life has value so long as one attributes value to the life of others, by means of love, friendship, indignation and compassion.
— *Simone de Beauvoir*

ACKNOWLEDGMENTS

To Laura Daly and to D.L. Savvides for their superb editing

To Charles Roth for his brilliant cover design

To Lisa McCallum for helping me with every aspect of this novel

To Jennifer Nelson and Leigh Ann Wilson for providing invaluable assistance in my research

To Talatha Allen, Shykia Bell, Dody Cox, PattiAnn Cutter, Eloise March, Jaidis Shaw, and Sheri A. Wilkinson, for their ongoing support and kindness

To my grandmother, who unwittingly inspired this novel many moons ago when she took me to brunch at the Algonquin Hotel

To my mother, who loved having fun with language

There are so many more people who have supported me in so many ways. I wish it were possible for me to thank each and every one of you. I hope you all know who you are. And last, but not least, thank you to my fellow authors for your support, advice, inspiration, and friendship. You all mean so much to me.

SABERLEE BOOKS BY LISETTE BRODEY

Crooked Moon
Squalor, New Mexico
Molly Hacker Is Too Picky!
Mystical High (Book 1, The Desert Series)
Desert Star (Book 2, The Desert Series)
Drawn Apart (Book 3, The Desert Series)
Barrie Hill Reunion

BARRIE HILL REUNION

Chapter ONE

April 4, 1986 – 6:26 p.m.

"I'm soaked! The mail is soaked. And more importantly, I need a drink." Leah Brent placed the mail on the marble table in the foyer and proceeded to take off her raincoat, watching as small puddles of water formed on the floor and as her husband, Colin, picked up the mail she had just put down.

"Wet out there, isn't it?" Distractedly, Colin leafed through the mail, stopping as a square beige envelope got his attention.

"Brilliant observation. Do you think helping your wife out of her wet coat might take precedence over the mail? For someone raised by such proper British parents, you're not exactly the poster boy for chivalry."

"We're not living in medieval times, and I wasn't raised as a knight. Apparently, you don't know me very well." Colin stuck the beige envelope in his jacket pocket, put the mail back on the table, helped Leah out of her dripping Burberry, then hung it on a nearby coat rack.

"I know everything about you, including the fact that your manners can be underwhelming. And what did you stick in your pocket?"

"Nothing important." Colin put a hand over his pocket to

protect its contents.

"The hell it's nothing. We've been married for over twenty years, and I've never seen you hijack a piece of mail. It's got to be something. Let me see it."

Colin silently counted to three, then four. "Leah, why don't you get out of those wet clothes? I'll make you a drink."

Stepping in the first puddle she could find, Leah screamed and fell to the floor. "Oh my God, my back!"

Colin rushed to his wife's side, and before he could help her up, she slipped her hand into his jacket pocket and grabbed the beige envelope. Proud of her impromptu performance, she stood, clutching the piece of mail to her chest.

"Let me have that, Leah!" Colin's face reddened. "And by the way, even the best stuntwomen get hurt."

"Holy crap!" Ignoring him, Leah's dour expression morphed into a wide grin as she stared at the envelope. "Now, *this* ought to be fascinating. I have no idea what's in this envelope, but I'm about to have the time of my life reading it. Hard to believe I'm holding a piece of mail from Clare Dreyser. Same last name. Ha! I'm betting the poor thing never married. No surprise there. Whatever could it be? Looks like an invitation going by the embossed stationery she used. Surprised she has that much class." Leah looked at Colin. "And why the hell did you try to keep this from me?"

Colin looked down at the wet floor, then at his wife. "Because whatever it is, I don't want to go back to the Barrie Hiller days. Not in my mind, not in the flesh."

"That would be rather impossible." Leah opened the envelope and scanned the page. "Well, maybe not! Clare has organized a twenty-year reunion for the Barrie Hillers. In May."

"And you can't stand the woman, and we won't be going."

Leah, still grinning, read aloud. "Greetings, Barrie Hillers. It's the founder of everyone's favorite college literary group. It's been over twenty years since we've seen one another. No doubt, we've all lived lives complex and crazy enough to rival our favorite literary works. Let's get together for a bit of socializing, a bit of intellectualizing, and a lot of catching up." Leah read on, beaming as if she'd just heard from a treasured friend, not from a woman she mocked regularly, despite the passage of two decades. "I've organized a weekend reunion. Where? At our old meeting place, the Vanessa Grand Hotel; where else?"

"Not sure who'll show up, but I'd imagine she'll get some sort of turnout. We won't be among the attendees," Colin said as he turned to go.

Leah's grin took over her face like a quickly spreading rash. "The hell we won't! Dinner on the sixteenth of May ending with breakfast on the eighteenth. I don't care what's on our calendar; we'll be there!"

"No, we will *not* be! Let's just leave the past alone. Why are you so eager to clear your calendar to see a woman you loathe?"

Leah looked incredulously at him. "Are you kidding? Clare is the most fascinating bore of a woman I've ever known. I'm a playwright. You're a playwright. Why would you want to pass up such a guaranteed wealth of material? And I don't need to remind you that it's been years since we've written something." Leah licked her lips like a cat that had just polished off a hearty meal that didn't belong to her. "Two decades in the life of a neurotic mess. No better muse than that. And whether you'll admit it or not, I know you hate her, too. Besides, there are several people I'd love to see. Like Bart."

"Why? Because he's famous? There's no guarantee Bart or anyone else besides Clare will show." Colin held out his hand. "Give me that invitation. I'll decline for us."

Leah stuck the envelope down the front of her blouse. "Darling, if you're laboring under the misconception that I won't go without you, enlighten yourself now. I'm going. With or without you. And I can't wait."

CHAPTER TWO

MAY 16, 1986 — 5:06 P.M.

Almost too calmly, Clare sat on the blood-red brocade couch that faced the entrance to the Parker Room. As she waited for her old friends to arrive, she was disturbed by the notion that everything around her seemed eerily sentient. The couch, one of three identical furnishings, along with two stuffed chairs, had been arranged in a square, eager for lively group conversation. A large antique coffee table with curved legs sat vulnerably in the middle. To her left, a black Chesterfield sofa rested stoically against the wall. A mere six inches from the right end of the sofa was a walnut bar on wheels. On it were several bottles of wine, whiskies, and a variety of mixers. Lined up to the right of the bottles were crystal dishes filled with lemons, limes, and olives. To the left, three types of glasses were turned down on a white linen cloth. Clare could feel it: the drinks and fruits were waiting nervously to be consumed, while the glasses feared breakage.

Get a grip, get a grip. Nothing in this room is alive but you. Just try to stay that way.

Clare hoped she had ordered enough for everyone. At a right angle from the bar, to the right of the room's entrance, was a table with two chafing dishes, and a stack of small plates, napkins, and forks. So far, everything inanimate was as she had planned.

Fatigued from suppressing her anticipation, Clare took a deep breath and turned to look around the room at the tired yet grand decor. Behind her, the massive velveteen drapes, adorned by gold tassels, had dulled over the long years, perhaps from the invasion of sunlight or possibly as a protest from the years of gossip that danced merrily and unmercifully upon their exquisite fabric.

Clare smiled wistfully at the magazines she had fanned out on the table before her. They all had one thing in common: actor Bart Younger's image on the cover.

"It'll be good to see you again, love." Clare touched Bart's forehead on the cover of *Hollywood Galaxy*. "Beautiful inside and out."

"Who the heck are you talking to?"

Clare looked up to find Betty, a weathered but lively member of the Vanessa Grand's staff, rudely invading her thoughts. Betty, without invitation, walked over to the table and grabbed the treasured copy of *Hollywood Galaxy*. "Wow, this is a collector's edition. Bart Younger. Sure, I remember this photo. It's just as he looked in *Windswept*. Remember that film? The way he kissed Holly Lyndworth in that movie made me ... well, I think I'll keep *that* to myself."

"Yes, please do," Clare said.

"He used to come here a lot before he got famous, you know. Lived right here in Connecticut while he was in college. I was working in the kitchen back then, in the sixties, so I never got to wait on him. But I hear he was a super guy. Huge ... tipper!" Betty laughed loudly, still holding Clare's magazine. "Thought I was gonna say somethin' else, didn't you?"

Clare tightened. "I didn't give it any thought. Are you here for a reason?"

"Just checking your setup. You're ready to go with drinks. Paul is bringing in the crude eat tays now. You want them on this coffee table, right?"

"The what? Oh, yes, please put the *crudités* and dip here on the table. The cheese and crackers, too."

"Gotcha!" Betty motioned to the waiter pushing a cart into the room. "All of that goes right here. Where the lady has her magazines. There's room for everything, I suppose."

Clare smiled politely as the waiter deposited the trays, then left.

"Now," Betty said, "just confirming that you want the fancy stuff brought in when your guests arrive. The hot horsey dervies."

"The what?" Clare paused to replay Betty's words. "Oh. The *hors d'oeuvres.* Yes. You've been working here for over twenty years, and you don't know how to say—"

"Of course I do. Just like having a little fun with names. Wordplay, as people like to call it."

"Yes. Wordplay and I are well acquainted." Clare surveyed the setup. "It looks like the lines of communication are successful. Now, I'd appreciate it if you leave that magazine where you found it."

Betty reluctantly laid the magazine on the table. "You look nervous. You okay? Need an aspirin?" She turned and whispered to the wall. "Valium?"

Clare corrected her posture as she addressed Betty. "I'm hosting a reunion of a college literary group that I founded. We haven't seen one another in over twenty years. Two decades ago, my friends and I did a lot of living in this room. Even just sitting here, I can't help being flooded with memories ... and a great deal of anticipation. I thank you for your concern and would appreciate your leaving me to my thoughts."

Betty nodded, rolling her eyes as she turned, then left the room.

Although she was several yards down the hall, Leah's voice

traveled without pity to Clare's ears. "You'll thank me for dragging you here. Wait and see. You'll have the time of your life."

"No, I *won't*." Colin looked longingly at the elevator that had just brought them from the tenth to the third floor. "I need to go back to our room and make a call."

"Is that so? Who do you need to call?"

"Leah, I don't have to report every move I make to you."

"No, you don't." Leah laughed. "We've been married so long I *know* every move you make."

Clare shivered. Hearing Leah's voice unsettled her. She took a deep breath, exhaled slowly, then straightened on the couch as she prepared for the Brents to enter the room.

Leah's eyes scanned the room in horror. "Don't tell me we're the only ones here. Worse, please don't tell me we're the only ones who are coming." Spotting the assortment of bottles and glasses, the chafing dishes, and the trays on the coffee table, Leah sighed with relief. "Well, it does look as if you're expecting a few more guests, though the thought of us being the sole attendees is rather frightening. That said, I'm dying to know who else is coming."

Clare stood to greet them as Colin walked over and gave her a stiff hug. "It's wonderful to see you again."

"You too, Colin. I remember you as if it were yesterday." Clare looked into his eyes then turned toward his wife. "Hello, Leah. I'm so glad you could make it."

"Oh, hello, Clare. I got so caught up in the emptiness of the room, I suppose I forgot to say hello. Silly me." Leah gave Clare a once over. "Somehow I expected you to still have that long straight brown hair. I never expected short and frosted. What a surprise."

Before Clare could choke out a response, Betty returned, wheeling a cart of hors d'oeuvres. "We never did discuss how many people needed to be here before I started serving, so I thought I should bring these now. Are these your only guests?"

Leah turned to Colin in a whisper. "God forbid I should start having the same thoughts as a hotel maid waitress person."

Colin tensed and turned away from his wife. "I'm hungry. And those mushroom caps look great."

As Betty placed the hors d'oeuvres into the chafing dishes, Colin walked over to the drink setup. "Clare, can I pour you something?"

"I'll have a Perrier, thanks."

"Leah, Chardonnay to begin?"

Leah turned to Clare. "When you're with someone for so long, he just knows what you want. Doesn't even have to ask."

Clare's eyes flickered with fury. "But he just did. Ask."

Seething, Leah was about to retort when Betty turned to Clare. "I'm finished here for now, Miss Dreyser. And if you're through with those magazines, I'd love to have one with Bart Younger on the cover."

"Actually, they all have Bart Younger on the cover. These magazines are treasured personal property. Collectibles. I'm sorry; they're coming home with me."

"Never hurts to ask." Betty shrugged and pushed the empty cart out of the room.

Leah shook her head at Clare, her nose twitching as a simpering grin contorted her face. "You haven't changed at all, have you? Still pining for Bart after all these years. Honestly, I would have thought you'd be over him by now." Cautiously inspecting the black Chesterfield before sitting on it, Leah left the empty seat next to the bar for Colin. "I suppose you'll play bartender like you always do."

Colin nodded as he peeled the foil off a bottle of Chardonnay. "Might as well."

Clare put a hand on each end of the fanned magazines and quickly pushed them together into a neat, unassuming pile. "These magazines were just part of the memorabilia I brought along. I thought they might be fun to look at." She watched as Colin stabbed the wine bottle's cork with more force than necessary, then looked away.

"If you like fossils, I'm sure those rags are great fun. But we're not here on an archeological dig." Leah looked at Colin. "Right, my darling?"

Colin picked up a bottle of Perrier, poured some into a glass, and handed it to Clare, then gave Leah a glass of Chardonnay. After pouring one for himself, he sat down. "Whatever you say," Colin said flatly.

Clare turned to him. "Afraid of rattling some skeletons in the closet?"

"Of course he's not!" Leah boasted. "We don't have any bony remains behind our doors, Clare. And, as you just heard, my husband agrees with me. We're here to find out what's happening in the here and now. Isn't that what your invitation said?" Leah turned to Colin. "Though, upon further reflection ... I suppose fossils can be somewhat fascinating ... and ... reunions *are* for reminiscing." Leah forced a laugh. "Provided there's something worthwhile to reminisce about. Therein lies the rub!"

Refusing to let Leah get to her, Clare smiled. "Well, I'm glad you could both make it this weekend."

"I wouldn't have missed this for the world," Leah said with a wicked grin. "Whatever made you do this, Clare? Colin and I would never have had the time to arrange such a gathering. We're far too busy."

"It was no trouble."

"If you say so," Leah replied, tasting her wine as if she were approving it. "But then again, you have a lot more free time on your hands than we do."

"I'm well organized." Clare took a few sips of water before answering. "As my mother always told me, if you want something done, ask a busy person. I don't have nearly as much free time as you think, Leah."

"Oh, somehow I doubt that!"

Leah's boisterous laugh took a moment to scorch Clare's ears before it darted out the door and down the hall to meet Dan Collier, who was fast approaching the Parker Room.

His horn-rimmed glasses crooked on his nose, the man with the thinning hair and kind face, rushed into the room.

"Dan!" Colin stood to embrace his old friend as Leah did the same.

"I'm so happy to see you both." Dan smiled broadly as he looked at Clare, eager to let her know he was happy to see her as well.

"Welcome, Dan." Clare was relieved to have a new face in the room. After waiting patiently for Leah to finish making a fuss, Clare hugged him.

"It's wonderful to see you all again. I just checked into my room and came down here immediately. My appearance most likely reflects that. There's a light rain falling off and on, so I'm a bit damp, but that's nothing. We were several days into talk of a strike at the paper, and I feared I wasn't going to make it at all. At the last minute, things were settled, and I made a mad dash to Grand Central Station. Caught the train here with about thirty seconds to spare. Lucky thing, too. The next train with a stop in Barrie Hill didn't leave for over two hours."

Colin stood and walked to the bar. "Name your poison, Dan." Colin grabbed a glass. "I'm not sure that getting here was worth all of the effort you put into it."

"Sure it was! I'll just have some club soda for now. Thanks, Colin."

Colin scooped a few cubes of ice into a glass, opened a bottle of club soda, and poured some. "At the very least, have a lime to liven things up." He pick up a quartered lime, dropped it into the club soda, then handed the glass to Dan before taking his seat.

"Cheers." Dan sat on the couch across from Leah and Colin, then turned to Clare. "Will Maggie be here?"

"She was supposed to be. But her housekeeper called last week to say she hasn't been feeling well. So, I really don't know, Dan. Not a word since. Let's keep our fingers crossed."

Disappointment washed over Dan's face. "Did she say anything else?"

"Just that Maggie really wanted to be here."

"Did you call to see if she was coming?"

"It wasn't my place. But trust me, I made sure to let Maggie's housekeeper know just how much her friends wanted to see her."

Leah looked impatiently at Clare. "Exactly who are you expecting to show?"

Dan took a big sip. "You know, Colin, I wouldn't mind if you poured a small shot of vodka in here after all." He paused. "No, stay seated. I'll get it."

"No you won't." Colin stood. He walked to Dan and took his glass.

Dan turned to Clare. "Well, I'm sure Maggie would have let us know if she were canceling."

"I'd like to think so." Clare smiled sympathetically.

Colin handed Dan's drink back to him, then sat down again. "We'd all like to see Maggie. Though clearly, no one will be happier to see Her Ebullience waltz into this room than you, my besotted friend."

An awkward silence momentarily filled the room. Sitting on the end of the couch closest to the door, Dan drummed his fingers on the armrest. Realizing everyone was watching him, he withdrew his hand, resting it on his knee. "So … what in the world has everyone been doing for the past twenty years?"

"You first, old buddy. Married with kids, yes?"

"That's right, Colin. I met Sally right after college." Dan picked up the lime in his glass and squeezed it into his drink. "She was the office manager at the first newspaper to have me, the *Connecticut Courier*. About a year and a half after we said our vows, our first child, Melissa, was born."

Dan noticed Leah's obvious disinterest. "After Melissa, we had Horatio, Hortense, and Aloysius."

Colin and Clare looked stunned, while Leah appeared to be reacquainting herself with the draperies.

"Pardon me, Dan," Colin said. "But those last three are some hellacious names."

Clare looked at Dan, then at Colin. "I think Dan is kidding."

Dan's silly grin confirmed Clare's suspicions. "Absolutely, Clare. I couldn't help but notice I was drowning Leah in boredom, so I thought renaming my last three, Daniel, Amanda, and Kevin, might regain her interest."

Leah, caught red-handed, turned sharply to Dan. "Really, Dan, that was not necessary. Being in this room again, one can't help but be whooshed back into the past. Sorry, my mind drifted."

"I see; so the four walls are more stimulating than news from an old friend."

"My wife is just very whooshable," Colin offered.

Clare suppressed a laugh. Leah tensed. "No need to make jokes, darling. I have apologized. Do go on, Dan. Of course I want to hear about your family."

"Well, for now, let's just leave it be. Sally and I have four wonderful children, ranging in age from thirteen to eighteen. Perhaps when the others arrive, it will be appropriate to share more."

Leah, unfazed by the gentle admonishment, rose to prepare herself a plate of hors d'oeuvres. Twenty minutes of awkward conversation later, a loud scream in the hallway was a welcome diversion to all. A medley of animated voices floated into the room, but the most exhilarated one belonged to Betty, who stuck her head in the doorway of the Parker Room to speak with Clare.

"It's Bart Younger! In the flesh. Keep your old magazine!"

Leah jumped out of her seat. "Bart is here! Clare, why didn't you tell me he was coming? It's not as if I didn't ask you several times. Why would you keep ignoring me when … oh, never mind! Of all people, I never thought Bart would show."

"Why not? Actors like to see old friends, too." Bart smiled broadly as he stood at the door. An attractive Asian woman stood by his side.

Betty, electrified by excitement, was bouncing behind him. "Actor? You're no actor!"

Stunned, Bart turned to look at the gushing woman in the hall.

"You're a star!"

"Oh! Thank you very much. And your name is?"

"Betty Jean Bruner, sir. You're so tall and muscular. And your hair is so thick and wavy." She blushed. "I guess you know that. I'm just so thrilled to meet you."

Bart took her hand and kissed it. "A pleasure to meet you, Betty Jean Bruner. You're very kind. Well, I'm sure I'll see you later. I'm going to greet my friends now."

"If I didn't serve food for a living, I'd never wash this hand again. Thank you, Mr. Younger!"

Bart smiled graciously and turned his attention to his friends.

Clare rushed to greet him first. "Bart! I'm so delighted you could be here."

Bart gave her a hug worthy of a twenty-year absence between friends. "It's fantastic to see you again." Bart gently put his hands on Aimee's shoulders. "Clare, I'd like you to meet my wife, Aimee Lee Younger. Aimee, this is Clare Dreyser. And this is Leah and Colin Brent, and this is Dan Collier."

Bart had just finished his introductions when Betty poked her head in the door. "Got one more coming!"

Dan's face lit up. "Maggie!"

Betty shook her head. "If this guy's name is Maggie, he probably had a real hard time in school."

"Oh." Dan's expression dropped, just as Larry Sullivan entered.

"Greetings, my long-lost, newly found friends. It's your favorite black Barrie Hiller, erudite man of the world, if you will … no hard feelings if you won't … ha ha … I have returned to see all of you lovely people. Dan the Man, why the forlorn look? Perhaps you're afraid I won't hug you first?"

Larry laughed as he wrapped his arms around Dan. "Why so unhappy, my man?"

Dan graciously returned the gesture. "It's great to see you, Larry."

Leah glanced unsympathetically at Dan before turning to Larry. "He's upset you're not Maggie."

Bart, trying to hide his annoyance with Leah's remark, edged in to greet Larry and introduce Aimee, as Clare and Colin waited patiently for an opportunity to reunite with a hug.

Leah, the last to receive Larry, did so with far less enthusiasm than she had mustered for Bart, though effectively managing a genuine hello.

After all introductions had been made and with drinks and hors d'oeuvres in hand, the six old friends and the newcomer seated themselves—Larry finding comfort in the lone stuffed chair next to the couch where Clare sat.

Bart raised his drink in Clare's direction. "Cheers to you, lovely lady. I couldn't be happier to be here. Reunions are the kinds of thing that most people want to attend, but want someone else to arrange. I'm delighted you took the initiative. Over the years, I've thought of you all so many times. It seems like a lifetime ago that we were all here together … discussing great literature … not-so-great literature, exchanging ideas, trading barbs, discussing everything from Vietnam to Martin Luther King to the Beatles, and standing united for truth and justice—"

"Talking about Vietnam was a whole lot easier than fighting there," Larry said. "Then, to come home to anger and disrespect …"

Horrified, Bart looked at Larry. "I had no idea, Larry. None at all. I—"

"You have nothing to be sorry for. I'm one of the lucky ones. I came home intact. Psychologically, I was kind of fucked up … but I made it. Some of my buddies … not so lucky."

"I'm so grateful you made it home, but I feel terrible that I never knew you served," Bart said. "We spoke by phone in 1975, when you started working as a critic, and you never mentioned Vietnam. I wish you had. But thank you for your service." Bart's forehead creased as he spoke solemnly. "I just *really* wish I had known …"

"Yes, thank you, Larry," Dan said. "I suppose you're the only one of us who served."

"There were others from our graduating class," Larry said. "But as far as I know, out of the four of us men here today, just me."

"I wish I'd known, too," Colin said.

"Oh, please. And you would have done what if you had?" Leah challenged him.

"Thanked Larry for his service. Checked to see if he was all right. Held good thoughts for him." Colin's disgust registered on his face. "Is that enough of an answer for you?"

Leah looked away.

"I'd really like to hear about your experience," Dan said.

"I appreciate that, Dan." Larry sighed. "But I really want my time in Nam … and the aftermath … to stay in the past. I don't say that lightly, either. It took me quite a while to get to a point where I could say that and mean it. I still can't be anywhere near fireworks or diesel exhaust. Hearing a chopper rattles the fuck outta me. Some experiences never leave you. I can't control the world around me, but I try to control *my* world as best I can. But the fewer memories that are triggered, the better."

"I understand," Dan said. "I respect that."

Larry turned to Bart. "Finish what you were saying to Clare before I interrupted you."

"I think I pretty much said it all. I was just going to add that Father Time has treated us well. Everyone looks pretty much the same."

"Except for you, Bart. You look even better."

"Oh, Leah, don't be silly."

"I suppose you have a staff of people taking care of you. An entourage of sorts."

Aimee shot a look at Leah. "I'm his only entourage. Just lil ol' me."

"Oh, you're an American," Leah said.

"Yes, I am. Any reason why you thought otherwise? There are millions of Asian Americans, you know."

Ignoring her, Leah looked right at Bart. "Surely you use bodyguards when making public appearances or traveling?"

Uncomfortable, Bart turned to Aimee, but she gave him a nod to carry on, so he answered Leah's question. "Not usually. Only when absolutely necessary. I think an entourage only draws attention."

Colin's eyes widened. "Isn't that what movie stars want? To draw attention to themselves?"

Bart laughed. "Fair enough. I can't speak for other actors, so I'll just answer for myself. I like the attention, but it can be inconvenient at times. Like when I'm out for dinner with my beautiful wife and an overzealous autograph hound approaches our table with a list of demands. Most people are respectful, though. For me, it's not the attention, but the acting that I really enjoy ... the chance to work at my craft and make a living at it. I love the challenge, the act of creating, the art, the freedom, and even the limitations. It all goes together. But to answer your original question, though I wouldn't necessarily say I enjoy 'drawing attention to myself,' I do appreciate positive reinforcement for a job well done. Doesn't everyone?"

Larry, settling in with a glass of red wine, turned to face Bart. "I know whereof you speak, Sir Bart of Younger. Since getting my film review show on weekends, local though it may be, I've had many a New York encounter with rabid film fans."

Leah snickered as she twirled a raw carrot in a bowl of artichoke dip. "Not exactly the same thing as what Bart goes through. And surely, you're not comparing fleeting local celebrity with established long-term movie star celebrity?"

Larry looked appalled. "Fleeting? I'm sorry, Leah. You know this how?"

Bart quickly intervened. "Who knows, Larry's Q score may surpass mine one day. There's nothing to stop my star from leaving the galaxy."

"Nonsense. There's nothing ephemeral about you, Bart."

"I take nothing for granted, Leah. Having followed Larry's progress over the years, I'm impressed by the following he's achieved. And you have me talking as if he's not here, and I hate that." Bart turned to Larry. "Excuse me. I've caught your show when I've been in New York, and I hear through the grapevine that something pretty special is going to happen. Not sure if that's public knowledge."

Leah raised her eyebrows. "Well, now I'm intrigued."

Pleased by Bart's knowledge, Larry continued: "There's no

better place to make the announcement than right here. You're right, Bart. I'm going to have a three-minute segment twice a week on a national entertainment show. I can't mention which network until I'm signed and sealed, but it'll be public knowledge by next week."

Leah pretended to cover a yawn. "I'll be sure to check the front page of the *New York Times.*"

Bart stood and extended his hand to Larry. "Congrats. Well deserved."

"Are you so sure you want to congratulate him, Bart? After all, soon Larry will be able to pan your films nationally."

Aimee looked at Leah with disgust. "What an unnecessary thing to say."

Leah's sneer made it clear she was not pleased to hear the stranger speak. "Nothing to worry about. Larry's only going to have six minutes a week; I'm sure he can find other films to pan besides Bart's."

Aimee tightened. "That was not my point."

"Oh, sorry, dear. I didn't realize you had one."

Shrugging, Aimee continued speaking without making further eye contact with Leah. "Congratulations, Larry. We've only just met, but good going. That's quite an accomplishment."

"Thank you, Aimee. I wish everything in my life were going as smoothly as my career. I'm rather—"

"Oh, really, Larry. You're not going to start whining, are you? You haven't even finished your first drink."

Chagrined, Dan turned to address the woman who had just shown equal disinterest in his life. "Leah, it was only minutes ago you said we've come together to find out what's happening in the here and now." He smiled and turned to Larry. "I'm proud of you, my friend. And, yes, although we'd like to come to a reunion with our lives all perfectly polished, I'm afraid sometimes life is dull. On other days, it just exists to make a mockery of those Currier & Ives cards we send out over the holidays." He looked at Leah. "Tell me, Leah, if we can't share our troubles as well as our successes, why are we here?"

Clare started to respond, but Leah, cut her off before she could say anything. "Oh, let's save the grumbling for later. Personally, I need time to warm up. According to the official reunion guidebook, at least one hour should be spent on pleasantries. After that, it's open season."

Larry grunted. "Are you sure you can hold out that long, Leah?"

"But of course, even though it's no secret that I'm not a fan of pleasantries."

"Define pleasantries," Aimee said.

Pleased by the challenge, Leah responded with a disingenuous smile. "Of course. Pleasantries are empty words. What you'd hear in an office at end of day Friday. 'Have a nice weekend.' 'You, too.' Fast forward to Monday morning, start of day. 'Hi, how are you?' 'Fine, and you?' 'Fine.' 'That's good. How was your weekend?' 'Great, and yours?' 'Fine.' 'That's nice.' Those, Mrs. Bart, are pleasantries. God, how I loathe pleasantries."

"Sometimes they're necessary."

Leah shook her head. "Maybe to you, Mrs.—"

"My name is Aimee."

"Well, maybe they're necessary to you, dear."

"Come on, Leah," Aimee prodded. "You've never asked someone how they're doing? How their sick grandmother is, how the kids are doing in school, or how the new job is going? Just to be nice?"

Bored with the conversation, Leah glanced in Aimee's direction but not long enough to make eye contact. "I suppose. No one is really immune from it."

Aimee sighed. "If I care about someone, I *want* to know if

they've had a nice weekend. I really do."

"That's true," Bart said, nodding. "I married a very caring woman."

Colin chuckled. "But what if a person's had a horrible weekend? Do you want to hear all of the gruesome details?"

Playfully nudging her husband, Leah continued. "Now, wait a minute, honey. Gruesome details can be interesting."

Aimee spoke through clenched teeth. "And so can pleasantries."

Dan handed his glass to Colin, who was motioning to refill it. "Way less vodka this time. Actually, you can't have gruesome details without pleasantries. Certainly, one must know another person well enough to say, 'Hello' and 'How was your weekend?' before spilling one's proverbial guts all over the table."

"Not necessarily," Larry said, as he put some cheese and crackers on a plate. "Last week I was on a train to Philadelphia, and this woman sat next to me and proceeded to tell me the story of her life."

Leah made no attempt to conceal her boredom. "What did you do? Swap war stories?"

"No, I told her I had to get off at the next stop. Then I moved to the next car. Unfortunately, that was a mistake."

"Why?"

"Because the guy in the *next* car told me the story of *his* life, too. How he graduated from college, got married, became a CPA, had an affair, sought counseling, sold floor coverings, and had another affair with his son's algebra teacher."

Still cloaked in ennui, Leah played with the conversation for lack of other toys at her disposal. "Wait, I know. His son got straight A's in algebra."

"Nope." Larry took a slow and elegant, almost affected, sip of his drink. "His son didn't get A's. That's what caused him to break up with her and find the Lord."

Colin roared. "Oh, Jesus. I didn't see that coming."

Dan reached for the glass Colin was handing him as he turned to Larry. "I guess you have one of those compassionate faces that make total strangers open up to you. I've always been told that I had a compassionate face. So, Leah, what else does your official reunion guidebook say?"

Perking up, Leah showed pleasure at the offer of center stage. "For starters, at least one of us is supposed to be a doctor, and one of us is supposed to be a lawyer."

Larry took another grandiose sip of his drink. "Obviously, we're not of the norm. But then again, this is the reunion of a literary group. It's not to be expected."

"It also says that one of us should be a down-and-out failure." Leah taunted Clare with every bit of her faux superiority. "But I can't discuss that for another hour."

Clare boiled internally, but her face remained pleasant. *You horrid bitch.*

Dan, who had not stopped checking the door for Maggie, stepped in to equalize the conversation. "Speaking of which, I'm sure everyone remembers Ralph Tomey."

Bart nodded. "Sure, I remember Ralph. He was the class comedian."

Dan looked forlorn. "Well, Bart, he's not so funny anymore. He's into politics now. Supporting some third-party candidate for the Senate. He came storming, unannounced, into my office a while back, demanding equal time for his candidate. After howling at me for ten minutes, he suddenly took a good look at me and stopped short. Apologized for not recognizing me, mumbled something about how I'd changed since college, then slipped back into his tirade. It was sad. All of that joviality ... gone. No more sense of humor. Not even a trace. Just an angry, bitter man."

"Hmm," Bart mused. "That's interesting. Ralph Tomey. Reminds me of a character actor I've worked with on a couple of films. I always pictured him telling jokes at the breakfast table and tall tales at dinner. Having beers with the guys—and the loudest voice in the crowd at Little League."

"Nope," Dan said. "I made some inquiries about him after he left my office. He's been divorced for ten years and has two sons he never sees. His wife filed suit against him numerous times for non-payment of child support. Ralph Tomey is what they call a 'deadbeat dad.' Shameful, really. No reason for it at all."

Leah laughed. "Horrors! A deadbeat dad! How interesting, Dan."

Unable to keep quiet, Clare stepped in to support Dan. "It's a very serious matter when fathers abandon their children, Leah. It's nothing to joke about. Not where I come from. I found what Dan had to say to be very interesting."

"Oh, Clare. You would find the Topeka, Kansas, phone directory interesting."

Not if you were in it.

"Well, I don't ever have to worry about Colin being a deadbeat dad. One of the reasons we never had kids is because our lives are just too busy. We have so little free time, and when we do, we spend it together. We want to make it count. Of course, there's always a play or two crying to be written, but we are always doing this, that, or the other. It's madness. When we graduated from Barrie Hill, I worked in the marketing department of my uncle Robert's law firm, while Colin was working crazy hours at a newspaper. I got bored … very bored … so I began fundraising for a hospital. Around that same time, Colin got a job as a student adviser at Columbia and worked full time while getting his master's. As I said, we were busy, busy, busy. We'd often go days and barely see one another. By the time Colin was ready to go into the school's doctoral program, I was positively sick of having to be anywhere on a regular schedule, so I started my own fundraising business. Meanwhile Colin slaved over his doctoral courses and dissertation for years while teaching as an adjunct. He finally became an assistant professor at Columbia in 1982, while I continued my fundraising and other philanthropic endeavors. I had to handle so much while Colin earned his post grad degrees, not to mention his weekend getaways with the guys. Who in the world had time for children?"

Despite her disinterest in *him*, Larry was particularly interested in what Leah was saying. "So would you say that you and Colin have had a conventional marriage?"

"In some ways. But if you mean, 'by the book,' then no."

Larry pressed on. "Do you think a couple has to be married to show true commitment to one another?"

Leah thought for a moment. "No, I don't. It just so happens that Colin and I did marry, but we don't play by the rules. Don't misunderstand me, Larry, we only have eyes for one another, but as for children, we both agreed our lives were more effectively spent on our careers. And since Colin's parents moved back to London, he visits them when time permits. I certainly have no desire to visit my in-laws. We also take separate vacations and have for years. "

"Really?" Larry asked. "Interesting."

"Why not? I'm an island girl. Give me a beach in Tahiti or Fiji, a cool drink, and a shining sun, and I'm happy. I work hard. Relaxation is my elixir. I traveled around the world before Colin and I ever met. I drank at Hemingway's haunts in Paris, strolled daily down Church Walk in Kensington past Ezra Pound's former home, partied in Dublin with men who'd known Joyce, and, well, as I told you all years ago, I once had dinner at the table next to Sartre and de Beauvoir. It was at the La Coupole. Simone dropped her pen, and I picked it up for her. I took advantage of that moment to engage them in conversation. Ah, existentialism! In those days, it was all about learning and twisting our thought patterns into pretzels. Now, I enjoy being pampered and savoring the fruits of my labor."

Rotten apples. Clare fought to keep her thoughts from turning into words.

"Colin never had those experiences, so he enjoys his getaway weekends with the guys and trots off to cultural hot spots on vacation by his lonesome. While he's getting his fill of foreign lands, bare-chested waiters are delighting me with pretty colored drinks."

Looking uneasy, Colin simply nodded.

"I'm sure we're not the only couple who take separate vacations. It's hardly shocking that enlightened people pursue different interests. And I do love my bare-chested waiters."

Still intrigued, Larry wanted to know more. "So, Leah, you don't believe that Colin needs to go everywhere you go?"

Colin and Leah traded glances. "Well, sometimes I do have to drag my husband to certain events … ahem … and I will say that in the beginning of our marriage, I did want him to accompany me on vacation. But honestly, Larry, I have a much better time knowing he's off sightseeing while I'm having the time of my life with my girlfriends."

Larry's eyes widened. "Only your girlfriends?"

"Yes, only my girlfriends. No doubt, we meet many men at the resorts, but it's conversation and laughs only. At least for me."

Soaking in every word, Larry studied Colin's face. "And I take it this arrangement is copacetic with you. You're not bored sightseeing alone?"

"Not at all. Everything is just as Leah said. And why, may I ask, would an erudite gentlemen such as Larry Sullivan be so fascinated by our independent sojourns?"

Larry glanced down, then looked up at his old friends. "Truth? I'm having relationship issues. Cassandra and I have been together for seven years. She wants to get married, and I don't see why a piece of paper is needed to solidify our commitment to one another. Furthermore, she wanted to attend this reunion, and I asked her to stay behind. She'd have been bored and felt left out."

Aimee smiled privately at Bart, not knowing Leah had been focused on her reaction.

"Well, it seems that Mrs. Bart can identify with that, Larry."

"Leah, my wife's name is Aimee."

"Of course, Bart," Leah said, brushing off the reprimand. "Perhaps you should have brought her, Larry. The two women could have gone off somewhere together."

Larry picked up a raw carrot and snapped it in half. "You're missing the point, Leah. She wanted to be a part of this because being a Barrie Hiller was such a part of my life back in college. Cassandra often enmeshes herself in the study of pop genealogy."

Clare, who had been trying to find her place in the conversation, took the opening. "Pop genealogy? I don't think I've heard of that."

Dan wrinkled his brow. "Nope, can't say I have either."

"Please, Larry," Clare said. "We'd love to hear about it."

"Oh, Clare, please speak only for yourself. '*I'd* love to hear about it, Larry.' You have no way of gauging anyone else's interest but your own."

You raging bitch!

Bart looked at his wife as if embarrassed to have her witness Leah's abrasiveness. "I would love to hear about pop genealogy. Wouldn't you, Aimee?"

"Yes, actually, I would."

Outnumbered, Leah pouted, while Larry happily took the floor. "I'm afraid my explanation is going to disappoint. Pop genealogy is Cass's term for learning about people she likes … or loves … and maybe a few that she doesn't. She doesn't care about bloodlines and great-grandfathers as much as she's intrigued by how those she knows spent their formative or earlier years. Childhood friends, classmates, first loves, old neighbors, former bosses … well, she loves learning what makes people tick."

Aimee gently nudged her way into the conversation. "She sounds like an interesting woman with a passion for psychology."

"She's actually getting her master's in it," Larry explained. "Cass says that her 'pop genealogy' is psychology without all of the complex theories."

"I call that 'amateur psychology' and nothing more," Leah said.

"I'm paraphrasing and doing a very poor job of it," Larry said. "In fact, I'm doing Cass an injustice by even trying."

"By all means," Leah said. "Stop the injustice! Save us all from the tedium of your failed effort."

Larry glowered at Leah, then turned away.

"Quite enough!" Colin said quietly to Leah, who pretended not hear him.

"So why didn't you bring Cassandra?" Aimee asked Larry. "Did the idea of her presence here threaten you?"

Larry clasped his hands behind his head and leaned back pensively. "Let's just say this, Aimee, I'm a man first. A specimen between two pieces of glass … never. I don't like being analyzed."

"I see," Aimee said. "I'm surprised you've stayed with a woman for seven years if being with her puts you in a position to feel that way."

"Oh, it doesn't," Larry replied. "But meeting all of you … well … that would have been an exceptional learning experience for her, but not one I wanted her to have. Dig it?"

Leah let out a loud sigh. "No, I'm not 'digging it.' But if we must dig anything, how about a hole where you can bury this nonsense."

As long as the hole doubles for your grave, I'm all for it.

Though Leah couldn't hear Clare's thoughts, the look in Clare's eyes left no doubt she was disgusted. "What's wrong, Clare? Was it something you ate?"

Larry jumped in. "Nine, ten, eleven."

"Wow," Clare said, picking up her drink. "I'd nearly forgotten that silly counting game. Back then, I thought it was beneath our collective genius." She smiled." Of course, that never stopped me from participating."

"Colin and I love it. Though I must say, we haven't played it in years."

Bart turned to Aimee and quietly explained what was going on. "It's just one of many word games we used to play. When someone ended a sentence in a word that could be or was also a number, we'd always count three numbers past it. 'Something you ate ... nine, ten, eleven.' Doesn't sound quite as clever as we thought it was back then."

Aimee squeezed Bart's hand. "When you told me you couldn't prepare me for this reunion, I had no idea how truthful that was. It's hard imagining you spending so much time with this group."

Leah's voice got loud. "I do believe the Youngers are whispering about us."

Clare cut Leah off. "I think Larry was trying to share his relationship issues with us."

Larry leaned forward in his chair. "Yes, actually, I was. I just don't see the point of taking a perfectly good relationship and turning it into a marriage."

"It's worked beautifully for Colin and me!" Leah said, popping a cherry tomato into her mouth.

"Yes, so it seems," Larry said. "How about you, Dan? Are you still enjoying the same wedded bliss as Leah and Colin?"

"I've really been blessed. A lovely wife and four outstanding children."

Colin chuckled. "But he hasn't stopped looking at the door since he got here."

Dan paused to parse his answer. "Well, no, Colin. I'm not going to pretend I don't want to see Maggie." He sighed. "Clare, are you sure there's nothing you forgot to mention? Knowing Maggie, if she weren't going to attend, she would have let us know. I'm sure of that."

"Honestly, Dan, I've told you everything. Her housekeeper said she wasn't feeling well but really wanted to be here."

Leah handed her glass to Colin. "Another Chardonnay, darling. Clare … who else did you invite?"

"Well, I did invite Madeleine and Henry Peyton. I'm very disappointed they couldn't make it. But they're currently living in Romania."

"What on earth for?"

"He's with the State Department. They move around a lot."

"Just as well they're not coming. We have a neighbor who does the same. Always rattling off his latest adventures, droning on about every event he and his wife attend, and he feels, for some inexplicable reason, that I must be captivated with tales of the dignitaries they rub elbows with. Who else turned you down, Clare?"

Clare looked squarely at Leah. "Wait. Let me get this straight: you have a neighbor, who, like Henry, spends his career living in different parts of the world. How incredible that, with all his globetrotting, he finds time to drone on to you. When is the last time you saw this neighbor?"

Leah looked contemptuously at Clare. "Oh, how the hell should I know? They rented out their house and moved to Tunisia three years ago."

"I see. So, the stench of his drone has just followed you."

Larry roared with laughter. "Must have been mighty

powerful."

Aimee turned her head so that Leah couldn't see her laugh. Bart smiled, heartened that his wife could find something to be amused about.

"Laugh if you must, Larry," Leah scoffed. "But I speak the truth."

"Colin, I must say, your wife is a treasure," Larry said.

One that should be buried. Clare struggled to keep her thought from turning into words.

"Oh, yes," Colin agreed. "And I never know what gem she'll delight me with. Mark Twain my words; every day is special."

Bart whispered to Aimee, "Another word game. Inserting famous authors into ordinary sentences."

"I see. And does one get points for these bon mots?"

"No, just the pleasure of having scored."

"Ah! Fascinating," Aimee responded dryly. "At least the author game has more room for creativity than the counting one."

Leah watched Bart and Aimee, annoyed by their natural intimacy. "The Youngers are yet again whispering among themselves."

Bart rested his hand on Aimee's knee as he spoke. "I was just explaining to Aimee about the word games we used to ... well, that we apparently still play."

Clare smiled warmly. "I can certainly understand that. It's not easy going to a spouse's reunion ... especially when it's this group. You're a brave woman, Aimee. No surprise that you needed Bart to explain a few things to you. But I'm really glad you came."

Leah snickered. "Clare, do you seriously expect anyone to believe that you're happy Bart has brought his *wife* to the reunion that you put together just to see him again?"

You have no idea how wrong you are, Leah.

Bart bit his lip before responding. "Leah, Clare arranged this reunion for all of us. I've been eager to see her for quite some time, too. Had she not arranged this reunion, no doubt we'd have met for dinner one of these days when I was on the East Coast."

"Oh. So you say," Leah retorted.

Weren't expecting that, *were you, Leah?*

Colin stood. "Who needs a refill? Larry, you were telling us about some relationship issues. I think you left off somewhere around not wanting to be a specimen between two pieces of glass."

Dan handed Colin his glass, then reached for a slice of cheddar. "No vodka this time. Heavy on the lime."

Putting his shoulders back, Larry postured. "Yes, I was. I don't understand. Why, after seven really good years, is Cass harping on marriage? I happen to know a lot of people who married after living together, and for some reason or another, the relationships fell apart after the I dos. So why not just leave it at 'Let's not' and go on with our lives?"

Colin handed Dan a fresh drink and sat down. "She's probably just going through a phase. Women go through phases. We all do, for that matter. Ride it out, my friend."

"I don't know … something is different this time. Cass has mentioned marriage over the years, but never so adamantly, never so consistently."

"Who knows," Colin said. "Maybe one of her friends put a bug in her ear. Like I said, ride it out."

Leah chuckled. "My husband is an expert on women."

"Really?" Larry said. "Having spent the last twenty years with you, he can't have had a very broad education." He smiled. "I'll pause while everyone appreciates my pun."

"You know, Larry, I could be insulted by that, but I'll take it as a compliment. Thank God I'm *not* like other women. I'm confident, secure, and, as you know, not afraid that if I take a vacation with my girlfriends, I'll come home to an unfaithful husband or divorce papers being served to me over breakfast."

Dan broke in. "But you *are* married, Leah. Would you be as confident if you weren't?"

"I'm fairly certain," Leah responded. "But I don't know for sure, because I've always had an adoring man by my side. Larry, have you changed your behavior in any way? Have you given this woman—"

"*Cassandra* ..."

"Yes, her."

Bart and Aimee looked at one another. Leah continued. "Have you given her any reason to feel a greater need for security?"

"Not that I'm aware of, Leah. No, I have not changed how I am with *Cassandra*. A friend of mine suggested my new position and upcoming national exposure might be threatening to her."

"I see. So you're thinking she wants some security."

"Something like that. Yes."

Nervously, Dan checked the door for the umpteenth time. "Sally and I have been married only a year less than Leah and Colin. Things do happen because one person changes, but usually, both parties evolve. I don't know many marriages that stay even over the course of years."

Leah turned her attention from Larry to Dan. "Well, Colin and I have evolved together. But I'm sensing the Collier Bluebird of Happiness is hoping to fly to another nest."

Dan had no wish to be as forthright as Larry. "Colin, tell me, is Leah the sole spokesperson for your happy marriage?"

"Well ... I don't really—"

"I take it the marital road has remained smooth, then." Dan said.

"Never a reason to repave," Leah told him. "Or even fix a pothole. As you can see, I take excellent care of myself and always look my best for Colin."

Dan looked at her oddly. "I see. After all, nothing is more important in maintaining a relationship than seeing to one's physical appearance." He glanced at Colin. "How do you fight off all the competition for your wife, who 'always looks her best'?"

For starters, there aren't many men out there who pine for a ball-busting bitch.

Noticing the emotion playing on Clare's face, Larry looked at her. "Something you want to add, Clare?"

Leah burst out laughing. "What in the world would Clare Dreyser know about relationships or marriage?"

Clare's eyes went black. "How in the world would you know anything about me or what I've been doing for the past twenty years?"

"Oh, please. I knew back in college you'd never marry. And you've worked at that *Kiddie World* magazine for how long? Too long. No doubt, knowing that children would never be part of your life's equation, you've lived vicariously through your job. And if you did have a husband, which is grotesquely implausible, you'd have dragged him here for us all to see."

"Apparently no one is interested in my situation," Larry grumbled, "and the help I had hoped to receive is nonexistent."

Leah groaned. "Larry, we have the entire weekend to hear your troubles. Loosen up. You don't have to be the center of attention all the time."

Clare shuddered. *And neither do you.*

All eyes turned toward the door as Betty knocked and entered. She turned to address Dan. "If you're looking for a crazy, rich blond lady wearing a purple-feathered boa on a bright purple blouse—one who couldn't be subtle if her life depended on it—she checked in over a half hour ago. Just saw her again in the lobby. She asked for all of you. Guess she'll be here in a moment."

"Maggie! Maggie's here!" Dan jumped out of his chair,

hurried out of the room, and raced down the hallway toward the elevator. As the doors opened, Dan threw his arms wide before enveloping Maggie in an exuberant hug. Maggie Bristol was every bit as happy to see him.

Chapter THREE

MAY 16, 1986 – 6:30 P.M.

Maggie hugged Dan passionately, her plum-colored boa draping over his shoulder. "Oh, Danny, how I've missed you! I want a hug for every day we've been apart. It feels like forever and yesterday all at the same time."

After a few moments, Dan reluctantly disengaged from the embrace to look at her. "My gorgeous Maggie. Clare and the others weren't sure you'd make it, but I knew you'd come."

"Of course, Danny. I couldn't stay away, because I knew you'd be here waiting for me. I was nervous about coming, though. Between you and me, I didn't just arrive. I've been down at the hotel bar calming my nerves. I'm afraid I've already had a bit to drink. Seeing you again … seeing the others … I just had to steel myself. I hope I don't say anything too outrageous. You know me when I've had a few."

Dan smiled warmly and gently put his hands on Maggie's shoulders. "No matter how much or how little you've had to drink, you're always a shining star in my eyes." He paused to look at her more intensely. "Are you all right, dear? Word has it that you haven't been feeling well."

Beaming, Maggie radiated happiness as she spoke. "I'm looking at my Danny; how could I be anything less than wonderful?"

Hesitant to press the matter, Dan smiled as a few tears trickled down his cheeks.

"Don't you start crying, or I will. And you know there's nothing pretty about smeared mascara. At least not on my face."

Dan laughed as he gently touched Maggie's face with one hand, the other still resting on her shoulder. "I think smeared mascara would look even worse on mine. I have a feeling I'd get lots of stares, too."

Maggie giggled, then looked into his eyes. "My friend. My special friend who is unlike any man I've ever known."

Dan smiled. "You're everything that is beautiful, Maggie." He let go of her and took a step back. "I could stand here and look at you for hours. But I think we'd better make our way into the Parker Room. No doubt they'll be out here within a minute if we don't show our faces."

"Indeed they will." Looping her arm through his, the two walked the brief distance to the Parker Room.

Elated to see her old friend, Clare jumped up, rushed to the door, and gave her a hug. "Oh, Maggie! You're just what this party needs. I'm so happy you're here."

"I'm the one who's happy to be here, Clare. And you are looking quite stylish! I never could get you to warm to wearing boas, but you fill out that dress quite beautifully. It's a classy look."

Leah, hearing Maggie compliment Clare, fumed.

Colin turned to his wife. "Be careful. You're leaking venom, and I have nothing on me to mop it up with. Besides, if someone slips, we could be sued."

"Oh, hush."

Aimee, who had been pretending not to overhear, smiled.

Still angry, Leah whispered to Colin, "Maggie must be blind not to notice Clare's pot belly. Nothing stylish about that!"

Ignoring her, Colin turned his attention to Maggie, who had

effortlessly commanded everyone's attention.

"Larry Sullivan! New York's favorite film critic! Maggie's impressed. How are you, darling?"

Larry looked down at himself, then, standing, looked at his arms and hands. "I'm still black and bodacious. Career-wise, things are looking up. Relationship-wise, hitting a smallish bump in the road."

Leah waved off Larry's response like it was a fly buzzing around her face. "The woman has just walked in the room. Perhaps you should let her finish her hellos before saddling her with your tale of misery and heartbreak."

Maggie gave Larry a hug. The moment they separated, her eyes fixed on Leah. "Leah, darling, you're exactly the same."

Pleased, Leah stood and showed off her trim figure. "Perhaps even better, Maggie. I do take care of myself."

Clare shivered. *That's not what she meant. Perhaps she should rephrase: you're still the same hateful bitch you've always been.*

Maggie hugged Leah briefly then reached for Colin. "How are you, my enigmatic friend?"

"Am I an enigma, Maggie? Why is that?" Colin asked as he walked to the bar.

Because she can't figure out why anyone in his right mind would stay with her *for twenty years.*

"Oh, darling, I suppose we're all puzzle pieces trying to fit into the big picture."

Colin looked over at Dan, who was still beaming. "Your presence today has made a new man out of Dan. Look, the color is returning to his face. I guess we can cancel the paramedics."

"Well, *I* might faint looking at the movie star in our midst." Maggie smiled warmly as she addressed Bart. "You were always so dedicated to the arts, and it's no doubt they have returned the favor." As she went to greet Bart, she nodded affirmatively to Colin who was pouring a drink. "Gin and tonic, please. Bart, is this your wife?"

Aimee put out her hand. "Aimee Lee Younger. I'm pleased to meet you, Maggie. Bart has told me some incredible stories about you."

Maggie laughed. "I hope you didn't believe any of them. But as you get to know me, I'm afraid you'll learn they're all true."

Bart embraced Maggie. "All good, Maggie. All good. So wonderful to see you."

Dan took the glass Colin had filled for Maggie and held it while she made herself comfortable in the seat he had saved for her.

"Well," Maggie said to Bart, "I don't know how in the world you've managed to become such a well-known and sought-after actor while simultaneously keeping yourself out of the tabloids. How un-Hollywood of you!"

"That's nothing. We don't even own a Jacuzzi."

Amused, Aimee feigned puzzlement. "A Jacuzzi, huh? I never heard the word, much less owned one."

Maggie took several generous sips of her drink. "It's this big hot tub, sort of like a whirlpool. Sometimes people get naked and they sit around together in the water, drinking and socializing. It's fun, except you have to watch out for venereal disease. Lots of people have been known to get nasty infections from those things. You see, disease breeds in warm water."

Aimee looked stunned. "I was kidding. I do know what a Jacuzzi is. They're ubiquitous in Los Angeles—"

Lost in her own orbit, Maggie rambled on. "Oh, don't look so surprised, darling. You can catch something from a toilet seat, and you still sit on that, don't you?"

Leah chuckled. "I would hope so."

Larry leaned back as if he were about to screen a movie. "And here we are, folks, at the corner of Awkward and Amusing. "Well, Leah, I'll bet your reunion guidebook doesn't recommend opening a conversation with a chat on venereal disease."

Maggie took several more healthy sips of her drink. "Venereal disease is a part of life, I'm afraid. I had a friend who swore she caught something from a new pair of underwear. She didn't wash them before she wore them—God only knows why. She thinks some poor woman tried them on in the store because she wanted to see what she looked like in black satin panties. That seems rather far-fetched to me, but I told my friend it was her own fault. She didn't want to hear it. She railed against the imaginary woman and started calling her horrible names."

"How awful," Clare said.

"Yes," Maggie agreed. "I never saw her again after that day."

Shaking her head, Clare continued. "The plight of the poor is not something to be taken lightly. Tell me, Dan, do your reporters cover the homeless crisis?"

Finishing her Chardonnay and handing the glass to Colin for a refill, Leah uttered a pained sigh. "Where would you say Clare has taken us now, Larry? Perhaps to the corner of Boring and Who Cares?"

Embarrassed, Larry looked at the tray of cheese and crackers, putting a few more on his plate. "No, I wouldn't say that."

Leah held out her arm to wait until Colin had refilled her drink. "Do go on, Maggie."

"Well, my late third husband, who was twenty-five years my senior, was a real- estate mogul. His son rehabbed houses and sold them for a profit. One day I was out with him, and he insisted on showing me a property he had just purchased for next to nothing, bragging about how he was going to make a fortune. It was a tenement. Ten people had been living in one room—five of them rats. Paint was falling in large chips from the ceiling. The pipes were rusted and corroded, and there were pigeons, hanging out on the ledge as if they were guests at some bird tea party. On the kitchen counters were several discarded oatmeal containers with little bitty insects nestled inside the remaining oats. How awful to have nothing but oatmeal to eat for every meal."

Aimee looked at Bart, stunned.

Clare reached for a stuffed mushroom cap on her plate. "Maggie, I see you're a real expert on the poor."

"No, I'm not. I know it's terrible, but I don't want to be. All I know is that I wish my former stepson had fixed that house and given it back to the family he legally stole it from. He could have afforded to do so, but if he were a decent person, he would have paid them a fair price from the beginning. Who knows what happened to them."

"I'm glad to hear you say that," Clare said. She paused to eat. "But you do know that poor people consume more than oatmeal."

Maggie finished her gin and tonic and passed the empty glass to Dan, who passed it to Colin for a refill. "Remember in *Oliver Twist* how those poor orphans lined up with those little bowls while some mean-looking brute slopped gruel into them? It's the same thing as oatmeal."

Larry was intrigued. "The gruel."

"Yes, darling. It's one and the same. Same dish, different name. I actually combine the words and call it 'groatmeal.' "

"You're quite the Dickens scholar."

"No, Larry, my sweet, but I know about gruel. And I suppose it is better than rummaging through garbage cans. The other day, I saw a woman take a half-eaten carton of banana yogurt out of the trash and—"

Larry knit his brows. "You got close enough to notice what flavor it was?"

Beaming with delight, Leah nudged Colin.

Maggie, appreciative of her attentive audience, continued. "There was a cigarette butt in it, and she just picked it out of the yogurt … like you pull an olive from a martini … and went right on eating. I was positively nauseated. Then, when she had finished feasting on some stranger's garbage, albeit with some difficulty, she lit the damp cigarette butt and smoked it. But at least she didn't hurt anyone by doing so."

Leah tittered with glee. "Maggie, how I have missed your unique observances of life."

Clare cringed. "Maggie, certainly that story is not representative of your average poor person. Dan, I'll ask again. Didn't your newspaper just run a five-part series on the homeless in New York and America?"

Dan pursed his lips awkwardly. "Well, yes, in fact we did."

Nodding, Larry gave Dan a thumbs up. "Nice job. I read that. Some powerful photojournalism, too."

"Thanks, Larry. The paper won several awards for that piece. It was a proud moment. Now … to do something for all of the people who suffer … that would be an even prouder moment. But I can tell you that some of the subjects of that piece, especially some of the veterans, ended up getting much-deserved help as a result of our work. We all felt good about that, but it's not enough. Not by a long shot."

"Yeah, nothing like going off to war and coming home to end up on the streets because society turns its back on you." Larry paused to let his anger cool. "Thanks for running that, Dan. Thanks for giving a damn."

Colin couldn't help but notice that Leah was disappointed by the turn in conversation. "Good work, my man. I happened to catch the series as well."

Clare smiled. "Ah, yes, I think I do remember seeing that. A superb job. Dan, maybe this would be a good time to discuss the problem. Maybe you could help clarify a few things for Maggie … for us all."

Aimee's eyes lit up. "I would love to hear about it. I've done some pro bono work for organizations that help the homeless. There are simply too many forgotten people out there. Nobody likes to think that the woman sleeping in the cardboard box is someone's mother, or that the drunk passed out in the doorway is someone's father, or that the man mumbling to himself is shell-shocked from the savagery of war. It's tragic. Too often, we don't think of homeless people as citizens who once raised families, thrived in business, or served in our military. Instead, we make the grave mistake of convincing ourselves they were born on the street and are content being there. We ignore them. Perhaps if we understood how they came to be there, alcoholism, drugs, trauma, mental illness, loss of income, depression, domestic violence, et cetera, we might begin to eradicate the problem."

Dan put his drink down and prepared to speak. "Well, if everyone would like—"

Maggie tugged at his sleeve like a small child asking a parent for something. "Danny ..."

Embarrassed, Dan stopped in mid sentence. "Perhaps this isn't the best time."

Colin threw out some bait. "Why not, Dan the man?"

"Well ... this *is* a reunion. I mean, it's a lot more interesting to share our lives and reminisce than it is to listen to me toot my own horn about the great editorials my paper has been doing."

Colin kept pushing. "It's not about tooting your own horn. It's about discussing a serious problem in this country and others for that matter. I'd like to hear about it. Clare would. Aimee would. And no doubt Larry and Bart—"

Leah shot daggers at her husband. "Dan is right. It's inappropriate talk for a reunion."

Larry stared coldly at Leah. "Your idea of what should take place in a reunion is based solely on your whims at any given moment. There is no logic whatsoever in what you have to say."

"I for one don't want to go back to the corner of Boring and Who Cares."

Larry sat up and leaned in Leah's direction. "You don't care about homeless people?"

"Oh, don't go all bleeding heart on me, Larry. We give to charity. And, no, I don't think a reunion is an appropriate place for a long-winded discussion about what's wrong with our society. We didn't come together today for that purpose."

"Then I suppose you don't want to hear about the volunteer work I do with my brothers in Harlem, helping recovering addicts and ex-cons transition back into society."

Bart's face shone with pride. "Wonderful, Larry."

Dan passed his glass to Colin. "Just a splash of vodka this time. I'm pacing myself. Listen, everyone, I say we save this for later. We have an entire weekend together. If anyone wants to talk about this, catch me later. Okay?"

Maggie radiated happiness. "Thank you, Danny. Later is better. I just don't want to talk about sad situations at the moment. I've seen far too many of them lately." She took a sip of her drink. "Bart, I'll bet you're worth millions by now."

Embarrassed, Bart responded quietly. "We live very comfortably. I consider myself quite fortunate."

Maggie downed a healthy swig. "I'll bet you do. Did anyone notice the doorman on duty?"

Colin shrugged. "I don't usually scrutinize hotel personnel, but what about him?"

"As my limousine pulled up, before he came over to open the door for me, I saw him pick his nose."

Aimee turned to Bart. "Oh my God."

Undaunted by the indirect reproach, Maggie continued. "... then he wiped his hands on his pants, opened the door for me, and had the nerve to hold out that same hand to help me out of the car. What do you think of that, Colin, dear?"

"Not very classy."

"No, it's not. That's usually why they make those guys wear white gloves."

Dan laughed. "You're as charming and dear as you always were."

Still looking at her husband, Aimee was incredulous. "She's kidding, right?"

Leah took it upon herself to respond. "No, she's not kidding." She turned to face Bart. "Tell us about your films. You must know what you'll be working on next."

Larry snickered. "I see, Leah. Bart's films are good conversation, but my work with my brothers in Harlem isn't. Is that how it goes?"

"You're a film critic. I would think you'd be interested, for God's sake. But apparently, you're a Leah critic as well."

Clare shot a dagger in Leah's direction. *A title anyone should be proud to claim.*

Larry bit his tongue and glared at Leah, then, softening his expression, looked at Bart. "I would like to hear about your films. Very much. It's just—"

Bart made a halting gesture with his hand. "I understand."

A phony smile slid across Leah's face. "Now that we've got that settled, Bart, deliver unto us the scoop on thy movie roles."

Clare smiled genuinely. "Yes, Bart. Please. I know I'd love to hear all about what you're doing."

"Well, of course you would, Clare. You've been obsessed with Bart since college." Leah turned to her husband. "You know that as well as I do, Colin."

Colin stared at his knees and said nothing.

"Not obsessed, Leah. Not even close." *You stupid, ignorant bitch.*

"Really, and what would you call those vintage Hollywood rags you brought with you?"

Clare glanced at the stack of magazines still sitting on the table. "I would call them precious souvenirs that celebrate an old friend and remind me that he has accomplished his dream and become a respected actor."

Bart turned to Clare. "I can't tell you how much it touches me that you saved those. You always believed in me, Clare. Often when no one else did. And I have always believed in you."

Leah laughed boisterously. "Oh, be serious, Bart. Have you? Do you have a private collection of all the issues of *Kiddie World* magazine Clare has edited or written for? I'm surprised a childless woman would even be given such a job."

Dumbfounded, Bart just stared at Leah.

Leah pressed the replay button on her laugh. "Ha! I didn't think so!"

"I didn't know where Clare works before receiving the invitation and her letter," Bart said. "Now that I do, I have every intention of not only reading the magazine, but subscribing to it for my niece and nephews."

"Thank you, Bart. I'm honored."

Maggie stood and twirled her boa. "Is it time for a group hug?"

Larry walked to the bar. "Not yet, but it's definitely time for another drink. Bart, do tell about your movies, brother man."

Bart's eyes sparkled. "Happy to do so. Well, let's see. I've just been signed to do a film in which I'm going to play a famous historical figure. But the movie is still hush- hush, so that's all I can say." Bart took a sip of his drink. "We've just wrapped on a film about two brothers who were an integral part of the political corruption in Chicago from 1910 well into the 1920s."

Larry, his glass full, took his seat. "Heard about that one. Look forward to seeing it."

Colin nodded. "That's definitely one I'd like to see, too."

"It's one *we'd* like to see, Bart," Leah said more loudly than usual. "Colin and I adore going to films together ... when we can find the time. Larry, I hope you won't be panning this one during your six weekly minutes of critique time."

"No, Leah. I won't. I'm going to spend the entire time critiquing your plays ...   only I don't think there are any in production. Well, there's always you."

Maggie laughed. "Well, Leah, it's a good thing our Larry is only a film critic. You've certainly given him a wealth of material should he decide to expand his critiquing."

Hasn't she ever! Clare nodded.

Maggie pushed a wisp of hair out of her face. "Bart, darling, do go on. Any more films?"

Bart twisted his mouth anxiously. "Well, there's one more that I'm ninety-eight percent sure I'm going to do. I suppose there's no harm in talking about it. It's called *The Garden of Lost Dreams.*"

"Of course!" Clare put her drink down. "I was just reading about that film. Holly Lyndworth is starring in it. You played opposite her in *Windswept* many years ago. About four years ago, I remember reading that you were going to do another reunion film with Holly. I kept my eyes peeled for more news, but there was nothing. Maybe my memory isn't serving me as well as it should."

"Actually, you're spot on. Honestly, I'm not really clear on what happened with the last film, but I was very disappointed. The project just fell apart. Actually, my agent pulled me from the film because there were some rumors about a scandal with the director. Once I was out, Holly's agent pulled her, too. Then the financing fell through, so the film was never made. I just let it go. I had to move on. But this one is nearly a go, and I'm looking forward to our onscreen reunion. The fans have been wanting this for a very long time, so we're going to give our all to deliver."

Maggie, who was now resting her hand on Dan's leg, looked at him. "Did you see *Windswept*, Danny? It was one of the most sensual films in cinematic history. I had the most glorious sex for a week after seeing that one. Nonstop!"

Colin interjected. "I do remember the film, Maggie. I didn't bask in the aftermath as you did, but it was indeed quite a window steamer!"

"You were probably on a mountain hike with your friend Ed," Leah groused. "Why don't I remember that one?"

"I don't know, Leah. Maybe you were off in Tahiti when I saw it."

Maggie mock fanned herself. "It was hot, hot, hot, Colin."

"It certainly was." Colin grinned. "Now, be careful. You're making Dan 'hot hot hot.' And jealous, too!"

Leah noticed that Aimee was gritting her teeth. "Mrs. Bart, I dare say you're not a fan of *Windswept*. Your polite exterior appears to be fading."

"I never saw it."

"I see. My, what crisp tones you have."

Aimee reddened. "I just said I never saw it. Don't read into what's not there."

Leah smiled gratuitously. "But that's exactly why I'm so intrigued. It's because I *am* reading what's there. So, tell me more about the two of you. Where did you meet?"

Aimee exhaled then continued. "Bart's agent, Kenneth Menhardt, was a client of mine. We met at a party Ken threw for his wife's birthday."

"A client?"

"Yes, Leah, I'm an attorney."

"Oh, I had no idea." Leah looked at her husband for

corroboration. "Did you know she was an attorney?"

"I kind of figured that out earlier when she said she's done some pro bono work for organizations that help the homeless. I added two and two and got four."

"Well, I didn't pick that up." Leah sighed as if she were broadcasting her boredom. "I said earlier that the official reunion guidebook said one of us should be a lawyer, but in this case, you're an outlier, so you don't count." Leah popped another cherry tomato into her mouth. "So, was it swoon at first sight?"

"No, it wasn't 'swoon at first sight.' I don't swoon."

Leah laughed. "Of course not. Lawyers never do."

"What is that supposed to mean? Is that some kind of dig at the legal profession? Why are you even asking these questions? You're not the least bit interested in me at all."

Dan stiffened his back and looked at Aimee with a sense of urgency. "I can't speak for Leah, but I'm certainly interested in hearing about how you and Bart met. Aren't you, Maggie?"

"Of course. I adore a good love story!"

Leah grunted. "Most lawyers never laugh, either."

Aimee clenched her jaw. "Sure we do, Leah. When something is funny, we laugh just like everyone else."

"Perhaps on your way to the bank," Leah mused. "But that's not necessarily a bad thing. My most-cherished relative, my uncle Robert, is a lawyer."

"Go on," Maggie said, "I want to hear how you met."

Bart put an arm around his wife. "Aimee and I had immediate chemistry. We started off making small talk, which quickly turned into hours of delightful and interesting conversation."

"I see," Leah said. "And how much delightful and interesting conversation was had before you got married?"

Can't you say anything civil to anyone without being sarcastic? Clare cut a piece of cheddar and put in on a cracker.

Bart smiled. "I think we were together about two-and-a-half years before we got married. But Aimee moved in with me after about fifteen months."

A loud knock at the door of Parker Room caused Leah to swallow the smart retort she was about to make.

Betty burst in and stood in front of the group. "Excuse me, folks. I hope I didn't interrupt the address of the Gettysburg or anything, but one of you people has a call. I can bring a phone in this room, or you can take it down in the lobby."

Leah's nostrils flared in disgust. "Are you going to clue us in?"

"Huh?"

"Are you going to tell us who the phone call is for—or is this a game of twenty questions? Is there a prize for guessing right on the first try?"

"You don't have to be so hostile. All you have to do is ask."

"And all you had to do was tell us. Who is the damn phone call for?"

Betty snickered at Leah. "That wasn't so hard, was it? Although I could have done without the obscenity. The call is for Larry Sullivan."

"For me, huh? I feel like I've just been chosen King for a Day. Who is it?"

"I didn't ask, Mr. Sullivan. I mind my own business. Some woman." Betty turned to Bart. "Hello, Mr. Younger. Are you comfortable? Can I get you anything?"

"I'm just fine. Thank you for asking."

"Please call me Betty."

"Sure thing, Betty. I'm just fine. Unless my wife would like something."

Aimee nodded. "No, thank you."

"Well, you just let me know if you do. I'm here to serve."

Betty turned to Larry. "Where are you going to take the call?"

"Tell the young lady you couldn't find me."

Leah, reenergized, was once again intrigued. "Larry, you're not going to give your girlfriend of seven years the brush-off, are you?"

Larry turned sharply to face Leah. "Oh, now you're interested? I told Cassandra this was one weekend I was doing alone. I asked her not to get in touch with me, and apparently my wishes aren't being respected."

Betty was eager to respond to Larry's request. "I wear a lot of hats here, but I'm not a secretary. And I'm busy."

"Can't you just tell the caller you couldn't find me?"

"Betty Jean Bruner doesn't like to lie."

Larry huffed in disgust. "I thought that it's your job, as a proud member of the hospitality team, as I'm certain you are, to graciously please your guests. All of them. I'm not asking you to swear under oath to the Supreme Court. What if you go out of the room, and I'll hide in the closet? That way, you can honestly say you couldn't find me."

Leah whispered loudly to Colin, "Maybe that's the real reason he doesn't want to marry his girlfriend."

"No, Leah. I'm completely heterosexual." Larry sighed. "Miss Betty, please honor my wish."

You don't even have the decency to be embarrassed. Clare lowered her eyes to avoid broadcasting her anger.

Betty put her hands on her hips. "I said I don't like to lie."

Larry stood angrily. "Fine. Just hang up the phone then. Don't tell her anything. Excuse me, friends. I'm going to have a talk with the hotel manager."

Maggie stood as well. "I need to go to my room."

Dan looked concerned. "Maggie, are you okay? I'll walk you."

"No need, Danny. I'll be just fine. I won't be long. I'll walk out with Larry."

Betty narrowed her eyes at Larry then rushed out of the room. Seconds later, Larry and Maggie left.

Colin raised an eyebrow. "I hope Larry doesn't get the poor woman fired."

Clare nodded. "I hope not. I think she should have done as Larry asked her to, but I don't want to see her get into any trouble. Anyway, Bart, you were telling us how you and Aimee met. How many years ago was it?"

"Aimee and I got married six years ago. We kept it low-key."

Leah sighed. "I assume there are no little ones, or you would have mentioned them by now."

"Perhaps. Maybe in the not-too-distant future. Aimee and I have been talking about having a family."

"Bart, your domesticity amazes me," Leah said, sprinkling salt on a stalk of celery. "Anyway, on a more scintillating note, I do hope you and Holly Lyndworth reunite on screen. I think some heightened sexual prowess would be good for your image. You don't want to be too squeaky clean now. Women like men with edge. Especially in the movies."

"Well, Leah—"

"And, Dan, how about you? Come on, you can be free to talk now that Maggie has stepped out. I've never met your wife, but I'd imagine she's a match for your somewhat old-fashioned countenance. I'm guessing she's homespun—the quilt-sewing, baby-loving, and biscuits-for-breakfast type. Tupperware parties with large turnouts, little shell-shaped pink-and-white hand soaps in the powder room, and homemade gingham curtains in the family room."

"How did you know? You have quite the intuitive gift. Sally also makes apple pie for the Little League bake sales."

Leah was proud of herself. "I knew it!"

Dan curled his lip to refrain from snarling. "Fascinating generalizations, Leah. Sounds like you've been reading old copies of *Women's Day* from the 1950s. But to my knowledge, Sally has never sewn quilts or curtains. Yes, she loves babies, so you got something right. However, I doubt she's ever cooked an apple pie in her life, and I have no idea if the Little League, with which we have no association, even has bake sales. I don't know what 'biscuits-for-breakfast type' even means."

"Simply stated, that she prepares homemade biscuits and daintily spreads marmalade and other jams on them."

"Fictitious and silly," Dan said.

"Neither. I think you're simply not paying enough attention to all her flights of fancy. I'll also bet she's perky and petite and wears floral prints."

Dan exhaled in frustration. "Sally is the twin sister of Big Foot. Fraternal twins, separated at birth. She's over eight-foot tall and wears no clothes at all because she's covered in hair. Nobody makes her size. Not even Lane Bryant."

"Hilarious, Dan. Why not just admit it. I'm right on the money. Homespun. Just as I said."

"My wife leads an active and productive life. She participates in several important community organizations and is a positive role model and a wonderful mother to our four children. I'm very proud of her."

"That sounds more like an obituary than a wife. I always knew you'd marry a woman like that," Leah said. "Even in the sixties, you were an anomaly ... the straight arrow who played by all the rules ... at least on the outside. But is Sally enough for you? When are you going to let that tiger inside you loose?"

"What tiger?"

"The tiger that's always been in love with the Maggie Bristols of the world."

"There's only one Maggie. And I do love my wife, Leah."

"But there's no way in hell you would have brought her to this reunion."

Dan stiffened. "Leah, just leave it alone."

Leah pouted playfully, but no one was amused. "Do I have to?"

Clare started to speak to diffuse the tension, but Dan wasn't finished. "You still love to speculate and stereotype, don't you, Leah? Still think you know what makes the whole world tick. You've got the inside scoop on us all. Our spouses, our friends, our children, our neighbors. You know it all, don't you? Tell me, are you that afraid to look in the mirror?"

"Whatever are you talking about, Dan?"

"My wife spends a great deal of time looking in the mirror, actually."

"Hush, Colin!"

Someone's got to be in love with her. Clare brushed a crumb off her lap.

"Thanks for the clarification, Colin." Dan paused to dampen his anger. "You know, Leah, confident and content people don't need to cut down others to feel superior."

"Oh, hush, Dan. I'm having fun. We're having fun."

Clare bit her tongue. *Speak for yourself. Just like you told me to do.*

"I'm just stirring the pot of memories and throwing in a bit of spice. We used to sit in this room for hours trading barbs and analyzing one another. It's what we do. Or at very least, it's what we did. What did you want? That we should all come back as curmudgeonly creatures with bad memories? It's quite clear you're thrilled to find Maggie just as she was, so don't be so harsh and hypocritical with me."

Clare stood. "Dinner is going to be served in a couple of

hours, at eight o'clock. There's a choice between chicken cordon bleu and salmon. Red bliss and baked potatoes. Asparagus and green beans almondine. Caesar and mixed green salad."

"My God, Clare. You always did know how to bring a conversation to a screeching halt."

Colin glanced sideways at his wife. "I think that was her intention."

Leah looked at Colin then at Clare. "You should have noted on the invitation that you were going to assume the role of censor."

And you should have noted on your RSVP that you were going to be a raging bitch from the moment you entered the room. "I'm not trying to censor you, Leah. And since you're such a fan of looking in the mirror, consider your actions. Instead of catching up with Dan, you're ridiculing him, his wife, and everyone else. Yes, we traded many a barb back in the day, but most of it was all in good fun."

Bart nodded. "Clare is right.

"Oh, nonsense, Bart. You're just defending the longtime honorary president of your fan club."

Clare started to speak but was upstaged by Larry's reentrance into the Parker Room.

"Well, I had a talk with the manager about that woman."

Bart frowned. "I hope you didn't do anything to jeopardize Betty's job."

"No, nothing like that. But her manager did agree that she should have accommodated me and will do so should a similar circumstance occur again."

Dan interrupted. "Where's Maggie? Didn't she come back with you?"

"No, man. She went up to her room. I'm sure she'll be back shortly."

Dan wrung his hands and drifted off into his own world.

Colin was curious. "Did you talk to Cassandra? Why was she

calling?"

Larry stood before his friends with a commanding presence. "I didn't speak with her. I would imagine she was calling to insist that she join me here in Barrie Hill or, on second thought, just to tell me how miserable she was without me. I wasn't about to get into a heated argument and let it color my good time."

"So, you are having a good time?" Colin said, reaching for a raw green bean.

Leah lightly punched Colin in the arm. "Of course he is. This is better than being a slave to the scripted dialogue of a film any day."

"I take umbrage with that word, Leah."

"What? Slave? Oh, Larry, please. Don't go all black on me, and for God's sake, sit down. You're not Othello, and this isn't a stage."

Larry continued standing. "You're diving into shark-infested water, Leah. Be careful."

Laughing, Leah turned away from Larry and gave Aimee a quick glance. "I've had a shark sitting nearby for quite a while now."

"All lawyers are not sharks, Leah. I'm certainly not."

"I never said *all* lawyers were. I was just talking about you."

"If I were a shark, I would have bitten your head off and spit it out the window, then watched as it fell three floors and splattered all over the sidewalk. Or maybe I would have taken the elevator to the roof and dropped it from there for a more dazzling and explosive spectacle."

Leah mock cowered. "Oh, dear, does that mean you don't like me?"

No doubt everyone in this room would like to have a piece of you. "I think—," Clare began.

Leah groaned. "Please, Clare, you're not going to try and save the moment with another ghastly menu recitation, are you?"

No, I was just going to suggest that Aimee brush her teeth with

Crest for Bitch Breath after biting off your head. "Actually, yes, I was going to say that perhaps your head served up on a platter might be quite the centerpiece."

Leah turned to Colin. "Alone for a lifetime, the despairing woman attacks the happy and successful woman she has always envied."

Aimee responded before Clare could defend herself. "As I'm the only other woman in the room at the moment, please, Leah, tell me: what exactly about you would Clare, or any woman for that matter, be envious about?"

"I'd be happy to answer that, Bart's wife."

"My name is Aimee."

Leah ignored her. "Clare wants what all women have and she doesn't. For starters, she's been obsessed with your husband for well over two decades. She's jealous of both of us for being size fours, and of *me* for being beautiful."

You're the ugliest woman I have ever known.

"Clare is jealous of my pedigreed background …"

My mutt Bentley has a better pedigree than you do, Leah.

"She is jealous of my world travel, my evening with Sartre and de Beauvoir, my playwriting, my longstanding marriage, my enormous popularity in college, and of all the things I have that she doesn't. Ha! Dare I say it! The loss of my virginity!"

Larry resumed his theatrical pose. "Whoa! Let's get some things straight here. Colin, satisfy my curiosity … do you agree with your wife?"

"My wife has her opinions. Clearly."

"You look mighty uncomfortable, my man. Is that the best answer you can give me? You have no issue with your wife lambasting Clare?"

"I think Clare can defend herself."

"That wasn't what I asked you," Larry said as he sat down.

"Oh, Larry. Be quiet. Of course Colin agrees with me. How could he not?"

Let me count the ways. Clare exchanged a brief look with Colin.

"Leah, I take it you and Clare have had no contact in twenty years," Larry said.

Clare piped up. "That's right, Larry. None."

"What a ghastly thought!"

Larry sat down and thought for a moment. "And yet, Leah, you can sit there and spout, with undeniable accuracy, all of the things Clare envies about you. You can spew invasive so-called truths about Clare's personal life based on no evidence whatsoever."

"It doesn't take a genius to see who she is. In this case, the past has been a great predictor of the present."

Clare rolled her eyes.

"Not really, Leah." Larry said. "Wanna know what I see? I think you may very well be projecting. I think *you* envy Clare."

Leah's laugh scorched the walls. "What in the world does Clare have that I don't have?"

Larry looked around the room as Dan, Bart, Aimee, Colin, and Clare waited for his response. "Oh, I don't know, Leah. Maybe the respect of everyone in this room."

Thank you, Larry.

Before Larry could respond, Maggie rushed into the room, her presence demanding attention.

"Maggie!" Dan said, his face brightening.

"Oh, Danny, did you miss Maggie?"

Leah winced. "Is there a bucket handy?"

Reluctantly, Larry sat. Maggie was more animated than when she had originally entered the room.

Dan patted the seat next to him. "Sit down, dear. You look upset."

"Oh, Danny. I'm way too flustered to sit. I feel like it's taken me longer to get to my room and back than it did from New York City."

Colin laughed. "Well, no doubt, Maggie. It was an eternity for Dan."

Dan looked up at Maggie. "I really do wish you'd sit down."

Maggie paused, then took a seat. "I suppose I will sit after all. Colin, be a love and pour me another gin and tonic. I need it. What a horrid time I've had."

"What in the world happened, Maggie?" Dan asked as Colin went to refresh Maggie's drink.

Maggie waited until Colin had finished pouring to answer Dan. "Well, I went to my room to call home and check on my poodles, Pierre and Amelia."

Colin handed Maggie her drink. "Standard? Miniature? Toy?"

"Amelia is a white standard poodle with a Continental clip."

Clare smiled. "Ah, the Continental clip. Isn't that the one where the hair is a bit like Little Richard on top, and the legs look a bit like they have earmuffs on them? Very puffy all over?"

Colin nodded. "I know that one. Have a friend with a dog just like that."

Leah looked questioningly at Colin. "We don't know a soul with a dog who looks remotely like the creature Clare just described. Why did you say that?"

"A colleague of mine has a dog like that. Just because we're married doesn't mean your eyes see every damn thing mine do."

Larry was all too happy to interject. "You do take separate vacations, Leah. I'll bet Colin's eyes see all kinds of things."

"What are you trying to say, Larry? That Colin looks at other women? Because I know my husband, and he only has eyes for me."

Are you sure? Clare smiled ever so slightly to camouflage her disdain.

"While the cat's away in Tahiti, the mouse might have a sweetie."

"Hush, Larry!"

Colin looked at Maggie. "I believe you had the floor. So, where were we? Right, your Amelia is a white standard. And your Pierre?"

"Thank you, Colin. Yes, my Pierre is a brown medium. He's my best boy!"

"Whoa. Careful, Maggie. Dan looks jealous."

Dan shot Colin a look.

"As I was saying, I called home to check on my babies. They're fine, thank goodness. But getting to my room was anything but. What a nightmare! There is some kind of enormous family reunion going on down the hall from us, and they're wearing the same green T-shirt that says 'Cutter Family'"

Colin laughed. "Must be a tight fit. All of those people in the same T-shirt."

Maggie ignored everyone's chuckles and continued speaking. "When I left here with Larry, he took the stairs to the lobby, and I stopped in the ladies' room. When I came out and walked to the elevator, the family reunion had taken a break, and about thirty of them were playing a game of elevator poker. Every time one of the elevators stopped on this floor, they'd whoop and cheer. Then several of them would jam in it like a New York City subway at rush hour."

Colin nodded. "Hmm. Interesting. I didn't think you would be familiar with our great subway system."

"Of course I'm familiar with it. Do I ride it? No. Anyway, I finally got onto an elevator with a Cutter family leftover who introduced himself to me as 'Pappy.' As if I cared. I pressed the button for the eighth floor, and it lit up, as elevator buttons do, and he clearly saw that. But he pushed the button again anyway. I hate that. I've always hated that. So I said to him, 'You see I've already pushed the button for the eighth floor. What do you think; you won't get there unless you push it again yourself? My push isn't good enough for you or what?'"

Leah laughed. "Oh, Maggie. Hilariously the same. And look at you, Dan, Glowing at her every word. You look positively radioactive."

Maggie was annoyed. "I am *not* finished. Where was I?"

Dan put a reassuring hand on her shoulder. "In the elevator, dear."

"Oh, yes! Why do people push buttons that other people have already pushed?"

Clare attempted a guess. "Force of habit, I'm sure."

"Well, as if that weren't bad enough, after introducing himself to me and after I chastised him for an unnecessary button push, 'Pappy' thought I would want to know that he's staying in room 623 and was just visiting someone on the eighth floor. Ugh. Just as I was about to let him know how uninterested I was, we had arrived at the next floor. The door opened, and several more people got into the elevator, giving the corpulent patriarch an excuse to push himself right into me. I was horrified. The noxious beast smiled at me as he took advantage of the situation and pressed himself up against me. Honestly, he was built like an oversized piggy bank. Someone should have cut a slit in his back and let him save spare change, but all I wanted was to get away from him. I wasn't going to let him get away with it, so I screamed, 'Get away from me, you letch.'"

Clare's eyes widened. "And did he?"

"Oh, Clare darling, a nephew grabbed him by the collar and yanked him away. He told him that being arrested at the last family reunion was enough, and if it ever happened again, he would be banned from the reunions for life."

Dan's face burned as he clenched his jaw. "I have a mind to go find that man and have a word with him."

Leah laughed. "Oh, Dan. Ever Maggie's knight in shining armor. Sounds like the man might crush you like an ant. Besides, I highly doubt you'd be able to locate him."

Maggie shivered. "Actually, the entire clan is whooping it up right down the hall, in the Kaufman Room. If he's gone back there, he's probably pressed up against some unsuspecting second cousin."

Bart, who had been quiet for some time, spoke up. "That's a very unfortunate story, Maggie. My younger sister often tells me similar stories about riding in the subway. I'm sorry you were violated in any way."

The corners of Leah's lips turned up. "Clare, perhaps you might like to ride a crowded elevator or two. Never know what kind of action you might get."

Clare was boiling. "Leah …"

"Yes?"

"Nothing, just nothing. But I am so tempted."

Colin looked uncomfortable but didn't speak.

Aimee nodded. "Right there with you, Clare. Believe me."

"Oh, please, Mrs. Bart. Maggie, I'm sure you will recover. And, Maggie, the world is full of people who will re-push your buttons. Learn to deal with it."

Larry gave Leah an unforgiving look. "Eloquently stated from the greatest button pusher of all."

"Oh, hush, Larry. If I'm a button pusher, then you're a pusher away. Pushing away your woman of seven years because you wanted us all to yourself. Because you didn't want to be a part of her 'pop genealogy' study. Colin, pour some water over our good man. He's a flaming hypocrite. Look at him. He's on fire!"

Bart stood. "Please, may I speak?"

Leah smiled and sat back. "Of course, Bart. The floor is yours. For as long as you like."

"Really. Are you sure?"

"Of course, I'm sure. I know Colin and I both are happy to hear anything you have to say."

Larry blew air through his lips in disgust. "Why are you giving in so easily to Bart? You're certainly not that nice to anyone else. Most especially his wife."

Bart put a hand up to stop Leah from speaking. "I can answer that, Larry. It's called 'Patronize the Movie Star.' Happens to me all the time. I'm quite sick of it. So please, Leah, say whatever your heart …"

She doesn't have one. Clare shifted on the couch.

"… desires. Out with it."

"Don't be silly, Bart."

Aimee motioned for Bart to sit down.

"Please, Aimee. Let me get this off my chest. Leah, pretend I sell insurance for a living. Now, what do you think of me?"

"I like you, Bart. I don't know what else to say."

"You think I'm boring."

"If you sold insurance, you might be. But you don't. You make movies."

Exasperated, Bart responded. "There are exciting people who sell insurance and some horribly dull ones who make movies. I know; I've worked with them. Forget my occupation, Leah. What do you think of *me*, Bart Younger, the man? Surely, you must have some inner desire to tear me to shreds as you have everyone else, including my wife."

Leah smiled unconvincingly. "I don't know what else to say; I like you."

"Really? Then why don't you respect my—"

"Maggie's hungry! Clare, darling, what have you ordered for

dinner?"

"Oh, God, don't encourage her!" Leah groaned.

Clare stood as Bart sat down. "Friends, we have one hour and ten minutes until dinner, which will be served in a private main floor dining room. I think we should take this time to tend to our personal needs then gather for what promises to be a memorable meal." *Maybe not a good one, but a memorable one.*

Leah sighed loudly. "For God's sake, isn't there any takeout? A *Moveable Feast* of sorts."

You could move your ass back home and let everyone enjoy dinner.

Everyone stood but Maggie, and nobody answered Leah.

Bart turned to Aimee. "Ready to go back to the room and strengthen our defenses for dinner?"

Aimee began fidgeting with her wedding ring and did not notice Leah was eavesdropping. "You know, sweetie, I got a brief look at one of the hotel staff who looks exactly like a good friend from high school. It's probably not her, but I'm going to go down to the lobby to find her. You know how compulsive I can be. It will drive me crazy if I don't find out."

Bart looked confused. "Oh, why didn't you mention it before?"

Aimee shrugged. "I was going to, but then you said something, I got distracted, and, well, I'm telling you now. It shouldn't take me much time at all. I'm sure I'm wrong. Do you mind? See you in ten minutes or so?"

Satisfied, Bart gave her a kiss. "Sure, honey. See you then."

Leah whispered something to Colin, who didn't care, and kept her eyes fixated on Aimee.

Dan helped Maggie up, and Clare, Colin, Bart, and Larry engaged in conversation.

As Aimee slipped out of the room, Leah followed, keeping

her distance. Leah watched the movie star's wife head for the elevator, then rushed to the stairway to beat her to the lobby, unnoticed.

Chapter FOUR

May 16, 1986 — 7:35 p.m.

The Vanessa Grand Hotel was packed with overnight guests, event attendees, and restaurant patrons. The lobby was bedlam, and it was easy to lose a face in the crowd, but Leah had made it downstairs before Aimee's elevator did and knew exactly where to stand to see and not be seen.

Aimee hurried off the elevator and looked both ways before spotting a bank of phones in a hallway just off the main lobby. She rushed toward the closest phone, put her bag on top of the shelf, then huddled close to the phone to make her call.

Satisfied that Aimee had her back to everything but the phone, Leah grabbed a discarded copy of the *Connecticut Courier* from a lobby table, walked over to the phone bank, then stood only one phone away from Aimee. Holding up the newspaper to cover her face, Leah pretended to read while she listened.

"Let me talk to him, Leanne. I don't really care what he's doing or what producer he's with; I want to speak to him. Now!"

Hearing Aimee's authoritative and demanding tone, Leah's eyes enlarged. Noticing that other hotel guests were walking toward the phones, Leah opened her bag, took a couple of dimes from her change purse, and dropped them in the coin slot. She was just about to change her voice and fake a phone call when Aimee's intended party got on the line.

"Hello, Ken. Thank you for taking my call. ... Yes, I'm here with Bart at this miserable joke of a reunion ... I'll explain later. Believe me, I didn't call to talk about my husband's old college chums."

Aimee listened impatiently, then broke in. "I want you to make *Garden* go away. Whether it languishes in the graveyard of films that never saw the green light of day, or ends up being produced with another male lead ... that's not my concern. But Bart's role in it needs to meet an untimely death, just like the first one did. You need to work your magic, or your ineptitude, and chop this project into little bitty pieces ... I don't care what stories you have to concoct. You're clever; you can do it. Just pull Bart from the fucking film!"

Leah could hear the male voice protesting loudly on the other end of Aimee's call, but she couldn't make out what he was saying. But Aimee's increasing agitation was clear, and Leah's jubilation was overflowing.

"No, I'm not *asking* that you do anything; I'm *demanding* that you do. I don't care if the role was written for him. I don't care if the millions of adoring fans are waiting with bated breath to see Bart and Holly reunite. This is about what I want and only about what I want. Understand? You pull Bart from the film and come up with a creative and plausible reason for doing so, because if you don't, there's a big bag of beans that are going to spill all over Hollywood when Sylvia and her father find out about your affair—"

Drumming her fingers loudly on top of a phone book that lay under the pay phone, Aimee impatiently listened. "Don't argue with me, Ken. I don't make idle threats. You of all people ought to know that. Now, I'm going to hang up. I know it's a weekend, so I'm giving you until the close of business Monday to kick this film in its gonads. Pull Bart! Holly's agent will follow; I'm sure. Got me? Read me? Over and out."

Aimee tuned out the protest on the other end of the phone then, slammed the receiver into the cradle. "You better not fuck this up, you son-of-a-bitch!"

"Oh, my! The real actor in the family isn't Bart at all, is it? It's Mrs. Bart. And I must say, the little Asian princess has a very foul mouth."

Rattled by Leah's presence, Aimee jumped, then gasped. Saying nothing, she glared at Leah as if doing so would make her disappear.

Leah smacked her lips. "I take it someone doesn't want her husband to ever kiss Holly Lyndworth again."

"Mind your own business, you interfering cow."

Leah laughed. "Moo moo. I'll bet Bart would be udderly grateful to this interfering cow for letting him know that his little wifey is sabotaging the most-anticipated film of his career. And I'm guessing it wouldn't be the first time. What do you think of that? Moo!"

"Don't you dare say a word to Bart!"

"You have no power over me, Mrs. Bart."

"My name is Aimee. That's A – I – M – E – E."

"Oh, an alternate spelling. Sweet, but completely irrelevant."

"Just keep your mouth shut, Leah." Aimee turned to go, but Leah grabbed her by the wrist. Aimee glowered at her as she tried to yank her arm away. "Take your filthy hands off me!"

Leah's eyes blackened as she let go. "You may have threatened someone named Ken on the phone, but you won't threaten Leah Brent. You're very good at giving ultimatums, but now we'll see how well you take them. You either cooperate with me, or I will not hesitate to tell Bart every single ugly word I just heard. Do you hear me?"

"Yes, I hear you. And I'm asking you nicely to please mind

your own business."

"Why would I do that? That's no fun."

"Please, Leah."

"No. Now, what is your name?"

"Aimee."

"No, no. Try again."

"Aimee Lee Younger."

"No. Again."

Aimee hadn't even noticed that she was grinding her teeth. She hesitated for a long time before responding. "Mrs. Bart."

Leah mock applauded. "Well done! Task number one completed. Now, for task number two … "

ˈ ✳ ˈ ✳ ˈ ✳ ˈ

"Maggie needs to freshen up! Please, walk me to my room, Danny."

"Of course." Dan stood and held out a hand to her.

"I need more than freshening up," Maggie said as she stood brushing invisible bacteria from her body. "I need a long, hot shower and a change of clothing after that horrid man pressed his poundage against my body."

A crash of thunder erupted, and everyone looked at the window to watch as a torrential rain began to fall.

Colin motioned to indicate the window. "God has heard you, Maggie. Not only will you be cleansed, but the taint of His Corpulence will be washed from the streets of Barrie Hill."

Larry laughed. "Perhaps, but no doubt the gent is still leaving his taint within this very structure."

Maggie looked wistfully toward the window. "I wish God were always so cooperative."

Dan frowned. "Why do you say that, Maggie?"

"No reason, Danny. Please, just walk me to my room."

As Maggie and Dan said their good-byes, everyone stood to do the same.

Larry walked to the window. "It's teeming out there. I guess that kills my nostalgic walk through the streets of Barrie Hill before dinner."

Clare smiled. "Maybe later, Larry. Though the prediction for tonight isn't very pretty at all."

"But not as ugly as it's turned out to be."

Clare looked at Colin and Bart, then at Larry. "No, definitely not."

Bart smiled with outstretched arms. "Come here, you. Give me a proper hug before you leave."

As Clare and Bart hugged, Colin made a quick saluting gesture and left the room. About a minute later, Clare was gone, leaving Bart and Larry alone.

"Let's sit down for a few. Just like old times, Roomie."

Larry took a seat on the couch next to Bart. "Won't your wife miss you?"

"I don't believe so. She had some business in the lobby. Thought she may have seen an old friend earlier. They're probably having quite the time catching up. Now, honestly, how is my former roommate doing?"

Larry leaned back, resting his head in his clasped hands, as he often did. "Don't know, my friend. Thought I was doing okay. For seven years I've been living with a woman who really understands me. And I've never cheated on her. Hell, before that, I had so many women I couldn't count them all. I was like an Olympic runner in reverse."

Bart nodded. "Running *away* from the finish line."

"Exactly. You still get me." Larry paused to listen to the sound the rain made as it pelted the window awning. "Not that I want to pass the buck on my character flaws, but losing so many close friends in Nam, well, I think I was afraid to attach myself to anyone again. If you don't let yourself get too close or care too much, how great can a loss or a breakup be, you know?" Larry sighed. "That was my thinking. I meant what I said earlier about not wanting to discuss the war, but you just don't come out of something like that being the same person who went in."

Bart looked at him sympathetically. "I'd imagine not."

"Anyway, after several years of therapy and self-introspection, I finally shed my fear of loving *one* woman and being loved in return. I get myself now. For good or for bad, I know who and what I am. When I met Cass, everything just made sense. To my credit, I hadn't just been running away from women; I'd also been running away from the *wrong* women. I just didn't know it."

"That's quite a breakthrough. So why the aversion to showing her off to the group?"

"We're all made up of many pieces, brother. Just like Maggie said earlier to Colin. Puzzle pieces. There are some pieces that fit with others and some that don't. Did you really want Aimee to be here?"

"She wanted to come. I was concerned she'd feel like an outsider. I never really factored in—"

"Leah."

"Right. Leah. I've been sitting here trying to remember why I once found her engaging. She was always sharp tongued, but she was nothing like this."

"In twenty years, bitter can grow some strong roots."

"You speak the truth, Lar."

"Any clue why she's the way she is?"

"A clue, yes. A good reason, no." Larry hesitated before speaking. "Let's see. I know that Leah's father was a high-ranking military man. Barked orders to Leah and her sister all of their lives. He died before Leah graduated from high school. Her mother fell to pieces and went emotionally AWOL. Leah was on her own with a very hefty inheritance. Reading between the lines of what she told me way back when, she was angry and entitled, so, she lived like the world and everything in it was her play thing. That's what I do know about her. As I recall, she and her sister were estranged. I think Leah tried to play boss, and her little sis wasn't having any part of it. No idea if they speak now, but I'd wager they don't. Anyway, twenty years ago, Leah's sense of entitlement didn't manifest itself into the callous woman we see today."

"Not at all," Bart mused. "She was palatable back then. Hell, she was likable ... most of the time. Irreverent, but funny, as I recall."

"Twenty years have passed. We've all changed," Larry said. "I'm not quite sure how similar or different any of us are ... not yet, but Leah has devolved. Clare, on the other hand, is more confident. Back when, she was as sharp as they come, but she underestimated her own worth. You could see it in the way she carried herself. Today, I get the idea she's more than capable of kicking Leah's ass, but since this reunion is her baby, class act that she is, she's holding back."

"Agreed," Bart said. "As I'm sure you remember, she and Colin used to be close friends. Clearly, that was a friendship that died once he got together with Leah."

"Hell, yeah. It had to die. There was nowhere for it to go. Damn shame."

"I'm not sure yet who Colin is today." Bart paused to think. "But I think I understand why Maggie called him her 'enigmatic friend.' He was always a hard worker, but he loved his down time just as much as the rest of us. I'm not surprised he has a PhD. Colin always had the fortitude to go after what he wanted. Question is, does he have the fortitude to get rid of what he doesn't want? Or is he actually happy with Leah? Because that would be the biggest enigma of all."

Larry nodded. "I hear you. I'm trying to figure that one out, too. Hard to imagine, but maybe he sees something we don't. Yeah, Leah has had some raw deals in her past, but who hasn't? I've met a lot of folks with truly tragic stories. And they're some of the best people I know."

"Agreed. So let's turn this conversation back to you, Lar. Why give this wonderful woman the brush-off? Especially after she called here for you."

Larry twisted his mouth and thought for a moment. "This probably won't make any sense, but things appear to have been going well for us. Scary well. But I think I needed to break up the routine. Shake things up again and see how they settle. You know, make sure it's all for real."

"Life is more than a pretty scene in a snow globe. That can be a dangerous game to play. Maybe you should have brought her along, especially if she had such a strong desire to be here."

Larry paused to consider Colin's words. "No, leaving her at home will only make Cass and me stronger. Reinforce our bond. Prove that we don't have to be physically together to have a bond. This is nothing new. She's just been very curious about my life before. About a month ago, she pulled out my old photo albums and was looking at photos of me as a kid. What was I like? Who were my friends? Was I a good kid? Damn, so many questions. And trust me, Cass is evasive about things in her life, too. Especially this past year."

"Maybe things haven't been going 'scary well,'" Bart suggested. "Maybe just scary."

Larry squirmed in his chair. "Yeah, I didn't want to think that, much less say it. Guess I'm trying to see the glass half full." He looked around the room to distract himself from unpleasant thoughts. "As for being here with us, I just wasn't ready to open that door and let her walk through it. Not ready to let her walk into my past and snoop around, especially when she's in a nosy frame of mind and has her own stuff going down."

"You've been together for seven years," Bart said. "Is she really asking too much?"

"Maybe not. But I didn't want her here all the same. There are days when she shuts me out … tells me to leave her be … and I do. So the way I see it, I'm not asking for any special favors or being a hypocrite."

"Just one more question, Lar. For now. You said Cassandra really understands you. Do you understand her?"

"Don't know, Bart," Larry said as his face contorted. "I thought I did. But now … I don't know."

The two old friends just looked at one another.

"Well, now that my head has been shrunk, it's your turn, Bart. You and Aimee seem firmly ensconced in your lives together. Thinking about children, huh? Seven Barrie Hillers at this reunion, all of us over forty, and Dan's the only one with kids. Either something's very wrong or very right with the rest of us."

"Never thought of it like that. And, yes, Aimee and I have talked about children. Haven't you and Cassandra?"

"Indirectly. Cass is nine years younger, so I figured maybe in about a year, if she was interested, we could talk."

"And that time frame works for her?"

Larry scratched his head. "Damn, Bart. You're making a brother's head spin. Let's go back to you for a while. Visit a neighborhood we haven't been in yet."

"Fair enough, Lar."

"So is your story anything like mine? Did you run from women until you met Aimee?"

Bart looked down. "Nothing like that."

Larry was intrigued. "I think it's time to get my shovel out and dig a bit deeper. I think I've hit something here."

"You have. I won't deny it."

"Aimee isn't your first true love."

"No, she's not."

"Okaaaay! Getting warmer. Is she your true love now?"

Bart sighed. "I hope so."

"You *hope* so? Okay, truth time." Larry raised an eyebrow. "Is there another 'true love' competing for your affection? Another flame in your fire?"

"Well, there was Holly."

"Yo, did you say Holly? As in Holly Lyndworth?"

"I did. I met Holly not too long after I moved to Los Angeles. We were in the same acting class, and she was my first scene partner. Oh, Lar, it was hot, steamy, and unlike anything this Jersey boy had ever experienced. At first, I thought it was just the scene we were doing. But it wasn't. It was Holly. Hot Holly."

"And was the heat reciprocated?"

"Hell, yes. She lit up my world and told me regularly that I scorched hers. I thought we'd be like Hollywood's few forever married couples. You know, like Paul Newman and Joanne Woodward. We worked together, played together. We were so good."

"And that's why you were so hot in that first film together."

Bart held up his hand. "You're getting ahead of me, Lar. We'd already broken up by the time we did *Windswept.* The passion that everyone talks about in that film—that's what you get when you take two people who've gone their separate ways but still want one another and put them together again."

"Whoa … why the hell did you two split?"

"I'll tell you the short version for now. We do have to meet the others for dinner in a while. It was this: I've always wanted to be an actor. I love my craft. Every day of my life I work toward being better. I live it. I breathe it. Hell, maybe the reason I've even tolerated Leah today is because I'm a people watcher. I learn by seeing what makes people tick. What gets under their skin. What they do to get under other people's skin." Bart took a sip of his drink. "Let me digress from Holly for a moment. It's easier to explain *me* before I explain Holly and me."

"Digress away."

"I've seen a lot of deviant behavior in my days. I never told you this before, but my high school math teacher, who was also our neighbor and family friend, turned out to be a sexual predator. He tried to molest my younger sister, but she got away from him, thank God … and then she spoke up. I was, and still am, so proud of her. Courage can be contagious. As soon as other people heard her allegations, they came out of the shadows with their own. The breadth of this bastard's crimes was stunning. Shortly after everything came to a head, he was arrested. Later, he was tried, convicted, and then went to prison. For a long time."

"Shit," Larry said. "That's fucked-up."

"Big time. It was a nightmare. I used to think about the S.O.B. a lot, even have nightmares about him, but it took me years before I could actually talk about him. I even blamed myself for not having seen through him, even though nobody else had, either. But once he was locked up, and I knew we were all safe, I started replaying his bizarre behavior. All of my memories, mixed in with stories from other people, coalesced into the picture of pure human perversion. I couldn't believe nobody had had a clue. Why did it take an attack on my little sister for us to figure things out? My thoughts scared the hell out of me while the actor in me wanted to learn from him and everyone else in my world. Problem was, sometimes still is, I was scared that too much study might poison me somehow. I'm not an emotional chameleon. I know who I am and I know that I don't have the potential to ever be like that man. But because he fooled an entire town, especially my family, I didn't want to get into his head. His crimes, literally, hit too close to home. I didn't want to sympathize in any way. I didn't want his soul to be sucked into mine, as is the case when I study a character I'm going to play." Bart looked around the room. "But the thing was, being so damn angry, I couldn't stay *out* of his head." Bart paused to play back his own words. "I'm not making a lot of sense, am I?"

"Not yet. In fact, I'm even more confused. But, hey, you're good. I've heard you ramble before. It's called 'working shit out.' Go on."

"Thanks." Bart glanced around the room, as if looking for inspiration. "I've always been okay on a stage or in front of a camera, but in my private life, things haven't been so easy. I've always felt this battle to 'see and not be,' and to 'learn but not yearn.' Ever since I moved to LA, I was checking myself every day to make sure I didn't turn out to be some Hollywood asshole or keep company with the wrong people. That's why I've never been into the whole Hollywood scene, and it's one of the reasons I had to be here this weekend. I needed to go back to me before I was famous."

"Are you sure you've chosen the right profession?"

"I'm sure. I've learned to repel crazy, but it's nothing I take for granted. Most of the time, I'm fine. But when something hits home for me, like my former math teacher and neighbor, as with Leah, my thought process is different. Although I try to be analytical, I'm a human first, an actor second. And humans have less of a tolerance for ugly than actors. Humans get angrier. Am I making any sense?"

"None that I can see," Larry said.

"Oh, shit. I'm sorry."

"Just messing with you, Bart. But I'm still not understanding why you needed to tell me this before explaining why you and Holly broke up."

"Sorry, that was some major digressing."

Larry smiled. "Okay. Take your time. I'm a patient man. At

least I'd like to think I am. Can you go back to you and Holly? What came between you and that very fine brunette of your same profession?"

"Well, as you well know, I love acting. The craft. It's what I live for. Even when I first became known, I wasn't enticed by Hollywood swag. You know, all the goodies that come along with fame. I didn't care about parties unless people I truly liked were going to be there. I didn't need to be seen or to see others. I didn't need all of the party favors, all of the extras, all of the excess. I didn't want to become any of that."

"I see. And the lady did."

"Big time. She wanted it all. She wanted to enjoy every bit of her celebrity. As beautiful as she is, she was considered a plain Jane throughout school. Didn't even get asked to the prom. She had a lot to prove to a lot of people, but mostly, I think, to herself. And the more she got swallowed up in the whole scene, the more I developed an aversion to it. That's why I told you the story about that pervert. After that happened, it scared me how easily the wrong people could become squatters in my head. I had learned that I could too easily obsess over degenerates. Not trying to imply that everyone in her crowd was that way. They weren't. But a few of them swam pretty close to the scum on the bottom of the pond, you know?" Bart paused to exhale. "Holly and I were together for four years and four months. We just wanted to live different lives, move in different directions. I couldn't bear to watch us crash and burn and end up destroying one another. Neither did she. So we just said good-bye."

"Day-yam, Bart. That's some heavy shit."

"Yeah. It is. About two years after we split, Holly married some producer named Kellan Jay Wood. Kind of ironic, you know?"

"What? Not following you."

"If she'd taken his last name, she would have been Holly Wood."

"Ah! Gotcha."

"I say 'ironic' because she finally had all the toys she'd been collecting, and she was miserable. She didn't have Hollywood; she *was* Holly Wood. From everything I heard, the marriage was tumultuous from the start. They divorced after three years. Not sure what took them so long."

"And you weren't interested in seeing if the two of you could try again?"

Bart shook his head. "No, she was coming off some bad times, and, honestly, I didn't know what she wanted from her life anymore. And I was still trying to figure myself out. Eventually, I started casually dating a couple of women, and then a few years later, I met Aimee at my agent, Ken Menhardt's, house."

"What attracted you to her?"

"Her sweetness … and her smarts. She's changed, though. Unlike me, I think she lets a lot of her environment stick to her while I try to repel mine. She had to toughen up to work on some of the cases she has, and I'm not sure that being married to a well-known actor, even one that doesn't cheat, has been great for her confidence. Just watching her do battle with Leah, for example, baffles me. The woman I married wouldn't have put her gloves on and gotten into the ring."

Larry wrinkled his brow. "Is that a bad thing? Giving it back to Leah?"

"Not necessarily," Bart said. "But it can be hard to battle evil and not be affected. Don't get me wrong; I admire Aimee for holding her own. "I'm just not sure I really know her the way I thought I did. And I think it's kind of important that I do. She is my wife, after all."

"I hear you. You love Aimee the way you loved Holly?"

"Different, Lar. Completely different."

"And when you and Holly do this movie again, what are you going to do if the old spark is still there? For both of you."

Bart shrugged. "I don't know. But I do know that Aimee and I aren't having any children until I find out."

Larry's eyes widened again as he sat up straight. "Wow. Does she know that?"

Bart paused, then looked at his former roommate. "I didn't know it myself, until I said it just now."

"You sure you love Aimee?" Larry cocked his head to the side. "What did you say earlier about the delightful and fascinating conversation you had the first night you two met? Nobody ever had to take a cold shower after 'delightful and fascinating.' Or sweet and smart. You dig?"

Looking past Larry, Bart stared blankly into space. "I've never said this aloud before. In fact, I've never even allowed myself to think about it. But I know what I did." He met Larry's eyes. "I overcorrected. Just this moment, I'm seeing this. Aimee is a wonderful woman, but without realizing it, I chose her because she's nothing like Holly. Aimee can exist within herself while Holly fills a room with her personality … her laugh … her smile … her sex appeal. Holly is more of a free spirit while Aimee takes inventory of everything in her midst and analyzes it. When I met Aimee, I really liked the fact she didn't need others to define her. But as time goes on, I get the sense Aimee is becoming more rigid and controlling. That sounds terrible to say aloud; I don't mean for it to." Bart laughed. "You know, sometimes it's really hard to write your own dialogue. Where's a damn scriptwriter when you need one?"

"You're doing just fine without one." Larry smiled.

"Honestly, I almost don't believe the words I'm saying are real. How is it that I didn't see these things before now?"

"Does Aimee know how you feel about Holly?"

"I've never really spoken to her about my past. Except to explain why we broke up. But that was as far as I took it. I certainly haven't said a word about my residual feelings."

"My man. People know shit. Especially in Hollywood. In New York. Anywhere shit is happening that's worth talkin' about. Gossip spreads like poison ivy."

"Probably because it's just that. Poison. You're right, Larry."

Larry put a hand on Bart's shoulder and gently shook him. "So I'm asking. Do you love this lawyer lady?"

Bart looked at his watch. "Holy hell, Lar, I've got just enough time to stop by my room and make it to dinner on time. Aimee must be wondering where I am."

"Oh, okay. I hear you. We'll talk later."

Looking confused, Bart stood to go, then looked at Larry who was still sitting. "Of course I love her."

Larry dropped his head in despair as Bart left the room. *Cass, baby, this is why I know we can get through anything. No hot-and-steamy women still hanging around inside my head. It's only you, sugar. Always has been.*

Chapter FIVE

May 16, 1986 — 8:35 p.m.

The maître d' graciously opened the door to the private dining room, holding it until everyone had entered the room.

Dan walked over to the round table and counted seven place settings. "Unless we're playing a game of musical chairs, we're missing one place setting."

Colin looked at the table. "Looks like the dish ran away with the spoon and didn't give a fork."

Bart laughed heartily.

"Is this a Freudian slip, Clare? Who is it that you were hoping wouldn't come?"

You, Leah. Who else?

"There must have been some confusion when I confirmed for seven with a possible eighth. That was when Maggie was unsure if she'd make it or not."

The maître d', hearing the conversation, made immediate apologies and motioned to a waiter to resolve the situation immediately.

"No harm done, Clare, darling. I would have just sat on Danny's lap."

Colin winked. "No doubt you would have felt his happiness."

Bart pulled out a chair for Aimee and sat down next to her.

Leah took a seat directly across from Aimee, to keep a watchful eye on her every move. Bart sat next to his wife, leaving one spot between him and Colin, which Clare took. Larry sat on the other side of Aimee, and Maggie sat next to him, with Dan on the other side.

Maggie unfolded the linen napkin and looked around the table. "Maggie's impressed. We have a perfect 'boy girl boy girl' setup!"

Clare agreed. "Indeed we do."

"Oh, Clare, what a surprise that you're sitting next to Bart. And my husband, for that matter."

Aimee, with momentary amnesia, started to defend Clare, but Leah gave Aimee a look that shut her down before anyone could notice she was trying to speak.

"I'm delighted Clare is sitting next to me, Leah. I asked her to."

"Oh. Of course, Bart."

Clare looked at her nemesis. "I'm sorry, Leah. Would you like Colin and me to trade places? Perhaps you'd like to sit next to me."

"The seating is just fine. I'm happy to sit between my husband and Dan."

Thought that would shut you up.

Clare turned to speak to Bart while others began private conversations as well. It took about ten minutes for drinks to be served, and another fifteen for salads. Well into his conversation with Clare, Bart turned to notice that Aimee seemed despondent. "What's wrong, honey? Are you not feeling well?"

Aimee looked up and caught Leah staring at her, pushing the corners of her mouth up to insist she smile. Repulsed, Aimee smiled at Bart. "I'm just fine. Don't worry about me. Take this time to talk some more with your old friend Clare. Maybe she'll get over her pathetic obsession with you."

"What?"

Aimee looked at Bart, noticing Leah bursting with glee.

"Aimee, I don't believe I heard you right. You sound exactly like Leah."

Finding it impossible to make eye contact with her husband, Aimee looked down at the table. "I don't like the woman, Bart. But she does have a valid point about Clare. I saw it from the moment we arrived."

Bart took hold of her arm until she looked at him. "Are you kidding me? You must be."

"No, I'm not kidding. I think she arranged this entire reunion just to see you again. You may not see it, but she's in love with you. I'm a woman. I can tell when a woman is lusting after a man. Especially when that man is my husband."

Bart laid his salad fork down. "I'm stunned. I really am. Clare may have had a little crush on me in college, but it was never more than that. And there is absolutely nothing to indicate that any vestige of those feelings, if they even existed at all, remain. But even if that were the case … Aimee, why so cruel? It's so unlike you."

"Honest, not cruel. Just see her for the sad case that she is, Bart. Open your eyes."

Leah beamed at Bart's incredulous expression.

Aimee turned to Larry, who was without a conversation partner. "Larry, Bart tells me you two roomed together the last three years at BHC."

"We did."

"Bart says it was a very special time in his life."

"We got along well. Respected one another's space and had a hell of a good time, too."

"I'm sorry," Aimee said. "You seem preoccupied. I hope my conversation isn't intrusive. I'm just interested in knowing my husband's friends."

Larry finished his salad and took a sip of his wine. "Funny, isn't it? Here you are, wanting to get to know *me* because I was, well, am, a friend of your husband's. And the love of my life is sitting at home because I wouldn't allow her the same opportunity. Tell me, Aimee. If you were me, how would you be feeling about now?"

"I think you're being too hard on yourself, Larry."

"Really?" Larry challenged her. "I ignored her phone call."

"Well, you can always ring her back. Invite her to join you for the rest of this weekend."

"Stupid me, I initially thought that was the reason for her call this afternoon. But after taking a few minutes to think about it … hell no it wasn't. For one, Cass knows me. And she knows I'll have told everyone why she's not here. Now you tell me, what proud woman is going to show up in the middle of a weekend event knowing each and every person is aware that she wasn't welcome from the beginning?"

"You've got a point. So call her and apologize."

Larry handed his salad plate to the waiter, who had just come by. "That's just it. While part of me is feeling bad, the other part still isn't so sure he's wrong."

"I see," Aimee said. "Well, let me ask you this: do you think that Cassandra tells you everything? While you're busy shutting her out of your past, she might be slipping all kinds of things under your radar screen. You know?"

Larry nodded. "I'm sure she is; I said so earlier. But still, it's food for thought. Ah, and here comes some more for the stomach. Chicken cordon bleu."

"I'm having the fish."

Suddenly, the lights flickered on and off. Then, for twelve seconds, the room went black. While the Barrie Hillers vocalized minimal upset, there was a loud collective groan of a hundred people heard through the wall.

"The green shirts must be in the next room. I hope I don't

run into that dreadful Pappy again." Maggie shuddered. "God only knows who he groped when the lights went out."

Dan put his arm around Maggie, who was trembling. "Don't worry. I'll protect you." A large clap of thunder sounded, rattling the table and everything on it. "My, that's some storm out there. I heard some people talking in the lobby; it's not expected to end any time soon."

"I'm a wrecky mess, Danny. My hands are shaking so much that I can't even cut my chicken."

"Louisa May Alcott that for you, Maggie."

Colin applauded. "Well done, Dan the Man!"

Pleased with himself, Dan proceeded to cut Maggie's chicken. A moment later, the lights flickered again.

Leah groaned. "That's all this party needs is a power outage. Then again, it might liven things up."

Bart, distracted by his wife's sudden change in attitude, was determined not to let his concern show. "Clare, this food is quite good. Excellent selection."

"Thank you, Bart."

Dan nodded. "It certainly beats our beloved Barrie Hill cafeteria. Please tell me no one here has forgotten its manager, Polly Hatfield. I think she had a real longing to be a writer. As I recall, she went overboard with that newsletter she put out. I'm blanking on the name of it. Does anyone remember?"

Larry raised his hand. "*Polly Hatfield's Cafeteria News.*"

Everyone except Aimee laughed.

Leah cut her asparagus and laid her fork on her plate. "She used to describe the week's fare as if we were dining in some exclusive restaurant. 'Sautéed string beans sprinkled with toasted almond bits, accompanied by savory meatloaf—"

Colin coughed. "Ken'l Ration."

Leah continued. "'…dancing in a rich mushroom sauce.' Oh,

and if the meal had even the slightest bit of spice, she had it dance the tango. 'Garlic shrimp dancing the tango in a broth of fresh tomatoes, jalapeño horseradish, sweet Vidalia onion,' and whatever the hell else was in there."

"Maggie remembers! Her lemon pie danced the merengue! And she claimed those unfortunate tacos were dancing the salsa."

Bart laughed. "Ah, yes! No need for details while we're eating, but let's just say I haven't had one since. I think those tacos enhanced the practice of every gastroenterologist in the area."

Maggie giggled. "Oh, and I do remember Polly had a suggestion box by the cash register."

Colin nodded. "And I suggested she get rid of it."

"An excellent suggestion." Leah nestled up to Colin's side as she smiled coquettishly. "So brainy. That's why I married you."

Noticeably uncomfortable with Leah's actions, Colin moved on. "Polly's claim to fame, if I recall, was an interview with James Beard."

Leah laughed. "He was her idol. No wonder. They looked so much alike."

Ignoring her, Bart leaned forward to address the group. "I met him several years ago while doing a film. Not many people know this, but he originally aspired to be a singer and an actor. We had quite an interesting talk. I told him that I had originally wanted to be a chef. Smart guy. Didn't believe me for a minute. He died a year ago January, if I recall."

Clare took a sip of her wine. "I never knew that. I guess Polly didn't include that part in her interview."

Maggie placed a gentle hand on Dan's wrist. "Danny, do you remember the little drawings she did in the margins of the newsletter? Little ice cream sundaes and hamburgers."

Dan grinned. "I was partial to the hamburgers. I liked the way she drew those little sesame seeds on the buns."

Maggie giggled. "Yes, darling, I do remember those. How about you, Larry? Do you remember?"

Larry took a moment to take the linen napkin from his lap and wipe his mouth. "Indeed I do. I was always very grateful that she didn't draw her own buns."

"Heavens, no! I do remember when she catered an event for the English department," Maggie continued. "That dear Dr. Markley, the one who had a crush on me, almost choked to death on one of her spinach croissants. I remember seeing him pull these green stringy things from the back of his throat, thinking to myself, seaweed?"

Dan laughed. "You never told me that story, Maggie."

Leah, eager to control the conversation, spoke up. "I don't know of another college in the country that has a newsletter for its cafeteria. Such a silly thing." She turned to Clare. "Polly Hatfield was a friend of yours, wasn't she? In fact, as I recall, you let her join our group for a few months. How disastrous!"

"She had a perfect right to join, Leah. She also wrote for the *Chronicle*. She wasn't that bad."

"Compared to you, I suppose she wasn't. Christ, Clare, even you shone next to her. Well, she did end up quitting the group, didn't she?"

Aimee, who had been silent, looked up. "With a little help from her friends, I'd imagine."

Leah flashed an ersatz smile. "How did you know? You weren't there."

"An educated guess."

Bart looked relieved to hear his wife speak. "I wonder what ever happened to Polly."

Leah shrugged. "Maybe someone gave her a stale cracker and she died."

Clare turned to address Leah. "She teaches social studies now at a very fine private girls' school."

"How in the world do you know that, Clare? Don't tell me you've kept in touch with her! At least you didn't invite her to our reunion. So how is it that you know her whereabouts and her whatabouts? Are you pen pals?"

"I know a young lady who had her as a teacher. Her name happened to come up in conversation."

Maggie raised her glass to a passing waiter, indicating her desire for a refill. "Okay, enough about Polly. Women can be such bores. Let's talk about men."

Larry raised his glass to toast Maggie. "That's flattering … I think."

Maggie rambled on. "I heard through the grapevine that Augie Van Horn was committed to a psychiatric hospital last year."

Finishing the last of her asparagus, Leah looked up. "Augustus Leopold Van Horn the Third?"

Larry looked surprised. "Day-yam. How many Augie Van Horns are there?"

Clare smiled. "Well, at least three."

"Four, five, six."

Clare turned to Leah. "Well done, Count Dracula."

Aimee whispered to Bart, "Was that the counting game again?"

"I'm afraid so. Not the most challenging activity, to be sure. But it was a staple of our conversation."

"So you said earlier."

Maggie was rapt to continue. "I have news! I recently ran into Van Schrader at a cocktail party."

Dan was surprised. "Vanessa Clark married Buzz Schrader?"

"That's ancient history, Danny." Maggie nodded her thanks as a waiter placed a fresh drink in front of her and took away her empty glass. "Let me go on. Buzz and Van, it seems, ran in the same circle as Augie and Joanna Van Horn for years."

Aimee whispered too loudly to Bart, "They must be one dizzy group of people by now."

Larry laughed while Maggie continued speaking. "To get on with what I was saying, Augie started gambling and eventually lost his job, obtained by nepotism, of course. His father-in-law gaveth, and his father-in-law tooketh away. Joanna left him, and that's when it happened."

"What happened, dear?"

"He tried to kill her, Danny!"

Colin chortled. "Perhaps Dan doesn't read his own newspaper. I remember that well."

Dan looked embarrassed. "Of course, I remember it. I just wasn't sure what Maggie was referring to."

"Three, four, five," Leah said, irritated when no one acknowledged her.

"Maggie can be an enigma," Colin said to Dan. "As she told me earlier: we're all just puzzle pieces … or something enigmatic like that."

Maggie paused to sip her fresh drink. "Exactly what I said, Colin. Anyway, clearly, Augie just went out to lunch and never came back."

Clare smiled. "Did anyone call the restaurant?"

Leah looked condescendingly at Clare. "You're kidding me. It's an expression, Clare. You know what expressions are, don't you?"

Clare dropped her chin and looked at her. "I was being sarcastic, Leah. You and sarcasm have quite the love affair. But while you weren't looking, I snagged your lover."

Laughing raucously, Leah leaned back, enjoying the attention as all eyes again focused on her. "Oh, Clare, even speaking metaphorically, that's absolutely uproariously funny. Don't you think so, Colin?"

Colin took the last two sips from his wine glass. "I think the waiter forgot to bring me another drink. Oh, here he comes now."

Maggie leaned forward. "To finish my story, it was then that they put Augie away. Van says he just sits in his room and sings."

Larry, finished eating and laid his silverware on his plate. "I may regret this, but what does he sing?"

Aimee, against her better judgment, answered before Maggie had a chance. "Looney Tunes, what else?"

Everyone laughed except Leah, who was eager to change the subject. "Bart, I've been thinking about your upcoming film. *The Garden of Lost Dreams,* isn't it?"

"Yes, that's it."

"It's based on the novel of the same name, right?" Leah snuck a glance at Aimee. "I think I read the book many years ago. Wasn't that about a beautiful woman who was married to a wealthy Italian man in Tuscany? He keeps her captive in her own home for years until the handsome gardener discovers her, and the two of them fall madly in love and plot to escape."

"Exactly! Great memory, Leah."

"Well, I think it will make the perfect film with you and Holly Lyndworth as the lead characters. There's not a leading man in Hollywood who's more right for the role. Don't you think so, Mrs. Bart?"

"Her name is Aimee, Leah."

Aimee sighed. "If she wants to call me that, just let her. It's okay."

Bart glanced at Aimee, but gleaning no clue as to the reason for her behavior, addressed Leah. "Well, thank you for the compliment. By three in the afternoon on Monday, Pacific time, the deal should be signed and sealed."

"That's wonderful news!"

"Thank you, Leah. I think so, too. The public demand for this film has been overwhelming. An exceptional scriptwriter has been brought on board, and it will be shot entirely on location in Campania or Tuscany."

Aimee's face fell.

Leah mock frowned. "Oh, no, Bart. I don't think your wife knew that."

Unaware of what she was doing, Aimee dug her fingernails into her thighs, but quickly regained control when she saw Bart watching her.

"Honey, please tell me what's going on. You haven't been yourself since we sat down for dinner."

Aimee picked up a fork and smashed her red bliss potatoes until they were mashed. Realizing Bart was watching her, she put her fork down and looked at him. "I'm sorry, Bart. When you told me it wouldn't be much fun for me to attend your reunion, you were right. I'm just a bit unnerved."

"Would you like to go home? Or maybe to New York for the weekend?"

"Oh, honey, I'd love to! Can we leave after dinner?"

"No, Aimee. I didn't mean the both of us. I meant that if you're not—" The lights flickered again but remained on. A bit rattled, Bart continued speaking. "Actually, I don't think it's a good idea for anyone to be traveling in this weather. If anything is even running."

"I'm fine, Bart." Aimee looked up to find Leah staring at her. "I'll be fine."

Clare rose from her seat. "Excuse me, friends. I'm going to check on the weather."

Leah laughed. "Clare, honestly, unless you have a pipeline to God, there's nothing you can do about it. Dan already said word has it the storm will last for a good while. Oh, wait, maybe you're going to go outside and recite a poem: 'Rain, rain, go away, come again another day.'"

"Cute, Leah. But, no, I thought I'd stand outside and sing 'Stormy Weather.' You know, make friends with the storm so it won't be so aggressive. That's what I usually do. I don't know why you care. I'd think you'd be happy to see me leave for a bit."

Maggie stood up and began to sing. "Don't know why, there's no sun up in the sky, stormy weather. Since my man and I ain't together, keeps raining all the time …"

Larry stood and put his arm around Maggie as the two of them sang.

Dan stood on the other side of Maggie, putting an arm around her waist, and joined in.

Perturbed that her fellow Barrie Hillers had successfully neutralized her attack on Clare, Leah sat, fuming, while Clare quietly slipped out of the room.

Colin turned to his wife. "You didn't want to sing along?"

"Shut up."

Rising, Colin glanced at Leah. "On that note, I'm off to the men's room."

As Colin walked away, Leah snickered, then turned her attention back to Bart and Aimee, who were applauding as Maggie, Larry, and Dan finished the song.

"Bravo, my friends! Beautifully done. Love that song. Never can figure out whose version I like better, Lena's or Billie's?" Bart looked at Larry. "What do you say, Roomie?"

"Gotta go with Lena, although Billie's unique emotive qualities sometimes surpass. Depends on my mood. If I'm morbidly depressed, I tend to go with Billie."

Bart was taken aback. "Hope that doesn't happen too often."

Leah watched as Colin disappeared from sight as Betty approached the table. "I just love hearing people sing Acapulco."

Leah wasted no time showing her distaste. "A cappella."

"You sing it the way you like it. I enjoyed the Mexican version. Didn't you, Mr. Younger?"

Bart smiled broadly. "I loved the Acapulco version, Betty."

Betty blushed. "I won't disturb anyone; I just am here to tell Mr. Sullivan that he had another phone call."

Larry's face dropped. "Cassandra is calling for me again?"

"I didn't say that. And her name isn't Cassandra. It's Mona."

"Mona? I don't know a woman on earth named Mona. I've only heard of two Monas in my life. One had her husband screaming her name in a deodorant commercial. The other one hangs in the Louvre. You must have gotten the name wrong."

Betty stood firmly and addressed Larry. "I didn't get anything wrong, Mr. Sullivan. I heard her just fine. She distinctly said her first and last name."

"Cassandra Jackson."

"No, she said her last name was Moore."

"You've got to be kidding. Are you sure she wanted *me*?"

"She said to tell you, 'I'm tired of playing mind games.' Then she said her name: 'Mona Moore.' And then she slammed the phone down on me. I don't take kindly to that. And you can tell her so for me next time you talk to her."

Leah smiled patronizingly at Larry. "Doesn't look like that will be happening any time soon."

"Good night, Mr. Sullivan. My shift ends in ten minutes. There, you have your message. No need to rat me out to my supervisor again." Betty's face lit up as she turned to Bart. "Good night, Mr. Younger. It's been a dream come true to meet you. I'll be the first in line to see you and Holly Lyndworth in your new film. In the meantime, maybe I'll see you tomorrow."

Aimee cringed.

Bart smiled. "Oh, you work Saturdays?"

"Yes, I do. Wednesdays and Thursdays are my weekend."

"Then most likely our paths will cross again. Good night, Betty. It was lovely meeting you."

As Betty turned to go, Larry leaned back and smacked his palm to his forehead. "Oh, holy shit! She didn't say 'Mona Moore.' She said, '*Mon amour.*'"

Leah let loose with unbridled laughter. "Oh, if that isn't a scream! Colin should be here to hear this! What a riot! Mona Moore."

Larry covered his face with his hands as Leah continued to roar with laughter.

Dan looked at Leah. "Under different circumstances, Leah, this might be amusing. But it sounds as if Larry's girlfriend may be leaving him."

Leah was still laughing. "But that doesn't make this any less hilarious! Oh, my stomach hurts from laughing so hard."

Ignoring Leah, Bart addressed his former roommate. "Really, Lar, maybe you should give her a call."

Larry thought for a moment, but waved off the suggestion. "Nah, she's just letting me know she's not waiting around our apartment for me. She likes it when I worry. She may even leave town for a few days, just to scare me. She's done it before. It's emotional blackmail, and I don't like it."

Aimee stiffened. "Nobody likes blackmail. Emotional or any other kind."

"Well, Mrs. Bart, I find that people who are the victims of blackmail have usually done something awful and are deserving of what they get. They're usually very hypocritical people as well."

Aimee ignored the retort. "Bart, I'm going to the ladies' room. I'm fine. I'll be back."

Bart looked up at her as she stood. "Okay, honey. Sure you're all right?"

"Oh, Bart, don't be such a fusspot over your wife. Let her use the little girl's room."

By the time Leah finished scolding Bart, Aimee had made her way to the lobby, where she tried to stop tears from flowing. She spotted Clare and Colin, standing near the phone bank, and made a quick detour into the ladies' room so they wouldn't notice her.

The attendant, seeing Aimee's distress, rushed over to her. "Ma'am, are you okay? Can I call someone?"

"No, but you can get me some tissues," Aimee said. She sat on a pink brocade bench and dropped her shoulders in defeat.

Within seconds, the kind attendant handed Aimee a box of pink tissues. "Here you go, dear. Are you sure I can't call someone?"

Aimee shook her head. "No, absolutely not. I need to stop weeping and return to my husband looking the same way I did when I left."

"If I can help in any way, just ask. My name is PattiAnn, by the way."

"Thank you, PattiAnn. Tell me, do I have any black streaks on my face? I can't bear to look at myself in the mirror right now."

"Just a few. I have some makeup remover on my tray. Will that help?"

"Yes, that would be great. I'd like to clean my face and apply some fresh makeup. But I probably need to stop crying first, you know?"

PattiAnn smiled sympathetically. "Yes, that probably would be best."

Aimee blew her nose. Within six minutes, she had managed to pull herself together, wash the damning evidence off her face, tip the gracious PattiAnn, and prepare herself for a return to the dining room.

In the lobby, Colin and Clare were still deep in conversation, but they had moved to another spot, and Aimee didn't know how to get around them without being seen. Still shaky and distraught, she didn't want either one of them asking her what was wrong, nor did she wish to interrupt them.

Look what these two have to do just to catch up for a few minutes without that monster ripping into Clare. I wonder if he's apologizing for his wife.

Aimee leaned against a wall, just around the corner, and waited for their whispering to stop. When it did, she watched as Colin headed toward the dining room, while Clare went to speak to someone at the front desk.

I guess there's no time like the present to return to the snake pit. Why didn't I just let Bart make this trip alone! My God, what kind of hell is this? This isn't Connecticut. This is the Twilight Zone.

As Aimee entered the dining room and walked toward the table, she saw Colin take a seat next to his wife. "What did I miss?"

"You missed the hotel maid waitress person delivering a message to Larry from a strange woman who said her name was Mona Moore. Only it was actually Larry's possibly now-former girlfriend who had actually said *mon amour.* Is that not a scream?" Leah paused to scrutinize Aimee as she resumed her seat. "Fast forward to now. Larry's obsessing over his girlfriend and what to do about the entirety of her semi-cryptic message. Larry says he's not going to fall prey to her manipulation, but look at him, Colin. Every bit of him wants to call her back and beg for mercy. His knees are bruised, and he hasn't even hit the ground yet."

Larry glared at her. "That's bullshit, Leah. You have no idea what I want to do."

Maggie smiled as Clare returned. "Our hostess has come back. Maggie loves sweets. What's for dessert?"

Leah groaned loudly and everyone ignored her.

"Apple pie à la mode."

"Ugh! How all-American and boring, Clare. Count me out!"

The waiter approached the table and addressed Clare. "Will everyone be having the French apple tart, Miss Dreyser?"

"All but one, Frank. Mrs. Brent will be having a mud pie." *In the face.*

"But you said ... I won't be having any damn dessert. Just coffee."

"Of course, ma'am. Coffee, tea, and after-dinner drinks will be served shortly."

As the waiter left, Clare sat, refusing to acknowledge that Leah was scowling at her.

Bart put his hand over Aimee's. "Are you all right, honey? I've really been concerned about you."

"I'm fine, Bart. Please. Don't worry about me, okay?"

Maggie smiled warmly at Aimee. "I'm so glad you came back, Aimee dear. I was afraid that being with Bart's old friends here at the Vanessa Grand might be too much for you."

"Not at all. Bart told me to prepare for eclectic and unexpected conversation. I've been primed and ready ... as ready as one could be ... for weeks."

"Maggie will start!"

Clare smiled. "By all means, Maggie. The floor is yours."

"Wonderful. Now, I have a question for everyone. If anyone thinks Maggie Bristol is shallow, you'll see how wrong you are ..."

"You're not shallow, dear. I know you. I've always known you."

Maggie gently touched Dan's cheek. "I know, sweet cheeks. When the waiter comes over, can you tell him Maggie needs a very old cognac? In a big old snifter."

"Of course." Dan raised his hand and motioned for the waiter who was preparing the dessert tray and coffee.

Leah rolled her eyes in Colin's direction, but he pretended not to notice.

Maggie pressed on. "This is a hugely hypothetical question, and certainly not the kind of conversation I'm known for, but I've been doing quite a lot of thinking lately."

Leah nudged Colin. "Did she say a lot of thinking or drinking?"

Colin, still ignoring her, paid rapt attention to Maggie.

"I've been wondering about all different things. What if this? What if that? And all of my what iffing has led me to the question I'm about to ask."

Leah whispered to Colin, "She's probably wondering if we all know that the carpet doesn't match the drapes."

"Just let her speak," Colin snapped, unable to avoid her a third time. "You're the one who insisted we come here this weekend. I could have stayed home and listened to your snide remarks. Or gone out to get away from you like I normally do."

"Oh, hush, Colin. What's gotten into you?"

Bart turned to Aimee. "Another snide aside from Leah."

Aimee suppressed a snigger. "What's a snideacide? The death of a sarcastic remark?"

"Yes!" Bart laughed. "Exactly what it turned out to be!"

Leah turned to Colin and spoke as softly as she could. "Don't you dare speak to me that way in front of everyone!"

"You asked for that," Colin told her.

"If Colin and Leah are done whispering, Maggie will continue speaking."

"My wife is done speaking, Maggie. Please, go on."

"Thank you," Maggie said. "Now, remember, I've been in deep thought about this, so check your flippancy at the door."

Leah saluted Maggie. "Aye, aye, Captain! Flippancy checked."

Dan eyed Leah sharply as he motioned for the waiter. "Show Maggie some respect! Show yourself some, for that matter."

Leah snarled and looked down.

As an unobtrusive waiter walked over and took Maggie's order from Dan, another approached with a rolling cart of desserts and a coffee pot.

"Thank you, Danny. Now, what if we, the human race, went back to the beginning of mankind and in place of everyone who has ever lived or lives now, a completely different set of human beings had been born. How similar or how different do you think our lives would be? If not for Alexander Graham Bell, who would have invented the telephone? Without Thomas Edison, Albert Einstein, Henry Ford, Jonas Salk, the Wright Brothers, Isaac Newton, Galileo, and all the other thinkers of our time, how would we have evolved? Would it have been only natural that someone would have thought of the very same things, in the very same progression of time? Would there have been another Hitler had that particular monster never been born? If another universe could have been created, parallel to this one, how similar, or how different, do you suppose it would be?"

Aimee brightened. "That's an interesting question, Maggie."

Colin agreed. "Well, I've been taken by surprise. Earlier in the Parker Room you wanted to talk about men; now you want to talk about mankind."

Maggie thanked the waiter, who had handed her a cognac. "Colin, darling, I do have my moments of extraordinary reflection. So, do you have an opinion?"

"Hmm," Colin said. "Talk about asking a question to which there is no simple answer!"

"If there were a simple answer, I wouldn't have had to ask. Clare, what do you think?"

"I know one thing, Maggie. There would always be monsters. Unless the fundamentals of human nature were somehow genetically altered, nothing would change in that regard. They'd just be monsters with different names. There already are monsters with many different names."

Leah looked sideways at Clare but was still smarting from Dan's admonishment.

Lost in thought, Larry surprised everyone by speaking. "I've often wondered if all races were in all places ... if the world were homogeneous in that respect, would that have altered racism and xenophobia as we know it today?" He turned to Aimee. "I don't know if your husband ever told you this, but he was a brave man to share a dorm room with a black man back in the sixties. A whole lot of people didn't like it. And even though Bart is too much of a gentleman to tell me, he took his share of flak for rooming with a brother."

"Lar, I was naive in those days and thought I could hide that small piece of ugliness from you, even though you encountered it on so many other levels. All I can say is this: if it mattered to people what the color of my roommate's skin was, then those people didn't matter to me. But let's not stray too far from Maggie's question. Please, continue, Lar."

Leah muttered to Colin. "Are you as deathly bored with this as I am?"

Colin responded quietly without looking at his wife, "You're only bored when you can't be offensive."

"To answer my own question about racism," Larry said, "I will begin by saying that I agree with Clare. Human nature, the good and bad of it, would be the same. I do think that a great deal of hatred comes from ignorance, from being taught to hate, and from not knowing those we profess to hate. From segregation and exclusion. On that level, I think some of what I despise most about the *human* race might be more palatable. Or perhaps I'd just like to think so. But that said, I think pecking orders will always prevail. I believe that people will always find ways to divide themselves into groups, and the less-confident, as they always do, will find ways to demean and diminish others to raise themselves up."

Leah pounded the table. "Really, Larry. Do you think I don't know you're pointing your gun directly at me?"

"Believe it or not, Leah, I wasn't thinking of you at all."

Dan looked directly at Leah. "You know, if you throw a stone at a pack of dogs, the only one who will yelp is the one who gets hit."

"And what the hell is that supposed to mean?"

Colin turned to his wife. "You know exactly what he means."

"What does my Danny think?"

Dan smiled, fighting the urge to caress Maggie's hair as he spoke. "I think you never fail to amaze me, Maggie. Without having had any time to think this through, first I would agree with Clare about human nature. I believe people would be the same. But it is very possible that our language might be very different. Especially if we were all mixed together, as Larry suggested. Our two parallel universes might not understand one another at all. And while it's likely that all of our miraculous inventions would have come to be, perhaps they may have evolved in a different timetable, thereby shaping our world in unimaginable ways. And while sadly there will always be monsters, if there had been different monsters, who knows how the course of history might be changed."

Leah cleared her throat. "This is all nonsense. Nothing would be any different."

Bart shook his head. "Well, I disagree. Every little thing we do in our lives sets off a ripple effect that can dramatically alter our course. There have been a ton of films about time travel that illustrate what I'm saying; I even did one early in my career."

"What does time travel have to do with any of this?"

"Everything," Bart said. "If humans had the ability to go back in time, say, for the purpose of changing a catastrophic event, even the smallest of unrelated activities could change the world and perhaps create another catastrophic event. It makes you think. If even one small event happens differently, the world can drastically alter course. If a man decides on a different seat on his morning commute on the train, he may or may not meet his future wife, and they may not have a child who will change the world, for better or for worse. Everything matters."

Leah sighed. "That may be true, Bart, but the point is that these two hypothetical universes wouldn't be that different, and I don't know why we're even discussing this."

"What should we be discussing, Leah? This is exactly the kind of thing the Barrie Hillers used to talk about. We'd philosophize into the wee hours over far less."

"We had more time back in those days, Bart. I'm not trying to play conversation police, but I just find our respective personal lives more interesting than contemplating what a parallel universe would be like."

Maggie frowned. "Well, I thought it was an interesting question."

Dan shot a look at Leah, then gave Maggie's hand a quick, comforting pat. "It was a very interesting question, Maggie."

Larry nodded. "It's got me thinking. Are we, as the human race, hopelessly doomed to fuck up our world? Is there something we can do to change the course of things? I feel as if everything humans do to move us forward also harms us."

Leah slapped her palm on the table. "Do you see the insanity of this question, Larry? I don't believe the greatest thinkers of our time could tackle this one."

"So what does that mean, Leah? That man, and woman, just keep selfishly messing with the planet, with each other, until we cease to exist?"

"Give me a break, Larry. Now you've got all of mankind ceasing to exist."

Clare smiled. *Larry's got a point. If you ceased to exist, that would be an immediate improvement.*

"No, Leah, I don't. But I think that technology will continue to produce amazing things we can't imagine today, in 1986. I think today's science fiction will be tomorrow's reality. But I think that some day we're going to take it too far. We may have to start all over again."

"Nonsense!"

"You don't know that, Leah. Neither do I. Not one of us will live long enough to prove my hypothesis true or false. Can you agree on that?"

"I'm bored by this, Larry."

"You weren't happy when I was talking about my issues with Cassandra. You're not happy when Maggie poses an interesting concept for us to discuss. Why don't you just tell us exactly what it is you *do* want to talk about? From where I sit, it seems like you're only happy when you can rip into someone. The condemnation of others seems to be a game for you."

Leah motioned to the waiter to refill her coffee. "You're wrong, Larry. I'm open for most conversation. I just don't want to be mired in the monotonous."

"You really are the conversation police. Let me address this question to Colin. Maybe he'll be more honest than you're being. Why did Leah want to attend this reunion? Do you know?"

Colin fidgeted as he mulled over various ways to respond.

Tell them the truth. She wanted to stick it to me.

Colin smiled as the waiter refilled his half-empty cup. "Leah's curiosity brought her here. I don't really know. As a playwright, perhaps she was interested in seeing how people were doing some twenty years later."

Dan was taken aback. "Really! That sounds like we're lab rats, not old friends."

Leah poured some cream into her coffee. "Pay no attention to the tripe my husband is uttering. I came here because I did have a strong desire to see old friends. And for every one of you who is questioning my intentions, you're all hypocrites. Attacking me while you accuse me of doing the same."

Bart stood and waved his white linen napkin in the air. "Everyone, please! Can we call a truce here? Can we start over? I can't speak for anyone but myself, but the time we spent together all those years ago was the most memorable, life-altering experience I've had to date. I learned a lot about myself and the human race in general. I had a freedom with my fellow Barrie Hillers that had never existed for me outside the walls of the Vanessa Grand Hotel. It was the freedom to strip down, metaphorically speaking, of course, to my naked, unabridged self. Before that time, and certainly since then, being constantly in the public eye, I've never had that kind of freedom. Even now, the laws state I have less of a right to privacy than the rest of you because of my celebrity. In a way, I'm public property, and I detest that. I came here this weekend because I wanted a tiny piece of my past freedom back. I genuinely wanted to know how each and every one of you was doing. Please, can we go on with this reunion the way Clare no doubt intended us to in her invitation?"

"Thank you, Bart. I did intend for something quite different." *Very different.*

Larry raised his coffee cup. "I'll drink to that, my friend!"

Maggie chuckled and took a sip of her cognac. "Maggie will drink to that, too!"

Leah murmured to Colin. "It looks like Maggie will drink to nearly anything."

Ignoring her, Colin raised his glass.

Picking up on Colin's anger, Bart raised his glass. "So, do we have a toast to starting over?"

Everyone but Leah and Aimee joined in the toast. As six Barrie Hillers held their cups or glasses high in the air, a booming crack of thunder sounded, again rattling the cups and glasses on the large round table. The lights flickered on and off, and just as the second crack was heard, the room went black.

Chapter Six

May 16, 1986 – 10:34 p.m.

Seven minutes later, the maître d' rushed into the dining room, along with two waiters. As he shone a flashlight, the waiters hurried to place candles on the tables and light them. "Sorry, folks. The power is out all over Barrie Hill and neighboring towns. The electric company is saying the outage is likely to last until tomorrow. We've got plenty of candles to light the room for you here, but I'm afraid the only way to the guest rooms will be the stairs. We're going to lend you flashlights, but we also have staff available to walk with you in the stairwells. Please be careful, and please do not use the stairs alone. We're going to leave this cart nearby, which should have more than enough flashlights for all of you to take to your respective rooms. There are also some extra candles for the table, in case you need more than what we've just put down. We had to use all of our battery-powered lamps to light the lobby. Our apologies."

Clare looked up to address the maître d'. "Don't you have a backup generator?"

"I'm sorry, Miss Dreyser. There's been a rather serious flooding issue in the basement, and I'm afraid our backup generator is of no use at the moment. Again, there are enough flashlights here for all of you. Unfortunately, the additional lamps we had are all damaged by water."

"Clearly, they were not stored properly." Leah groaned. "I hate power outages. I guess that means no hot showers. Well, that's good news for you, Dan."

"Really," Dan said flatly. "How's that, Leah? No, never—"

"Taking that cold shower you're going to need after spending the day with Maggie will be a breeze."

"Don't you ever stop?"

"Oh, hush! Just having some fun with old friends."

Dan shrugged off a chill. "Damnedest fun I've ever had."

The maître d' turned to Clare. "We will do our best to accommodate you in whatever way we can. The last time a storm caused an outage in the area, the power was restored much sooner than promised. Maybe that will be the situation this time. In any event, giving our guests the worst-case scenario leads to fewer disappointments. I hope you'll excuse us; we've got several other guests to tend to at the moment. I'm very sorry, Miss Dreyser. But please ask for me if there's anything you need. I'm more than happy to be of service."

"Thank you. I will," Clare said kindly as the three men nodded, then hurried away.

Leah laughed. "Well, Clare, there's an offer for you. You should have taken him up on it. Find out what it's all about."

Distracted, it took Clare a moment to play back Leah's words. "What are you talking about?"

"Sex, of course. He told you to let him know if there was anything you needed."

"Remember this, Leah." Bart waved his linen napkin in the air. "Truce. Why don't you give it a rest? Your remarks to Clare are extraordinarily inappropriate."

"That's when I'm at my best, Bart. And I don't respond to the waving of dinner napkins, nor do I agree to silly truces. Not tonight or twenty-something years ago. I'm not a truce toaster. Never was."

Clare gently touched Bart's arm as he sighed in disgust. "Thank you, my friend. I can handle this." She looked at Leah. "Okay, for once and for all, let's get this insanity over with. What is your morbid fascination with my sex life?"

"But you don't have one, Clare. You never have. What's it like to be a virgin at forty-three?"

Bart started to speak, but Aimee stopped him.

Clare looked unaffected and bored. "I wouldn't know, Leah. Why don't you find a forty-three-year-old virgin and ask her?"

"Oh, Clare, everyone here, whether they'll admit it or not, knows I speak the truth."

Bart was furious. "Do *not* speak for me or anyone else!"

Aimee whispered to her husband, "I'm pretty sure Leah is right."

"Ah, I heard that! Mrs. Bart agrees with me."

Embarrassed and confused, Bart sighed and looked down at the table.

"Well, Maggie is certainly not interested in the sex lives of others, and I know my Danny isn't either. I agree with Bart, Leah. Please speak only for yourself."

Larry, who had been lost in thought again, spoke up. "Right now, I'm wondering about the future of my own sex life. I can't imagine why Clare's private life or anyone else's should be of interest to me."

"Oh, Larry, you're just in a funk since Mona Moore left that sad message for you. Ha! Mona Moore. That is simply hilarious."

Clare turned to Leah. "If there's something you want to say, Leah, just get it out of your system now, okay?"

"I have no interest in getting anything 'out of my system.' I just don't know why you won't admit you're a virgin. You were an anomaly in the sixties. No free love and all that for you. And clearly, you're an anomaly today. I'm guessing you're the only one of the group who didn't fool around back then. Except maybe for Dan. But as I mentioned earlier today, he was an anomaly, too. Of course, had Maggie been willing …"

Dan shot Leah a dirty look but said nothing.

"How you know so much about me … or anyone else … is mind boggling," Clare said.

"You've never been married, have you?"

"No, I haven't."

"Of course not. As I said before, if there was any man in your life, you'd want him here by your side. And alas, you're here alone."

"What does that prove?"

"Clare, honestly, have you met any new men of interest since college?"

"No, Leah. I haven't. Not one."

"And you're hardly the type to engage in casual sex."

"You're absolutely right. I am not."

Leah was beaming. "I think I can rest my case."

"Fine. Now, can we move on?"

"Absolutely, Clare. That was easier than I thought."

Maggie, who was staring into the flame, turned to Dan. "This flame makes me think about that beautiful poem by William Blake."

"You always did love poetry, my dear. Which one?"

"Tiger, Tiger, burning bright, in the forests of the night; what immortal hand or eye, could frame thy fearful symmetry?"

"Beautifully spoken, Maggie."

Leah, still demanding center stage, piped up. "If you'll recall, Dan, earlier, in the Parker Room, I suggested you let the tiger inside you loose. You might want to take my advice. As you can see, Maggie loves tigers."

Maggie, cognac in hand, looked directly at Leah. "Tell me, dear, are you still upset because Clare won the Adeline C. Harter award in our senior year? And you didn't?"

"Don't be absurd. But it was a ridiculous choice on the part of the judges."

"I don't think so at all," Dan said with conviction. "Clare was the perfect choice."

"Thank you, Dan."

Bart turned to Aimee. "The Adeline C. Harter award was given to the senior who showed the most promise for excellence in writing."

"Oh, I see."

Leah groaned. "Well, twenty years after the fact, it's clear that the awards committee made a grievous error. In 1970, Colin and I won two awards for our play, *Home for the Winter.*"

Larry twisted his lips into a half-smile. "But you co-wrote that, Leah. Any lauded work done on your own?"

"No, but—"

"I didn't think so." Larry spoke in a higher pitch as he mimicked Leah. "My God, that is simply hilarious."

Great comeback, Larry. I could kiss you for that.

"Oh, hush, Larry. The point is, Clare won an award for the most promise in writing, and as far as I know, the biggest feather in her cap is being the editor of *Kiddie World.*"

"I do run a prominent national magazine, Leah."

"But it is *Kiddie World*, Clare. Not exactly a great work of art. It's not the *New Yorker.*"

"No, it's not. But it's a quality publication. I'm very proud of my work, of the magazine's reputation, and of having started as a part-time staff writer and worked my way up to editor."

Bart interjected. "I think it's a wonderful accomplishment."

"Yes, Bart. As you told Clare earlier. You're going to subscribe for your niece and nephews. Very sweet. Tell me, Clare, did you go to *Kiddie World* right after graduation? What job did you snare with your prestigious award?"

Clare paused to maintain her composure. "I freelanced for two magazines on a regular basis."

"You freelanced? And then you got a job as a part-time staff writer."

"That's right."

"Couldn't you find a full-time job?"

Larry stood to motion to a waiter who had just entered the room. "Leah, I think we've discussed Clare plenty for one evening. Let's talk about you. I have a question."

"Just ask away, Larry."

"Do you have any friends? I mean, *real* friends."

"Colin and I know oodles of people."

"I didn't ask you about oodles of anything. Nor did I ask about Colin. I asked *you* if you had any friends. Girlfriends, to be precise."

"I socialize with many people. I see them when I like, on my terms, and I have no obligation to hear their troubles or listen to them whine."

Larry clasped his hands behind his head and leaned back. "Wow, what a response. For one, it's quite a degrading statement to make about members of your own sex. Second, I have to wonder: who do you call when you have something on your mind?"

"I have a husband, Larry. And since you're so interested, I used to have a so-called best friend, but that relationship died a long time ago."

Larry stopped to ask the waiter, now standing behind him, for an after-dinner drink, then returned his attention to Leah. "Did you take a gun and shoot it?"

Another good one, Larry!

"No, I did not. She did."

Maggie was riveted. "Please, Leah, darling. You must share with us. What happened?"

Leah took a sip of coffee. "Well, I met Laurel at the local gym. She was an artist, a potter, to be exact, and we shared many of the same tastes. She lived only minutes from Colin and me, and we ended up doing a bit of everything together. Everything was nice for a couple of years until her husband, Mario, decided to cheat on her. I did everything I could to help Laurel. *Everything.* But she was in denial. And in the end, she took him back and dumped me. She became angry with *me* for all of the things I said about that no-good louse. I tried to protect her and her children, and it backfired. I promised myself right then that I would never give so much of myself to a so-called friend."

Maggie raised her glass of cognac to the waiter who had just taken Larry's order. Satisfied he had seen her, she turned back to Leah. "That is an upsetting situation, I suppose, but certainly not a reason to be friendless all of these years. I'll admit, I've always had more male friends than female, but there are times when another woman understands what most men cannot."

"Well, Maggie, that's what works for you."

Larry wasn't satisfied. "I'm still curious, Leah. You said earlier this evening that you and Colin take separate vacations. You said he goes to Europe and other places, while you bask in the island sun with your girlfriends. Is that right?"

"I suppose that's the gist of what I said."

"So you travel with acquaintances?"

"When I said I laugh with my girlfriends, I was referring to the women I meet on my trips. We end up being chatty and forming our own little groups. Sometimes you see the same people year after year. But they're temporary friendships, and they serve a purpose. No strings. No drama. No extra people on our Christmas card list."

God forbid.

Larry, with one elbow on the table, dropped his chin into the palm of his hand, then looked at Leah in disbelief. "I see. So, no need for people of substance in your life?"

"I never said the people I socialize with lack substance. I'm a busy woman. I'm on the board of seven different organizations, and that requires me to attend many social and business functions. I must talk to over fifty people a week. They're all highly successful."

"I didn't mean 'substance' in that way. I'm talking about people with whom you have a personal relationship, people who you can call on when you need a friend. People who can call on you for your support as well."

Leah grunted. "Oh, really, Larry. Like your girlfriend what's-her-name, who you have not only chosen to leave at home, but whose phone calls you have ignored? Is that how you support those who need you?"

"Touché, Leah. What the hell do I know? I'm a rotten bastard. But despite the choices I made this weekend, I am there for Cass. I needed her to be there for me, to give me some breathing room, and she has clearly refused. I'm not necessarily the one rejecting her."

Maggie looked unapologetically at Larry. "I'm afraid you're giving a good impression of it, dear."

"Why, Maggie? Don't I have a right to some personal space? Don't we all?"

"Absolutely, sweet man. But you did ignore her calls."

"Well, technically, just one, Maggie. The second time she called she just left a message."

"Same thing, sweetie. The fact is that you didn't respond to either one."

"But we spoke about this for weeks after I got the invitation. And it's not like I don't give her space, because I do."

Leah burst out laughing. "Yes, whether she wants it or not."

"Well, if you take separate vacations," Larry countered, "it stands to reason that you and Colin don't do *everything* as a duo.

Obviously, you do write plays together."

Colin fidgeted nervously, and everyone noticed.

"Or maybe you don't. What's the deal, Colin?"

Leah narrowed her eyes at Colin, her body tensing.

"Actually, Leah and I haven't written plays together for over a decade. More like nineteen years ... and even then ..."

Clenching her teeth, Leah wore her wrath like Dracula wore his cape.

Bart sighed. "I must have misunderstood. I thought you two had been writing plays for over twenty years."

"No, Bart. We *started* writing them over twenty years ago. We wrote *Home for the Winter* the year we graduated. That was the only play we really finished."

"What happened to the collaboration?"

Still seething, Leah was threatening Colin with her eyes but he wasn't paying any attention to her. "As Leah mentioned yesterday, not long after I got my first job, I went to work on my master's degree. I took only a short break after that, and then dove into my doctoral studies. I finally got my PhD, but it took many years. And only since last April have I been a tenured professor. It's been a long and exhausting haul. So as you can see, there hasn't been a lot of time to collaborate on plays. I suggested years ago that Leah give playwriting a whirl on her own. It was never really my thing anyway."

"Congratulations on all of your hard work and success, Colin. I know getting your doctorate was no easy feat." Bart turned to face Leah, who had grown fangs since the revelation. "What about it, Leah? Did you give the solo writing life a whirl?"

"No, I did not."

Clare tried to stay mum, but she couldn't resist. "You told me you were far too busy to do anything like arrange this reunion. Apparently, maybe you could have done so after all."

"I am on the board of seven different organizations. That requires copious amounts of my time."

Clare nodded. "I see; so you really *wouldn't* have the time to write plays."

"If Colin's schedule would ease up, I would easily be able to reduce my workload with the organizations. It's that simple."

Maggie smiled at the waiter, who handed her a fresh drink before making his way to Larry. "So, Leah, darling, what activities do you and Colin partake in … together? Aside from the obvious."

Leah looked spitefully at her husband. "Maybe you'd like to tell our old friends about Ed?"

Colin feigned having to think. "No, don't think so."

Larry, whose mind had been drifting in and out of the conversation, reentered it. "Colin, my brother. You're not—"

"Hell, no, Larry."

"Oh, then who's Ed?"

"He's our neighbor. Good guy. We spend a fair amount of time together. Time Leah would prefer I spend with her; that's all."

Leah shot him a dirty look then turned to glare at Aimee, who had been silent for a long time.

"Leah, we'll have to talk," Aimee said, picking up the cue. As an attorney, I also sit on several boards."

Maggie giggled and turned to Dan. "Every time someone says that, I always want to respond with 'I hope there are no nails in them.'"

Dan laughed. "Very funny."

"Maybe that's what she's got stuck up there," Larry mumbled to himself.

"I didn't hear what you said, Larry. Mrs. Bart, you're sitting right next to him. What did he say?"

Aimee looked at Larry. She noticed the corners of his mouth were turned up in a smile that only she could see and that his dark brown eyes were laughing.

Larry, quick to translate Aimee's prolonged stare into a well-received compliment, winked at her.

Leah fumed. "Well, Mrs. Bart, what did he say?"

Aimee looked at Leah and smiled. "Did Larry say something? I didn't hear a word. But getting back to you, Leah, I think it's wonderful that you do so much for charity."

Colin suppressed a laugh. Leah began to fidget but stopped when she realized what she was doing.

"Leah," Dan said, breaking the silence, "I think Aimee was paying you a compliment. I, too, think it's quite admirable that you sit on the board of seven charitable organizations."

"They're not charitable organizations, Dan. They're businesses."

"Oh … I see."

"No, you don't see. Although they're not charities per se, each and every company I work with does do something charitable. Like the bank, for example. My uncle Robert is the chairman of the board, and it's an honor to work alongside him. He's the finest human being I've ever known. He's not a dilettante of any kind. He's a true philanthropist with more awards and commendations than one could count. He's a very powerful man, and I have the greatest admiration for him. And it's mutual."

I doubt it. Clare put one hand on the candle within her reach and turned it around, staring at the flame as she did so.

"Sounds like a fine man." Dan turned to Aimee. "Tell us about your work, Aimee. Any charitable organizations?"

Leah smoldered as the spotlight shifted to Aimee.

"Oh, yes, Dan. All of my board memberships are with charitable organizations. The one dearest to my heart is a shelter for battered women."

Clare smiled. "I'd love to hear about the organization. A

friend of mine on Long Island, along with a committee of people, is working on founding a shelter. Any advice would be greatly appreciated."

Leah cleared her throat.

Aimee took a deep, uncomfortable breath, then looked at Clare. "I have no advice for you, Clare. Sorry. Except to maybe get over my husband. It's been, what … twenty-something years?"

Bart was mortified. "Aimee! Seriously? What the hell is wrong with you? Where is this nonsense leading to?"

Feeling the knot in her stomach grow larger, Aimee continued. "Three, four, five."

Leah howled with laughter. "Ah, Mrs. Bart is now an honorary Barrie Hiller."

Bart, realizing that everyone was watching him, lowered his voice and spoke directly to his wife. "What the hell has gotten into you?"

Maggie waved her boa in the air. "Attention, everyone! Aimee isn't an honorary Barrie Hiller. She's an honorary Leah."

Dan whispered to Maggie, "She certainly has caught the ugly bug."

"I'm horrified," Bart said to Clare. "I have no words except 'I'm sorry.' My wife has never shown this side of herself before. Not ever. It's baffling and humiliating. I apologize to you for her."

Leah cleared her throat again.

Aimee turned to Bart and Clare both. "No apologies for anything I've said. I mean every word. Clare, I can see by the pathetic look on your face that you're milking this for all it's worth."

"Aimee! Stop it!" Bart roared. "Enough!"

Aimee stood. "I'm going to leave the seven of you to yourselves. I'm going to sleep. It's been one hell of a day."

Bart stood alongside her. "I'll walk you up to the room. It's not safe to go alone in the dark."

"Please, sit down, Bart. I'll have one of the hotel staff escort me. I really just want to be alone. I insist!"

Larry jumped up. "I'm on my way to the men's room, Aimee. I'll walk with you and make sure you find an escort. Is that okay?"

"Yes, Larry. I'd appreciate that. Thank you." Aimee smiled and mumbled "good night" to everyone before hurrying away.

As Larry and Aimee left, Bart sat down, picked up his napkin and wiped his brow. "Will someone tell me I'm hallucinating and that none of this is happening?"

"Sorry, Bart." Leah pouted. "No can do. Perhaps your wife isn't the sweet little woman you thought her to be."

You have something to do with this, Leah. I know you do. I don't know what it is, but you won't get away with it. And that's a promise. "Don't worry," Clare whispered to Bart. "There's a good explanation for Aimee's unfortunate behavior. It just isn't a pretty one."

"Do you know what's going on?"

"I believe Leah has somehow forced her hand. How or with what, I have no clue."

Bart looked at Leah, who was wrapped tight in her smugness. "I think you're right. I should go find out what's going on."

"I don't think so, Bart. I would give things time to cool down. My God, it's hot as hell in here."

Chapter SEVEN

MAY 16, 1986 — 11:46 P.M.

Aimee stood in the lobby and waited for Larry, who had excused himself to go to the men's room.

Mayhem filled the Vanessa Grand. Guests were complaining about the outage as if the hotel had caused it. A tanned man in a Brooks Brothers suit at the front desk was screaming about the broken backup generator and threatening to sue. At least thirty of the green-shirted reunion attendees were milling about aimlessly, one of them crying because she couldn't climb nine floors to her room with a sprained ankle. Her inebriated mother, meanwhile, was demanding the bellhop "do something about the rain." When he suggested she "pray for it to stop," she went screaming to a beleaguered concierge that the bellhop had imposed his religious values on her. And she was going to sue.

Mesmerized by the madness, Aimee welcomed the numbness that had taken over mind and body. She was startled to hear a voice behind her.

"This is some crazy shit going on here. People who are staying here are screaming because the power's out and people coming off the streets who need a place to stay are upset at being turned away. It's a house full of nuts. No vacancies at the inn. Not a one."

Aimee turned around. "Oh, Larry, I didn't see you come back … which would make sense since the lights are out. These battery-powered lamps they've scattered about are helping, but not by much. Yes, this is crazy indeed. I feel like I've stepped out of one nuthouse into another." She paused to further survey the chaos. "This is quite a litigious-minded group. Everyone wants to sue the hotel. Too bad there isn't one legitimate suit in the bunch. I could make some extra pocket change by picking up a few new clients."

"Pocket change, huh? What is pocket change to a lawyer these days, anyway?"

"I was making a joke. It just wasn't very funny."

Larry spotted two green-shirted guests vacate a loveseat nearby and began walking toward it. "Quick, let's grab these seats while we can."

Aimee followed and sat next to him. "I'll tell you something; this madness is nothing compared to this loathsome reunion." She looked directly into his eyes. "Tell me, Larry. Was Leah such a monster back in college? Why in the world would anyone *ever* come to a reunion to see her again? That would be like wanting to be reunited with the bubonic plague. Only that would be preferable."

"Bart and I were discussing this earlier, when you left to find your old school chum."

"When I what?"

"Didn't you see an old friend in the lobby earlier? Or thought you saw one?"

Aimee quickly recovered. "Ah … yes. I'm originally from New York, you know. It wouldn't be the first time I've seen an old friend on a trip back East. But in this case, no. Turns out it wasn't her after all. They say everyone has a doppelgänger. Guess I found Mary's. And lost her again in the crowd." She laughed nervously.

"Oh … okay." Larry paused to recall their previous conversation. "Well, to answer your question about Leah, she was quick-witted and clever, but never evil. Sure, she could be cutting and sarcastic, but that was the language we all spoke back then. When we were together, there was a freedom we had with one another that didn't exist in the outside world. If you don't mind, Aimee, I'd like to ask you a question."

"Sure, what is it?"

"If Leah's the bubonic plague to you, why the hell are you trying to *be* her? What's up with that?"

Embarrassed, Aimee looked away and said nothing.

"Come on. You're not going to go all shy on me now, are you? What gives?"

Flustered, Aimee turned to him. "What you heard me say—aloud to everyone, or even to just Bart, well, it sickened me. Can you leave it there?"

"Hell no! I'm not leaving it anywhere. Talk to me."

"I can't. You're Bart's friend."

Larry gently touched her leg. "Maybe I could be yours, too."

"Why would you want to be my friend?"

"For starters, you look like you could use one. Also, the woman with Bart in the dining room tonight was a completely different person from the one I met in the Parker Room earlier."

"Look, Larry, if I told you the bitch blackmailed me into trashing Clare, would that be enough for you?"

Larry took his hand away. "Nah. I figured that part out on my lonesome. But the two of you just met. What I can't figure out is how she could possibly know anything about you, much less enough to squeeze that kind of ugliness out of a fine woman like yourself."

"You're Bart's friend. If I tell you, you'll tell him. I've already told you way too much. I should have just said good night to you and your assumptions and left it at that."

"Hey, I'm not judging you. Look at me. I refused to bring my woman here this weekend, and Bart brought you without a second thought. Maybe you're thinking I'm not so nice."

Aimee shook her head. "Nope. Actually, I'm thinking you've done Cassandra an incredible favor. If Bart had been a little bit more like you, I wouldn't be in this miserable situation."

"Which is what?"

"I can't tell you."

"What if I give you my solemn word that I won't tell Bart? I promise. I know you don't know me, and there's no reason you should trust me. I may be a man who has his faults, but I'm upfront about them."

"If I don't confide in you, Larry, will you tell Bart I'm hiding something?"

Larry waved off the question. "Sugar, I don't need to tell Bart anything of the kind. The man is clearly aware that his wife has done a one-eighty and turned into a Leah monster. He's going to ask you what's up no matter what you say to me now. I can't stop that. But, as I just stated, I can be a friend to you, too. And from all that's gone down, looks to me like you could be using one right about now."

Aimee sighed as she wrestled with her conflicting thoughts. "All right. It's like this. When I left the Parker Room, it wasn't to look for an old friend in the lobby. It was to make a phone call. To Bart's agent, Ken Menhardt. I'm no better than Leah, maybe. I called Ken to strong-arm him into pulling Bart from that film with Holly Lyndworth. Bart's been the perfect husband. He's never given me any reason to doubt his love. But there's something missing. I lied about seeing *Windswept.* I watched it when Bart was out of town. That passion, the kind he's got on screen with Holly, that's more than good acting. That's the real thing. And he's *never* been like that with me. And if this film goes through, I'm going to lose him, Larry. I know it."

"You know, somehow I think my old buddy would understand this. Why don't you just be straight with him?"

"Believe me, I've thought about it. But a few years ago, I went behind his back, and I did, quite successfully, get his agent to pull him from the last film. Then, thanks to a natural domino effect, it died without any more help from me. That's the part my husband isn't going to understand. He was deeply upset for months after that picture fell through, especially because the explanations he was given didn't make as much sense as they could have. But even greater than my fear of his learning of my hand in all this, I'm afraid that once I broach the subject of Holly, he's going to tell me that he still has feelings for her, and we'll never ever get back to where we've been."

"How in the world did Leah find out about this?"

"She followed me to the lobby when I left the Parker Room … and, obviously, to the phone bank. I was going to call from the privacy of our room until I remembered the long-distance call would be on the bill, so I used a public phone. Unfortunately, I was so absorbed in the threats I was making, so wrapped up in the emotion that drove me to it, that I didn't see her sidle up to the phone next to me. She heard every word I said."

"Damn." Larry exhaled. "Nasty grows some bitter roots."

"What?"

"Oh, nothing. Just something I was saying earlier to Bart about Leah. You know, we all have baggage. We all have crazy shit in our past that shapes the lives we live as adults. I know folks with brutal childhoods, and they're nothing like the nasty that Leah is. Don't know how Colin stands it. But, you know, the more I think about it, the more I remember Leah always comparing herself to someone else. She was one gorgeous woman back then, hot damn, yet, it was never enough. Always had to be prettier, better dressed, smarter, funnier, and more successful than anyone else. And Clare was always her target."

"That's interesting, Larry. Seriously. But it doesn't help me with Bart. What should I do?"

"Do you feel as passionate about Bart as you want him to feel about you?"

"Yes, and I think maybe that's the problem. I'm always wondering if he's got more to give that I'm not getting. And even though he's never been anything but loving, I feel like I have to be a ruthless competitor for his love. The man I was with before I met Bart was an accountant. He was very successful, but women didn't fawn all over him. I breathed a lot easier in that relationship, but I felt so much sameness in our daily life together. I was bored. Being Bart's wife is the best thing that ever happened to me. Life is much more exciting, but I've had to pay a price for that. Am I making any sense?"

Larry challenged her with a look. "Is it the excitement you love?"

"No, it's the man. I love my husband, Larry. Very much. That's why I don't want his lips to ever touch Holly Lyndworth's. Even in a movie. That's it. At least when I threatened Ken, it was to save my marriage. I feel like I stepped out of my body to make that call. Blackmail is not something that comes naturally to me; I felt threatened and compelled to protect what is most important to me. Leah, on the other hand, blackmailed me just for the sheer enjoyment of it."

"Not judging, Aimee. Just asking: was blackmailing Bart's agent the best way to protect yourself?"

Aimee looked down. "No," she said quietly. "I'm so ashamed. And the thing is, in my moment of reckless impulsivity, I put myself in a very dangerous situation."

"Aside from the obvious, what do you mean?"

"Well, even if Ken doesn't do as I … um … demanded, there's no way I can follow through with my threat. If I do, Bart will not only hate me for destroying his movies, but also for trying to destroy his agent's life. And no doubt, other people will find out, and my reputation will be shattered into little bitty pieces. I'm not only jealous, Larry, I'm about as stupid as they come."

"Why didn't this occur to you four years ago, when you first threatened his agent?"

"Because the situation I'm using to blackmail Ken with was so raw back then … brand-spanking new. He was running scared, and I knew there was no way he wouldn't do as I said. But now … well, I have no idea what could happen. I'll tell you, Larry: if this floor were able to swallow me up into some black hole of nothingness, I'd willingly go. I'm a horrible person and a complete idiot. I tell my clients all the time not to act on impulse. Do I take my own advice … of course not."

"Stop! Don't beat yourself up. You were hurting. You were scared. I can't advise you how to handle Bart's agent, but I think there's an excellent chance you can work something out. If the guy did something worthy of blackmail, then maybe he'll understand making impulsive mistakes. I don't know. As for Leah, I'll say this much: stop being her puppet. I'm not so sure she'll rat you out."

"Are you kidding, Larry? Have you listened to the woman? She has no filter whatsoever. Maybe some coffee filters in a kitchen drawer at home." Aimee paused to take a deep breath. "She doesn't care who she hurts."

"No, but she doesn't want to hurt herself. And if she goes far enough to destroy lives, well, she might just lose Colin. Have you read between the lines of their conversation? Separate vacations … haven't collaborated in umpteen years or more. I'm not so sure she's ready to risk everything. But, hey, it's not my head on the guillotine. Just trying to provide some helpful information. Don't want to sway your thinking."

"Thanks."

"Sure. Can I walk you to your room?"

"No, I'll get a flashlight at the front desk. I really need to be alone. Besides, if you're gone any longer, Leah might start talking about us ... if she hasn't already. She'll have us hot and heavy in a stairwell or something."

Larry smiled. "Not the worst thought someone could have."

Aimee looked at him as if she were imagining the possibility, then abruptly spoke. "I appreciate the advice, Larry. Good night. And I hope you and Cassandra work everything out."

ˋ✷ˋ✷ˋ✷ˋ

"Nearly a half hour in the men's room? Thought you might have gone off with Mrs. Bart."

"No, Leah. We were just chatting in the lobby. Observing all of the chaos that comes with a power outage in a hotel."

"Oh, I suppose."

"Lar, how's my wife? How did she seem to you?"

"Very tired, Bart. I think a good night's sleep will do her well."

"Did she get someone to escort her to the room?"

"She was on her way to the front desk when I left her."

"Maybe I should—"

Larry held up his hand. "No, you shouldn't have. She made a point to tell me that she really needs to be alone."

Bart frowned and looked at Clare. "I suppose."

Larry resumed his seat. "So, what did I miss?"

Colin, who was now drinking coffee, poured himself a fresh cup. "I was just filling Dan, Maggie, and Bart in on the joys of being an academic."

Clare forced a smile. "And me, too. He was telling me, too."

"Oh, right. Of course, I was telling Clare, too."

Leah sighed and gave Clare a dirty look. "Colin was explaining the road to tenure. Not always an easy one, but I was with him every step of the way."

To trip him, maybe.

"Teaching is easily the best part of being an English lit professor. Writing scholarly papers, well, once in a blue moon I'm inspired, but digging into research makes my head hurt. Publish or perish and all of that rot. Not enough hours in the day."

Larry nodded. "It's no wonder you don't have time to write plays."

Maggie agreed. "You really should be writing on your own, Leah, dear. It doesn't look like your collaborator is going to be freed up any time soon."

"With all of my board activity, there's no time. I'm sure I already said that."

Colin turned to Clare. "Didn't you have some interesting news about writing?"

Leah huffed. "When did Clare say anything about having interesting news?"

Colin took a slow sip of coffee before responding. "Earlier. After you dashed out of the Parker Room."

"Oh, I see."

"Go on, Clare. Tell my wife and everyone else your good news."

Clare hesitated. "Okay, if you insist … I was telling Colin that my first novel is going to be published. And I have a deal for two more."

Bart stood. "That is stupendous news! I need another hug."

Clare stood and embraced her favorite movie star. "Thank you, Bart. I'm pretty excited about it."

"Maggie is, too. Isn't that wonderful, Danny?"

"You bet it is! Clare, what genre are you writing in?"

"Contemporary fiction. Literary fiction."

Leah sat up straight, her face red with rage as if she wanted to put her fist through a wall, but she recovered quickly. "Oh, being editor of *Kiddie World*, I was sure you had written middle-grade novels or perhaps some teen romance."

"Oh, no, Leah. Very much for the adult audience."

"Well, since writers are at their best when they write about what they know, I'm sure your stories—"

"Novels!"

"…that your novels will be sans any sex."

Clare laughed. "You'll just have to read them to find out."

Leah groaned while Bart beamed.

"I'll be reading them, for sure. Who knows? Maybe they'll be turned into films one day. Is there a role for me?"

"Ah, funny you should say that, Bart. Now that you mention it, there is one character you could portray masterfully."

"Don't tell me, Clare." Leah sniggered. "You've written a Bart character and a Clare character who fall madly, passionately in love."

Maggie, reenergized by Clare's news, smiled broadly. "Clare, darling, I think you've just proven to everyone who voted to give you the Adeline C. Harter award that you indeed were the most deserving."

"How the hell do you know that, Maggie? Nobody has read her work."

"My publisher has, Leah. My major, prominent publisher. Enough to give me an impressive advance and a three-book deal."

Leah tensed. "Well, it's no wonder you've had time to write, coming home to an empty house and a typewriter as you do every night. I guess with oodles of free time, it's not surprising you've turned out a book in your isolation."

Dan stood and walked to Clare. "I'm terribly proud of you, dear friend. What a wonderful achievement! Working a full-time job as an editor and finding time to write novels. I'm inspired by you."

"Oh, Clare! I hope you don't do your novel writing on the

job! You could be fired for that."

"I certainly do *not,* Leah. I write on nights and weekends when I can find the time."

"When you can find the time! Ha! That's so hilarious, it just kills me!"

I wish it would.

"Leah, darling, I'm fascinated by how much you know about Clare's life, having had no contact since we graduated."

"Maggie, it's always been painfully obvious to me how lonely Clare's life would turn out to be. I'm surprised none of you could see it. Perhaps I'm just more intuitive. Or, maybe, I'm just clairvoyant."

Clare laughed heartily. "Nice to meet you Clair Voyant; I'm Clare Dreyser. How wonderful that we share a name. Perhaps we share a W. Somerset Maugham and dad, too."

Everyone but Leah laughed.

Larry raised his glass. "Ah, perfection!"

Angered, Leah turned to Colin. "I think it's about time we call it a night. Time to use those flashlights the maître d' left for us and retire to our room. Don't you think?"

"Victor Hugo on without me. I'll be up later."

Raising his glass again, Larry's voice got louder. "Ah, the Barrie Hillers as I remember them!"

"I want to go now, Colin. Do you not hear me?"

Colin turned to his wife. "You insisted we come," he said softly. "I gave in to you. So, if you want to go to our room, by all means, go. But I'm actually having a good time now. I'll leave when I want to leave. And not a moment before."

"All right, have it your way. We'll stay."

"Well, my darlings, you stay and enjoy yourselves. Maggie is tired, and Danny is going to walk me to my room. I'm not looking forward to those eight flights of stairs. My goodness! This is no time for a workout."

"If you're not comfortable with only flashlights, grab a couple packs of matches and one or two of those candles over there." Clare nodded toward a rolling cart. "You'll both probably need one in your rooms. I'm not feeling optimistic about this outage being over any time soon."

Dan walked to the cart and picked up a small fat candle and a pack of matches and put them in his pocket. "Thanks, Clare. I'll be fine, but Maggie may need the extra light."

Maggie and Dan wished everyone a good evening, and within moments they were gone, leaving Larry, Bart, Clare, Colin, and Leah.

Larry watched Leah's face glower. He studied her eyes as they darted around the table at the four remaining, then turned her attention toward the door where two had just departed. To the observant, her mind was on fire, her day's work far from done.

"If everyone will excuse me, I don't think I'll wait for my husband after all." Leah stood. "I'm quite sleepy all of a sudden. It's been a hell of a day. We can skip the nocturnal pleasantries."

While everyone, including him, simply watched Leah get up and leave, Larry remained fixated on the woman who had caused so much pain as she swiftly made an exit. *Bitter grows some ugly roots, and they're getting longer all the time.*

Chapter EIGHT

May 17, 1986 – 12.31 a.m.

Maggie, her arm linked with Dan's, felt content as they headed for the stairwell, through the still-chaotic lobby.

"Larry wasn't kidding. Look at this madness. You would think these people's lives had been disrupted forever. They're so loud and tacky. But this isn't nearly as bad as the New York blackout in 1977."

"That was a horror. I spent the night in my office. Better than some of my colleagues, who were trapped in elevators and subways. Ah, here's the door. Hold onto me, and I'll point the flashlight all the way. Just be careful where you step."

"I'm with you, Danny. I'm not worried."

Dan looked longingly into Maggie's eyes, then, realizing what he was doing, turned away.

The duo had climbed five floors without seeing anyone. "My goodness, Danny, I thought there would be more people. I guess they're already in their rooms or among those screaming cretins in the lobby." Maggie looked down. "What in the world is this?"

Dan shone the flashlight on the fifth-floor landing. He reached down and found a small heap of green cloth and picked it up. "Someone is missing a T-shirt."

"Oh, my, Danny! I hope it's not that wretched Pappy's. Hold

it open for me."

Dan handed Maggie the flashlight, while he held the shirt open with both hands.

"No, that can't belong to that letch. Not nearly large enough." As soon as Dan placed the shirt in a corner of the landing, Maggie shivered in disgust as she handed the flashlight back to him. "Ugh! I'm sorry I asked you to hold that thing a moment longer than necessary." The words just out of her mouth, Maggie and Dan heard the excited squeal of a woman. Alarmed, Dan shone the flashlight up the stairs right onto the size DD breasts of a woman wearing nothing but a skirt that was halfway down her hips and a bra around her waist.

Mortified, Dan gasped and redirected the light back to the landing, where he was standing with Maggie.

The woman called down to them. "Don't mind us! Just getting ready to have some blackout fun! Come on up. You can pass. You can even take a peek." She giggled.

"Oh, what a repugnant woman!"

Dan looked apologetically at Maggie. "I'm so sorry, dear. I'm afraid we're going to have to make our way past."

"Yes, I know. Just don't let her pestilent flesh touch you."

Maggie and Dan had gone no farther than seven steps when Maggie saw Pappy Cutter, pants unzipped, his large stomach hanging over, heading down the stairs and toward the bare-breasted woman.

"Oh, you horrible man! Why aren't you at the very least doing this in your room?"

Seeing Maggie, Pappy lit up. "Hello again, blond bombshell. You gorgeous specimen of a woman!"

"Keep your filthy words for this woman you are pawing. Again, why aren't you doing this in your room?"

Pappy laughed. "Well, now, that would wake my wife up. I

wouldn't want to do thaaaat! Susie and her don't get along too well."

"You're married? Your wife is here? Remove your debauchery from my path, you rotting piece of scum!"

"I'm not scummy, mummy. I'm keeping it all in the family. This is my cousin's lovely wife. Not like I hired a whore, though I have—"

"Keep that to yourself, you loathsome swine!"

"Hurry up, dear," Dan said. "Don't talk to him. It's only upsetting you more."

As they climbed three floors past Pappy and his cousin's wife, the squeals and groans emanating from their antics followed Maggie and Dan all the way to their destination.

Maggie cringed as she heard Pappy talking to someone below. "Hey, join us! The more the merrier!"

"That horrid man is trying to recruit an innocent bystander to turn his shameful tryst into a ménage a trois! In a stairwell of all places."

"Try to forget him, my dear. We've reached our destination." Dan opened the door to the eighth floor and shone the flashlight down the old, but regal carpet. "Two doors down to the left, if I remember correctly."

Maggie reached into her handbag and handed Dan the key. He opened the door easily and shut it behind him.

Dan turned off the flashlight and laid it on top of a suitcase that rested on a stand by the door. They stood, face-to-face, familiar with the yearning they'd come to know so well over the long years, and then, unplanned by either, embraced in the privacy of the dark room. Dan started to say something, but Maggie reached up and put a finger to his mouth, which he gently kissed. Maggie threw her arms around his neck, and within moments, the two fell into the unrelenting and passionate kiss they had always coveted.

After two minutes had passed, they pulled apart, but only

ever so slightly. "Oh, Danny, I'm so sorry. I didn't know that would happen."

Dan grabbed the flashlight, switched it back on, and walked Maggie over to the bed, where they sat. "I didn't either. Only because I thought I had more self-control. I've wanted to do that since the moment I first saw you nearly twenty-five years ago. I've never stopped wanting to do that. And, to be quite honest, dearest, much more."

Maggie moaned in despair. "I'm no better than that cow in the stairwell who was exposing her udders for that pig to suckle on."

Dan laughed as he stroked her hair. "I've never known anyone to express herself with the colorful language that you do." Dan looked wistful. "I asked you once in college why you often used 'unorthodox vocabulary,' and you told me you did so because you never wanted to sound like anyone else. And you don't." Dan paused to look at her. "There is no one who can make me laugh the way you do. To make me feel what I'm feeling now."

"Aren't you happily married, Danny?"

"I haven't a bad word to say about Sally. She's an exceptional woman. And we have four extraordinary children and a functioning partnership." Dan paused uncomfortably. "But our romantic life faded away years ago. Sexual intimacy is not a priority for Sally ... or even a desire ... and I suppose I didn't help matters by letting my mind wander ... to you. What satisfies Sally is an active, busy life. But I go on, letting her believe I am complacent with the limits of our relationship."

"Why haven't you spoken up and told her what you desire?"

Dan looked into Maggie's eyes before he responded. "Because she can't give it to me. All I would succeed in doing is making her feel as if she's failed me. When our romantic life began to fade, I tried to resurrect it. But I stopped because it dawned on me that it wasn't that she didn't love me, but she didn't want that kind of relationship—with anyone. So I stopped wanting any kind of intimacy from her. I think she told herself we were both the same. Only we're not. That was years ago. I love her, but I'm not in love with her anymore. Those days have long passed."

Maggie blanched. "Is she in love with you?"

"I don't know that she couches love in those terms. I believe she's happy with the life we have. Sex was merely a necessity to have children. Being in love is not a part of her world. Love and family, yes. Romance, intimacy, sex … no." Clasping Maggie's hands in his, Dan went on. "I still remember that night you and I met for dinner in 1971. We had a corner booth by the waterfall in Trattoria La Fontana. The owner, Stefano, assumed we were madly in love, so he made every dish special for us. Remember? We never ordered from the menu."

"You felt guilty about that night, Danny. And we only had dinner."

"No, I didn't feel guilty."

"Then why did you tell Sally I was Stan Boyle from Dallas?"

"I didn't know if she'd understand. It was easier. But I didn't feel guilty. It was the most memorable night of my life."

"Oh, Danny. Your wedding night should have been the most memorable … even if the intimacy didn't last forever." Maggie looked down. "Not dinner with me. And now, it's all …" Tears began to trickle down Maggie's cheeks.

"Dear, there is something wrong. You alluded to something before, in the Parker Room, and it's been nagging at me all night."

"I'll be okay."

"Please tell me what's wrong."

"I can't bear to do that."

"Please, Maggie."

Wiping away her tears, Maggie looked at Dan and smiled, her blue eyes sparkling. "Did I ever tell you that I have the most beautiful view from my penthouse? I can see all of New York. It's just fabulous." Maggie stopped to blot her tears as Dan handed her a tissue from a brass box on the nightstand. "Thank you. Really, Danny, some nights, I feel like I own that skyline. Oh, it's pretty here in Connecticut—but I'd rather be in that penthouse than anywhere else in the world. All the buildings are like little trophies to me. I know exactly where the *New York Journal* building is, too. 'Cause that's where you work. And even when you're not there, I feel close to you just by looking at it. You bring a smile to *my* face." Maggie took a moment to tamp down her emotion. "Tell me, did Melissa choose a college yet?"

Choked up, it was Dan's turn to fight back tears. "She'll be going to American University. Wants to be a political correspondent." Dan looked into her eyes. "Maggie, I had no idea you thought of me so much throughout the years. I wish I had known. I wish you hadn't stopped calling."

"It was better, for both of us."

"Because you were married as well?"

"Oh, sweetie, you know I've had four marriages. When we had dinner, I'd already been divorced from my first husband, James. He was a player. He cheated on me six months into our marriage. I was married to Leon, who was overseas at the time. He traveled the world on business and never had time for me. He should have hired a social secretary, not married me. I wasn't dumb enough to think a globetrotting CEO wouldn't cheat, so when I got the goods on him, I asked for a divorce. I wanted to call you so much during that time, my darling. Just to talk. Just to see how you were doing."

"Oh, Maggie, why didn't you?"

Maggie paused to consider her words. "Because one day, I was in the ladies' lounge at the Waldorf. I was at the hotel to attend some stuffy charity luncheon. My friend Marilyn dragged me to it. There I was, Danny, fixing my blush in the mirror, when I heard this woman say 'Excuse me.' I was taking up the entire mirror—you know me. So I turned around, and there she was. She was wearing one of those dumb stickers on her blouse. It said, 'Hello, I'm Sally Collier.' I just stared at her. I didn't mean to be rude, but I had to take a good look at the woman who married my Danny. She seemed really baffled. She looked back at me with this blank look in her eyes. Then big-mouthed Marilyn says, 'Come on, Maggie. The car is waiting.' That's when the look in her eyes changed. Marilyn never said my last name, and I don't wear dumb name stickers, but she knew, Danny. She just knew. I'll never forget the way she looked at me."

Dan's face went blank. "I wish I had known that. But I'm not so sure she had any idea who you were. Not once did I ever tell her about my feelings for you. Maybe she recognized you from old photos in our yearbook. But as I said earlier, my photo albums aren't in our home. Who knows?"

"Maybe I imagined it, Danny. Now that I think back, maybe she only looked at me that way because she saw me looking at her. That would make sense. But I didn't see it that way at the time, especially the way her look changed when Marilyn said my name."

"It doesn't matter now." Still holding Maggie's hands in his, Dan squeezed them then let go. "So what happened to you then, Maggie? You never called me again, and you divorced the CEO."

"I was sick of being married to men who slept with other women." Maggie looked embarrassed. "So, although subconsciously, I made sure it would never happen again. I did a Judy Garland and married a gay man."

"Oh, no!"

"Yes, Danny. I did. Obviously, I got nothing but friendship from him, and when I realized he married me for my social status and money, I quickly dissolved that marriage. I was single about a year when I met Drake. He was a lovely man some twenty-plus years my senior. He worshipped me. He never had eyes for anyone but me. He was the first husband I'd had who made me feel special, who made me laugh, and who made me feel loved every day."

"What happened, sweetheart?"

"Oh, Danny, it was dreadful. I woke up one morning, and he was lying next to me. Gone. He had died in his sleep. I was traumatized. I still miss him. I'm forty-three and I've been married four times. And now I'm single. And alone."

Dan looked sadly into her eyes. "What a fraud I am, Maggie. I should be telling my dear friend that I believe she will find her true love. But I can't say that, because if I'm painfully honest with both of us, I want to be that true love."

Maggie reached up and gently caressed each side of Dan's face, her fingertips barely touching his skin. "My sweet Danny. If ever I thought I could have made you happy, I would have let you sweep me away after college. But I'm an Oscar Wilde child, and you're so much more respectable—"

"Dull and boring …"

"No, my darling. Not at all."

"Maggie, if I weren't married to Sally, would you feel differently about me now, all these years later?"

Maggie took a moment to mull over Dan's question. Within seconds, her vision became blurry.

"What is it, Maggie? Why are you crying? Tell me what's wrong. I want to hear all about your life, but, please, don't change the subject again. Just tell me."

Maggie took Dan's right hand in hers. "I am more comfortable holding the hand that doesn't wear a wedding ring. Danny, I have been dealing with some medical issues. I have a very small lump in my breast. It is quite miraculous I discovered it so soon, but I'm still very frightened. I'm having a biopsy next week. My doctor says it is likely a cyst and that I have every reason to be very hopeful, but I'm scared. Your Maggie has been deeply depressed. This scare has made me realize how very alone I really am. That is why I've been drinking so much, to get myself through this. And that's not a good thing to do." Maggie paused to catch her breath.

Dan squeezed Maggie's hand as he scrambled to find the words. "But you—"

"Have so many friends? Yes, I do have many friends, but their well-meaning words are upsetting me even more. They're telling me horrid stories about people with cancer … not even knowing if the lump is malignant or not. Several have asked who my doctor is and insist they know a better one. Again, I've had no diagnosis, yet they're suggesting all kinds of alternative treatments, analyzing my diet, and on and on. I've asked every one of them to please step back. I made the mistake of telling one friend, and she told everyone. It never occurred to me she wouldn't keep my confidence." Maggie stopped to calm herself. "They are making me crazy, Danny … I've never felt so alone in my life. I'm smothered by advice I didn't ask for and deprived of the love I crave."

Dan's mouth opened, but no words came out. Incredulity and pain overcame him. Maggie could feel his hand trembling in hers. His brown eyes, deeply pained, touched her soul. His despair, coexisting with his desire, maddened him.

"Take me, Danny."

Dan blinked, as if he could not believe her words. Squeezing Maggie's hand, he looked into her eyes as if to clarify what he'd just heard.

Maggie took her hand out of his and caressed his face again, this time her fingers moving down the side of his face as if they were making delicate lines in sand. "Take me, Danny." She put her other hand on his leg, slowly inching upward.

Dan's breath quickened, and he reached into his jacket

pocket and pulled out the candle he'd taken from the dining room. Standing briefly, he placed it on the nightstand and sat down again. Maggie looked at it and smiled, her hand resuming its course. "Oh, yes, take me by candlelight."

Dan, fumbling less than he would ever have expected, reached into his pocket for the matchbook, opened it, struck a match, lit the candle, and quickly returned the matchbook to his jacket pocket. With newly found assertiveness, he gently clutched Maggie's shoulders. "Are you sure?"

Maggie leaned forward. "I've never been more sure. But you're the one who must be sure for both of us. I feel like a hypocrite. Only a few minutes ago, I was disparaging married men who sleep with other women, and here I am, asking you to make love to me. But you would not be a man who sleeps with other women, only a man who loves me. That's all—only a man who has always loved me. Maybe I am a blatant hussy who should retract her false virtue."

Dan let his fingers roam through Maggie's blond curls. "I told you, my darling. Sally and I—"

Maggie reached up and grabbed Dan's hand, locking her fingers with his. "You may not have intimacy with her, Danny, but you have a life that is comprised of way more than what we both want at this moment. I can't destroy that, yet I'm asking you to bear the burden of sin for both of us. Shameless."

Dan put his index finger on Maggie's lips. "No. No, you are not. Darling, listen to me. When I arrived earlier, I told everyone that there had been a threat of a strike at the newspaper, and that I almost didn't make it."

Maggie looked curiously at him. "But that's true. I heard it on the news all week."

"Of course it's true. But what I didn't tell anyone was that I wasn't able to focus on the strike. No, I was conjuring up ways to feign illness to get here. That sounds crazy and irresponsible, but that's how desperate I was not to let this chance to see you again elude me. And when I thought you might not be coming, well, I'm afraid I didn't hide my distress very well. Colin had a fine time pointing it out to everyone."

"Oh, Danny." Maggie sighed. "It wasn't illness that made me late, as my housekeeper told Clare. I didn't see any point in coming if the negotiations were ongoing. How ironic that would have been if you'd come and I hadn't. Like something out of 'The Gift of the Magi.' I was glued to WINS radio all day, and as soon as I heard the strike wasn't happening, I called my chauffeur. I had packed my bags days ago. But as I told you earlier, when I arrived at the hotel, I was so nervous that I went to the bar before the Parker Room."

Dan's desire intensified. "That's not important now. What matters is that we both ached to reunite. And we have. Now, don't you worry about a thing, dear." Dan removed his glasses and put them on the nightstand. Taking both of her hands in his, he stood and helped Maggie to do the same. Letting go of her, he turned to the bed, taking a corner of the bedspread, and turned it down. Then, grabbing the neatly tucked-in sheet, he pulled it out. As he did this, Maggie watched, feeling her entire body tingle as if thousands of tiny needles were gently stimulating her.

Dan removed his jacket and draped it over a nearby chair. Standing there, confidently, he removed his shirt and tie, never breaking eye contact with her.

Smiling, Maggie admired his muscular chest, incongruous with his thinning hair and horn-rimmed glasses. As Dan unloosened his belt, Maggie began to unbutton her blouse, as if dancing in time with a partner. Dan stopped to watch her. In no time at all, her blouse had been removed and laid on the bed. Within seconds, she unhooked her bra and laid it on top of the blouse.

Careful not to break the connection, she reached around, grabbed the bra and blouse, and drew nearer to Dan, who took her clothes and placed them on the chair with his. Now his turn, Dan quietly kicked off his shoes then stepped out of his pants as if such a maneuver were part of his everyday repertoire.

Maggie grinned hungrily at the bulge in his underwear, gasping as he stepped out of it, revealing more than she had ever hoped for. "Oh, Danny," she whispered. "My, my, Danny." Staring at him, she fumbled at the zipper in the back of her skirt. "Darling, I think you need to help me with the rest."

Within moments, the two old friends, standing naked before one another, breathed in unison then fell onto the bed. The candle's warm glow merely accented the passion that filled the room as their bodies pressed together. Their loud sighs were filled with yearning … their souls set immutably on fire.

Chapter NINE

May 17, 1986 — 8:31 a.m.

Dressed in a cobalt blue dress and matching heels, Maggie sat in the chair and smiled as Dan emerged from the bathroom.

As he looked at Maggie, he beamed. "My goodness, you are beautiful. In the history of the Vanessa Grand, I'm certain no woman has ever dressed so stunningly for breakfast."

Maggie looked longingly at him. "Danny, last night was the best night of my entire life. Bar none. I've never had a better lover, and I've never felt more loved." She grinned. "I'm certainly glad the power came back on so we could take a hot shower together."

Dan kissed her forehead. "It was the best night of my life, too. It was an awakening of my soul and a validation that I have never wasted a moment in yearning for something or someone that doesn't exist. Oh, my love …" He stopped to slow his breathing. "I should probably go to my room, change my clothes, and have a shave. No one will be the wiser." He knelt in front of her. "Are you all right, darling?"

Maggie tenderly ran her index finger across his lips. "I am more than all right. Are you? No regrets?"

"Absolutely none, my dear. Would it be wrong of me to say I want to do it all over again tonight?"

Leaning forward, Maggie locked her hands behind his neck.

"I think I would die if you didn't." She paused to soak in the moment. "You'd best be going. We'll meet in the dining room."

Dan kissed her, then stood. "See you soon, my darling."

Maggie watched Dan leave. He had no sooner unlatched the security chain, then turned the knob, when, with the force of a tsunami, hell burst through the doorway, pushing Dan back into the room and slamming the door in front of him.

Maggie screamed in horror. "Something wicked this way comes! Leah! What are you doing here? How dare you!"

Looking haggard, her clothing rumpled, Leah snarled as she leaned against the door. "I thought you two would never emerge from this den of iniquity!"

Aghast, Dan took control. "You waited outside this door? All night? In the dark?"

"Just for two hours after you went in. I followed you from a distance up the stairs. Heard your charming encounter with Sir Corpulence and his slut. Quite amusing! Except for the part when I passed him and he asked me to join them."

"Oh, that was you!" Maggie said. "Following us! Tracking us like prey."

"Yes, that was me," Leah responded gleefully. "And, yes, prey you were ... and still are." Leah took a second to revel in her glory. "Anyway, when I realized the still-smitten newspaperman wasn't going anywhere, I went back to our room and got some shut-eye while I assume my husband was wasting the night away in the dining room with the pot-bellied spinster, the soon-to-be-single critic, and the truce-toasting movie star. Probably drank himself silly."

"Surely Colin must have come in at some point and wondered where you were," Maggie said. "He must be wondering right now."

"Hell, no," Leah said. "He got another bloody room because he was too inebriated to walk up ten floors. Paid a lowly bellhop to slip a note under the door letting me know. I'd say that worked out pretty well for me, wouldn't you? As for Mr. Movie Star, he must be covered in drool, having sat next to that pathetic slobbering virgin all night." Leah paused to fume. "Whatever. But you two … that's a different story. I've been back here since six-thirty. Waiting for you."

Dan looked over at Maggie as if to reassure her that he would handle everything. "Leah, I'm asking you to leave Maggie's room. Now. And don't come back again."

Leah roared with laughter. "No, no, no, no! You don't make the calls around here. I'm in charge. Okay?"

Maggie looked at Dan, then at Leah. "What do you want?"

Glancing at the unmade bed, Leah simpered. "That's right, Maggie. Ask Leah what she wants. Because what Leah wants, she *always* gets."

Dan moved to the chair where Maggie sat and stood behind her, his hands firmly resting on her shoulders. "Get this over with, Leah."

Leah smiled. "Well, Mr. Dan the married man, I don't think I have to tell you what will happen if the two of you don't cooperate, do I?"

"Oh!" Maggie covered her mouth in horror.

Struggling to stand up straight, Leah leaned against the front door, one hand on the suitcase that sat on top of the rack to the left. "'Oh,' is exactly right. No need to go into any pesky details now, is there?"

Maggie tried to stand but felt Dan's hands keeping her in the chair. "How could you, Leah? How could you want to hurt Danny like this? Or me! What have we ever done to you?"

Tired of standing, Leah began to pace. " 'How could you want to hurt Danny like this?' says the woman who just put out all night long for the married man. Oh, that's rich! Well, speaking of rich, your money can't buy you out of this one, Maggie."

Dan, preparing to speak, rubbed Maggie's shoulders as she stared at Leah.

The momentary silence came to an abrupt end as the phone rang, startling everyone. Maggie jumped up. "I'll get that."

Leah glared at her as she walked to the phone.

Tentatively, Maggie answered. "Hello?"

"Maggie?"

"Yes?"

"This is Aimee Lee Younger. Bart's wife."

"Okay … "

"Listen, I only have a brief moment while Bart is taking a shower. As you know, I left the party early last night. I was asleep when Bart came in. Just now, he was telling me about his night with old friends. He told me you left early and that Dan walked you to your room."

Maggie gulped. "Yes … and?"

"Well, Bart mentioned that Leah left almost immediately after the two of you did. I'm so afraid she caught up with you, in the lobby, perhaps, and that she may have told you things about me that could … well, cause me great pain. Yesterday she was a stranger to me. Last night and today she is an enemy threatening to destroy me. If she said anything about me, I implore you to keep it to yourself. Please let me sort out my own life. Sorry to be so cryptic. Please don't mention this to anyone else. I have to go. Bart just turned the shower off. Good-bye."

Maggie held the phone to her ear as she heard Aimee hang up. "I see. Okay, Colin, certainly, if you want to speak to me privately, you're welcome to come up to my room. Yes, I'm on the eighth floor … right … that's the number. It should only take you a minute or two to get here now that the elevators are working again. I'll gladly wait." Maggie paused. "See you in a few. Good-bye."

Leah stood straight, her body becoming rigid. "What the hell does my husband have to talk about with you? Privately, for that matter."

Maggie approached Leah while Dan followed and stood by Maggie's side. "I don't know, Leah, but I suppose I'll find out. Maybe he knows what you're up to. Maybe I should tell him."

"Let me tell you both something," Leah spat. "My husband deplores infidelity and would be every bit as disgusted as I am, though, really, how you two cavort doesn't really interest me. I'm here to recruit you, not to judge you."

"Recruit us for what? Shall I tell Colin about this when he arrives?"

"No!" Leah shouted. "You should not, if you know what's good for you. But my husband will join forces with me, if anything. We're a team. Clearly, I cannot say what I came here to say. Not now. I'll catch up with you both later. Don't convince yourselves for a moment that you've weaseled your way out of anything."

Maggie and Dan said nothing as Leah opened the door and shut it behind her. Dan walked over and refastened the latch. "I don't want Colin bursting in here the way Leah did."

Waving her hand, as if to negate the worry, Maggie sat on the bed as Dan took a seat beside her. "Don't worry, Danny. Nobody else is coming to this room. Certainly not Colin. And he would never burst in. He would knock."

"Of course he would. But if he's upset by something, he—"

"That was Bart's wife, Aimee, on the phone. She was terrified that Leah had caught up with us last night and spilled some ugliness about *her*. She begged me not to listen to it. Then she had to hang up. After she did, I pretended to be talking to Colin, just to get that wretched shrew out of the room."

Dan put a comforting arm around her. "Quick thinking, dear. And now, we have to do some more quick thinking."

"Danny, do you remember how Aimee was behaving

yesterday? When Bart introduced her, she was perfectly lovely. Then, later, there was an abrupt change as she began to cast aspersions on Clare ... as if possessed by the devil."

Dan and Maggie spoke in unison: "Leah."

"I don't understand it," Maggie said. "But this is about hurting Clare. And because no one will willingly enlist in Leah's army, she's drafting us. *Recruiting us*, to use her pitiful verbiage. Fiendish wench. You must go, my love. I'll meet you downstairs for breakfast as we planned. Best you take the stairs to your own floor."

Dan nodded. "Of course. That was already my plan. I don't want anyone who knows us to see me on this floor when the elevators doors open." Squeezing her tight, Dan kissed Maggie on the lips, lingering only a few seconds, then stood to go.

MAY 17, 1986 – 8:55 A.M.

Sitting at the same table where they'd had dinner, Colin and Clare looked around the near-empty room, then at each other.

"Most people have long finished breakfast, and we haven't even begun ours," Colin said. "The Barrie Hillers were always known for having breakfast at a civilized hour." He looked up at the waiter, who had just wheeled a beverage cart over to the table and was standing at Clare's side with a coffee pot. Colin turned to Clare. "We're the first ones here. Does that make us the least civilized in the group?"

Clare answered him with a look that said, "Guess so," then looked up at the waiter. "Actually, I'd prefer some chamomile tea with lemon, please." She turned back to Colin as the waiter prepared her tea and placed it in front of her. "Speaking of the least civilized one, she must be frantically looking for you."

Colin looked up. "Coffee for me; thank you." He resumed

looking at Clare. "I doubt it. I'm sure she got the note I had the bellhop slip under her door. I made it clear that I was in no shape to walk up ten flights of stairs."

Clare smiled. "Nothing like an unexpected blackout to liven things up. Great evening." She squeezed a wedge of lemon into her tea and stirred it. "I wonder if the others will be here soon."

Colin took a sip of his coffee. "If I weren't so damn hungry, I wouldn't care."

"Me, either."

Colin sighed. "You're right; last night turned out to be pretty terrific. Today worries me. I still wish you'd never arranged this damn thing. We could have—"

"Well, well, you two! Back to enjoy another day, and this time a full day," Larry said, startling Clare and Colin as he rounded the table and took his seat. "You almost look surprised to see me." He paused, as if he were preparing to make an announcement. "Will the Barrie Hillers survive another day? Who will run screaming from the room first? Will everyone get through breakfast in one piece? Will all eight attendees make it back to the Parker Room for an afternoon of playful, demoralizing, and scathing banter? Will Leah's scorching barbs leave permanent scars? Have they already? Ah, yes, but upon whom? Stay tuned, folks! We're back live after a commercial break." The lone waiter, who had been waiting for Larry to finish, offered him coffee, then hurried away.

Clare looked at Larry from across the round table. "There's cream and sugar here."

"Thanks but don't need 'em," Larry said. "I drink my coffee black. Just like me." He looked at his watch. "Nine o'clock on the dot." He paused to think. "Punctual and habitual; that's me. A souvenir from my time in the military." He looked up. "Apparently, we're all resuming our same seats from last night. How quickly human beings fall into patterns. I'm sure everyone else will feel most comfortable sitting exactly where they were seated last night. I wonder why human beings *are* so damned habitual."

"If you really want to know," Clare began, "I'm certain it's because habits help us survive. By doing something the same way we've done it before, we don't have to think about it or make a fresh decision. If you think about your average day, which I grant you, this is not, it's likely filled with hundreds of habits you don't even acknowledge as such. Good or bad, habits are part of our makeup. They're humanity's little time savers."

Colin took another sip of his coffee. "Yeah. What she said. Especially the 'good and bad' part."

"Makes sense," Larry said. "I can't help but think of the habits that Cass and I have together. We're an integral part of one another's lives. And now ..."

"What's going on, my friend?" Colin asked. "You're every bit as preoccupied as you were last night, but what I don't know is whether or not you've called her."

Clare and Colin both looked intently at Larry, who hung his head. "I did. Called this morning when I woke up. She wasn't answering the phone."

"Hmm," Colin said. "Maybe she didn't answer because she wasn't there."

"No, no. I'm sure she was there," Larry said. He paused to think, then spoke with greater calm. "It's just that nobody else would call that early, so she damn well knew it was me and didn't pick up. I'm being punished. I'm sure of that. Cass always ..." Seeing Bart and Aimee approach the table, Larry stopped.

Colin whispered to Clare, "I think she left him last night."

Clare nodded while smiling at Bart and Aimee.

"Good morning, friends. I was just telling Aimee what a fantastic evening she missed." Bart held out Aimee's chair for her, unaware that her tense countenance was visible to all but him.

Taking his own seat, he nodded as the waiter approached with the coffee pot, gesturing to him to fill Aimee's cup before his own.

Colin whispered to Clare, "The waiter's face looks as tight as Aimee's. He knew whose cup to fill first."

"So," Bart said, once the waiter had poured his coffee and stepped away, "I take it everyone made it back to their rooms."

Clare smiled. "I had a lovely gentleman escort me to my room by flashlight. Just as the maître d' suggested."

Bart looked at Colin. "As I recall, you and Leah are on the tenth floor. Must've been quite a haul. You had a lot to drink."

"We are, it wasn't, and I did." Colin smiled. "I still have connections here. Got a room on the second floor."

"Lucky you," Larry said. "You must have snared the last one in this grand old inn."

"Actually, that's exactly what happened," Colin said, picking up his coffee cup. "There were a lot of people in town for the evening who couldn't get home and wanted a room. And there were people who were supposed to check out and refused to leave. You must have seen the pandemonium in the lobby. Normally, there would have been more rooms, but that family of green T-shirts has taken up half of the hotel."

The waiter walked over and put another sugar and creamer set next to Larry, in front of Maggie's empty seat. Larry nodded thanks and turned to Aimee. "Hey, how are you doing? Need something to sweeten your morning?"

Aimee glanced at Bart, happy to see that he was engaged in conversation with Clare and Colin, then spoke in a low voice. "All of the sugar and cream in this hotel couldn't make this hellish situation any better. Not unless it was gathered in a heaping pile and then shoved down Queen Schadenfreude's throat until she was rendered forever mute ... or shoved somewhere else."

Larry laughed quietly. "Kick-ass vision you got there."

Aimee looked at him, unsure of how to respond. "I'm really afraid she caught up with Maggie and Dan last night and told them what she knows. She left so abruptly after they did; I think she wants to poison Bart and his friends against me."

Larry thought for a moment. "Nope. Don't think so. Not as you've just laid it out. Bitter has grown some ugly roots with Leah, but spilling to others only dilutes her poison."

"Oh, just great!" Aimee blurted out, attracting everyone's attention.

Alarmed, Bart turned to Aimee. "Everything all right, honey?"

Larry watched as Aimee transformed her anger into radiance. "Sure. Everything's fine, Bart. Sorry. Go back to your conversation, please. Larry just mentioned something that reminded me of a business call I forgot to return. But it can wait until Monday. All's good."

"Okay then, sweetie."

"That was fascinating to watch," Larry said, once Bart had resumed talking with Clare and Colin.

"What?"

"You know, how you turned those poker-hot flames of fury into little rays of sunshine." The corners of Larry's mouth turned up into a near smile.

Aimee said softly, "He's already suspicious, and Lord only knows what will transpire when that witch shows her face again." She paused to make sure Bart was still talking. "Your comment about not wanting to dilute her poison scares the hell out of me, Larry. Just how far do you think she is capable of going? Just how poisonous is she?"

Larry took a sip of coffee and motioned to the waiter for a refill. "Twenty-plus years ago, I could have assured you nothing would come of it. And although there's been a significant increase on the ugly scale, I still don't think she'll do anything. It would be game over. No leverage and certainly no praise from Colin. Like I told you last night in the lobby, I'm not sure how copacetic things really are between the two of them. I'm betting she'll stay mum."

Aimee sighed as she considered Larry's words. "Well, I wish I could take that to the bank, but I can't. Last night you talked about the past … how she always had to be better than everyone. Sounds like she's making up for lost time. She's a loose cannon, and I can't bet that she won't fire."

"Stay strong. Stay in control. She sniffs out weakness the way a K-9 sniffs drugs. Smile at her like you've got a secret." Larry touched his index fingers to each side of his mouth, pulling it up into a brief smile. "You can do it; I've already seen evidence of your acting talent."

Aimee bit her lower lip. "I'm not sure how to respond to that."

Larry started to touch her hand, then thought better of it. "I'm just saying, I think you're a strong woman who can be a fierce adversary when she needs to be. I'm right, yes?" He smiled at her. "You wouldn't be a successful attorney if you weren't. Come on. Don't let her win." Leaning closer, Larry whispered, "My bet is on you. And don't worry, I've got your back."

"Thank you," Aimee said softly. "Oh, look. Here's Dan."

"Dan the man!" Colin said cheerfully. "Top of the morning to you. Wish you and Maggie had stayed with us last night. Reminiscing by candlelight proved to be quite the elixir for us weary and wayward Barrie Hillers."

"I've no doubt," Dan said, resuming his seat from last night as the waiter rushed over to pour coffee. Dan looked up at him. "Thank you!" Dan looked around the table. "Good morning all."

As Dan's greeting was being returned, Colin gave a nod toward the waiter as he walked away. "He's been Johnny on the spot this morning, stands over there in the corner by his station like he's guarding Buckingham Palace, but each time one of us comes in, he glides effortlessly across the dining room to pour some freshly brewed java. His fully stocked tray sits nearby, however, for those who, like Clare, prefer a spot of tea or a glass of juice."

Clare looked blankly at Colin. "That was riveting. Thank you."

Colin laughed. "Glad you approve. Just thought some color commentary might enliven the morning for our rather sullen newspaper editor. I had to come up with something. I'll admit the pouring of coffee isn't a very stimulating topic."

"I know," Clare said, smiling. "That's precisely why it's rarely discussed."

Colin exhaled. "Well, there was the time Leah poured hot coffee on a research paper I'd just finished—on purpose."

Clare shivered in disgust. "And that should have been grounds for divorce."

Bart laughed while Aimee pretended to do the same.

Uncomfortably, Colin looked down. "Probably shouldn't have brought that up." He paused and looked up at Clare. "Or handed you a straight line."

Larry guffawed. "Glad you did. I love it. Back-and-forth banter just like in the old days. Barb-wise, you and Clare were always a great match."

Dan picked up his coffee cup, then, noticing that his hand was trembling, put it down.

"Morning jitters?" Colin asked.

Embarrassed, Dan pressed his lips together as he searched for the right words. "No, no. I'm just fine. Perhaps a bit worried about Maggie."

Concerned, Clare made a sympathetic face. "You did walk her to her room last night, didn't you?"

Aimee stared at Dan, looking for some sign that he had heard her secret.

Dan stirred his coffee. "Of course I did. I just worry how she fared in the dark room during the blackout."

"Didn't you call her this morning?" Clare asked.

"I was …" Dan stopped mid sentence as he saw Leah enter the room. He glanced at her, then at Colin. "Well, your wife is here."

Aimee drew a breath so loudly everyone heard as they simultaneously pretended they hadn't. She looked hopelessly at Larry, who reminded her to be strong by sitting up straight, putting his shoulders back, and wearing an ever-so-slight grin. Following his example, Aimee sat up straight and put on her best poker face.

Leah, who, in her haste, had inexpertly over applied concealer to hide the bags under her eyes, walked briskly over to Colin, snickering as she saw Clare sitting next to him, then sat in her seat, looking around the table, like a queen surveying her subjects. Before anyone could speak, she turned to Colin and said, "I had no idea you were here. I thought you would be … oh, never mind."

Dan, whose nerves had only gotten worse, continued to stir the coffee he so desperately wanted to drink.

Composed, Colin looked at Leah. "You thought I would be where? I take it you got the note I paid the bellhop to slip under the door last light."

Leah gritted her teeth. "I got it. Almost slipped on it. No doubt when you greased the bellhop's palms, the lubrication transferred to the note. And nearly killed me!"

"In your delusions …" Colin mumbled.

We should have all been so lucky. Turning her head to hide her smile, Clare traded looks with Aimee, whose smile had taken refuge behind the palm of her hand.

"And you survived like a champ," Colin repeated, happily unaffected by his wife's scorn and silliness. "So why would you be surprised to see me here in the dining room? Isn't this exactly where I'm supposed to be?"

Leah stared at Dan, who only had eyes for his coffee cup.

"Well," Larry said, breaking the tension. "Good morning to you, Leah!"

"Good morning," Bart chimed in.

"Good morning," Leah grumbled. "Where the hell is … oh, there you are." She looked up at the waiter holding the coffee pot. "Please. Pour me a cup. It *is* fresh, I hope. And hot!"

Clare looked at the waiter. *Pour it on her head and see how loudly she screams. If she shrieks, it's hot enough. If not, heat it up and try again. Go for scalding.*

Aimee noticed disdain wash over the waiter's face. For a moment, it validated her pain, though, sadly, it was of no practical value.

"Thank you," Leah said to the waiter. "This had better be hot."

"Very," the waiter said. "It's a fresh pot. I'd suggest letting it cool."

Leah smiled condescendingly. "Thank you, but I think I can gauge the proper temperature of my morning coffee without waiterly advice. I've been doing it all my life."

"As you wish," the waiter said, barely holding in his contempt.

As if to shake off his presence, Leah shuddered as he walked away, picked up her coffee cup, and took a sip. To her shock, it was much hotter than she expected. She spit it out, creating a large stain on the front of her gray blouse. "What the hell—"

"You were warned," Colin told her.

Leah picked up the linen napkin in front of her, dipped it into a glass of water, then touched it to her lips to cool them. After a few moments, dipping a second time, she applied the wet napkin to her blouse, working on the stain until it dissipated. "Just shut up." Sensing that everyone wanted to laugh, she began shooting verbal bullets. "Well, I hope we're not holding up breakfast because one of us is late."

"You were late, too," Colin said.

"Horrors! Did I miss one of Clare's ghastly menu recitations?"

"No," Colin said, "not that there's anything wrong with letting everyone know what's on the menu. What you did miss was my less-than-extraordinary description of the waiter crossing the room to pour coffee."

Leah huffed her disgust. "Well, sitting next to a bore can make you one."

Colin looked directly at Leah. "I'm doing everything I can to stop that from happening."

Unnerved by the jab, Leah refocused on Dan. "Where in the world is Maggie? I know she's not a morning person, but no doubt we could all use a jolt of that electricity between the two of you to jump-start the day."

Steadying himself, Dan straightened the silverware in front of him. "I'm sure she'll be along soon."

"I know she went up rather early last night, as did you and I, but perhaps she didn't get the sleep she had hoped for. Ah, as Robert Burns said, 'The best laid schemes o' mice an' men, Gang aft agley …' I suppose that includes women, too. You know, there are so many ways in which one could interpret Burns's quote. John Steinbeck certainly—"

"Much of life is open to interpretation," Dan said.

"Yes, true," Leah said devilishly. "But when Burns says, 'The best *laid* plans—'"

"Ah," Larry interjected, "here's the lovely Maggie now. A vision in … boysenberry, I believe. Dress and shoes alike. But no boa."

Dan stood immediately, smiling at Maggie as she walked toward the table in a tailored dark violet dress with matching shoes. "Good morning, dear. You look beautiful."

"Thank you, Danny," Maggie said, sitting in the chair he held out for her. "Good morning, everyone."

"Coffee?" Dan asked, indicating the waiter standing by her side.

"Yes, please. Thank you," Maggie said, smiling warmly at the waiter.

As the waiter poured the coffee, another waiter appeared with menus and handed them out.

"Oh," Leah said, "does this mean we actually get to choose our own breakfast fare?"

"There are three choices," the waiter explained. "And, of course, a continental breakfast is always available." He looked at Clare. "Should I stay, Miss Dreyser, or do you all need time to look over the menu?"

"I don't know about everyone else," Colin said, "but I'm ravenous. I'd like to order now, if that's okay."

As everyone agreed, Dan doted on Maggie. "Some Francis Bacon and eggs, dear?"

Maggie laughed. "Sounds wonderful. But I think I'll just have a toasted blueberry bagel and cream cheese. And a glass of grapefruit juice."

As soon as everyone had ordered, Leah quickly resumed the spotlight. "You know, Maggie, I had a vision of you in bright blue this morning." She looked at Dan. "Didn't you see Maggie in blue this morning?"

"You know what I see, Leah?" Maggie said.

Leah looked annoyed. "What?"

"I see someone who has tried to hide her sleeplessness with

way too much concealer. Unless you're trying to hide raccoon eyes, it would be prudent to blend."

"Tread lightly, Maggie," Leah said, using bombast to hide her embarrassment.

"Well," Bart said loudly, "let's not begin our morning with subterfuge. I, for one, had a wonderful evening last night. Clare, Colin, Larry, and I reminisced into the wee hours." He turned to Aimee. "I'm so sorry you left early. You would have had fun."

"I'm sure it was a great time for all of you, Bart. But other people's memories are never as much fun as your own, you know?"

"Mrs. Bart has a point," Leah said.

Bart looked at Aimee as if to let her have the pleasure of correcting Leah, but she said nothing.

Colin motioned for the waiter to refill his cup, then turned to face everyone. "Last night, I was trying to think of a story, but for the life of me, I couldn't. And this morning, it's as clear as a bell. Does anyone remember Janis Jacobs Nolten, who was a Barrie Hiller for all of four months?"

Maggie giggled. "Oh, yes! Barrie Hill's bird lady!"

"I remember her," Larry added. "She was president of the local ornithological society, and, as I recall, it was a very big deal to her."

"Yes," Colin continued. "I'm not sure if any of you remember this, but she was hosting this regional meeting of members of ornithological societies throughout Connecticut and parts of New York. She invited hundreds of bird lovers. Quite confident that most would attend, and not wanting to be bothered opening acceptances from all of those members, she decided to put 'Regrets only' on the invitation. But then, she got the bright idea that 'Egrets only' would be hysterically appropriate."

"Oh, yes," Maggie added. "I remember! Nobody got the joke or RSVP'd at all. Only a handful of people showed, one of them being that dreadful boyfriend of hers, Leonard Waxmiller."

"Leonard Waxmiller!" Clare repeated. "I do remember him. She brought him to a meeting, and he told that hideous bird joke: what happens when you have sex with a woodpecker?"

Maggie burst out laughing. "You get splinters!"

Bart and Larry laughed.

"You know," Bart said, wiping a tear from his eye, "we're all laughing now, but I remember we just looked at the guy like he had two heads when he told that joke."

"He probably had a wood pecker himself," Maggie said. "He was such a dummy."

Leah looked at Maggie. "Quite the authority on peckers, you are. In fact—"

"Here comes our food," Dan said.

Quickly, the waiters placed food in front of all eight guests, then walked to their station in the corner of the room.

"Eggs Benedict exactly as I used to order them," Leah said, looking at her breakfast. "Clare, I'm wondering if perhaps your reason for not liking the pecker joke was your unfamiliarity with them. My reason for not laughing at the joke, of course, was its pedestrian quality."

Larry nodded. "Yes, Leah, I think we all shared your snobbery."

Clare started to respond to Leah, then thought better of it.

Cutting a bite of eggs Benedict with her fork, Leah smiled and looked at Dan. "Dan, I hope you were able to reach Sally last night. Being the wife of a newspaperman, I'm certain she heard about the power outage. She must have been quite concerned."

Dan, not meaning to do so, dropped his fork on the plate, startling everyone.

"No need for concern, Leah."

"You know," Leah said, trying to camouflage her smirk,

"when you first told us the names of your four children, I'm afraid I was rather distracted … being back in the Parker Room after so many years. But now that I've got my bearings, please do tell me about your children … and your wife."

Sitting up straight, Dan smiled pleasantly at everyone and looked at Leah. "I've already spoken about my family several times, Leah. I don't think you were listening. I'm not going to repeat myself because you were distracted. If anyone wants to know anything, I'll be happy to answer."

Leah let go with a dismissive laugh. "I don't think I'm distractible in the same way you are, Dan."

Colin looked curiously at his wife. "What's this about, anyway? It's odd, even for you."

Ignoring him, Leah focused on Dan. "Perhaps Sally would like to come up here and join us for the rest of the weekend. I for one would love to meet her. Wouldn't you, Maggie?"

While Dan ignored the comment, Bart broke the troubling silence. "Clare, I hope you brought photos. I have albums filled with them, but they're tucked away in my parents' attic." He looked around. "Please, friends, tell me someone has photos."

"I'm glad you asked," Clare said, noting the unfamiliar change in Maggie's demeanor. "As a matter of fact, when I booked this reunion, I requested that a thirty-five-millimeter slide projector be sent to the Parker Room this afternoon. I had a good many photos converted into slides, but I didn't spend too much time looking at them. I wanted to enjoy them for the first time in twenty years like everyone else."

"Oh, God!" Leah groaned. "Is it any wonder that your idea of a swell time is boring old friends with photographic fossils."

"Stop it!" Colin said quietly. "Just stop. This is a reunion that *you* insisted on attending."

Bart looked disgusted but quickly regained his enthusiastic

countenance. "Maybe you'll be bored, Leah, but I for one can't wait. I packed up everything when I moved to Los Angeles all those years ago. Haven't seen so much as an old snapshot. I'm excited. I'm guessing everyone else feels the same."

"Absolutely," Larry said. "I'm not sure if I'm prepared to revisit that 'fro I had the last two years." He laughed. "It had a life of its own."

"And a name, too," Bart added. "Lawrence Senior the Magnificent."

"Day-am," Larry said. "I'd completely forgotten that. I don't think anyone knew that but you, Roomie. And you were supposed to keep my secret forever."

"Was I?" Bart laughed. "Sorry about that."

"That's the thing about secrets," Leah said. "They never stay secret forever. What do you think about secrets, Maggie?"

"I think they can kick you in the posterior if you're not careful," Maggie said. "In ways you never imagined. Painful ways."

Leah bristled, but said nothing.

Not missing a beat, Maggie turned to Larry, who was seated next to her. "Do you remember the long flowing golden locks I had back then?"

"Absolutely!" Larry said. "Goldilocks!" He paused. "I'm sure you, too, must remember my 'fro."

Maggie smiled. "Larry, dear, of course I remember Lawrence Senior the Magnificent. Only I always assumed it was the name for another body part—"

"Ah, that had yet another name," Bart told her, then laughed. "But I'll keep that to myself."

"Okay, okay! If anyone wants to see a black man turn red," Larry interrupted, trying not to laugh. "Now is your opportunity."

Bart laughed again. "It's all in good fun, my friend."

Playfully, Larry buried his face in the palms of his hands,

then looked up. "Moving right along. Can we talk about our beautiful Goldilocks here while I recover from embarrassment?"

"Oh, don't be embarrassed, Larry," Leah said. "My husband has named his appendage 'Ed.'"

"Really?" Larry said, looking at Colin. "Didn't you mention earlier you had a neighbor by that name?"

"Yes, I did," Colin said, turning red. "My wife is just playing silly games that amuse only her and irritate only me. Pay no attention." He turned to Leah. "Just stop. Now."

"Well, we were on the subject, so I just had to share."

The awkward silence that ensued was quickly broken. "I remember your golden locks well. Just beautiful," Dan said to Maggie. He looked across the table at Clare. "I'm excited to see the photos, too." Dan paused to reminisce. "Besides, I haven't seen myself with a full head of hair in a long time."

Leah finished her bite of eggs, then spoke. "I'm guessing you don't pull out the old photos much at home, Dan."

"No, Leah. I don't. Like Bart, I'm afraid they're tucked away somewhere in my childhood home as well."

"Well, I suppose looking at some old photos might be interesting, though I hope we'll be treated to more than Clare's vast collection of Bart photos. Ah, so in love with him you were, Clare. Still pining now. Clearly."

Clare stiffened, then looked at Colin, but didn't respond to the remark. "I have photos of all of us and, of course, some others who aren't here today."

Leah turned to Aimee. "I know you're wishing you were in that group, Aimee—'some others who aren't here today.' You must be dreading this slide show."

Aimee took a moment to swallow the coffee she had just sipped. "I'm actually looking forward to it. I'm eager to see Bart in his college days."

"And …" Leah pressed.

"And nothing," Aimee said.

Larry looked at Aimee and then at Leah.

"Bart," Leah said, "I'd love to hear more about that new film with Holly Lyndworth you were talking about yesterday."

"Not much more to share until the powers that be green light it."

"I see," Leah responded. "Well, I hope for your sake it's a go. I'd hate to see a nasty red light sneak in there."

"I sure as hell hope not. As I told you all yesterday, having the first film fall apart was one hell of a disappointment. To this day, I'm not sure what happened, and I won't lie; it's a persistent thorn in my side. I'm used to the ups and downs of this business, but that just was a tough loss. This time around, however, I have every reason to be confident. Very confident." Bart thought for a moment. "At least, I hope I do."

Aimee glared at Leah, who glared menacingly back.

"Something you wanted to say, Mrs. Bart? Perhaps you wanted to offer words of support for Bart's new film … at least, I hope there will be a new film … or maybe you'd like to express your enthusiasm for seeing Clare's old drool-covered photos of your husband."

"Stop!" Bart said. "Leah, can we call a moratorium on the childishness?"

Ignoring him, Leah stared at Aimee, then spoke. "You were going to say …"

Aimee's face turned ashen. "Um … I was going to say 'Not really,' Leah. You're right. I'm not actually interested in Clare's old photos at all."

Leah smiled. "I just knew it. How did I know that? And why is that?"

Sneaking his hand under the table, Larry surreptitiously

squeezed Aimee's leg above the knee, offering undetected moral support the only way he knew how.

Aimee turned her head to meet Larry's eyes ever so briefly, before looking straight ahead again. "Ah, here comes the waiter. I think it's last call for coffee."

Annoyed by the interruption, Leah shot a dirty look at the waiter as he refilled Aimee's, Dan's, and Larry's cups. "Miss Dreyser," the waiter began, "I just want to confirm that you'll be having a light lunch in the Parker Room, then a late dinner down here this evening."

"That's correct," Clare said. "Speaking of late, our breakfast was a bit delayed this morning, so if the lunch service upstairs can be pushed back a half hour or so, that would be fine."

"Thank you. I'll let my boss know," the waiter said, stopping to return Leah's glare before he left.

"What a rude man," Leah snapped.

"Why?" Colin asked. "Because his face reflected the glow of your condescending treatment? That makes him rude?"

Leah snarled and looked away.

"If you'll all excuse me," Bart said, standing, "I need to call my parents. I'm going down to Jersey to see them tomorrow night after we've parted ways." He looked at Clare. "Should I come back here, or are we heading upstairs to the Parker Room?"

"I suspect we'll be here another fifteen minutes or so," Clare said. "Then, we can take a break to freshen up, redo our eye makeup, or attend to pressing matters before we reassemble in the Parker Room."

"Okay," Bart said. "See you here or in the Parker Room." Bart bent down, kissed Aimee on the top of her head, then hurried out the door.

Leah turned around to watch him leave. "Bart's in quite a hurry to talk to his parents." She refocused her attention on Clare.

"Redo our eye makeup? How dare you?"

Clare laughed. "Seriously, Leah. After everything you've said to me, I'm not allowed to have a little fun? Besides, what makes you think I'm talking about you?"

Maggie giggled softly, agitating Leah.

"Okay, okay. If the pot-bellied virgin wants to play, I won't stop her. Go on, Clare. Make my day."

Larry stood. "I think I need to make a call, too."

"I can't imagine who *you're* going to call," Leah said. "Oh, Cass, alas alack, please, my love, take me back! Oh, Mona Moore, open thy door. I miss you so; where didst thou go?"

Glaring at Leah, Larry thought for a moment. "Nah … but damn, I'm tempted," he said, then walked off.

Aimee, no longer flanked on either side by Bart or Larry, excused herself, leaving Dan, Maggie, Leah, Colin, and Clare to make small talk for another ten minutes.

"Ah," Dan said, seeing Bart reenter the room. "Our star has returned."

Bart smiled awkwardly as he sat. "Where did Larry and Aimee go?"

"Larry went to call Mona Moore, and Aimee didn't offer an explanation," Leah said. "I don't think she wanted to be here without you, Bart."

"That would be understandable."

"So," Leah continued, "that wasn't a very long talk with your parents."

"They weren't home. I left a message. I would have been back here sooner, but I stopped to sign a few autographs in the lobby."

"No rabid fans, I hope," Colin said. "You don't look quite as cheerful as the guy who left."

Bart looked pensive. "Oh, sorry. I'm fine. Just a lot on my mind. I can't wait to get upstairs to the Parker Room, see those photos, and go back to the old days when life was simpler."

Dan nodded knowingly. "It's funny, when I think of my college days, I can so easily see how simple life really was … but to my young mind, it was extraordinarily complicated. If I make it to old age, I wonder how I'll view the life I live now."

"You know, Danny, it's sort of like being in an art gallery. Everyone stands back to take in the picture as a whole, but imagine if the people in the paintings could talk. They'd see things very differently, being a part of it, than the spectators would. As time moves on, I think we're all just spectators as we look back. We certainly can't change our past."

Dan smiled. "Well said, dear."

"Hmm," Leah mused, "are you saying that a person cannot accurately assess her circumstances while she is living them? Or make moral decisions? Interesting. A good way to absolve oneself of any wrongdoing."

Maggie looked at Leah. "It's merely a concept, not a blanket statement."

"No, of course not." Leah stretched her arms in front of her. "But could it be pillow talk?" A wicked grin appeared on her lips. "Golly, I'm so excited; it's almost photo time!"

MAY 17, 1986 – 10:20 A.M.

Exiting the ladies' room, Aimee turned the corner and saw Larry standing at the phone bank. There was a look of devastation on his face. He slowly placed the receiver back in the cradle, but made no move to walk away. He only stared at the phone in disbelief.

"Larry," Aimee said quietly, "I won't ask you if everything is all right. I can see that it's not. What can I do to help?"

Startled, then relieved to see her, Larry looked toward the

lobby, then turned back to Aimee. "Things aren't so great for either one of us at the moment, are they?"

"No, they're not."

"Listen," Larry said softly, "down that hallway, to our left, there's a side exit to the parking lot. If you cross the lot, just around the corner, you'll find a small park with some benches, hidden behind some trees. Used to sneak off there all the time in the old days. Can we go there and talk? Breakfast is over, and everyone will be headed to the Parker Room in a half hour or so. You can just tell Bart you went outside for some fresh air, and it'll be the truth. Sound good?"

Aimee thought for a moment. "That sounds perfect, Larry. Yes. Lead the way."

Taking one final glance around the lobby, satisfied that no familiar faces were watching them, Larry nodded toward a hallway with an exit sign overhead and began walking. Just to be on the safe side, Aimee walked behind him until Larry reached a heavy door, put his hand on the push bar to open it, then gestured for Aimee to pass through first.

"Ah, I can breathe!" Aimee said as the door shut behind them. "Metaphorically speaking."

"Literally speaking, too. The air is always so fresh after a good rain."

"I was just going to say that." Aimee looked around. "So, where is this hidden spot you're taking me to?"

"Follow me." Larry pointed into the distance. "See the trees over there? It's just behind them. Watch out for cars." He grinned. "The moving ones."

Aimee laughed as she walked across the lot with him. "I'll be careful. Thanks."

"Used to come out here to think things out back in the day ... *and* smoke weed," Larry explained. "And an occasional cigarette.

The Barrie Hillers were never big on smoking, unlike most people. Probably because our favorite English lit teacher died of lung cancer at thirty-eight. Chain smoker. Kind of hit us hard. But that didn't quell our cravings for cannabis, you know?"

"My husband, too?" Aimee asked, as they stopped to let a dark blue sedan pass.

"Ah … Bart was good for an occasional toke. But Colin and I more than made up for his negligence."

Aimee laughed as they walked between two parked cars and onto the grass. "Negligence, huh? Such legalese for a film critic."

"Guess so." Larry smiled. "Bart neglected a lot of good stuff. Yup, let many an opportunity go to waste."

"Maybe because he didn't want to go to waste with it?"

Larry stopped to look at her. "You don't smoke the stuff, I take it."

Aimee smiled. "Did I say that?"

"You're okay, Aimee Lee Younger," Larry said, as they continued walking. "We're almost there."

As they rounded the corner past a copse, Larry smiled to see that the space was nearly as he remembered it. Three wrought-iron and wood benches formed a U around a concrete table whose base was crafted with colorful square tiles, forming a 360-degree image of the town of Barrie Hill. Bordering the table were hundreds of purple, pink, and white impatiens. The tiny park was set on a square of grass with an ornate lamppost in one corner and a wrought-iron trashcan in the other. To Larry, it still had the feel of a hidden garden that had run screaming from the stresses of a world that had the audacity to keep turning.

Larry walked over to inspect one of the benches. "Just a few drops of rain on this one. Not sure if I have—"

"Not a problem." Aimee reached into her purse. "I always carry tissues."

Taking a couple of tissues from the package she held out, Larry wiped off the bench, offered Aimee a seat, then walked over to the trash can to get rid of them.

Sitting down, Aimee looked around as Larry returned and sat beside her. "You like it here?" he asked.

"Very much. This is peaceful. A port in a storm."

"Good. I'm glad."

"I could just sit here all day." She turned to look him in the eyes. "Actually, I was thinking about hopping on a train to New York to escape this nightmare."

"I'm not sure if that's a good idea or not, but you'll never run out of things to do in the Big Apple."

"Oh, I know. Remember I told you last night ... I'm a native New Yorker. I grew up in Chinatown. Right off Canal Street. My parents still live there."

"Of course. I don't know why I was still thinking you were from California."

Aimee laughed. "Nobody is from California ... except maybe the millions of native Californians I haven't met. Honestly, I think there are about two people in my firm actually born in California, and one's from Palo Alto and the other from San Diego. Not a soul from Los Angeles on the legal team."

"What made you decide to leave New York?"

"Our LA office asked me to come out to work on a big case. I was supposed to be there a year. But the case dragged on, and by the time I was planning to come back East, I'd met Bart. So I stayed."

"Ah, I see." Larry reached into the inside pocket of his jacket and pulled out a joint and a disposable black lighter. "In the interest of going back in time, or merely escaping the now, I'm going to indulge. Two questions: will it bother you, and if not, would you care to join me?"

"Sounds like a good interim solution for what ails us. You

didn't bring any bug spray, did you?"

Larry appeared concerned. "Oh, hell, did something bite you?"

"Yeah," Aimee said, smirking. "Not too long after we arrived yesterday."

"Ah," Larry said. "I hear you. Listen, I know you didn't ask for my opinion, but I think it would be a big mistake to hop on a train to New York."

Aimee sighed. "I'm thinking you're right. But what are your reasons?"

Larry put the joint in his mouth, flicked the lighter, cupped his hands around the flame, and inhaled a long toke before passing the joint to Aimee.

"Thanks," Aimee said.

Larry exhaled. "I'm just thinking that there's nothing to stop Leah from biting you in absentia. Knowing her, she'd perceive your departure as a victory and you as a coward. Granted, she would be angry you weren't here to torture, but she might take revenge by flapping her gums. I think your presence is a powerful deterrent. Can't guarantee you that; just my gut talking."

Taking a toke of the joint, Aimee inhaled and passed it back to Larry. After a few moments, she exhaled. "You're right. I know you are. Besides, I don't want to leave Bart. I just can't help but think my days with him are numbered. And you know what? I have only myself to blame. I never thought I was a jealous woman, but my behavior says otherwise. I don't like myself very much right now, but I'm not giving up."

"Good," Larry said before taking another toke.

Aimee sighed. "I just can't bear the thought of living with the threat of exposure hanging over my head."

Larry blew out the smoke, then watched it dissipate into the air before speaking. "Would it be so wrong to call the left coast and put a stop to that kill order or whatever it was that you issued yesterday?"

"I don't know," Aimee said worriedly. She stood up and began to pace. "I don't think it would matter. The fact remains that I decimated the first film, and I can't undo that. Nor can I undo the fact that I threatened Ken yesterday. As harsh as I was, I'm sure he's already put the deed into motion. Like I told you last night, I'm pretty much doomed no matter what happens. I can't believe I let jealousy get the better of me. I had no intention of doing that, Larry. I swear I didn't. It's just when Bart started talking about the film, with such enthusiasm, my brain went haywire imagining him and … I just did the unthinkable … again! Stupid, stupid me! And I promised myself I would never do that again. I despise the woman who called Ken. I don't want her to be me." Aimee stopped to think. "Being a lawyer forced me to be tough in business, but out of the office or the courtroom, I was nice. I really was." She looked off into the distance. "I'd like to think I still am." She turned to look at Larry again. "I know Bart is not a player, but simply having a husband that so many women want, well, it's hardened me. I was never jealous or suspicious before. In fact, I hated those traits in others. But it's true that we often hate traits in others that we most dislike in ourselves. Maybe I was always that way and didn't know it. What I do know is that some days, I don't even recognize myself. I'm so—"

"Try to calm down. We're here to get mellow, remember? And you're still nice. I mean that, Aimee. Come on, sit."

Ignoring his request, Aimee continued pacing. "The other thing I wanted to say: you must hate me for the things I've said to Clare … and probably will continue to say until I find a way out of this mess. She's your friend. It must make you sick listening to me, even if you know what my reasons are."

"Hmm," Larry said. "I can't deny what you're saying. And no, I'm not thrilled with what you've been blackmailed into doing. But I think Clare is a strong lady who can handle whatever comes her way. And something tells me that when all is said and done, Leah will have more regrets than anyone."

"Do you know something you're not telling me?"

"Nope. Not a damn thing." Larry smiled through his sadness. "Just try not to get too ugly, okay?"

Aimee stood for another moment, then, feeling drained, sat down and looked at Larry. "I never thought I'd find myself in such a despicable situation. So sorry, Larry, not only for how I've been behaving toward Clare, but also for my preoccupation with this nightmare. You're going through hell, too, and here I am just blathering on about myself. Forgive me. What happened with Cassandra?"

Larry sighed and handed the joint to Aimee. "I thought she wasn't answering her phone, so I called her sister, Belinda, in Hoboken to see if she would tell me what was going on. Color me surprised when Cass answered Bel's phone."

"Is it that surprising that she would visit her sister?"

"No. But she informed me … straight away … that she's left me. Lock, stock, and rotten barrel. She's moved into her sister's place and is taking over the lease when Bel gets married next month. She made a point to tell me that she took every last possession out of my place so she'd never have a reason to come back. Ever."

"Oh, Larry. I'm so sorry," Aimee said before taking a last toke.

"There's more. I think she's back with her ex. Or headed that way. He lives in her sister's building. Regardless, she said we're over. And I'll tell you something else. I know for a fact she's been in touch with him for a while. I think she pushed me into bringing her along this weekend knowing that I'd say no and she'd have a reason to leave me. That way, the breakup would be my fault … not hers. Manipulative shit, you know. People do it all the time. Yeah, I really believe she tricked me into giving her a reason on a silver platter. Color me a sucker, too!"

Exhaling, Aimee handed the joint back to Larry. "But why would she ... oh no ... what if Bart has been waiting for a reason to leave me, too? What if he still has feelings for—"

Larry gently stubbed out the joint on the ground, then put it back in his pocket. "Don't get ahead of yourself."

Aimee looked into Larry's eyes. "If Bart had told you he still had feelings for Holly Lyndworth, you'd never betray his confidence, would you?"

"I never betray anyone's confidence. You can trust that. Hey, I'm feeling a good buzz. How about you?"

Aimee looked at her watch. "Yes, me too. I hope it lasts a good long time, too. It's nearly eleven. If we don't head off to the Parker Room ... separately ... and soon, I think we'll regret it. I really want to hear more, Larry. I know you need to talk. And so do I. But we've gotta go."

MAY 17, 1986 – 10:25 A.M.

Maggie looked through the peephole as she put one hand on the doorknob. As soon as she opened the door, Dan dashed in, closing the door quickly behind him.

"Danny, you look flushed! Was Leah following you?"

"No ... I don't think so."

Taking Dan by the arm, Maggie walked over to the bed, where they both sat. "Catch your breath. Tell me what's going on."

"When I got up from the breakfast table," Dan said, "Leah was nattering away with another mindless critique of Clare. As I was leaving, which was about five minutes after you left, it was obvious she wanted to follow. Her eyes were glued to me, and she started to get up as I began to walk away, but Colin admonished her to stay and let Clare respond to the ridiculous allegations she was making. It was then that Leah shot me a look that said, 'I'll get you later.'"

"Leah was never a candidate for Miss Congeniality, but her abuse of Clare has been brutal, not to mention her disrespect to Bart's wife, Aimee, and whatever vile blackmail scheme she's waiting to spring on us. But she taunts Clare so openly!"

"She does," Dan agreed. "And I was so angry I nearly stayed, but Clare was handling Leah quite admirably, and it was far more important that we have this time together before we have to rejoin the others."

"Yes, Danny. It is."

Dan put one hand behind Maggie's head and drew her face to his, then kissed her. After two minutes, he reluctantly pulled away. "I could do that all day and all night. Later this evening our time will be ours to do as we please, but now, we need to talk."

"Yes, I suppose we do." Maggie sighed. "Danny, there's only one thing Leah can do to hurt me, and that is to hurt you. It was all I could do to sustain my composure this morning when she started in with that nonsense, most especially when she asked you if Sally would like to join us."

"Her sadistic taunting rattled me, but she's not going to call Sally. We have an unlisted number, *and* nobody is home. Sally's family has a home in the Catskills, and she and the kids are there now. I wish I knew for sure what Leah wanted from us, but at the same time, I'm loath to give her an opportunity to tell us. I think it's pretty clear; she wants us to hurt Clare." Dan paused to acknowledge his growing anger. "I despise that, and I despise the way she's crashed our bliss. It's such a violation."

"It is. And maybe I should be ashamed of what I'm doing, but I'm not." Maggie looked down.

"I'm not either. But it is our business, not Leah's." Dan

tenderly touched Maggie's leg. "Please look at me."

Maggie met his eyes. "From the moment I saw you again, I wanted to make love to you, Danny. That's the truth. The bigger truth is that I've been dreaming about it for years. About us."

"That's my truth, too. A hundred fold. If I had only known …" As Dan's voice trailed off, sorrow filled his eyes.

"Then maybe it's better you didn't. You're a married man. Do you feel guilty? Tell me the truth."

Dan lowered his eyes. "Oh …"

"Please, Danny. I need an answer to my question. Whatever your truth is, you can tell me."

Dan put an arm around Maggie and squeezed her tightly. "All right, I will. Though my truth is neither appealing nor noble."

"Let me be the judge of that, Danny."

Dan shifted on the bed to face Maggie. "How do I put this into words?" He stopped to reflect. "I've said many times that I'm blessed to have such a beautiful family and a successful career. But I'm a man who wears an invisible cloak of mediocrity. My cloak is no lighter a burden than Jacob Marley's chains are to him."

"Oh, no, Danny! Marley was a tormented ghost because he was a greedy and selfish man who cared about no one but himself. Marley lives in infamy beyond the confines of *A Christmas Carol.* Just like Ebenezer Scrooge, he is legend by his lonesome. Jacob Marley … what a dreadful comparison."

Defeated, Dan continued. "I haven't committed the sins Marley did, but my burden, this mediocrity I carry around with me, I visualize as a close relative to Marley's chains."

"Mediocrity? Not you, Danny. Why do you feel that way?"

"I told you, Maggie … Sally and I do love one another … a kind of love that when examined closely is more accurately a great fondness and abiding respect. Yes, it began as more, but even then, it was not much more. Rather, I hoped a romantic love would evolve.

But it didn't. Just the opposite occurred. I was never foolish enough to expect Sally to be you. That would have been brutally unfair. In fact, I'm sure I chose someone very different so that I would never be tempted to compare and because I wanted to see Sally for the woman she is. And she's a fine woman. But I am bereft. If not for you, I might have wondered all of these years if I even had the capacity to want … to rage, to burn, to desire a woman with every breath in my body. But wanting is not enough. Until last night, I've had to satisfy myself with mere thoughts … craving the intimacy of melding into one with the woman I have always loved.

"I've worked hard all of my life. Done everything expected of me. So, no, I don't feel guilty for allowing myself to feel alive for the first time in my life. Lust is grand … but lust mixed with love is the peak of existence. I have lived in the nadir of my being. If I'm a cheater, then so be it. But I've thought long and hard about the sin of cheating myself. To some, that is a shameful rationalization. To me, it is part of my truth."

Maggie took her index finger and dried the lone tear on Dan's cheek, then kissed the spot where it had fallen. "My darling, Danny, I've played so hard and fast and traveled so far and wide that people have always envied me. Maybe not my multiple marriages, but friends have often remarked that I am lucky because I haven't wasted life as they have … or as you say, lived in mediocrity. If you insist on using that word as a touchstone, then I have to say that my wild-child ways were no different from your life as a stand-up husband, father, and newspaperman. You have accomplished far more than I have, Danny. I thought some day I might try to publish my poetry, but after graduating from Barrie Hill College, I wrote so little of it and lost faith in what I'd already written. I have a life swathed in glitter, but it has never been gold. That is another form of mediocrity. Don't you see that? Everyone here at this reunion, even Leah, has done more than I have."

"No! Whatever small accomplishments she has are diminished by her ever-present cruelty and rancor. Before you arrived yesterday, Leah was cheerfully telling us she and Colin take separate vacations because they have separate interests. He likes to see something of the world, while she, having traveled so extensively at a young age, is content to bask in the sun with a fancy drink. I took that at face value yesterday, but today I'm convinced she was lying ... mostly to herself ... and that Colin's vacations are all about getting away from her. And, quite frankly, I don't care, my love. But I point that out just to say that her life, as I see it, holds little to no amount of pride for her. I've never known content human beings to behave so despicably toward others without provocation."

Maggie looked into his eyes. "So why, Danny, when you see that wretched woman for who she is, can you even mention yourself and mediocrity in the same sentence? I don't understand that. You are so much more, as a human being and as an accomplished and honorable man."

Dan smiled and took Maggie's hands in his, then raised them to his lips and kissed them. "Thank you, my dear. Let me try to explain." Letting go of her hands, he reached for a tissue on the nightstand and wiped his brow, then stood long enough to toss it in a nearby wastebasket. "As far as the world sees me, or judges me, I've done quite well. All four of my children have a father they're very proud of ... and Sally hasn't endured any of the horrors with her spouse that some of her friends have had with theirs. She's quite content in every way. I'm proud of my work ethic, my awards, my promotions, and of the way I treat my fellow human beings. But, you see, only I know what I have wanted and needed since becoming a man, and having merely brushed the periphery of that want, I feel I am a mediocre counterpart to the man I want to be."

"Oh, Danny! Is this because of me? Would you feel this way if we'd never met all of those years ago?"

Dan thought. "Yes, I would. Only I wouldn't have a name or a face for the woman I had been missing. And if that were the case, probably not as strongly. Or perhaps I'd think such a woman didn't exist for me. What I do know is that last night was the first time in my life I felt like the man I've always wanted to be. I'm sure that sounds like my needs are nothing more than one man's grand desire to fill a ravenous sexual appetite, but it's so much more. With you, I can give everything that has been locked up inside me forever. With you, I'm the man no one sees or would ever guess even exists. And you know what? That's as it should be. This man is not for the world to see. But I need to see him. I need to know he will not die from mediocrity. The greatest need of all human beings is validation. Being with you allows me to give that to myself … and so much more."

Maggie put her hands on Dan's shoulders and drew him to her. "No man has ever made me feel so wanted or so loved. No man." As they kissed, their bliss was destroyed by an intense pounding on the door.

Dan and Maggie exchanged glances. Dan stood, but Maggie took hold of his arm and pulled him down, electing to go to the door herself. Once again, she peered through the peephole. Surprised to see a bellhop, she opened the door just a crack.

The apologetic man in the burgundy uniform smiled nervously. "I'm so sorry, Miss Bristol. Our manager received an urgent call from a Mrs. Daniel Collier. She couldn't locate Mr. Collier with the group or in his room. She was convinced that he might be here and asked me to deliver the message that—"

Opening the door a bit more, Maggie looked suspiciously at him. "When Mrs. Collier called with the 'urgent message,' did she, in her haste, reach through the phone and shove that twenty-dollar bill into your pocket to have a message delivered?" Maggie stared down the suddenly mute bellhop. "Oh, for goodness sake, what is the name of the manager who took her call?"

Gulping, the bellhop looked down at the bill sticking awkwardly out of his side pocket. "Uh ... um, you know, it was so busy that I ..."

"Save it, you useless bottom feeder!" Leah barked as she rushed to the door from her hiding place around the corner. "At least you got her to answer the door. I suppose you're good for something. But you're hardly worth twenty dollars, you minimum-wage-earning punk."

Horrified, the bellhop hurried down the hall as Leah forced her way into the room and shut the door behind her.

"Well, what a shock to see the two of you fully dressed. I was sure—"

Now standing angrily at Maggie's side, Dan scowled at Leah. "What the hell do you want from us? What was that charade all about?"

Leah laughed. "I was trying to do you a favor. I thought I might scare you into calling dear Sally and remembering—"

"What do you want, Leah?" Dan's face reddened, but he was determined to retain control.

"All right, I'll tell you. And if you do what I ask, your sordid little secret will be safe with me. Quite honestly, I don't give a damn what the two of you do or don't do. But I need allies. I need you both to help me knock that insidious Clare Dreyser back into the vermin infestation she was born into and crawled out of. You will both cease treating her like she is someone worthy of your friendship. You will treat her for the execrable horror she is. Do you hear me?"

Maggie looked at Dan, then at Leah. "What in God's name has Clare ever done to you? Is this because she founded the Barrie Hillers, and you didn't? Because she won the Adeline C. Harter award that you so coveted? Is it because everyone here respects her? Just what is your problem, you miserable wench?"

Leah glowered at Maggie. "Don't you ever speak to me that way again and expect not to pay the price! You've been warned."

Dan twisted his fisted hand into the palm of his other. With a slow burn, he approached Leah, cognizant of a rage he had never felt before, but not intimidated by its nascent existence. With a cold stare, he took a step toward her. "Don't you ever threaten Maggie again, Leah. Do you hear me?"

"Like a lover of laughter hears a good comedian. I don't need to explain anything to either of you. I just want to bring that woman down. That's all I want. And if you think I won't follow through on my—"

"Get out of here," Dan said, moving next to Leah as he walked toward the door, forcing her to do the same. "Go on. Get the hell out of here!" He opened the door and glared at her.

"See you in Parker Room!" Leah said, laughing. "Bye now."

Maggie, fixed on Dan, jumped as the sound of the shutting door morphed into a ringing phone.

"It's okay, darling," Dan assured her. "Answer it."

Maggie picked it up. "Hello?"

"Hi, Maggie. This is Aimee Younger again. I'm in the lobby. I was just outside for some much-needed fresh air. I was hoping you were still in your room. I had to hang up so quickly this morning and never got to finish what I was saying."

"Go on, Aimee. Please, tell me. I'm listening."

Dan exhaled hearing that it was Aimee on the phone.

"Well, as I said, I know Leah left almost immediately after the two of you did last night, during the blackout, and I was afraid she may have given you an earful about me."

Maggie grimaced. "No, I can tell you that Leah has never spoken a word about you to either me or Danny. Has she threatened you in some way?"

"I know you're both longtime friends of Bart, so maybe I—"

"Aimee, dear, if Leah is threatening you, please tell me. I won't tell Bart. I promise."

"Well, she purposely overheard me on a phone call and found out some things that would make my husband unhappy. Very unhappy. I'm sure you noticed that I haven't been very nice to Clare, and that's because—"

"Because Leah is blackmailing you?"

There was a brief silence on the line. "Yes, exactly! I'm sure you're wondering—"

"What you've done?" Maggie asked. "No, I'm not. That's none of my business."

"Thank you!"

"Try not to worry. Evil often has a boomerang effect. Just wait it out. Go to the Parker Room and join Bart. I'll see you there in a bit."

"Thank you, Maggie. Thank you so much."

As Maggie hung up, Dan rushed to her side and embraced her. Silently, they held one another for minute. As they broke apart, Maggie was the first to speak. "As you heard, Danny, we're not the first Leah has approached with her vile blackmail scheme. My goodness, do you think she could have interfered in Larry's relationship as well?"

"At this point, I don't know, my darling. But I do know that this time with you is the most precious gift I've ever been given, and she will not take it from me, from us." Dan sighed. "I suppose we should wend our way down to the Parker Room … separately."

Maggie nodded. "Danny, one more thing. Hear me clearly. If events should go a certain way, and if you should witness me acting in a way that stuns you, in a way that makes you question everything you know about me, don't blame it on the booze or on my wild-child ways. Just trust in me."

Dan put his arms around her waist. "Of course. But what are

you thinking?"

"You may never need to know. But if circumstances require me to act, you must trust me and reserve all judgment. And we will have another glorious night. I promise."

Dan pulled her close and kissed her. "I would never judge you harshly."

"I know. You go now, Danny. Everyone knows how I take forever fussing with my makeup. It's important that you get there first. We're already running late, but that's okay. We're here to visit old friends … not catch a train."

Chapter TEN

May 17, 1986 — 11:11 a.m.

"Despite being eleven minutes late for the party, we're the first ones here again," Colin said, taking a seat on the same black Chesterfield sofa he'd sat in the day before. "But this time, Leah and I will be switching places. I'll be closest to you, and she can have the seat next to the bar."

Clare cracked a smile as she resumed her seat on the red brocade couch. "She'll love that. Wanna lay bets on whether she'll make drinks for anyone?"

"She won't. She forgot her arsenic. What fun would that be?"

"Well, she brought along enough verbal poison to make up for it. Don't you think?"

"That's something she doesn't have to remember to pack. It's a staple of her lifeform." Colin looked at the door, then at Clare. "Are you still glad you arranged this thing? You had to know she'd make everyone miserable."

"Hello, Larry!" Clare said, smiling, as Larry walked in the room.

Colin turned around. "Hey, there. How's my woebegone friend?"

Larry walked to the bar and made himself a drink. "Well, as

long as your wife isn't here to ridicule me, I might as well tell you: Cass has left me."

"Oh, bloody hell," Colin said as Larry resumed his seat on the stuffed chair that sat to the right of the couch. "Are you sure? Did you talk to her?"

"Sure did. I called her sister, Belinda, in Hoboken, and Cass answered. She's already moved her things out of our apartment."

"I'm so sorry," Clare said. "That's insanely sudden. It was only less than twenty-four hours ago that you didn't take her call. Who in the world makes a life-changing decision, packs her belongings, and moves out that quickly?"

"Oh, I don't know." Larry twirled a straw in his drink. "Someone who had this victim bullshit planned for a long-assed time and set me up as the bad guy. That's who."

Clare looked confused. "Why didn't she just leave you if that's what she wanted to do?"

"Because," Larry said, "some people prefer to be pushed out the door rather than just stroll away on their lonesome. Some folks don't like lighting a fire under their own ass. Need someone else to do it, you know? To shift blame."

"Oh, yeah," Clare said. "Truer words … oh, here's Bart."

"Ah, if it isn't my treasured late-night inner circle of old friends … here first." Bart looked at Larry, then at Colin and Clare. "I'm going to grab a Perrier. Lar, I see you're good for the moment. Clare, Colin … what can I get the two of you?"

"I'll have the same," Clare said. "With a lime. Thank you."

"Me, too," Colin added. "I'm saving my brain cells for later. I might need them. I'm still trying to replenish the ones I lost on the day I married … oh, hell."

Larry laughed as he, Bart, and Clare looked at one another. "Well, there's a conversation stopper for you … or perhaps a starter!"

Placing Colin's and Clare's drinks on the table in front of them, Bart took his seat on the couch that backed the entrance, then put his drink on the table. Turning to Larry, Bart looked at him quizzically. "Something's different, Roomie. Your eyes look a little …"

"What? Like I've been crying? Hell, no. But Cass has left me. For good."

"Oh, Lar, I'm really sorry to hear that. Shocked, actually. But, no, I wasn't thinking you look like you've been crying … more like maybe glazed …" Bart pantomimed smoking a joint and saw by the half-grin on Larry's face that he was right. "Whatever works, my friend. I'm sure we can find a quiet moment to talk later."

"Yeah, yeah. I'd tell you the whole sordid story now, but I don't want to dominate the conversation, nor do I want be ridiculed by—"

"Leah!" Colin said loudly. "I was wondering where you'd gotten to."

"You're in the wrong seat," Leah said, walking briskly into the Parker Room. "Move over."

"Not in the wrong seat," Colin corrected her. "Just a different one. Same couch, though. And I quite like this seat. Easier for me to catch up with Clare. It's been twenty years, after all."

Leah, mired in a snit, marched over to the bar and grabbed a bottle of Chardonnay. Annoyed that it was unopened, she stared at it, hinting with a pained sigh that someone else should open it for her.

Clare's face remained blank. *Go screw yourself.*

But there were no takers. Trying to disguise her annoyance, she grabbed a corkscrew and did the deed herself. After pouring a glass, she left the cork lying on the bar and sat down. "Well, isn't this cozy?"

Steeling herself, outside the door to the Parker Room, Aimee recalled Larry's supportive words, then walked through the door with a pleasant smile.

"There you are." Bart scooted an inch or so to his left as a symbolic gesture to give Aimee more space to sit.

"I was just outside for some fresh air." Aimee took the seat beside him. "I love the air after it rains."

"Good afternoon, everyone." Dan walked into the room and sat on the couch opposite Colin and Leah. "Sorry I'm running late."

"Oh, we understand, Dan," Leah said. "After all, you're the only one of us who has children. I'm sure you wanted to talk to all four of them … and your wife."

Dan smiled pleasantly at Clare. "I take it we haven't begun looking at photos yet."

"I'm expecting the slide projector and screen within the hour. But there's no rush to start, especially when we're not all here yet."

"My, my," Leah said. "I wonder what could be keeping Maggie."

"You know, Maggie," Clare said, "She always takes her time to look her best."

"Clare," Larry began, "I was wondering if you invited Wally Decker to our reunion."

"I did, but the invitation was returned unopened. Someone had written on it: 'Return to sender: cheating scum slash loser no longer at this address. Doing you a favor by not forwarding.'"

Everyone but Leah laughed.

"Ah, his ex-wife, Sasha, must have written that," Larry said. "And I think she did do us all a favor. The reason I asked is because I ran into the guy on Seventy-ninth and Broadway a couple of years back. He recognized me because he's seen me on TV; I wouldn't have known him, that's for damn sure."

"Why is that?" Bart asked.

"Well, Roomie, for starters, he was wearing some loud-ass

shirt practically unbuttoned to his navel. All I saw was chest hair walking down the street. The guy's a poster child for midlife crisis."

Leah looked sideways at Clare, who pretended not to notice.

"Did you two talk?" Bart asked.

"On the street. Dude wanted to go for a drink, at some singles' bar, nonetheless, but I nixed that. Didn't shut him up, though. Told me he felt old age creeping up on him, so he found some twenty-two-year-old side action—a receptionist from the Bronx at the small advertising company where he works. That lasted all of a month. Two weeks after his wife kicked him out, the young woman came to her senses and dumped him, too."

"Any kids?" Clare asked.

"Yeah. He's got a daughter who's in her second year of college at Adelphi. Apparently, she doesn't want much to do with him."

"Well, well! Looks as if Maggie has decided to join us," Leah announced.

Dan, who was sitting on the couch that backed the entrance, turned around, smiling brightly.

Everyone except Leah greeted Maggie as she took a seat next to Dan. "Sorry I'm late. Did I miss anything?"

"Larry was telling us about running into Wally Decker on the Upper West Side," Dan said.

"I'm certainly glad he's not here," Maggie said. "He had a very lascivious nature."

"I had no idea," Dan said, standing. "What can I get you to drink, Maggie?"

Maggie looked around. "I'll just have Perrier like everyone else. For now."

"Do tell," Leah said. "Did you date him?"

Dan, who had just taken the cap off a bottle of Perrier, turned to look at Maggie, who was horrified by the question.

"Goodness no!" Maggie said. "I wouldn't have done so if I had more lives than a cat. He was an unctuous sort with roaming fingers, like someone playing an invisible guitar. His stubby, hairy fingers were always everywhere but where they belonged."

"You are so right," Clare said. "I must have completely repressed that. If I hadn't, I never would have sent the invitation. He sat next to me at a party once. I kept feeling something on the side of my thigh but thought I was imagining it. When I looked at him, he appeared to have some kind of nervous twitch. But it didn't take long after that to realize that every time I looked away, he was trying to cop a feel. That's when I got up and left."

"Exactly the deviant behavior I remember!" Maggie said, as Dan, Perrier in hand, resumed his seat next to her. "Smarmy weasel."

"Well," Leah said with a shrug, "he never tried to touch me."

"Even a letch knows hot coal will burn," Maggie said.

"Or," Leah said, "maybe he didn't have a palate for fine wine and just wanted to chug some cheap hooch." Leah looked directly at Clare. "Little did he know, you can't even make cheap wine with unfermented grapes."

Ignoring Leah, Bart looked at Larry. "Was that the extent of your conversation, Lar? About his ex-wife and girlfriend?"

"Not quite. Ran off at the mouth for about ten minutes after that, showed me the gold chains around his neck, then bored me to death with some long-ass story about the diamond initial ring on his pinkie. I'll spare you the recap. He's the type who would wear a toupee except he's got plenty of hair. Paints his nails with clear polish, too. Ah, yes, and was jonesing for some Russian manicurist named Olga. Another twenty-something-year-old."

"Sounds like you're right about him being the poster child for midlife crisis," Clare said. "Though I think he was damaged a long time before that."

Aimee looked at Clare. "How would you define midlife

crisis?"

"I suppose," Clare said, "it's when some people reach a certain age and suddenly believe the best is behind them and life is passing them by. They long to do all of the things they've never done and question the things they have done. It's a time in their lives when the grass seems greener on the other side. But even when they're given a chance to make their grass just as green as the lawns they covet, they're not sure it's what they really want. It's a time of personal confusion and internal disorder."

Bart continued. "And in desperate moments, although they'd never really want it that way, they long to be like the complacent ones—those folks who've mapped out a life for themselves and follow it to the letter. They never wonder what might have been."

"Bores," Larry said.

"Maybe they do wonder," Aimee said.

Bart nodded. "In secret, perhaps. But things never seem to get out of control."

"Outwardly," Dan said. "And when things *do* get out of control, you read about them in the paper. 'Loving husband of thirty-four years commits suicide. Friends and family never had a clue.' When people are too complacent, you've got to wonder."

"Interesting thoughts," Colin said.

"Oh, more than interesting, darling," Playfully, Leah squeezed Colin's arm. "I think we might have some true confessions here." She redirected her focus to Aimee.

Uncomfortably, impelled by the sting of Leah's glare, Aimee addressed Clare. "Do you think you might be having a midlife crisis without knowing it? Or maybe you do know it?"

Clare poured the last from the bottle of Perrier into her glass. "I'm quite content, actually. There may be a thing or two I'd like to change, but for the most part, I've got everything I ever wanted."

"Really?" Aimee asked uncomfortably. "Would you admit it

if you were unhappy? Would you tell us if you were still longing for my husband, as I'm quite certain you are?" Feeling sick as her words echoed in her mind, Aimee lowered her voice as if to dilute the offense. "You said before that you hadn't met anyone since college."

Maggie and Dan noticed as Leah attempted to disguise her pleasure while Bart simultaneously wrestled with his discomfort.

"And I spoke the truth," Clare said. "But you don't know if I'm with someone I knew from childhood."

"Now, that's just silly," Leah said. "While that could technically explain your answer, the point I made earlier was spot on. There's no way in hell you wouldn't have brought him along for everyone to see."

Uncomfortable with her words, Aimee continued. "Not if she's settled for some loser like the one we were just discussing. Besides, who would bring a spouse or friend if she or he still had feelings for someone here?"

"Good point, Mrs. Bart." Leah licked her lips. "What do you think, Dan? Do you agree with our movie star's wife? Because I'm very sure you have unexpressed opinions just waiting to be shared. You and Maggie both. It would be prudent to share them."

"Prudent?" Colin asked. "Why is that?"

"Maggie and Dan understand me."

"Well, since this conversation appears to be all about me," Clare said, "I'm truly happy and content in every aspect of my life. A few tweaks are needed, but they'll come in time. Most likely, sooner rather than later."

"Tweaks?" Leah asked. "More like major readjustments."

"Use whatever verbiage suits you, Leah. It all works. My happiness is truth no matter what words you use to describe it."

"Delusional. You can't possibly be happy."

Ignoring her, Clare looked at the doorway as Betty entered.

"Good afternoon," Betty said, smiling warmly at Bart. "I have a message from you to call your mother. She didn't want to stay on the line while I found you. She just asked that you call her back as soon as possible."

Clare looked alarmed. "I hope everything is okay, Bart."

He smiled. "All is fine. My mom is just returning my call from earlier."

"Of course," Clare said. "I'd forgotten you placed that call."

"You can use any one of our private phones," Betty said cheerfully. "I'll be glad to escort you to an unoccupied meeting room down the hall."

"I'll bet she would," Leah whispered to Colin.

"Thank you," Bart stood. "Excuse me, everyone. Lead the way, Betty."

MAY 17, 1986 – 12:07 P.M.

"Hello?"

Bart smiled as he sat in the sage-colored wingback armchair in a corner of the Woollcott Room. "Hey there, stranger. It's me. Thanks for calling me back."

"Oh, Bart! I'm so glad you called again. Would it be inappropriate of me to tell you just how good it is to hear your voice?"

"Not at all. It's every bit as good to hear yours. I've really missed—"

"I've been rather desperate … in an uneasy sort of way … to talk to you and wasn't quite sure how to go about it, especially knowing you were back East. I was so relieved when I got your message, so I'm assuming you know something … especially since you asked me to leave word that I was your mother."

"Are you saying that before I left that message, you already knew I was back East? How? Why were you so eager to talk to me? Tell me: exactly what is it you are assuming I already know?"

"Are you telling me this is all just a coincidence? It's way too serendipitous … too fluky … too bizarre … too—"

"Holly, as much as I appreciate the assorted adjectives, please, talk to me."

"I will. But if you don't mind, due to some circumstances that you seem to know nothing about, can you just go first? Please, Bart, tell me why you chose today of all days to call me. I'll tell you everything you want to know after that. I promise."

Feeling a knot in his stomach, Bart began. "Okay. Well, as you know, I'm at the Vanessa Grand in Barrie Hill, Connecticut."

"Yes. You said so in your message, but I was so surprised to hear from you that it didn't register. When I called a while ago and the hotel operator answered the phone, I recognized the name of the hotel immediately. I know what fond memories it holds for you. Are you at a college reunion?"

"A very small one. Just me and six other members of our beloved literary group."

"Ah, yes! You talked about them all the time. You always said it was the best time of your life until you met me." Holly laughed uncomfortably. "Then you'd go on about how comparing the two was like comparing apples and oranges. And I could never get you to tell me if I was an apple or an orange."

Bart laughed. "But I did tell you that together we were a pear."

"Yes!" Holly said. "Exactly! And as adorable as that was, it drove me nuts. Or maybe bananas."

"Ha! I remember. And you wouldn't tell *me* which one." He paused to let a happy memory float by. "I don't think there's anything about the two of us I don't remember."

"Me, too. As much as I want to talk … well, about most of the past, tell me about today."

Bart paused uncomfortably as he stared at the phone that sat on a small mahogany table in front of him. "Well, I haven't seen my old friends for twenty years. Naturally, one of the first things they asked me was about my films and what's coming up."

"That makes sense."

"So, I told them about *The Garden of Lost Dreams*, how it was nearly green lit, and how our first hope for a reunion film had inexplicably died."

"Right. Go on."

Bart felt his body tense as he spoke. "Well, the more I started thinking about what happened four years ago, the more I got this uneasy feeling that history might repeat itself. I started thinking about how Ken told me he pulled me from the film because some mysterious scandal was about to explode regarding the director. But it never did. Bruce Knight has made numerous films ... great films since then, and I've never heard one bad word about the guy. And I checked. Not even a parking ticket. So why were we told otherwise?" Bart exhaled in frustration. "Getting back to today ... I kept trying to push the uneasy feelings away, but they kept festering. This morning I woke up from a nightmare. *Garden* was dead in the water, and nobody would tell us why. My heart was racing, and I was perspiring. I hopped in the shower and tried to steam away the bad vibes, but they weren't going anywhere. I nearly scalded myself but realized that wasn't a solution. That's when I decided I was going to call you the first chance I got."

"Oh, wow. I can't believe this ..."

Bart waited for her to finish her sentence, but there was only the sound of her breathing. "Come on. Keep your promise. Tell me what you know."

"Sorry. Oh, shit. I don't know how to say this, Bart. Coming from me of all people, it just seems so wrong."

"Hol, you're killing me, honey. You know that, right? Whatever it is, just tell me. I called you first. Remember that. Now, tell me. Is *Garden* dead, too?"

"No! It's not. It's actually very much alive, and that's going to be confirmed on Monday morning. It's going to happen, Bart. We're going to be together again … on screen."

Bart felt a swell of relief and joy as he looked around the room. "Thank God. Okay, then. So why am I feeling you've also got news I'm dreading to hear?"

"Oh, Bart!"

"C'mon, Hol. Talk to me."

"Okay, okay. Listen, yesterday I was at Ken and Sylvia's. Just a small get-together to celebrate Syl finally getting her certification in interior design."

"That's great. I know she's worked hard toward that … and you're really taking the slow boat to China, aren't you?"

"I am, Bart. But not intentionally. It's just so damn awkward." Holly hesitated before continuing. "Hear me out. We were in the living room. The phone rang. Ken's assistant, Leanne, answered it. She told the caller that Ken was busy … well, because he was. The caller got very insistent, so Ken took the call in his office. This person threatened him and told him that if he didn't kill *Garden*, well, he would live to regret it for numerous reasons. I'm paraphrasing, of course. I didn't hear the caller … nor did I hear Ken's side of the conversation."

"First things first. You're saying the film is a go?" Bart asked, sweat beading in his palms and on his brow.

"Yes. It's a go. When Ken got off the phone, he came into the living room, looking really nervous, and asked Syl to join him in his office. They were gone a good forty-five minutes. Then, he came and asked me to join them. He looked wrecked, and when I stepped into his office, I could see Syl had been crying. He explained to me that about five years ago, he and Syl went through a very rough patch in their marriage. In that time, Ken had a brief affair with a young actress. I won't go into detail, but this person blackmailed him with this, threatening to expose everything to Syl. When the blackmail attempt was made again, Ken wasn't about to let *Garden* die a painful death. So, he decided to tell Syl what had happened and beg for her forgiveness. Long story short, she not only forgave him, but it seems she had an indiscretion of her own to confess. The blackmailer actually did them both a favor. Their respective secrets had been so burdensome.

"Ken apologized profusely to me, said he needed to do the same with you. He said he wished he'd had the courage to speak up four years ago, but everything was too raw then. He and Syl really do love one another. He said he couldn't risk losing her."

Bart exhaled. "Okay, so as angry … make that furious … as I am to hear this, I can live with that explanation. But now we know that some SOB wants to kill *Garden* for whatever reason, and Ken's not letting it happen. That's despicable, Hol, and I guess my gut was right, but there's no reason in the world why this news is wrong coming from you. Actually, I can't think of anyone I'd rather hear it from."

"Oh, Bart …"

"The only thing I want to know is who the bastard is, what he stands to gain, and without sounding like some cheesy character in a sci-fi film, if the threat has been neutralized?"

"Yes, because Ken refuses to be threatened again, but …"

"What? Is it someone I know and trust? A friend of mine?"
Holly paused. When she finally spoke, her voice was much softer. "Worse, Bart. It's your wife. Aimee."

"Say what? Please, Hol. I need you to repeat that."

"You heard me."

Bart picked up the base of the phone from the table and

stood, pacing the short distance the phone cord allowed him. "Okay, then I'll be the one to say it. Did you just tell me that my wife is the one who killed the last film and that she wants to kill *Garden*? And that she called Ken yesterday and threatened him? Again? Stop me any time, Hol."

"Yes. That's what I said. I'm so sorry, Bart. Listen, don't take my word for any of it. Call Ken if you want. He can explain it much better than I can. Besides, I'm sure he wants to tell you everything in his own words."

Overcome with dizziness, Bart sat and put the phone back on the table. "I have every intention of calling Ken, but not right now. If the film is still a go, then calling Ken is not my priority. Or at least not my *immediate* priority. But believe me, I have every intention of having a long talk with him."

"Aimee is there with you, right? I don't mean at this moment, I mean … Ken said she mentioned something about being at a 'miserable joke of a reunion' with you. Sorry … I shouldn't have repeated that."

"I'm glad you did. Knowing what I do now, that seems the very least of my worries. Besides, from her perspective, I can understand that, 'that' referring to her pejorative comment. Nothing else. I don't understand anything else!" Bart took a deep breath to calm himself. He paused for several moments before speaking again, doing so more softly. "But suddenly, some things are starting to make just the slightest bit of sense in a very warped-reality kind of way."

"I hope that's a good thing. It's really none of my business."

"Depending on how you see it, it's very much your business."

"Not the things between the two of you. At least in a personal sense. What she did to the first film and tried to do to this one, well, yes, messing with my career is definitely my business. But my involvement ends there; at least, I think it does."

"I'm guessing you have your own relationship to worry about, too."

"Uh … actually, I'm not in a relationship now. It's been a while for me."

Bart closed his eyes and replayed the words he had just heard. "You're not?"

"No," Holly said softly. "I'm not. My priorities have shifted … a lot … and I'm just working on the new-and-improved version of myself."

"Really? You are? That's great to hear. Good for you." Bart paused, unsure of what to say next.

"You still there, Bart?"

"I am … sorry. You know, Hol. I think I just need to sit here for a while and digest all of this conversation before I rejoin the reunion. I want … I need … to talk to you more … a lot more, but this isn't the time or place. I can only promise that I'll be in touch soon and let you know how things are going."

"Because you know I'm really concerned about you, right? Because you know your tone changes when you're upset and does that crackly thing."

"Ah," Bart said, feeling the onset of poignant memories, "yes, I always outed myself with that 'crackly thing.' At least with you."

Holly laughed. "Hey, we're human beings first, actors second. We can't fake our way out of everything. And as much as we try to glue ourselves together, we break."

"You always got me," Bart said. "Like nobody else ever did."

"And you me."

Bart paused as he drifted back in time. "By the way, Hol, since you brought it up earlier, this awkward moment might finally be the time to tell you: you were always the orange."

"Sweet and juicy?" Holly asked.

"Yeah," Bart said with a smile she could only visualize.

"Something like that."

"Thanks, Bart. Knowing that will get me through some stuff. Call me when you can. When it's right."

"I will, Hol. Just as soon as I can," Bart's heart beat faster. "I really want to hear more about you … about the changes in your life. I really … look, for now, until we talk again, you just take care of yourself, honey, okay? And thank you. I know this call wasn't easy for you."

"Anything for you. Bye, Bart. Hug yourself for me."

Letting go of the wistful smile he could not allow to remain, Bart hung up and stared straight ahead. *Whatever do I do now?*

Chapter ELEVEN

May 17, 1986 — 1:11 p.m.

After sitting in solitude for nearly an hour, thinking about the unsettling news he had just received and wondering how it would change his life, Bart looked at his watch. Startled to see how much time had elapsed, he stood, braced himself for whatever was ahead, then walked out the door and down the hallway.

As he turned the corner to return to the Parker Room, he stopped as he saw Larry approaching.

"Ah, there you are!" Larry said as the two men stood face-to-face. "No, I wasn't coming to look for you ... on my way to the men's room ... but I can tell you that everyone was beginning to wonder. And maybe worry. Thought maybe some crazy fans kidnapped you."

"Ah, nothing so exciting. Three of my cousins were visiting my parents. Took a while to talk to all three of them after chatting with my mom and dad. I probably would have spoken to my parents longer if I weren't heading there tomorrow. Unfortunately, my cousins are flying back to Chicago tonight, so we had to do our catching up on the phone."

Larry gripped Bart's shoulder. "Hey, I wasn't asking for an explanation. Sorry if I came off that way."

"Never crossed my mind." Bart smiled uneasily. "Listen, Lar, I'd really like to find some private time to talk to you later, though. A follow-up to yesterday's conversation. I need the ear of a good friend."

Larry pointed to the side of his head. "That's me. And I've got an ear to prove it. Two of them, in fact. You choose."

Bart smiled and looked him in the eyes. "Looks like you've found a way to maintain some long-lasting mellow after all of the mess with Cass … and—"

Larry laughed. "To my pleasant surprise, what I brought with me is particularly and powerfully potent. You know me. I'm never more than a toke away when the going gets rough. Just hope nobody else noticed."

"Doubt it. Nobody else roomed with you for three years. I've had practice reading your face. Especially your eyes. It's an actor thing."

"Right," Larry said, averting his eyes to study the wallpaper design. "Well, they're bringing some tea sandwiches and other edibles into the Parker Room, so I have to be careful not to let my acute case of the munchies give me away."

"Your secret is safe with me," Bart said, staring at Larry until the two resumed eye contact. "Catch you in a few."

＇✳＇✳＇✳＇

Steeling himself, Bart walked back into the Parker Room, passing the two waiters who had just set up a light lunch buffet. Everyone was standing, looking over the food or freshening their drinks.

"Perfect timing!" Clare said with a smile.

"Indeed," Bart said. "Looks tasty!"

"Your wife was afraid you'd left town without her," Leah said, as she delicately placed three tea sandwiches on her plate. "She just couldn't help but share her worry with all of us."

"Not a word of truth in that," Aimee said politely. "But I'm glad you're back, honey."

"No such worry reached *my* ears," Maggie said.

"Or mine," Dan added.

"Ditto," Colin said, pouring a short glass of white wine. "Can I get you something, Bart?"

"Whatever you're having," Bart replied. "Thanks."

"Warning!" Leah said, addressing Bart. "Notice the trays on the cart. Clare decided we should dine on our laps. Isn't that so … well … proletarian?"

"I think it's a great idea," Colin said, walking over to hand a glass of wine to Bart. "It's a lot more than we did back in the day. We didn't use trays then at all."

"Nope." Bart took the glass and nodded his thanks. "I like the idea of trays. Going down to the formal dining room is a bit much three times a day."

"Maggie agrees, too!"

Annoyed, Leah put a spoonful of salad on her plate and took a seat. "I guess I'm the only one here who regularly eats at a table."

"That's not true," Colin said. "You often eat dinner in front of the TV."

"On a tea table," Leah said. "The operative word being *table.*"

Colin laughed and said nothing.

Making a point to stay out of any conversation, Aimee, after partially filling her plate, grabbed a tray and sat on the couch to wait for Bart.

Maggie and Dan, back on their couch, waited for everyone to sit before eating.

"I hope y'all left something for me," Larry joked as he reentered the room.

"Plenty for you," Bart joked. "I know how hungry you are."

Larry winked and began to fill his plate, as Bart smiled and resumed his seat next to Aimee.

Discomfited by Bart's lack of conversation, Aimee looked up at him. "Obviously, you know I didn't say anything to anyone about how or what I was feeling, but I was a bit worried. Is everything okay with your parents?"

"Just fine," Bart said, picking up a cucumber and watercress tea sandwich. Looking at everyone but Aimee, Bart continued. "I haven't had one of these sandwiches in over twenty years."

"Oh, I have," Maggie said. "Very popular with the ladies who lunch. Not that I'm a regular member of any ladies' group."

Leah looked up. "I can't imagine you spending too much time with the female species."

"No, dear. But at least the members of my own species will have me."

"Not prudent," Leah said sharply to Maggie.

Colin looked oddly at his wife, but said nothing.

"She will not intimidate me," Maggie whispered to Dan.

"No," Dan whispered back, "but she'll keep trying. And we'll hold our ground."

As everyone broke up into smaller groups, Aimee, relieved, turned to Bart. "You were gone over an hour. What's going on in New Jersey? I know your dad had the flu last month."

"He's been over that for two weeks," Bart said, barely looking at her.

"Are you upset with me?" Aimee asked uneasily. "Are you okay?"

Bart stopped eating and turned to face her, looking into her eyes. "Actually, I think I should ask you if *you're* okay. Your eyes look a bit glazed and bloodshot."

"Um … I have no idea why that would be except that I did have some trouble sleeping last night. Just thinking of all of the unpleasant barbs sent my way courtesy of your old friend. You know, I may only have gotten a few hours' sleep, come to think of it."

Bart said nothing, then looked over at Larry, whose glazed eyes looked back at him as he smiled. He turned back to Aimee. "I've known you to do many an all-nighter during a big case. Funny, though, in all of those situations, you had your eyes glued to documents and law books until the wee hours … and yet, they never looked as they do now. Funny, isn't it?"

Aimee shrugged. "Who knows. Maybe because I'm out of my comfort zone here."

"Could be." Bart smiled pleasantly. "Have you gotten to know my old roommate?"

"Not really," Aimee said, looking at her plate.

"You know, honey, forgive me, but I never asked you about your old friend."

"What are you talking about?"

"Yesterday," Bart reminded her. "You excused yourself to go down to the lobby, because you were nearly certain you saw a friend from high school."

"Ah, right! False alarm. I'd already forgotten."

"You couldn't find her? Or you did find someone, and it wasn't her?"

Aimee bit her bottom lip. "Uh … I did find the person. And she did resemble my old friend. But it wasn't her. As I told Larry, everyone has a doppelgänger."

"Wait … so you have gotten to know my old roommate a bit."

"Not really," Aimee said, angry with herself. "I bumped into Larry in the lobby last night. It was a very brief encounter. Hardly what I'd call 'getting to know him.'"

"Yes," Bart said. "Larry did mention to us that you were together. I was going to come after you, but he told me you were fine and wanted to be alone."

"Um … yes … I was rather insistent about that."

"Well, I'm sorry the friend you were seeking turned out to be someone else. What's the name of the person you thought you saw?"

Flustered, Aimee put her tray on the center table and looked at it as if it were poison. "I thought it was … Shirley. Yes, my old lab partner from biology class."

"I see. I remember talking about biology class with you once. We were comparing dissection horror stories."

"Oh, yes. We had a lot of laughs about that."

"My memory must be failing me, though. I remember you saying that you took biology in the eighth grade, in junior high."

"Well, yes, Bart. Shirley was my lab partner in junior high, and then we went on to high school together. Nothing very interesting or unusual about that. Besides, I didn't even like her."

"Really? Yet you hurried down to the lobby to find her."

Aimee sighed and looked helplessly at Larry, who was busy eating.

"It was just curiosity. Not that different from your wanting to come to this reunion, actually."

Bart, finished with his food, grabbed Aimee's plate and put it on top of his empty plate. "I strongly beg to differ. I didn't come all of this way to spend a weekend with people I didn't like. Everyone here was a close friend. Granted, there might be one person here I'd no longer cross a street to see, but we're talking about two very different situations."

Before Aimee could respond, Bart, plates in hand, stood, then walked over to discard the trays and dirty plates on the cart, just as a waiter was coming in the room to get them.

Once again, Aimee looked at Larry, who was taking the last bite of his sandwich. Disturbed by her obvious distress, Larry made a sympathetic face, which he quickly lost as Bart glanced in his direction.

MAY 17, 1986 – 2:21 P.M.

"Bart, I was just thinking, while Clare is setting up the screen, this might be a good time for me to sneak out of here, go to the room, and take a nap. As I said earlier, I didn't sleep too well last night."

Leaning back on the couch, Bart contemplated her words. "Oh, okay. I thought you were interested in seeing our old photos ... my old photos. I know it's not your reunion and vastly less interesting than if it were, but you did say you wanted to see how I looked in my college days."

"I do. I meant it. But I'm just so wrecked."

"You're free to do as you wish, Aimee. You can see the photos *and* sleep. After this, we have a couple hours free before dinner, so you can nap then if you prefer."

"I'm really worn out; I'd rather not wait."

Bart shrugged.

At the end of her couch, a short distance from Aimee and Bart, Leah's ear stretched all the way to the Youngers' conversation. "Oh, Mrs. Bart, I don't like hearing that you're leaving us. Why do you want to do that? Do you have an important call to make?"

Aimee's eyes bulged, while Bart contemplated Leah's sarcasm.

Fidgeting with her wedding ring, Aimee looked up, barely making eye contact with either of them. "I'm tired. I'm just really tired."

"That's interesting," Leah said. "It's not like you were part of the late crowd last night. I really think you should stay, partake in all the fun we're going to have."

Bart watched curiously as Aimee, with laser focus, began pushing back her cuticles.

"Okay, whatever," Aimee mumbled. "I'll stay for the photos."

Leah slapped her palms together twice in sarcastic applause.

"Oh, goodie. It's so much more fun when you're here."

Feeling unsettled, Bart turned to speak to Dan and Maggie, who were sitting at a right angle from him. Aimee leaned forward and spoke softly to Leah. "I'm only staying because I do want to see my husband's college photos. You do not tell me when I sleep or don't sleep. I'm not your bitch."

Leah chortled. "Oh, that's hilarious! You're pathetically ineffectual and simultaneously ridiculous when you make such meager attempts to assert free will."

Aimee, gritting her teeth, shot a dagger at her, only serving to widen the contemptible smile on Leah's face.

"What are you so gleeful about?" Colin asked, noticing his wife's expression.

"I'm just looking forward to seeing the photos."

"I see. Now you're looking forward to them. You change your story every few minutes. Maybe you should be a politician. Actually, that would be difficult. You'd have to get enough votes to win."

"Hush!"

Clare, who with Larry's help had finished adjusting a projector screen behind the Youngers' couch, stood as she addressed the group. "It looks like we're almost ready to go. Bart and Aimee, unless you have eyes on the top of your head or want a case of whiplash, you might want to join me on my couch. There's room for two more."

Bart turned to see the screen directly behind them. "Absolutely," he said. Standing, he put out his hand for Aimee. "Let's go sit with Clare."

As Aimee walked with Bart to the other side of the small room, she noticed Leah, who was no longer close enough to whisper insults or threats, seething.

Returning to the couch, Clare sat next to Bart, remaining at a close right angle to Colin on the other side. Aimee sat at the end of couch, proximate to Larry's empty chair.

Still standing, Larry waited until everyone was seated. "All comfy? The curtains are already closed. I'll just flip the lights, and we'll be good to go."

"Go for it," Clare said.

Larry turned off the lights and hurried back to his chair.

Clare fiddled with the slide projector on the coffee table in front of her, then checked a few slides to make sure they were correctly inserted. "We're ready to rock n' roll. Just a warning: I tried my hardest to put all of the slides in correctly … that means upside down and backward. Please forgive me if I messed up any of them."

"Blah, blah, blah, blah, blah."

"Exactly!" Clare said to Leah. "I'm glad you were able to translate the concept into your native tongue."

Leah fumed as she heard sniggers in the darkness.

Maggie inched closer to Dan. "I feel like we're about to tell ghost stories."

"We are," Colin said before Dan could answer. "Many ghosts of Barrie Hill past are in that slide box." He turned to Clare. "Who's going to haunt us first?"

"Well," Clare said, clicking the remote, "in the interest of fairness and not to single anyone out, I thought we'd start with a group photo."

"Well look at that!" Maggie blurted out as the first image appeared on the screen. "My twenty-first birthday party. Right here in this room, too!"

"Sure is! Where did you get that black-and-purple boa?" Larry asked. "I'd forgotten all about it."

"I gave it to her," Dan said.

Maggie giggled. "Indeed you did, Danny!"

Colin laughed. "Got to ask, Dan the Man, where did you find that? Not exactly a staple in the shops of Barrie Hill."

"No, certainly not. I visited several vintage clothing stores in Manhattan but couldn't find what I had in mind. Then I stopped into Joe Allen's restaurant for lunch. The place had just opened. My waitress, also an actress, told me where I could find the best shop for boas. After lunch I took her advice and came upon exactly what I'd had in mind."

"A costume shop for the theatrically insane," Leah mumbled to herself.

"Oh, Danny!" Maggie said. "That was lovely of you to go to so much trouble. I never even thought to ask. I simply adored it, though."

"But I've long since thrown it down the incinerator," Leah said.

Clare pressed her lips together to ensure her thoughts wouldn't manifest into words. *Someone should have thrown you down an incinerator decades ago.*

"Not at all, Leah! In fact, I brought it with me," Maggie corrected her.

Leah's brow furrowed in defeat.

"Let's see," Bart said. "Who all is in this photo? Is that Henry Peyton with the tie-dyed peace shirt? His eyes look strange."

"Oh, don't you remember?" Leah said. "He had this weird issue with his eyelids."

"Ah, yes," Bart said. "But Henry's eyelids are nothing compared to those bellbottoms Larry and I are wearing. Holy hell!"

"Those bottoms have more flair than I do!" Maggie said. "Well ... almost."

Everyone laughed except Leah.

"That's warped," Larry said. "Look at mine with the orange, yellow, and red peace-sign stitched in there." He looked at Bart. "At least your bellbottoms were all denim. How could you let me go out wearing those things?"

Bart burst out laughing. "If you'll remember, I was so envious. I wanted a similar pair, and you refused to tell me where you got them."

Larry wiped tears of laughter from his face. "If only I'd have known how embarrassed I'd be today, I would have swapped with you. Damn, those things are hideous. And that orange Nehru jacket I'm sportin'? Fricking A, man."

"But everything goes so well with 'Lawrence Senior the Magnificent,'" Bart told him.

"My beloved 'fro," Larry said. "The least embarrassing part of me." He smiled and shook his head. "Clare, is that you and Colin standing by the drapes?"

"It is," Clare said.

"Where's Leah?" Maggie asked.

"Over in the corner, right next to where I'm sitting now," Leah said. "I was having a glass of wine … and observing. You know me, Maggie. I'm *always* watching."

"Well, everyone's too polite to mention how dashing I looked with hair," Dan said, ignoring Leah.

"You not only had a lot of hair," Colin said. "It was practically down to your shoulders."

"It was." Dan sighed.

"You look even better now," Maggie said to him.

"Maybe because you've seen more of him," Leah said to her.

Through the peripheral light of the projector, Dan's eyes narrowed as he glanced at Leah, then quickly looked away.

"Aimee," Maggie said, "we haven't heard from you. What do you think of Bart's sixties' attire?"

"Amazing, in the sense that the fashions of the time seems so outlandish, but everyone looks so comfortable … so proud. I'm just a bit younger than all of you, but I remember wearing some pretty scary looking graphic prints in the early seventies." She studied the photo on the screen, then turned to Bart. "It's almost like someone pasted your face under that long, crazy hair. I know it's you; but it's hard to believe. Know what I mean?"

Bart paused before answering. "Yes, I do. Sometimes it's hard to recognize someone … even when you're married to that person."

Clare, sensing Bart's agitation, clicked the forward button on the remote control. "And who's next? Well, look. It's Polly Hatfield and Leah!"

"What the hell!" Leah exclaimed.

"You and she look rather chummy," Colin said.

"Who took this photo?" Leah asked accusingly. "No doubt you did, Clare."

"No, Leah. I didn't. Mark Towers took it. You remember him. He was the senior photographer for *The Hiller.* He often gave me prints of photos when anyone from our group was in them."

"Hard to believe," Leah spat.

"Seriously?" Clare asked. "Are you actually crediting me with having the foresight to snap a photo of you and Polly in 1964 so that I could taunt you with it twenty-two years later? If I'd known it would bother you so much, I'd have asked Mark to take more."

"You know the year it was taken," Leah said. "That alone is suspicious."

"Only because when I saw Polly, she reminded me that she was in the Barrie Hillers for four months … in 1964."

Leah looked in Clare's direction. "You never said before that you actually saw her again. You just said that her name came up in … never mind … I certainly don't give a damn." She looked at the screen again. "That green-and-orange muumuu she's wearing is nauseating me. That pathetic woman had the bad taste to brag that she owned authentic Hawaiian clothing. More like haute couture for the homely. I think it belonged to her mother in the fifties."

"No, that dress never belonged to her mother," Clare said.

"Polly bought it herself on winter break in Hawaii. I remember. She was very proud of it."

"Who the hell cares? Just like you, one thing she could never get in Hawaii was a good lei. For God's sake, let's move on," Leah demanded.

Clare clicked the remote, the darkness nearly masking her smile. "Oh, look, we have a side view of our favorite stoners, Larry, Bart, Colin, and Henry squeezed onto one couch—everyone's feet are up on this very coffee table."

Bart sighed, then laughed. "I'm glad we had enough class to remove our shoes." He paused to examine the photo. "We look absolutely ridiculous! What's with those gold-patterned socks I'm wearing? They're hideous."

"Can't say much for those argyles I'm sporting," Colin added. "And those are some shockers you're wearing, Lar. Let's see if I can make this out. Looks like two lines of double-red stitching with black shapes in between. Sort of looks like a diagram of the New Jersey turnpike."

Maggie giggled. "Oh, I'm sorry, Larry, dear. But Colin is spot on."

"Hey, those were crimpled nylon, made in England," Larry said, smiling.

Leah turned her neck slowly so everyone could appreciate her disdainful expression. "How the hell do you remember that?"

"Easy. It was printed on the socks. I had several pairs of them. My grandfather gave them to me."

"Charming," Leah said.

"Too bad Bart's feet are blocking Henry's socks," Colin said. "They were probably real humdingers, too."

"Tragic," Leah added as everyone ignored her. "Henry was a real humdinger. I'm sure his socks were, too. Use your imagination. You're not missing anything."

"Henry was a doll," Maggie said. "He broke a lot of hearts when he fell in love with Madeleine."

"He did," Clare agreed. "But I was happy they got together. A lot of gold diggers were after him. I was happy he chose someone who loved him for himself."

"Well," Colin said, "Bart's feet may be blocking Henry's socks, but what's with his eyes?"

"He had eyelid issues," Leah said. "I told you all that just a while ago."

"I don't think that was the issue in this photo," Larry said. "Henry was seriously stoned."

"Whatever," Leah mused. "It's probably how he got the damn eyelid problems in the first place."

Clare pressed the remote.

"Santa and Mrs. Claus!" Maggie shrieked. "I had completely forgotten!"

"I recognize you, Maggie," Aimee said. "But who's Santa?"

"Your husband," Leah said. "You don't recognize him?"

Aimee looked embarrassed. "That's you, Bart? It doesn't look like you at all."

"Well," Bart said, "I wasn't just wearing a costume. I was applying the tricks of the trade I'd learned in stage makeup class. I'm wearing prosthetic jowls, for one. Like I said before, being married to someone doesn't mean you'll always recognize him … or her. You know?"

Aimee squirmed, not knowing how to read Bart. "This may seem like a funny time to ask," she said nervously, "but I never did understand something about this group."

"What's that?" Larry asked.

"You were all students at Barrie Hill College, and I know you formed this group out of a mutual love of literature. But what I don't know is why you met here at this rather expensive hotel, instead of somewhere on campus."

"I should let Maggie answer that," Larry said.

Maggie smiled. "First, Aimee, I should ask you if you're familiar with the Algonquin Round Table. You know, the group of witty people that included writers, critics, actors, and other sorts that met for lunch every day for about ten years. I believe they began in 1919, so they were far before the time of anyone here, but their legacy has lived on."

"Actually, yes, being a New Yorker, I do." Aimee tried to shake off the vibes from Bart she didn't understand. "I've had dinner at the hotel. Go on."

"Well," Maggie said, "my grandfather was part-owner of this hotel when it was built in 1924. He and one of his partners, George von Bulu, were great literary fans and were endlessly enamored of the Round Table members, some of whom they knew personally in New York. When they opened this hotel in Connecticut, they partially modeled it after the Algonquin and named the meeting rooms after some of the original members. We're in the Parker Room now, which is named for Dorothy Parker. The Woollcott Room, named for Alexander Woollcott, is down the hall. The Kaufman Room, named for the playwright and director George S. Kaufman, is easily the largest room on this floor. It's where those green-shirted relatives and that dreadful 'Pappy' have been whooping it up."

"That's fascinating," Aimee said. "I should have tied all of this together. I feel like a bit of a dummy for not having done so."

"Don't chastise yourself," Bart said. "Some things are right in front of our faces, and we don't see them."

"Right," Aimee said, her heart thumping wildly. She looked at Maggie. "So, how did all of you end up meeting here?"

"After my grandfather died, my father inherited his share of this hotel. That enabled us to meet here for a modest fee. Literary snobs that we were, I must say, we relished the idea of meeting off-campus and trading our witticisms in rooms named after legends. We rather fancied ourselves to be legends."

"Oh, yeah," Larry said. "We so did."

Colin laughed. "I'd love to deny that part, Aimee, but Maggie is telling the truth."

"Indeed I am," Maggie said. "It's more than a bit embarrassing, isn't it? You know, this hotel itself should have been named after one of the Round Table members, but George von Bulu, who owned the greatest share, named it after his daughter, Vanessa. My grandfather wanted to name it after me, but it didn't go that way."

"Does your family still own part of this hotel?"

"No, my father sold his share in the late seventies."

"I wish this hotel had been named after you," Dan said.

"Oh, Dan," Leah groused. "You would redesign the Statue of Liberty in Maggie's likeness. And it would be hilariously fitting, because she still holds a torch for you … and you for her. Perhaps we should elaborate on—"

"Did I answer your question, Aimee?" Maggie asked.

"You did. Thank you."

"Good," Maggie said. "Now, have we all seen enough of the Santa photo?"

"I *would* like to know why you and Bart dressed up like the Clauses," Aimee said. "If you don't mind …"

"My, my, Mrs. Bart is suddenly a virtual chatterbox."

"It was for a local children's hospital Christmas party," Maggie said, ignoring Leah. "Lots of fun for a great cause … or should I say 'a great Claus.'"

Laughter drowned out Leah's useless groan.

"Let's see what else we have," Clare said, advancing to the next slide. "Ah, Bart and Larry, wearing their buckskin vests, enjoying a beer with Ralph Tomey and Wally Decker."

Larry burst out laughing. "Holy shit, Roomie. Talk about fringe lunatics. Where the hell did we get those matching vests?"

"It'll come to me," Bart said.

Clare looked curiously at Bart, noticing he seemed distracted and ill at ease.

"Ah," Larry said holding up his index finger. "Your mother sent them to us after your parents returned from a trip out West."

Bart tried to lighten up. "Well, now that's just plain embarrassing. You're right. My parents bought them in Colorado. And we loved them … fringe and all."

"We did," Larry said. "Speaking of embarrassing, I still have mine. Cass found it in my storage trunk a few years ago."

"Did she like it?" Maggie asked.

"She actually loved it," Larry said. "Asked where it came from and insisted I wear it."

"Did you?" Dan asked.

"Of course. Anything for the love of my life."

Leah chortled. "Well, that's a bold-faced lie, Larry. 'Anything for the love of my life' would means she'd be here with us now, yes? Oh, poor Mona Moore! Languishing at home by her lonesome … or is she?"

"So, you actually wore that vest on the streets of Manhattan?" Colin said, annoying Leah with his quick change of subject.

"Not exactly," Larry said, trying not to give way to melancholy. "I wore it inside my apartment. All night long. Until I took it off."

"You wore it until you took it off," Leah said. "We all wear our clothing until we take it off. What do Maggie and Dan think? Don't we all wear our clothing until—"

"I think the fringed buckskin vest was all the rage back then," Dan said adamantly. "Bart and Larry were real style setters."

"Yes, I would agree with that completely," Maggie said.

"Maggie," Clare said, "look at Wally Decker. He's not really paying attention to Bart, Larry, or Ralph. He seems to be staring at someone."

"He does," Maggie said. "All I can see is a yellow leg with white squares on it."

Clare saw that Leah looked annoyed. "That was you, wasn't it? That was your Louis Vuitton pantsuit."

"If Wally Decker was looking in my direction," Leah said, "it's because Maggie was next to me." She looked through the dim light toward Maggie. "I remember that night so well. You were complimenting me on my designer suit, and, dare I say, I was admiring your outfit. You were wearing a bright teal dress with matching go-go boots. And a boa."

"I was," Maggie said. "And my hair was long and flowing. Later that night, that lascivious man did try to proposition me, but I rid myself of that wretched being before he could finish his sentence, 'Hey, babe, how would you like to ...'"

Clare advanced to the next slide. "Oh, my! Look at me; I barely remember having hair that long. And why was I wearing such a drab beige pantsuit? Though I suppose I'd rather see myself in this than neon green."

"I can answer that, Clare," Leah said.

"Because I'm dull and boring," Clare said. "There. I said it for you."

"You're nothing of the sort," Colin said. "And I liked you with long, shiny hair. And that outfit was very much in vogue back in the sixties. Pretty cool beaded necklace, bracelet, and matching earrings you had on, too."

"Oh, for Christ's sake," Leah said to Colin. "Clare finally gets it right, and you correct her."

"Why is your arm up in the air like that?" Aimee asked Clare.

"It looks like a railroad crossing arm, doesn't it?" Clare said, laughing. "I think I was trying to get everyone's attention for one reason or the other. Darned if I can remember. But this photo was taken on campus, not here. As you can see, we're in an auditorium. Ah, that's right. I was the emcee for a poetry reading. I remember now. Over a hundred people turned up."

"You read your poetry that night," Dan said to Maggie. "I remember."

"I did," Maggie said softly.

"Next!" Leah demanded.

As Clare hit the remote, Leah screamed as the next photo appeared on the screen. "You did that on purpose, Clare. Don't tell me you didn't!"

Everyone laughed to see an upside down photo of Leah standing alone, looking disapprovingly at someone as she posed with a lit cigarette in her hand.

"I remember that dress," Colin said. "It looked like a Mondrian painting, and it was tight, tight, tight."

"I'd say so," Larry chimed in.

"I didn't do this intentionally," Clare said to Leah. "Would you like me to fix the slide?"

"Oh, bullshit!" Leah said. "Of course you did. Just move on. Don't bother to right the damn photo."

"Why so glum?" Colin said. "Things could be worse. If you'd been wearing pants in this photo, loose change would be falling all over the floor right about now."

"Hilarious ... not! Hush. As for loose change, that's about all you'd have," Leah whispered to him. "If I hadn't—"

"Well, the dress was an artistic masterpiece," Colin told her. "Be proud."

"More like a messterpiece," Leah grumbled. "Or a piece of—"

"Oh, look," Colin said as the next photo came up. "Bart and

Clare waltzing … right here in this room."

Leah looked at Aimee. "Now do you see exactly what I mean? Look at the way she looked at your husband back then. Wouldn't you say nothing has changed?"

Bart watched Aimee look down and say nothing.

Angered by the lack of a response, Leah cleared her throat.

Maggie whispered to Dan, "We may have to join forces."

"What?" Dan whispered back.

"Tell you later," Maggie whispered. "Oh my goodness," she said loudly as the next photo appeared. "That's the ugliest dress I've ever seen! And I'm wearing it. I can barely count the number of colors and patterns on that piece of fabric. Look! Triangles, polka dots, squares, rectangles, and lines … in purple, mauve, yellow, green, blue, and orange, and whatever those other colors are in there … screaming to get out. Look at those poufy sleeves! Why in God's name was I wearing that monstrosity? What do you get when geometry knocks up art class and they have a child together? That dress! Ugh! I must have totally repressed that reprehensible garment!"

"You really don't remember that dress?" Clare asked. "I do."

"Goodness, no!" Maggie said. "And I apologize to any mirrors I may have cracked and to any eyeballs I may have burned. Simply dreadful! Not to mention that my hair is teased and sprayed to high heavens!"

"Ah, the sixties," Larry said reflectively. "Nothing like that time. And if we're all lucky, nothing ever will be like it again."

CHAPTER TWELVE

MAY 17, 1986 – 5:26 P.M.

"Ah, light!" Colin said as Larry flipped the switch. "And look, we're in the eighties again! I really do feel like we were transported back in time for the past two hours and change."

"We were." Clare got up and stretched. "Bart, would you mind unplugging the projector for me?"

"Sure thing," Bart stood. "Clare," he whispered, "could we talk for a few minutes when everyone clears out? I'd really like to speak to you privately."

"By all means," Clare said.

As Bart unplugged the projector, Larry hurried over to him. "Hey, my man, you said out in the hallway earlier that you needed to talk."

Bart, holding the unplugged cord in his hand, smiled at his former roommate. "I'm okay, Lar. False alarm. But thanks."

Larry looked strangely at him. "You sure? You—"

"Very," Bart said. "All's good."

"Okay then. But I'm always here if you need me. Now, if you'll excuse me, I'm going to collapse the screen and get it out of everyone's way."

"Good man," Bart said as he turned around.

As Larry approached the screen, Aimee casually sauntered

over to him, but didn't look directly at him as she spoke softly. "Do you think we could meet outside? Whenever you can get away?"

"Um … yes. See you in a bit."

As if she hadn't said anything at all, Aimee walked back to Bart. "You know, honey, I've got a second wind. I don't think I'm going to take a nap after all. If I do, I won't sleep a wink tonight. I just need some alone time. This is such a charming town; I think I'll take a stroll and get a feel for it."

"As you wish. Enjoy yourself. Anything special you want to see?"

"Not really. A little of everything, I suppose."

While everyone else milled about, Dan and Maggie remained seated. Leah, standing by the bar, fixed her gaze on them.

"What were you trying to tell me, dear?" Dan whispered.

"I think we must tell Aimee that Colin's shameful fishwife is blackmailing us, too."

Dan laughed. "This isn't a funny situation, but your colorful epithets bring much-needed humor." His amused expression turned to one of concern. "You know, we've been sitting in near darkness for quite a while, but even through the little light we had, I could see her giving Aimee the same type of cold stare she's been directing at us. Making the same kind of veiled threats, too. This was going on yesterday, but I didn't see it clearly, as I didn't know. Leah—"

"Is revolting," Maggie said, finishing his sentence. "Danny, Aimee looks as if she's ready to leave. Please, be quick and find a reason to talk to her. I think we should tell her not to let Leah get the better of her. If you agree, I'm thinking, without saying why, that we should let Aimee know she's meddling in our business, too. Meanwhile, I'll talk to Leah and distract her while you do that. We'll meet as planned afterward. But only if this is what you want, too."

"Absolutely. I'm on it." Dan stood. "Aimee!" he called across the room. "May I speak to you for a moment?"

Dan walked to Bart and Aimee. "I'm sorry to trouble you, Aimee. Yesterday, when this reunion began, you mentioned something about the pro bono work you've done for the homeless in LA. As a newspaperman, I'd really love to ask you a few quick questions before our weekend is over and I forget. I won't take much of your time at all. I promise."

Aimee smiled. "Well, sure, Dan. As I was telling Bart, I'm going to take a walk through town. But I certainly have a moment to talk to you before I do."

As Bart spoke to Dan and Aimee, Maggie got up, then hurried toward the bar. As she stood before Leah, she did so as to block her view of them.

Leah glared at her. "If you're here to beg for mercy, I'm merciless."

"I think that's been well established. Nothing to be proud of."

"If anyone has committed acts not worthy of pride, that would be you."

"You know nothing."

"Oh, really? Convince me that you and Dan were playing tiddlywinks all night. Tell me, how many winks did he shoot into your pot?"

"You vile woman!"

"Speaking of the pot, aren't you calling the kettle black?"

"I am not! Whatever you think of me, I have never purposely set out to inflict pain and suffering on another human being for the mere sport of it."

"I've asked you to pay a very small price for your actions. And I've yet to see a proverbial cent. Dinner tonight will be your last chance. If you don't do as I say, your knight in sooty newspaper ink will pay dearly. Which means you will, too."

Angrily, Maggie tossed her blond curls over her shoulder. "Do you really consider the trashing of my dear old friend to be a 'small price'?"

"Considering we're talking about someone as worthless as Clare Dreyser, yes."

"Do you consider the decimation of lives to be merited … simply because your childish bullying didn't go as planned?"

"We wouldn't be having this discussion if you had any morals." Leah craned her neck to look around Maggie.

"Depraved woman," Maggie hissed. "What are you trying to look at, anyway?"

Leah took a few steps to her right, only to find that Dan and Aimee were gone. "Where the hell did they go?"

"Where did who go?" Maggie asked. "I have no idea what you're on about now."

Leah grumbled as she stared at the spot where Aimee and Dan had been standing.

"See you all later," Larry said as he headed out the door. "Clare, the screen is propped up against the wall, to the right of the door. Do you need me to move it somewhere else?"

"No, that's fine," Clare said. "Once the projector is ready, I'll put it there, too, and let the staff know they can take it away. Thanks again!"

"My pleasure."

"Larry!" Maggie called after him. "Wait up, will you?"

Larry turned to see Maggie rush over. "Always a pleasure to wait for you, Maggie."

"Walk out with me, will you, Larry? I need to get away from that loathsome creature."

"Wow," Larry said, as he walked down the hallway with Maggie. "Nobody is safe from her vitriol. I'm not asking, but like I keep saying, 'Bitter grows some ugly roots.'"

Leah, angry that Maggie had left with Larry, stood by the bar, seething, unaware she was balling her fists until she felt her nails digging into the palms of her hands. Upon realization, she unclenched her fists, but internally, her rage escalated.

Clare walked over to Colin, who was now seated, taking the slides out of the projector. "Thanks for helping, but I can finish this myself. You can do me a much bigger favor by taking your wife out of here. Anywhere. For whatever reason, her animus is boiling over. Bart has asked me for some private time to talk. I'd like to be able to do that here."

Colin nodded, stood, and walked over to Leah. "Let's go. We're going to get some fresh air and perambulate through the streets of our misbegotten youth."

"Shakespeare you're not," Leah said angrily. "Hush!"

"Let's go," Colin said, as he quickly led her out of the room.

ˈ✷ˈ✷ˈ✷ˈ

Dan opened the door to the Woollcott Room and held it open for Aimee. As she crossed the threshold, she smiled apprehensively.

"This is the third-largest meeting room on the floor." Dan closed the door and walked into the room behind Aimee. "As Maggie told you earlier, the Kaufman Room is the largest. She forgot to mention the Ross Room, named for Harold Ross, the editor of *The New Yorker*. That's the second largest." Dan looked around. "Take a seat, Aimee. As you can see, we have the place to ourselves."

Aimee walked to the closest couch and took a seat on the end of it. Dan sat in the wingback armchair next to it.

"You didn't bring me here to talk about any pro bono work I've done," Aimee said matter-of-factly. "There would be no reason to seclude ourselves from the others. There's nothing cloak and dagger about helping the homeless."

"No, there isn't." Dan paused to collect his thoughts. "Aimee,

I'm sorry for not being upfront with you in the Parker Room, but that was impossible. If my reason for bringing you here is wrong, there will be no shortage of apologies from both me and Maggie."

"Go on," Aimee said cautiously. "I'm listening."

"Maggie has told me Leah is trying to force you to condemn Clare on her behalf."

"You can say the word, Dan. Blackmail."

Dan exhaled. "Yes. That awful word. Maggie and I thought we should tell you she's playing the same ugly game with us. We thought that knowing this might help you to find strength … knowing others are with you in this fight." Dan looked nervously down at his lap, then again at Aimee. "I'm sorry if I've spoken out of turn or brought you here foolishly."

Aimee looked around the room, her eyes examining everything from the draperies to the paintings on the wall to the furniture. "A lot of history in this place." She looked at Dan. "No, you didn't bring me here foolishly. I'm really sorry to hear this. I just don't know if it changes anything."

Dan straightened his glasses. "I see."

"You know," Aimee said, "I sensed Leah was toying with you and Maggie. At least, I thought I did. But that didn't seem to change the situation, as her threats to me are still very real." Aimee sighed. "I hope you know I'm not interested in your personal business, Dan."

"Nor are we in yours. What we want to tell you is that you shouldn't let Leah control you. I have no right to ask you to call her bluff, as neither of us can take responsibility for the consequences. But that's what Maggie and I intend to do. Maggie may have a trick up her sleeve that even I know nothing about. But we will not be giving in. If you feel the need to do so, we won't blame you, Aimee, but we hope you won't. We also hope that knowing we're also dealing with a situation, and that we don't intend to let Leah win, will give you some kind of moral support, as feeble as it may be."

"I really like Clare," Aimee said, "and she's been dear to Bart's heart for decades. I despise the things I've said, and you may have noticed, for now, I've stopped saying them. I can't promise what I'll do, but being aware of your predicament does help. For one, I don't feel so alone, but that said, I'm sorry. I just want to say that I think Maggie is one hell of a strong woman. Leah is a craven bitch. My money's on Maggie."

ˋ✶ˋ✶ˋ✶ˋ

"Finally, we're alone." Bart stood. "Do you mind if I open the drapes? I'd like to enjoy what sunshine is left in the day."

"Please do."

"Physically and emotionally, I feel like I've been in a cave," Bart said as he walked to the large windows and pulled on the gold-braided drapery cords. He smiled as sunlight poured into the room. After taking a moment to look wistfully onto the street below, he walked back to join Clare on the couch. "Thank you, my friend—for staying behind to talk to me. I'm sure you had something else to do."

"Nothing that could possibly be more worthwhile than having some alone time with you."

Bart kissed Clare on the forehead, then sat down next to her. "You've always been there for me, Clare. It's easy to make friends these days, but real friends, not so much. Everyone loves a movie star." He shivered. "I strongly dislike using that term. I prefer 'actor,' but it doesn't describe how most people see me. They think I'm larger than life. I'm not. I'm just me."

"You're every bit the man I remember," Clare said. "I just knew you wouldn't change. I knew that when I saw you again, you'd be just as genuine as you always were."

Bart blushed. "Thank you. I'm not sure if I deserve that." He took a moment to reflect. "Back in 1962, when you and I first met, Marilyn Monroe had just died two weeks before college began—on August fifth."

"I remember it well."

"Her death really shook me. In many ways, before I came to Barrie Hill, I was a starry-eyed kid who saw actors in the same fictive light others see me now. I thought Marilyn Monroe, Cary Grant, Gregory Peck, Joan Crawford … all of them … were somehow superhuman. I knew better, I really did, but I worshipped them. When Marilyn died, I was reminded we're all mortal, flawed beings. I never slipped back into that crazy mindset. And I'm very grateful for that."

"You know, Bart, even if Marilyn hadn't died so tragically, I don't think you'd be any different than you are now."

Bart reached for his glass of Perrier on the table. "Thank you. I'd like to think that. And I do realize I was only eighteen at the time, so in that respect, I should cut myself some slack." Taking a few sips of his drink, he looked around the room, then put the glass back on the table. "There's so much I want to say and so little time.

"First, before anything, I need to say thank you. Back in the early days, you were one of only a handful of people who believed in me. When most of the world was admonishing me for not having a plan B, you were telling me I could achieve plan A. You never deviated from your faith in me. Ever. You believed not only in my talent, but, even more so, in my perseverance."

Clare smiled self-consciously. "I did. But, hey, how many times did you tell me I'd be a great novelist some day, that I would succeed in anything I set out to do? Well, I'm not published yet, but I will be. I've finished my first novel and hope it will be well received. There's a lot about my life you don't know, Bart, but I hope you'll approve."

Bart looked quizzically at her. "I would. I know that." Gently, he touched her knee. "Clare, I'm just so damn sorry we didn't keep in touch. I've regretted that for years, and it took this reunion to change things. And I hope that from this day forward, we'll be friends in every sense of the word."

"I'm counting on that." Clare sighed. "Don't feel bad; I should have written or called, too. My life has been a lot more complicated than most people know. As for you and me, time just got away from us. In the future, we'll just have to be better at carving more of it out for one another. Sounds good?"

Bart smiled as he looked at Clare. "That's one deal I intend to keep."

"Good. Now, speaking of our friendship, even though twenty years have passed, I still know you. When we saw one another for the first time yesterday, you were quite cheerful, fully focused on being here. Today, when you came back from talking with your mother, it was like a different man entered the room. I felt a distinct pain emanating from you … perhaps confused agitation is more accurate … I don't know. But it was as if an intrusive force had wrapped its arms around you. I could feel you trying to wrest yourself from it." Clare stopped to exhale. "Then there's the theory that I'm completely delusional, reading too much into nothing, and talking too much. And that is entirely possible, because I'm finally able to do so freely."

"This is the problem with having literary friends," Bart said, grinning. "They can read you like a book."

Clare looked thoughtfully at him. "What's wrong?"

"Well, I guess I should start by saying that I wasn't talking to my mother, nor did I ever call her when I said I did."

"Oh … okay."

"I wasn't trying to deceive anyone, Clare. It was all of the talk about the movie I'm supposed to be making soon … the one with Holly. The more I thought about the first one dying a sudden death, the more I began to relive the events of four years ago. I'm a nice guy, and sometimes, too nice. If I trust someone, sue me, I tend to take his or her word at face value. I won't go into the details, but let's just say I reassessed the facts and came to an unsettling but baffling conclusion that there was way more to the story than I knew. Naturally, I began to worry that the new film might suffer the same unfortunate and mysterious fate as the first."

Clare furrowed her brows as she studied the sadness in Bart's eyes.

"I wasn't going to call my agent, Ken, because I believed if anyone was complicit in whatever happened, it might be him. I called someone I knew I could trust: Holly. She wasn't in, and I left a message for her to call me back … and, yes, I asked her to say she was my mother."

As Bart picked up his glass and finished his drink, Clare stood. "I don't want to stop you, but you look like you could use a refill, even if it is Perrier. Or would you like something stronger?"

"Not now," Bart said. "But yes, I would like another Perrier and lime. Thank you."

Clare, wasting no time, walked to the bar and fixed two fresh glasses of sparkling water. Returning to the coffee table, she placed a glass and a chilled bottle in front of him, then went to get her own. Once seated again, she took a sip, then looked at Bart. "Are you okay to continue?"

"I am. Thank you." Bart picked the lime wedge off the side of his glass, cupped his hand around it, then squeezed it into the drink. "Because we're short on time, I'll hop on the express train here and get to the point. Holly gave me some information that I haven't been able to digest. The good news is that the new film should be green lit on Monday. The bad news is that my agent, though unwillingly, did have something to do with the demise of the first one. But someone else was the mastermind, and that same person made a call yesterday, once again, attempting to blackmail Ken into having the current film killed."

"My God, that's horrible! Who would do such a thing?"

Bart's face tensed. "What if I told you that the call came from this hotel?"

"Leah!" Clare exclaimed. "Are you kidding me?"

Bart just looked at her.

"No, that's stupid. It wouldn't have been Leah. While she's capable of doing such a thing, she was nowhere in your orbit four years ... my God ... Aimee?"

"Yes." Bart sighed. "It was my wife."

"Clearly, somehow Leah got wind of this ... overheard something ... and that's exactly why Aimee has said such awful things to me. I knew Leah was behind it. But forgetting about her for a moment, tell me about Aimee. Why would she do that, Bart?"

"Only one reason comes to my mind: jealousy."

"If you don't mind my asking, not that it excuses anything, has she had any reason to be jealous?"

"I've seen Holly exactly once since I married Aimee. I was having lunch in Hollywood, at Musso and Frank's, with a producer, and Holly stopped by our table. We invited her to sit with us. She stayed for all of five minutes and then left. Holly and I talked on the phone after our film fell through, but that was it. Until today."

"How are you feeling? Hurt? Angry? Sympathetic? Confused? Deceived?"

Bart hesitated before responding. "All of the above. Only not equally. Any feelings of sympathy might be five percent of the pie; the other emotions take up ninety-five percent."

"That's totally understandable."

"Honestly, Clare, if it weren't for a chat I had with Larry yesterday, I would have no sympathy at all."

"How's that?"

Bart looked around the room, to check they were alone.

"Because when Larry asked me if I had any residual feelings for Holly, well, let's just say I wasn't the only one surprised by my answer. But that doesn't negate the fact I've been true to Aimee since the day we met. It doesn't negate the fact she not only set out to destroy my film, she blackmailed my agent. I just never dreamed she was capable of anything like that. I can't even count the number of lies and deceptions … damn … this is so overwhelming. Who the hell am I married to?"

Seeing the angst in Bart's eyes, Clare watched, knowing that he was struggling to find the words. She watched his indrawn breath as he looked around the room in pain, searching for something he would not find. After a few moments, Bart met her eyes again.

"People have been telling me for years that I'm too nice. Sorry, I'm not going to be some Hollywood asshole because I'm famous or because I know a lot of them. And, yeah, as angry and disappointed as I was about the first film, it was dead in the water. What was I going to do, rant and rave forever and make myself sick over it? Obsess over it instead of putting my energy into new films? I had to move on. I *did* move on. But this, Clare … I don't know what to say. I could *almost* understand if this happened four years ago, and Aimee went on to regret it. But clearly, she had no remorse over committing those crimes; she was on her way to another masterful deception. When I think of the conversations we had … how she comforted me … shit, how she lied to me … and *she* was the cause of all of the misery. My *sweet* wife."

"I'm so sorry, Bart. I don't know what to say. I know you're probably in more pain learning this news than you were about that first film … because this is personal …that, or so you thought, was business."

"Exactly!" Bart said, leaning back on the couch. "I have no idea what I'm going to do."

"Well," Clare said, putting a comforting hand on his, "don't do anything until you talk to her. Hear her out, because as angry as you are, you wouldn't be you if you did things any differently."

Bart sat up straight and looked at her. "Yeah, once again, I should be the nice guy. I should play that role I'm so damn good at."

"It's not about being nice, Bart. And it's not even about Aimee. I know that as hurt and angry as you are, hearing what she has to say is part of who you are."

"Yeah. It is. I used to take pride in that. Now I wonder …"

"Bart, you're always going to be one of the good guys, whether you like it or not. That's you. What you ultimately do about this has nothing to do with who you are. You've got to allow some time for this to settle in. Don't make any life-changing decisions when you're this angry … when everything is so raw … you know? I know that it's easier said than done … but try to calm down, and when you're able to do that, give yourself some time to think it all through."

"You're right, Clare. Maybe I should start by taking a walk. It might help clear my head a bit. Except that's what Aimee is doing, and I might run into her."

"Would that be a good or bad thing?"

Bart picked up his glass and took a sip of his drink. "Damned if I know. I'm just such a mess right now that I can't even ask you about your life while we have a Leah-free environment."

"There's time for that. Whether it's this weekend or a phone call next weekend. We made a promise to be the friends we once were."

"We did, and we will be." Bart leaned back and closed his eyes for a moment. Opening his eyes, he looked at Clare. "Can I ask you something?"

"Anything."

"If I'm honest with myself, and if I figure out that I have feelings for Holly that aren't going anywhere, would I be a horrible person for seeing a silver lining in all of this?"

MAY 17, 1986 — 6:26 P.M.

Larry leaned back on the bench and looked up at the tops of the trees. "You babies have grown since I left you. Lookin' good, too!"

"Do they ever answer you?"

Startled, Larry sat up straight. "Aimee!" He paused to catch his breath. "Damn, woman. I *was* expecting you, so how is it that you still managed to scare the bejesus out of me?" He patted the empty space next to him. "Have a seat. And to answer your question, sometimes, after I've had a few tokes, we have indeed had some good talks."

"Ah, interesting." Aimee sat down. "That tree over there," she said, pointing, "the one with the two giant burls on it, I'm thinking he looks like he can be a bit argumentative."

Larry smiled. "You think so? He's cool. His bark is worse than his bite."

Aimee groaned. "I gift wrapped that one for you. Sheesh." She took a moment to breathe in the fresh air. "Being outside never felt so good. How are you, Larry? Did you try to reach Cassandra again?"

"Nope. I'm just sitting here thinking about flags."

"The kind you hoist up flagpoles?"

"No. The red ones that spring up to warn you that something in your life is fucked up … or is going to be. The kind you don't look at when they're right in front of your face because you're in denial … or worse."

"I hear you. Any revelations since we last spoke?"

"More like confirmations," Larry said. "I really believe Cass pushed so hard to come this weekend because she knew it was the one place I wanted to go alone … and for good reason. The more I think about everything, the clearer my vision. You know what they say about hindsight." Larry sighed. "About three weeks ago, she was going through all her clothes, putting some in bags to donate to Goodwill and getting rid of things she didn't need. When I asked her about it, she said the closet had been a mess for too long, and it was time for some cleaning and purging. That was one big red flag I didn't see. She was getting ready to move out, and the biggest thing she was purging herself of was yours truly."

"I want to tell you you're wrong," Aimee said, seeing the pain in his eyes, "but the fact that she's moved out rather confirms you're not."

"Yeah," Larry said, staring off into the distance.

Silence hung between them for a few minutes until Aimee broke it. "Bart knows what I've done. I'm sure of it. And I think he may do exactly what Cassandra did to you. Use my actions to justify what he's wanted to do all along: leave me."

Larry turned and put his hands gently on her shoulders. "Don't let what happened between Cass and me warp your thinking, Aimee. These are totally different situations."

"With a whopper of an ending in common."

"Don't you think you're jumping the gun?"

"You were his roommate and close friend. Do you think he's okay with what I've done?"

Larry shifted uneasily and clasped his hands on his lap. "I don't know that he knows, Aimee. Really, I don't."

"Didn't you hear the things he was saying during the slide show? About not recognizing the person you're married to … et cetera, et cetera?"

Larry shook his head. "I'm afraid I was somewhere else— some weird plane of existence that consisted only of life in the sixties and life with Cass. I must have tuned everything else out."

"Bart doesn't talk in innuendo like that. Not his style. He did it because he's angry, and he wants me to know that he knows … shit!"

Larry reached over and brushed away a tendril of hair that had fallen in front of her eyes. "Even if he does know, and I have no idea, that doesn't mean he's going to leave you."

"He's going to use this in the same way Cassandra used the reunion." Unable to hold the tears at bay, Aimee let them fall freely.

"Aw, honey," Larry said. As Aimee buried her head in his chest, he rubbed her back. She was still sobbing when he looked up and saw Bart standing by the farthest trees, watching them. As soon as the two old friends made eye contact, Bart turned and hurried back toward the hotel.

⁍ ✳ ⁍ ✳ ⁍ ✳ ⁍

"I'm so glad you thought to change rooms," Dan said, as Maggie closed the door behind him. "When did you do this?"

"Right before I joined everyone for breakfast," Maggie said. "That vile 'Pappy' was good for something!"

"How so? What in the world does he have to do with this?"

Maggie took Dan by the hand and walked him to the loveseat, where they sat. "Just a handy excuse, Danny. While I was waiting at the front desk to talk to the manager, I heard him whispering with the front desk clerk about that dreadful man. He's made quite a name for himself. So, when the clerk asked how he could help me, I told him Pappy had made advances toward me, and to my distress, had seen me leaving my room, leaving *me* to fear for my safety. The manager intervened immediately and offered me this room, which, as you see, is even nicer than the previous one. I quickly packed everything up and had a bellhop move my things when I knew the fishwife was with the group. I also made sure no one is to be given this room number. Only my housekeeper knows it. And you."

"That is a relief," Dan said. "This room is fit for a queen. For you."

"No royal thrones here, Danny—only this loveseat. How perfect for us."

Dan's eyes radiated yearning as he gently ran his fingers through Maggie's hair. "You are insanely beautiful, Maggie. I don't know how I'll wait until tonight to make love to you again."

Maggie looked down at his lap and smiled. "Oh, Danny, I want to touch you … I want to in the worst way … but it will take me way too long to put myself together again if we do anything now. And if we do anything, they'll all know."

Dan took a long, calming breath. "Just the thought of being together again will carry me through until tonight. Besides, being with you is nothing I want to do on a deadline. Deadlines are for newspapers. Not making love." He looked at her with concern in his eyes. "You haven't had second thoughts, have you?"

"Certainly not because of anything that woman has said. Naturally, Danny, being with a married man is not something that ordinarily rests well with me."

Dan's pain momentarily distorted his face. "A married man who has been celibate for years … whose wife is not in love with him."

"But she's in love with your life together," Maggie said. "I know she is, Danny."

"Perhaps she is. Believe me, Maggie, I've thought long and hard …" Dan blushed at his unintentional pun, and smiled at Maggie's recognition of the surprise wordplay. "As I was saying, I've given this a great deal of thought … long before this weekend, and as I find myself more deeply in love with you than ever, there is only one reason I will deny myself, and that is if you tell me to do so. For forty-four years, I have done everything this world has asked of me. Everything." Dan looked around the room, then back into Maggie's eyes. "You know, when Sally's interest in our romantic life began to wane, which happened long before it stopped for good, I tried numerous times in numerous ways to revive it. But she would never talk about it. Not ever. She would only tell me she was happy and that I should be, too.

"I tried living with that, but it didn't sit well. I thought that perhaps conversation wasn't the answer. I tried all sorts of romantic gestures. Nothing made any difference. As time wore on, I knew I was falling out of love. Then, after a while, I gave up and allowed my fantasies of you to live ... to thrive ... in my imagination again. And they were more fulfilling than my physical or emotional relationship with Sally had ever been. But then, last night, it was nirvana. I have never been more satisfied while simultaneously finding myself insatiable. How's that for a mess? Or as Stan Laurel would say to Ollie, 'another nice mess.'"

Maggie laughed. "I wish all the messes in my life were as nice as this one. When we were looking at the photos earlier, so much of the past came flooding back to me. I could have made love to you with wild abandon back then. Oh, Danny, you have no idea how much I wanted to do that."

"You shouldn't have held back, Maggie."

"Oh yes, I should have. That's one regret I don't have. You might not have your four wonderful children now. I would have taken you down a path you didn't deserve to go. I didn't have the flower-child idealism that so many of our peers at Barrie Hill College did—not about myself or about the world around me. And I knew I was unable to settle down in any traditional sense. I knew the ways of the world would tangle with the best of my intentions and go 'Splat!' on the sidewalk like a person who had just ended it all by jumping from the top of a tall building." Maggie paused to collect her thoughts. "I hope I'm making even a sliver of sense. I knew, from a very young age, that I would subconsciously pick the wrong men so that suburban life, motherhood, and monotony would never claim me as one of their own. I knew I would be desired more than I would be loved. You, Danny: you're the only man I ever desired who I would not allow myself to have. You truly loved me, and I knew that."

Dan put his hand behind her neck and drew her lips to his. After kissing her for a minute, he looked soulfully into her eyes. "Oh, Maggie. I had no idea you were in so much pain." He kissed her again. "And I still love you, more than ever. More than words allow me to describe."

Maggie took Dan's right hand in hers and kissed it. "There's so much more to say. It seems like a cruel joke to have to join the others now, but it's what we must do. It would all be so much more palatable … enjoyable … without those horrible threats. But we will not give in to her, Danny. Looks can be deceiving. Remember that."

Perplexed, Dan cocked his head slightly to one side. "What does that mean? Does this have something to do with what you said this morning? Do you have a plan?"

"I wish. But I do have a seed of an idea, and I hope with all my heart that I don't have to plant it. It will be unpleasant, and I'm not at all certain of what might grow from it."

"You're not going to tell me any more than that." Dan smiled. "Are you?"

"No. I'm not." Maggie kissed him. "Let's hope Leah's bluster is nothing but a cruel bluff."

Chapter THIRTEEN

MAY 17, 1986 —7:21 p.m.

"My grandmother always told me, 'If you admire a famous person, don't meet them.' She said people always disappoint you in real life. But you're so nice! I wish she were still alive so I could tell her."

"I'm honored," Bart said to the fifty-something woman handing him a nursing brochure to sign. "Are you a nurse?"

"Yes, I'm an ICU nurse from Wilmington. I'm here for a convention that starts Monday morning. I got here early so I could relax."

"I've always admired nurses," Bart said. "My aunt Ruth in Chicago is a nurse. What's your name?"

"Kathy. With a K."

As Bart stood in the lobby and signed the brochure, he looked up and gasped. Larry was standing next to the woman, his face expressionless, just staring at him.

Kathy gushed. "You're so wonderful; even the men are eager to meet you."

"Ah, you're too nice." Bart handed the brochure and pen back to her. "This man is actually an old friend of mine."

"Who really needs to talk to you," Larry said urgently.

Bart extended his hand to the appreciative fan. "Lovely meeting you, Kathy. Please tell your fellow nurses they've got a big fan in Bart Younger."

"Thank you," Kathy said, treasuring the handshake. "I will do that. They'll be thrilled. Good-bye."

"Take care, Kathy." Bart smiled.

Larry waited a couple of beats until she had walked far enough away to be out of earshot. "Bart, can we go somewhere and talk? There's an empty meeting room just down the west hallway. Please."

"All right," Bart said, as he began walking. "I need to get out of here anyway. Most days, I love meeting fans, but I'm not up for it now. They're not always as respectful as that lovely woman was."

The two men hurried out of the lobby and turned down the hallway to the left of the reception desk.

"This room is empty," Larry said, nodding to the right. Bart and Larry entered the meeting room, and Larry closed the door behind them.

Seeing over a hundred chairs stacked against the wall, Larry grabbed two and placed them on the floor. "Not the most comfortable, but they'll do."

"What's up, Lar?" Bart said as he sat down.

"I hope you're not upset with me."

"Why?" Bart said flatly. "Because my wife was crying on your shoulder in our not-so-secret garden spot?"

"That, and because earlier you asked to talk to me, and then you didn't want to. And that was before you saw Aimee 'crying on my shoulder.'"

Bart sighed. "When I first asked to talk to you, I didn't know then that you and Aimee had been sharing your respective woes. When I found out … well, sorry, Lar, you dropped out of contention for confidant. Which is fine, because I really wanted some time with Clare, too."

"How did you know Aimee and I were talking?" Larry asked.

"Oh, I don't know. Maybe it was that stoner glaze in her eyes that was such a perfect match for the one in yours."

"Oh, shit. Mr. Observant." Larry sighed. "You're pissed, aren't you?"

"At you? Not really. I'm glad Aimee has someone to talk to, but at the same time, it's a bit awkward that her confidant and my old friend are one and the same. Then there's the part where I asked her if the two of you had gotten to know one another, and she said you had just briefly met in the lobby last night. But that's small potatoes on the plate of big lies."

"Bart, look, you knew I ran into Aimee in the lobby last night. When I came back to the dining room, I was open about that. She was really distraught. And so we started talking about Leah … about everything."

"Quite the non conversation you two had. Is that when she confessed that she had blackmailed my agent for the second time and why?"

Larry's mouth fell open. "Oh. So you do know."

"I know. And I'm pretty sure Aimee knows that I do and that she's told you as much. She wouldn't have been crying otherwise. Honestly, that was only the second time I've ever seen her cry. The first time was when her beloved grandmother died. For the most part, she's rather unflappable." Bart stopped to rethink what he'd just said. "At least on the exterior."

"This is awkward." Larry sighed. "I never meant to do anything behind your back. Nothing you said to me yesterday has passed my lips. I haven't given Aimee any information. I've just listened to her talk, and, yes, she listened to me."

"How nice that you found each other."

"Damn," Larry made a fist and pounding his thigh with it. "I hate when you talk in that voice where I can't tell if you're being sarcastic or not."

"I hate not understanding things, too."

Flustered, Larry paused to assess his options. "Listen, Bart, I'll talk to Aimee. I'll tell her that despite my best efforts not to get stuck in the middle, that's where I seem to find myself."

"Stuck in the middle with you," Bart said, drifting away. "I loved that song. Stealers Wheel, right? Early seventies."

"Yeah. Right on both counts."

"Don't do that, Lar. But let me ask you this: does she know I saw you two together?"

"No. I didn't say a word. Not my place. Despite the way it looks, I'm only trying to be a friend. As you've seen, I suck at handling my own relationship. Not trying to fuck up yours, too."

"Aimee is such a capable woman. She did a fine job of that without help from anyone."

"Oh, damn. You two have to—"

"Whoa, I know you weren't just about to tell me that we should talk."

Larry shrugged. "Who me? Not a chance."

"I didn't think so."

"Just tell me this hasn't killed our friendship, Bart. Please."

"Lar, I have to ask myself how I would have handled things if Cassandra had come with you and Aimee had stayed home. Honestly, I'm not sure what I would have done had the situation been reversed. So for now, let's not go there. We've got one more dinner and a breakfast to get through. As upset as I am, I want to enjoy this time. Aimee's a fish out of water. So if you want to give her a little pond to swim in, do it. Just don't repeat anything I've said, and we'll leave it there for now."

"Sounds good, my man. Thank you."

"Where is she, by the way?"

"I don't know. After I saw you, I told her I had some calls to make, and she said she was going to take a walk. I rushed in here to find you and have no clue where she went."

Bart stood. "Okay. If we're done here, I guess I'll see you 'round dinner time."

'✳'✳'✳'

Walking into the Parker Room, Colin found Clare sitting on the couch, her head back and her eyes closed. He looked at her for a moment before speaking. "Hey, are you asleep, awake, or somewhere in-between?"

Clare's head moved ever so slightly before her eyes opened. She looked at Colin and slowly sat up. "Somewhere in-between. I was floating in this big gray void where I could see no evil … or anything else, for that matter. Then two gorgeous kids in a canoe paddled by and waved."

Colin sat next to her. "Ah, I should have let you stay there. I'm sorry. Did the kids look happy?"

"Very. Serene and happy." Clare rubbed the sleep from her eyes. "Thank you for taking her out of here. Did you actually go for a walk?"

"Yes, and it was hellish. She has the same animus for the town that she has for everyone else. Walking north to the top of Barrie Street reminded her of the winter that she fell and tore her black Pierre Cardin trousers. When I reminded her of how beautiful the view was from that vantage point—the farmland to the east, the villages to the west, the church, and the vista of our beloved alma mater in the middle—she told me to hush. I was then reminded that she not only tore her trousers that day, but also scraped her knee so bad it bled all the way home."

"Tragic. So much suffering in the world, but none greater than Leah's." Clare leaned back on the couch. "Well, I love that view.

It's most beautiful in the winter and the fall. Picture-postcard gorgeous. I miss it."

"Me, too. Oh, guess what? The old stone schoolhouse down the street is now a daycare center. It looks exactly the same. There are still children's drawings taped to the windows just like there used to be."

"That place is very special. Such a beautiful historical building; how lovely to know it's still in use. Especially by children."

"Leah was surprised it hadn't crumbled by now."

Clare exhaled in disgust. "No surprise there. So much I could say to that. But I won't."

"No, save your breath. I'll spare you the rest of the walk down Misery Lane. But it didn't deviate any from what I've just told you."

"Of course not."

Colin looked at her. "You're still not regretting doing this?"

"No," Clare sat up again. "I'm not. I'm really happy to see everyone else. I've missed them. Haven't you?"

"More than I knew." Colin looked around the room. "What good times we had here. But leave it to Leah to pour a bucket of sludge over everything. I would have stayed home to avoid this, but she would have come on her own."

"You needed to be here. It wouldn't be the same without you. And you would have been really sorry if you'd missed seeing everyone."

"You're right. But she's even worse than I imagined she'd be." Concerned, he looked into Clare's eyes. "Are you nervous that things might escalate tonight?"

"Do I look like I'm afraid of your wife? More to the point: are you?"

"No! Make that a 'bloody hell no'. But I am going to rest for a while before dinner and try to reenergize. I already told Leah I'm keeping the room I got last night. Boy, did that piss her off. Anyway,

I'm headed to the room to lie down. Maybe I can doze off and see the kids in the canoe, too." Colin smiled. "Glad you're okay. I wanted to check on you. Leah took off like a bat out of hell half a block before we got back, and I wanted to make sure she hadn't gone gunning for you."

"Not that I'm aware of."

"Everything okay with Bart? When you asked me to take Leah out of here, he looked very un-Bart-like, and you looked stressed."

"Some rough stuff going down. I'm hoping it will work out."

"Sorry to hear that; I won't pry." Colin smiled. "I'm just glad you found time to decompress."

"Decompression is good for the soul."

"Yeah. It is. So, the game plan is dinner downstairs again?"

"Yes. But instead of hanging around the dining room like we did last night, we'll come back here. Far more cozy. Besides, it's Saturday night, and that was always Barrie Hiller night."

"It was." Colin leaned sideways and kissed Clare on the cheek. "But I have a feeling tonight will be unlike any night in our past ever was … and unlike any night in our future could ever be."

'✱'✱'✱'

Oblivious to the world around her, Aimee hurried through the lobby toward the elevators.

"Mrs. Bart! Wait!"

Freezing in her tracks, unbridled rage coursed through Aimee's veins. Without turning around, she stopped, ever so briefly, then kept walking.

"I said wait!" Leah barked as she caught up with Aimee, gripping her upper arm.

"Let. Me. Go," Aimee stared into Leah's eyes as she jerked her arm loose. "And don't you *ever* touch me again!"

"Oh, dear. Ever since I observed how pathetically ineffectual you are at asserting yourself, you've dialed it up a notch. Are we role-playing? Who is Mrs. Bart now?" Leah clasped her hands together like a sadistic schoolmarm. "High-powered Hollywood attorney? Macho Marine drill sergeant? Burly nightclub bouncer with a hundred pounds to lose?"

Aimee glared at her, barely able to restrain from getting embroiled in an ugly exchange of words. Seeing the elevator open in her periphery, Aimee turned and hurried toward it, frustrated as a group of people got in before she did.

"There's room for one more," a well-dressed man shouted to Aimee.

Nodding thanks, Aimee jumped on the elevator as Leah stood in front of it, snarling like an angry dog. Just as the door was closing, Aimee surreptitiously slid her hand up her chest and raised her middle finger at Leah, seconds before the doors sealed shut.

MAY 17, 1986 —7:46 P.M.

As classical music sounded from the clock radio by the bed, Bart, with only a towel around his waist, lay on the bed with his eyes closed. Borodin's Quartet No. 2 in D major transported him to a place of contentment. Swept away, he did not hear the door open, but its closing was enough to yank him out of his euphoria. Startled, he opened his eyes to see Aimee standing at the foot of the bed.

Slowly, Bart sat up, slid back, and rested against the diamond-tufted headboard. "Are you just back from your walk?"

"Yes."

"What was your impression of the town?"

"Small, quaint, historic, wealthy," Aimee said with a staccato rhythm.

"Do you want to sit?"

Without responding, Aimee walked around the corner of the bed and sat on the edge of it, as far away from him as she could.

"That's better. So tell me, did you see anything of particular interest?"

"Not really."

"Did you happen to notice Tim Finnegan's Pub two blocks south of here?"

Aimee shrugged indecisively.

"It's a brick building with beautiful mahogany bay windows with vintage beer mugs in them. It's got a huge sign with Celtic-looking green letters. Right outside the double doors there's a large wooden statue of an Irishman holding a mug of beer in one hand and a menu board in the other. We used to call him Seamus. The place hasn't changed in all these years. We passed it on the cab ride in, but I neglected to point it out to you. You can't miss it."

"Apparently I did."

"Oh. Well, it was our favorite gathering place back in the day, second to the Parker Room. On the nights we deigned to mix with commoners."

Aimee looked blankly at him.

"I'm kidding," Bart said. "That was a joke. Apparently you missed that, too."

"Apparently." *Why don't you just come out and tell me that you know? You must know. Don't you?* "What did *you* do during the break?" Aimee asked.

"I had a lovely visit with Clare, talked to some fans in the lobby, then came up here to take a shower and relax before dinner."

You have to know. You wouldn't have made those innuendos during the slide show if you didn't. Maybe I'm wrong, but I don't think so. If you didn't know, you'd be asking me what was wrong and why I'm acting so differently ...but how would you know? That's the million-dollar question.

"I'm done in the bathroom," Bart said. "I don't know if you want to freshen up before we go down to dinner."

"Yes, definitely. A hot shower is exactly what I need."

"Good. Well, I guess I'll get up and get dressed. Unless there's something you want to talk to me about."

"Like what?" *Are you waiting for me to confess?*

"Anything. You seem very unsettled. Are you okay?"

"I just want to get through this weekend. I wish you'd warned me about Leah."

Bart sighed. "I wish I had known. Larry and I were talking about this yesterday. The Leah we knew back then was quick-witted, but she was funny, and as strange as it sounds, likable. As I see it, she could have grown out of whatever youthful resentments she had, or, as she has done, chosen to entangle herself in the unsweetened passage of time. In other words, she's turned into a bitch ... a monster."

Aimee cracked a smile. *Maybe you don't know after all.*

"If I had even the slightest idea how she was going to treat you, I would have come alone or strongly warned you to endure at your own peril. I would never have thrown you into the swamp with a hungry alligator."

"An alligator would have been easier to handle."

"Yeah, I know." Bart got off the bed. "For that, I'm very sorry."

What does that mean? For that *you're very sorry.* "Thanks. Well, I guess I'll take a shower."

"I'm going to get dressed," Bart said, "then sit in that comfortable chair over there and read the script I brought. I'm ready when you are. Dinner is at eight-thirty."

Hell resumes at eight-thirty, you mean. "I'll be ready."

CHAPTER FOURTEEN

MAY 17, 1986 — 8:34 P.M.

"I'm only four minutes late," Maggie said, walking to the table where everyone but Clare was seated. "Maybe one day I'll actually be on time for something." Wearing a black V-neck dress with a black-and-purple boa around her neck, Maggie smiled as Dan stood and pulled out a chair for her. "Thank you, Danny."

Dan's eyes looked misty as he gazed at her. "You're wearing the boa I bought you over two decades ago. You are a vision."

"Indeed," Bart said. "Beautiful, Maggie."

Larry and Colin offered words of praise as Maggie blushed.

"And I was so sure that thing died in a trash compactor all those years ago," Leah blurted out.

Too bad you didn't. "Hello, everyone," Clare said. "I was just talking to the head waiter. Our drinks are being brought in now. Dinner service will start in about fifteen minutes."

Looking at Clare, Larry shook his hand up and down in a cooling gesture. "Wow, Clare, you look hot, hot, hot in that black dress!"

"Gorgeous!" Colin said, beaming.

"Like a leading lady on the red carpet," Bart said. "You look stunning."

"She really does," Aimee agreed, as Leah shot daggers at her from across the table. "That dress really suits you, Clare."

"What do they say about great minds?" Maggie said to Clare. "Both of us chose black for our last dinner together. *Trés élégante.*"

"Perhaps you thought you might be going to a funeral." Leah stared at Maggie and Dan, then Aimee. "Sometimes, when you play with poison, you die."

"Not if you pass it on to someone more deserving than you are," Maggie said.

"Chardonnay for the lady," a waiter said, putting a glass of wine in front of Leah.

Aimee looked at the wine glass and laughed. *Great timing.* "Drink up, Leah."

Leah turned sharply to the waiter. "I meant to order the Sauvignon Blanc. Take this away immediately."

The waiter, already well acquainted with Leah's unique charm, smiled insincerely as he picked up the glass. "As you wish. I'll be right back."

As another waiter came over and served the drinks, taking Maggie's order in the process, Leah whispered to Colin, "Don't you ever compliment her like that again!"

"Or what?" Colin said sharply. "What exactly will you do?"

"Hush!"

Within five minutes, when all of the drinks had been served, Bart rose to make a toast. "I don't think any of us have arms long enough to reach across this big round table, but cheers to all of you, with a special toast to Clare for making this reunion possible. My four years in this town, the precious three and a half years as a Barrie Hiller, hold a treasured place in my heart. I will never have such a special and exclusive group of friends again. As you said, Maggie, '*Trés élégante.*'" Bart lifted his wine glass. "*À votre santé, mes amis.* To your health, my friends!"

As they all raised their glasses, Dan noticed a flicker of fear in

Maggie's eyes. "You are going to be as good as new, my dear," he whispered. "Everything will be fine. You'll see."

Maggie smiled as everyone else except Leah offered cheers. "I believe I will be, Danny. Because my heart is full again; love is a great healer."

Dan swallowed the lump in his throat, making every effort to be discreet.

Bart continued speaking as he sat down. "I was just telling Aimee about Tim Finnegan's Pub. I don't know if any of you have passed it in your wanderings, but our boy Seamus is still out front."

"Ugh, I thought that hideous wooden thing would have rotted by now."

"Seamus!" Larry exclaimed, ignoring Leah. "My man Seamus! Who here remembers the night we stole a girlfriend for him? The perfect partner: Wally Decker's blow-up sex doll. He thought she was his dirty little secret. Poor sap never had a clue that his roommate knew and had ratted him out to the entire dorm on the same day he bought her at some sleazy sex shop in Times Square. Decker had hidden the doll in his underwear drawer, but stupidly had thrown the packaging in the trash. Didn't even think to hide the telltale evidence … only the doll! Anyway, most of the time, she was a puddle of plastic, deflated, yet waiting to serve."

"Oh, shit!" Colin said. "I'd completely repressed that!"

"I remember." Clare laughed. "But I'd forgotten until just now."

Bart broke up laughing. "We stole her from his dorm room, carried her to Tim Finnegan's, and left her outside to smooch with Seamus."

"What a caper!" Dan said. "Seamus was too shy to meet anyone on his own. Wally's doll may have been a bit too Jane Austentatious for him, but it was a match made in heaven."

"A snatch made at a factory." Leah snickered. "I can think of a real-life twosome who fit that heavenly description."

Clare laughed. "Dan, I've got to hand it to you. You were always better at the name game than anyone else."

"Really?" Colin asked. "With such a Sylvia Plathoria of uttered gems, wouldn't you say I came in a close second?"

Groans emanated from around the table. "That was bad," Clare said. "Dan was, and still is, the champ."

"Charles Darwin or lose, you've always been a great sport, Colin," Dan said.

Colin pointed his finger at Dan in mock anger. "That was unfair. Now you're just showing off. And I think Sylvia Plathoria was every bit as good … or as bad … as Jane Austentatious."

"Let's call it a draw," Dan said, laughing.

"Who remembers the doll's name?" Bart asked. "Did she even have one?"

"BJ," Larry told him. "Because every time Wally wanted to do whatever the hell he did with her, he had to give her a blow job, which is a hell of a lot more than she ever gave him."

"Oh, my," Maggie said. "Was she inflated or deflated when you bad boys stole her for Seamus?"

"Fully inflated, dear," Dan assured her. "Had she not been, we probably wouldn't have thought about her. See, Wally had gone down to the commissary for dinner and forgot to lock his door. Larry happened to be passing Wally's room as he was leaving and saw the doll's legs sticking out from under the bed. That was probably the first time Wally had been too lazy or rushed to deflate her. Anyway, we'd always thought Seamus should have a girlfriend, so when Larry discovered a golden opportunity to make our wish for Seamus come true, the four of us purloined the plastic lady."

"Fully inflated! Just like you, Dan," Leah said.

Ignoring her, Dan continued. "As it turned out, Wally didn't go back to his room after dinner and came straight to Tim

Finnegan's. When he saw his doll outside, cozying up to Seamus, he went ballistic. He stood outside the double glass doors for about five minutes, cursing up a storm, then he grabbed the doll and stashed her in the shrubbery on the side of the building when he thought no one was watching. Only we were all inside howling with laughter, watching his every move from the side window."

"Remember how he pulled her plug before shoving her into the hobblebush?" Colin asked.

"Oh, yeah. He sure as hell did." Larry picked up his napkin to wipe tears from his eyes. "But when he came inside, he couldn't accuse any of us, because he didn't want to admit BJ belonged to him."

"I just remembered something," Bart said, laughing. "Henry had been in the back, at a booth, having dinner with Madeleine when the whole thing went down. They just happened to run into Wally, who was headed back to the men's room. They had finished dinner and were heading up front to the bar. When Henry saw how forlorn Wally was looking, he said, 'Who let the air out of your tires?' Henry's question convinced Wally that Henry had to be the culprit … and was taunting him … so he told poor confused Henry, very loudly, to fuck off. He stormed off, and we never saw him again that night. Anyway, when Henry and Madeleine approached the bar, Henry asked if we'd heard what Wally had said and if we knew why he was so angry with him. After we explained everything, they both fell out laughing. We all did. Henry was more than happy to let Wally think he was the bad guy."

Colin laughed heartily, as did Dan and Larry. "I never understood how Decker could have that thing and believe for a second he could keep her a secret. Especially in a college dorm, of all places."

Larry picked up his wine glass. "My stomach hurts from laughing. It's a good thing I didn't remember this story on that day I saw him on Seventy-ninth and Broadway. I might have brought up the incident in conversation."

"I'm very glad you didn't," Colin said. "Henry was always honored to be the guilty party. The truth about BJ's travels that night are better left a secret forever."

"Nothing stays a secret forever," Leah said loudly. "There's always someone who will see that it doesn't. Especially when that person is betrayed … and angry."

Aimee exchanged brief glances with Maggie and Dan, but nobody said a word.

"Secrets can destroy people," Leah said, looking disdainfully at her three uncooperative targets.

Disgusted, Clare watched Leah carefully. "I think it's time for a ghastly menu recitation. Don't you, Leah?"

"No, I don't. Besides, I was speaking."

"To whom and about what?" Colin asked.

Lost for a response, Leah's eyes became threatening, and her face twisted in rage as nobody acknowledged her.

"What's on the menu?" Maggie asked. "I think we're all very hungry. Whet our appetites."

"Arugula and feta cheese salad," Clare began, "followed by chateaubriand, haricots verts, and nouvelles pommes de terre."

"Well, aren't we all so fucking French tonight," Leah spat.

Colin pressed on her forearm until she turned to look at him. "If you don't want to eat with us, if you'd prefer the hotel restaurant, Tim Finnegan's, or the Barrie Hill Diner, no one's stopping you. Have at them."

"I'm not going anywhere," Leah said loudly. "This meal sounds positively delicious. And if it isn't, you can be damn sure I'll enjoy dessert. Every last lick. That's a promise."

"She'll choke on it," Maggie whispered to Dan.

Aimee looked at Maggie and Dan, then glanced at Larry, who

gave her a reassuring wink.

"Fine," Colin said. "*Bon appétit!* Ah, here come our salads."

As the waiters served the salads, Aimee took advantage of the moment when Bart turned to speak to Clare, to turn to Larry seated on her other side. "I'm standing up to this bitch because I'm nearly convinced Bart knows, and therefore I have nothing more to lose. I hope I'm not making a mistake. Am I?" she whispered.

Larry looked nervous. "Just trust your—"

"Aimee," Bart said as he nodded toward the waiter. "This gentleman would like to know if you'd like another glass of Cabernet."

"Yes. Yes, I would. Thank you." She turned to Larry and whispered again. "You would tell me, right?"

Knowing he was in Bart's line of sight, Larry merely smiled.

As she quickly assessed the situation, Aimee turned away and focused on the waiter placing a salad in front of her.

"Clare," Bart said picking up his salad fork, "did you happen to invite that tall woman with the long hair who was with us for six months? Nancy … why do I want to say 'Whiplash?'"

"I remember her!" Larry said.

"Everyone called her Nancy Whiplash," Clare explained. "Her last name was Whipple, and her fiancé was named Guy Lash. Together they were Whiplash and Eye Lash. What names! Anyway, that's the reason." Clare took a bite of her salad. "No, I didn't invite her. I had read in our alumni magazine that she has a New Age shop in the Village somewhere. She does past-life regressions, tarot card readings, sells crystals … and pretty much anything of that ilk you can name. A friend of mine had actually been to the shop and met her. She said that Nancy is completely obsessed with what she does and can't talk about anything without bringing the conversation back to her own interests. So there's that. But mainly, this reunion was really about all of us, not the people who came and went for a few months. I just wish Henry and Madeleine could have joined us."

"I do, too," Maggie said. She paused to enjoy a forkful of salad. "I have a friend who talks about past lives a lot. And heaven. I've engaged in discussion with her, and while I find it all fascinating on one level, I find it very confusing on another."

"How is that, dear?" Dan said. He looked at Clare. "This vinaigrette is superb."

"She didn't make the damn dressing," Leah barked.

"I'm glad you like it," Clare said to Dan. "Maggie, I'd be interested to hear what confuses you."

"Everything!" Leah said, annoyed as she noticed the act of ignoring her had become a polished art among the others.

Maggie took a sip of her drink and laid her salad fork down. "Well, for one, imagine a couple who has been very happily married for many years. First the wife dies. A few years later the husband dies. After he is gone, many of their friends and family console one another by saying how happy they are knowing the two have reunited in heaven."

"That's pretty common thinking among most folks," Larry noted.

"Yes, I'd agree," Bart said. "Do go on, Maggie."

"Well, take the same situation and change it a little. After the wife dies, her loving husband mourns for her. But, unlike in the first scenario, he doesn't die a few years later. Instead, he lives and goes on to meet another woman. He falls in love, and they live happily for many years."

"Not an uncommon story," Clare said.

"Exactly!" Maggie said. "So after they've all gone to heaven, what happens? Do they sit around and play gin rummy together?"

"You've made an excellent point," Dan said. "And the examples you've cited are very simple. Life is usually a lot more convoluted, thereby making the understanding of these situations exponentially more complicated."

"But even if you simplify everything again, it becomes complicated in a different way if, for example, you believe in reincarnation," Maggie said.

"Oh, I can't wait to hear this," Leah mumbled to herself.

"Let's hear it," Colin said.

"Well," Maggie began, "let's go back to Couple A, the man and wife who have only been married once and are happy in heaven together. If you believe in reincarnation, what happens when one of them gets transplanted into some baby to start all over again?"

Leah choked on a piece of arugula and started coughing. She picked up a glass of water to wash it down. "'Transplanted into some baby!' That is positively hilarious and simultaneously ridiculous, possessing not one iota of plausibility or sanity."

"It may sound ridiculous to you," Colin said, "but Maggie is making a very valid point."

"Oh, is she? I don't see it," Leah said, still laughing.

"Have some more salad," Aimee said. "Maybe it will come to you."

Larry burst out laughing and saw that everyone else looked like they wanted to do the same.

Leah glared at Aimee as she shoved her salad plate away. "The night is still young. Don't you forget it!"

As Aimee turned away, Leah repeated the ominous glare for Maggie and Dan. "I hold the cards; remember that."

"Well, if that's the case, dear," Maggie said, "you should warn the others that you're not playing with a full deck."

"Hush!" Leah snapped. "You can't afford not to!"

Colin looked at his wife. "What's going on here?"

"Never mind."

"I'd like to get back to what Maggie was saying," Bart said.

"You have some thoughts on all of this?" Larry asked.

"A few," Bart said. "We could be here for years and still not exhaust mentioning all of the theories we mortals have about the afterlife, reincarnation, heaven and hell, or the absence of everything. No one knows. Not really. Maggie broke it down for us in a really simple way. It's all quite thought provoking. But I think the problem is that we apply mortal standards to our vision of the other realms."

"Have another drink," Leah said. "Then maybe we'll be able to understand what the hell you're jabbering about."

"I hear you," Larry said. "And you're right. As long as we're all mortal, I don't think we can know. But there's room for everyone's beliefs, as long as we respect one another. And therein lies the rub 'cause that's just something that a whole lot of folks don't do very well."

"If there is an afterlife," Maggie said, "it may be as different for people after death as the perception of it is before death. I don't think it's a one-size-fits-all deal."

"That makes a lot of sense," Dan said. "I never looked at it that way before."

"I'm still grappling with the mystery of how we all got here," Colin said.

"We came by car," Leah said. "For starters."

"And here comes our dinner," Colin said. "By rolling cart."

Chapter FIFTEEN

MAY 17, 1986 – 9:54 P.M.

"That was one hell of a good dinner," Larry said to Clare as they walked into the Parker Room"

"Agreed!" Bart said. "But I'm royally stuffed. That crème brûlée did me in."

"But worth every calorie," Clare said.

"It was, but I'll have to jog ten miles when I get to New Jersey tomorrow. Hmm. Let me rephrase. Maybe I should jog *to* New Jersey tomorrow."

"Just a brisk walk there ought to do it," Clare said, smiling. "Help yourselves to coffee, tea, cognac, or a variety of after-dinner drinks, everyone."

"I'll do just that." Colin walked to the bar. "Who wants what?"

As everyone sat down and gave their drink orders to Colin, Larry stopped to look at a framed poem on the wall, just right of the door. "Ah, 'Comment' by Dorothy Parker." He read aloud:

> Oh, life is a glorious cycle of song,
> A medley of extemporanea;
> And love is a thing that can never go wrong.
> And I am Marie of Roumania.

"Completely on target," Larry noted, putting on a sad face. "Especially this weekend."

"I'm sorry," Maggie said. "I know you're really hurting."

"I am." Larry sat in his usual chair. "But I'll be damned if I'm going to be a downer."

"You mean *continue* to be one," Leah corrected.

Colin stopped mid-pour and slammed the cognac bottle down on the bar. "There's only one downer among us, Leah, and it's not Larry. We're all growing very weary of it … no one more than me."

Leah sat back on the couch and folded her arms defensively. "I'm just the only one here with the courage to be honest. While not everyone may like hearing the truth, at least I'm not holding dark secrets with revelations that would hurt others."

"No," Aimee said. "You're as pure as the driven snow. Sin-free Leah. You would never exploit the pain of others for your own amusement."

"Whatever are you talking about?" Leah said in a Southern accent. "I do declare, Rhett, I don't have any idea what she's yammering about."

"Okay, Leah," Clare said. "Let's give you the floor once and for all. Go on. Have your say. I'll be your first target: what's your reason for hating me all of these years? We're all listening."

Feeling empowered, Leah sat up straight and uncrossed her arms. "I'll happily take you up on that." She took a moment to collect her thoughts as a smug smile crept across her face. "Let's go back to the beginning of our history, shall we? You founded this group, Clare, because you were lonely and because you knew of Bart's interest in literature and the arts. It was your way of spending time with him. You knew he was using you—"

"Speak for yourself, Leah! Using Clare? For what?"

"To publish your essays and articles in The *Chronicle*, to write about your theater work, to stroke your ego before you had a legion of adoring fans to do it for you."

"Bullshit!"

Leah turned to Clare. "You did have some clout in those pre-*Kiddie World* days. You could never deny Bart anything!"

"That's a lie," Clare said. "For one, he never asked me for anything."

"Oh, nonsense! No, he never asked you for what you *really* wanted to give him. But no man wanted *that*! Now, hush up and listen. I speak the truth. You used to truckle before Bart's pretty pink lips could form the 'P' in please. We'd be discussing Kierkegaard or Sartre—and you'd be drooling at the bulge in his pants …"

"Would you shut up," Bart said. "You're insulting me every bit as much as Clare. Neither of us deserves it, and neither of us will stand for it."

"Oh, dear me. Then stay seated." Leah paused to run mental victory laps, then continued to address Bart. "Yesterday you were almost begging me to tell you off. So sick of, what did you call it … oh, yes, 'patronizing the movie star.' Now you're begging me to stop. Guess your eyes were bigger than your stomach."

"This isn't what I had in mind," Bart said. "But you're right; it's more than I can stomach."

Colin, still standing at the bar, handed out all the drinks he had poured for everyone but Leah, then sat down.

Noticing, Leah snarled at Colin, then turned her anger back toward Clare. "You played the obsequious fool with all of us. You knew you were at the bottom of the social pecking order, but you were so desperate for company, so anxious to be included in something besides that masthead, that you let us ridicule you, play Pin the Tail on the Donkey with you … you took us any way you could get us."

"You're not speaking for me, I hope," Larry said. "Or any of us."

"Thank you, Larry," Clare said. She shifted in her seat to face Leah. "That's a bunch of nonsense, but nonetheless, that statement says a lot less for your behavior than it does mine."

"Let me finish!"

"You've said far too much already," Bart said. "And none of it with a speck of truth."

Maggie turned to Dan. "Remember what I said earlier, Danny," she whispered. "Nothing is what it will appear to be. Trust me."

Dan nodded, feeling fearful of what was to come.

"Let Leah speak!" Maggie said loudly as everyone turned to look at her. "The truth needs to be told." She paused to look at Clare. "Doesn't it?"

Confused, Clare looked at Maggie. "Is this your idea of 'truth'?"

Leah tried to hide her grin. "I knew you'd come around, Maggie."

"Go on, Leah," Maggie said. "Spill your guts!"

"Don't you dare!" Bart said to Leah.

"Put a lid on it, Bart," Leah snapped. She looked sadistically at Clare. "I'll give you a perfect example of how it was. I remember one Saturday night meeting in particular. Right here in this room. I was criticizing an article you'd written on the drug scene. Hell, you researched the damn thing, put long hours into it, and amazingly you turned out a pretty exceptional piece of journalism. You knew a lot more about the horrors of LSD and the long-term effects of weed than I did in those days."

Uncomfortable with the subject matter, Larry looked down.

"So," Leah continued, "Buzz Schrader and I made a bet. We decided to rip the article to shreds. We threatened to quit the group because we were so 'damn angry' at your 'lack of realism and focus.' We ranted and raved about not wanting to be associated with someone so socially ignorant. Buzz accused you of having a 'pathetic lack of integrity.' I called your article 'embarrassing for the Barrie Hillers.' We weren't even making sense. We were just throwing out words. Nothing penetrated that brain of yours. You apologized profusely and then turned to Polly Hatfield to engage in some inane conversation about the school cafeteria. You didn't even tell us off! We wanted to respect you. You never let us!"

"Jesus!" Bart said. "Is this your way, Leah? To set someone up, torture her, just so she can prove, by your warped standards, that she's worthy of your respect? Clare may have been insecure in those days, but she was good and kind—and talented—just as she is today. It seems, however, that you were, and still are, the most insecure of the lot. Just as you did back then, you're doing now: going to extreme lengths to feel superior over someone else."

"Oh my! Bart is defending your honor," Leah said. "Shall we wait while you go upstairs and change your underwear?"

"Enough!" Bart said. "You're disgusting."

"Don't you agree with me, Mrs. Bart?" Leah said.

Aimee shrugged. "I have nothing to say. You're on your own."

"And for that, you'll soon be as well," Leah barked, before refocusing on Clare. "Do you even remember the night I'm talking about?"

"You tell her, Leah!" Maggie said. "Let 'er have it! I'm with you all the way."

Stunned, Clare looked at Maggie but said nothing.

Leah glared at Clare. "So, do you remember that night?"

"I do," Clare said calmly.

"And you have nothing to say?" Leah turned to Colin. "Pour me a damn drink already."

"Get it yourself."

"Maggie will get it for you! What would you like, Leah?"

"A snifter of cognac. Remy. Thank you."

Bart, Colin, Larry, and Clare looked stunned as Maggie rose and went to the bar to pour Leah a drink, handed it to her, then sat down again.

"Thank you, Maggie," Leah said, taking the drink.

Larry turned to Maggie. "What's wrong with you? Why are you turning on Clare like this? How can you encourage Leah to spout such vitriolic crap toward someone who has never been anything but a good friend to you? Why are you trying to make Clare a victim of public obloquy?"

"Oh, my," Maggie said. "I'm afraid big O words won't obfuscate the truth about Clare."

"Just *stop*," Clare said. "Stop!"

"Why should we?" Leah said. This is more excitement than you've had in years. I'll wager it even makes up for the lack of any sex."

"You witch," Clare said.

"Oh, live dangerously," Maggie said. "Call her a bitch. Call me one, too. You know, if I didn't know for a fact that you had an insatiable desire to climb into Bart's pants, an overwhelming desire to feel his sexy manhood between your chaffed thighs, an uncontrollable passion to feel his plump lips on your blistered mouth, to feel his tongue whirling like a rinse cycle in your mouth … God, I'm turning myself on … I'd think you—"

"*Brava*, Maggie!" Leah cheered gleefully. "Ever the eloquent one!"

"*Enough, Maggie. Enough, Leah*, "Bart said, his face flushed with anger."

"Enough?" Leah asked. "We've barely begun. We're just telling Clare the way it was and the way it is." She looked at Clare.

"I'm sorry if you had dreams of getting us together so you could rewrite ancient history. Alas, alack. Here you sit in the Parker Room of broken dreams. Gone are your high hopes that the embarrassing memories of your pitiful past would dim with the passage of time and that we wouldn't remember how you groveled and begged for acceptance in those days." Leah sighed. "And, really, I don't give a damn that you're still a virgin!"

"Agreed," Maggie said loudly. "Nobody cares that you're still a virgin, Clare."

"No," Leah said to Maggie. "Nobody cares. But said knowledge does explain her rather lamentable countenance. Always longing! Never satisfied."

Clare stood and looked around the room, then turned to Leah. "Are you quite finished?"

"For now," Leah said dismissively.

"Fine. You've said your piece … piece of … now it's your turn to listen. I hope your ears are wide open, because I've got more to tell you than I'm afraid your decrepit brain will be able to handle."

"How utterly hilarious!" Leah laughed. "Oh, goodie. Clare's going to tell big, bad Leah off. I'm quaking in my very stylish shoes as you stand there in your old-lady flats."

Clare turned and looked at Colin. "You or me?"

"You start," Colin said. "I'll take it from wherever you stop."

Maggie squeezed Dan's hand. "Everything will be okay now."

Clare sat down and looked at Leah. "You'll excuse me if I sit. First of all, and of least importance, yes, I remember the night that you dragged Buzz Schrader into your web. Did it ever occur to you Leah, that Buzz was only pretending to go along with you, as Maggie just was?" Clare turned to address Maggie. "I don't know how you knew, or how much you know, but just this moment, I realized you were performing. And I know why. Thank you, Maggie. You've always been a true friend."

"What the hell?" Leah said. "Maggie wasn't putting on any performance. She meant every word she said. Tell her that, Maggie."

"I think it's Clare's turn to speak," Maggie said.

"Buzz wasn't a fan of yours, Leah," Clare continued. "And you weren't anywhere near the sorry excuse for a human being that you are today. But Buzz studied you. He thought you were a bully and, as he put it, 'his pet psychology project.' He explained to me that you had a very fragile ego, and that you needed others to agree with you. He told me that agreeing with your nonsense was akin to putting gas in your emotional tank. He confessed you'd tried pulling him in on your rants many times, but he'd refused. He asked me if I minded, if just once, he pretended to go along with you. He wanted to see how far you would take it. So, yeah, that night, knowing Buzz was playing you, I didn't pay any attention to that gibberish you were spewing about my drug piece. Just as you've been ignored many times this weekend, you were ignored then."

"Liar!" Leah snapped. "Convenient that Buzz isn't here to confirm that."

"I didn't bring his name up just now. You did. But you were right about something. At least partially. Sadly, I was insecure in those days. But not in the way you were and still are."

"I am *not* insecure!" Leah said.

"No, I wasn't glamorous like you and Maggie were," Clare continued. "I didn't think I could compete, and I nearly lost everything because of it." Clare stopped to catch her breath, then turned to Colin. "I've rehearsed this speech for years, even though I never thought I'd have a chance to deliver it. And now …"

Colin stood. "And now it's high time I take over. You need to preserve your strength."

"Are you fucking kidding me?" Leah said to Colin. "Why does this delicate virgin need to preserve her strength?"

"Hush!" Colin said. "Well, as I think Maggie might know,

Clare and I were seeing one another even before the Barrie Hillers were formed." He looked at Maggie. "Am I right? Did you know?"

Maggie nodded.

"You were seeing Clare?" Leah raged. "That's a joke. You may feel sorry for her now, but to make up such a lie so that she can save face is insane."

"No joke. Clare was editing The *Chronicle* then, and she published my writing. Often. Not because she loved me, but because she loved what I wrote."

Leah smacked the side of her head as if to unblock whatever had rendered her unable to hear correctly. "This is crazy."

"And," Colin said, "she told me that because she was publishing my work, it might be better to keep our relationship a secret. She also said that if anyone got the mistaken notion that she had a thing for Bart, well, she let that *one person* go on believing that."

"Silly me," Clare interjected. "Colin's work was worthy of being published. But I was just so afraid … so stupidly afraid that I'd be told to stop publishing him so much … or that I'd lose my job … that I encouraged the man I loved to hide in the shadows with me."

"*The man you loved*?" Leah screamed. "What kind of sick joke is this?" She turned to Colin. "You've colluded with her to make up this insane story as payback for whatever wrongs you have fallaciously judged me guilty of! This is bullshit. No need to proceed; I know you're both lying."

"No, they're telling the truth," Maggie said. "I saw them together on more than one occasion. They were very much in love. But I knew they were keeping it secret, for whatever reason, and so I respected that."

"You're lying, too!" Leah seethed. "Payback because I discovered your dirty secret!"

"Thank you for that," Clare said to Maggie. "I almost wish

you hadn't been so considerate. Things would have turned out so differently, but at least they turned out right."

"They did," Colin agreed.

"I was a wimp in many ways," Clare said. "If I had been open about my relationship with Colin, maybe … or maybe not … Leah Kasper would not have come on to him as she did."

Leah turned to Colin. "You expect me to believe you were seeing Clare when I first met you?"

"I was," Colin said.

Clare's face turned red with anger as she dug her palm into the arm of the couch. "I was so ridiculously insecure because I had been badly hurt in high school. And I thought that because you were rich, flashy, and halfway funny back then, that no matter what I did, even if Colin and I became public, that I would eventually lose Colin to you. I kept telling him I couldn't compete with your come-ons and constant ploys to win his affection. He told me that I didn't need to. He told me he loved me and always would." Clare wiped a tear. "He told me over and over. And every time you came on to him, I just didn't believe him. I didn't believe that, in the end, he would choose me. I believed your hyperbolic nonsense. I believed in my insecurities like a religion. And, eventually, I just walked away from the relationship. I didn't want to lose him publicly. I couldn't handle the humiliation that I was so sure I would endure. So I ended everything myself. Privately."

"Is this the nonsense you put in that novel you claim to have sold? Because this is one hell of a work of fiction."

"You wish," Colin told Leah. "You ain't heard nothin' yet." He turned to Clare. "Do you want to continue, or should I?"

"I'll take it for a bit longer."

"How long have you two been planning this charade?" Leah asked, scowling. "Since last night when I left the dining room? Is this what you were doing, sitting up until the wee hours, colluding by candlelight?"

"Right," Colin said. "We came up with all of this last night. Bart and Larry helped, too."

Still in shock, Larry nodded affirmatively. "Oh, yeah."

Bart, dumbfounded, said nothing, waiting for Clare to continue.

"Eventually, my worst fear became a self-fulfilling prophecy. Colin was worn out from trying to convince me that I was his chosen one, so he started seeing you. I was devastated but had only myself to blame. I handed him to you on a silver platter. Toward the end of our senior year, a year into his relationship with you, he came to me and told me he missed me. He brought a bottle of scotch to my dorm room."

"I wanted her to loosen up, let go of her fears, and hear me," Colin added.

Leah laughed boisterously. "I'm sorry, Colin, but if you wanted me to believe this absurdly tall tale, you might have injected a dose of realism into it. We've been madly in love since we began dating! And you expect me to believe that you went to Clare's dorm room with a bottle of scotch because you missed her? That is absurdly hilarious."

"Laugh yourself silly," Colin said. "I mean, the four of us worked really hard at concocting this exhaustive story last night. So you be sure to enjoy the fruits of our collective labor to the fullest."

"Oh, I am, believe me. Let the masquerade continue. I'm dying to see where you go with it."

"Well, after a night of the most incredible love making, I really thought Clare knew, once and for all, how much I loved her."

"Wild sex with the virgin," Leah howled with laughter. "Oh, my sides are splitting."

Colin pressed on. "To my extraordinary disappointment, once sober, Clare hadn't changed her mind and told me to go on with my life. Despite being hurt, saddened, and disappointed, I did. You and I began collaborating on a play, we all graduated, and you and I got married."

Leah mock applauded. "Well done! Kudos to the storytellers! I'd like to say I almost believed your tall tale, but I'm sorry to disappoint; I didn't. If you want to fool Leah Brent, for goodness' sake, people, try to be a bit more plausible with your farce."

"Who said we were finished?" Colin said. "There's much more. Hey, we were all up really late last night. You think this is all we came up with?"

"Oh, please," Leah rebuffed him. "I've heard enough."

"But I haven't even gotten to the good parts," Colin said.

"Whatever amuses you," Leah said. "Nobody can say I'm not a good sport."

"Six months into our marriage, you turned into the woman you are today, and I realized I had made the biggest mistake of my life. But your uncle Robert had helped me get a job at the university, and I was working like hell to get my master's and move on to my doctoral studies. I know you sensed my unhappiness, because even that early on in our marriage, you began making your veiled threats, subtly reminding me your uncle would pull any strings that you asked him to … and that what had been given to me could be taken away, and I had better be grateful for our marriage … and you."

Leah swallowed a lump in her throat as her face fell. "I did no such thing."

"Oh, yeah, you did," Colin said.

"You're twisting this tale. And you're doing what all liars do so well. You're taking little pieces of truths and weaving them into the lie to give it authenticity."

"It's no lie that I was miserable," Colin said. "So I called a friend in the Barrie Hill alumni office. I told her I'd dropped my address book in a puddle, and it was hopelessly unreadable. Without any hesitation, she gave me Clare's phone number and address, because she knew we'd been such good friends ... and Barrie Hillers." Colin paused and took a few sips of his cognac. "I didn't want to call her; I was afraid she'd turn me away, and I missed her way too much to be rejected. So I went to her apartment one night after work. When she heard my voice, she opened the door immediately. I wanted to throw my arms around her, but she was holding something and I couldn't."

"Oh, let me guess," Leah said, laughing. "A big, fat bacon cheeseburger dripping with grease."

"No," Colin said. "Our baby daughter. Colleen."

"Oh!" Maggie clasped her hands together. "I'm so glad you kept the baby."

"You knew I was pregnant? How did you know? I didn't tell a soul."

"We went to the same ob/gyn," Maggie said. "Sophia Kennedy. I was in an examination room waiting for her. A nurse opened the door to come in and take my vitals but got called away immediately and didn't shut the door behind her. You had just come out of the room next to me, and Dr. Kennedy was walking you to the reception area. You were sobbing. She told you that many single women successfully raised babies and that she could refer you to a counselor." Maggie sighed. "That's all I heard, Clare darling. I never stopped wondering if you had the baby, put her up for adoption, or kept her. But I knew it was Colin's baby. I knew he still loved you. When you didn't mention her, I assumed you'd probably given her away. That makes me an ass, I guess."

Leah stood, grabbed her empty glass, stormed to the bar, and generously refreshed her drink. "You are every bit the ass, Maggie! You will pay for your part in this cruel charade. And you know exactly how!"

Dan put his hand on Maggie's. "Don't worry, dear," he

whispered. "It's all going to be okay."

Colin looked up at Leah. "You're making not-so-veiled threats. This must mean you believe us."

"*No*! I don't believe a word. What I believe is that all of you are ganging up on me because none of you can deal with the fact that I see you all clearly for who and what you are! That's what I know!"

"I was so happy to see Colin," Clare said, looking at Maggie. "When I said …"

"… meet your daughter, Colleen Clare Brent," Colin said, "the tears started flowing and never stopped."

"Oh, bullshit!" Leah said angrily and took a large swig of her drink.

"One *sips* cognac, dear," Maggie said.

"Hush!"

Colin looked at Clare. "Do you want to continue, honey? Or should I?"

"Honey? Did you just call her 'honey'?"

"You're doing great," Clare told him. "Go on."

"I couldn't believe we had a daughter. She was … she is … beautiful."

Clare looked at Leah. "You were wondering how I knew what Polly Hatfield was doing these days. I know because she's a teacher at the private high school Colleen attended."

"Such clever insertion of some tripe you spoke of yesterday," Leah said. "I'll give you that. But despite the little details you're throwing in, this feeble fabrication is still without any merit."

Colin looked around the room at everyone. "Let me continue. After I told Clare how miserable I was, she told me how wrong she'd been, how much she'd changed, and that she'd never love anyone else nor disbelieve how much I loved her."

"I did," Clare confirmed.

"I wanted to leave Leah that day, but Clare told me not to. It wasn't because she was still insecure; it was because she wasn't. Having Colleen changed everything. She didn't want Leah to use her connections to get me fired. And I agreed, because I needed to help provide for my child and continue my studies."

Clare turned to Leah. "Yesterday, you wanted to know why I only worked part-time freelance after college … why I couldn't get a full-time job. Now you know!"

"Yes, Leah. Now you know." Colin paused to enjoy how light his body felt after years of pent-up tension had disappeared. "Clare and I have been together ever since that day. Five years later, we had our son, Michael."

"Bullshit! Liar!" Leah screamed.

Clare put her hands gently on her stomach. "A word about this pot belly of mine that you've made reference to more than once … and quite rudely, I may add. Sorry to disappoint you, Leah. I haven't lost my figure. I'm pregnant with our third child. A surprise, but a happy one."

Aimee gasped and covered her mouth, while everyone else traded looks of astonishment.

"You have not been with her for all of these years! You've been married to me."

Colin looked at everyone in the room except Leah. "I hope you will all forgive my forthcoming vulgarity, but I do have something to say to Leah." Steeling himself, Colin slowly turned and glared at Leah. "Have you not noticed that I haven't fucked you in over nineteen years?"

"Oh my God!" Leah screamed.

Once again, Colin addressed everyone in the room. "Yesterday, Leah made a couple of references to my friend 'Ed.'"

"Leave that out of it!" Leah said.

"I remember," Bart said. "Leah asked you if you'd like to tell your old friends about Ed."

"Hush!"

"Precisely," Colin said. "One time I said no, another time I said Ed was a neighbor that Leah wished I didn't spend so much time with. But there is no neighbor named Ed. E D, Ed, stands for erectile dysfunction. A story I told Leah so that I never had to touch her again. As you can see, she bought it: hook, line, and sinker. And, as you also saw, she was threatening to expose me in front of all of you … just to humiliate me."

"You horrible, cheating piece of scum!" Leah shouted.

"I don't understand, Colin darling," Maggie said. "Why in the world did you stay with Leah for all these years?"

"Because he loves me and won't admit it! We have something special nobody can understand," Leah cried.

"Because as time went on, Clare and I had two children. Leah, though *she* is unable to admit it, knows damn well I don't love her. I not only didn't have sex with her, I never kiss her or show any kind of affection. And I sleep in the guest room. And while she knew nothing of my other life, she has always known that I wanted to leave her."

"Liar!"

"No, I'm not lying, Leah." Colin continued to address Maggie and the others. "She has openly and consistently threatened to have me fired if I left her. When I got my doctorate and became a professor, she would routinely remind me that if I even thought about leaving, Uncle Robert would see that I didn't get tenure or keep my job. So I stayed. Last year I finally got tenure. I was ready to leave then, but Clare wanted me to wait until this year, when Michael graduated from high school, to leave, so that Leah wouldn't be able to interfere in any way. Colleen's in college now, and Michael will be in the fall. This weekend, they're both away on a canoe trip with friends in the Adirondacks, blissfully unaware of all of this."

"Well, damn," Larry said. "Everything you said yesterday

about separate vacations makes sense. While Leah was off sunning herself, you and Clare were seeing the world with your kids."

"Indeed!" Colin said. "They're world travelers. And they've been to England to see their grandparents five times."

"Six," Clare corrected.

Leah put her hands to each side of her head and screamed. "Look at you horrible people, enjoying every bit of my misery!"

"What was that, Queen Schadenfreude?" Aimee said.

"Your wife is the one who killed your film!" Leah screamed at Bart. "And she's doing the same thing to this one. If you don't believe me, call your agent, Ken Boy. She's a conniving, lying, jealous little twat!"

"Is that all?" Bart said without emotion.

Aimee looked at Bart, but he would not meet her eyes.

"Okay, don't believe me! But it's the truth."

"*The Garden of Lost Dreams* will be just fine, Leah," Bart said. "I've seen to that. I'm sorry to disappoint you, but you haven't told me anything about my film that I don't already know."

Aimee looked at Leah, then at Larry, who hinted at a sympathetic smile.

Enraged, Leah turned to Dan. "If you think I won't call your wife, think again! I will!"

Colin looked at Leah and waved her off. "You know what the ironic part of all of this is? I had only briefly met your uncle at our wedding and not again until three months ago. He was on campus meeting his cousin for lunch." Colin refocused his attention on the group. "Let me explain. Leah's uncle, Robert Kasper, is a very powerful, and, may I say, very nice man. His business partner is on the board of trustees at the university. This is the connection that Leah used all these years to blackmail me with. But here's the thing. I ran into this kind man when he had just come from a private lunch meeting with some board members. When Robert ... he asked me to call him Bob … and I began to chat, I could tell by the questions he asked that he hadn't spoken to Leah in quite a while, nor had he much of a clue as to what she was doing or not doing. But he's none the wiser because of me. I spoke highly of my wife, because I know that Robert Kasper is the one person in the world Leah admires and actually respects." Colin turned to Leah. "I don't have any idea what you want to tell Sally Collier, but if you do anything to hurt anyone in or out of this room, I won't hesitate to call Bob, who asked me to 'keep in touch,' and let him know exactly the kind of person you are and have always been."

"You wouldn't dare!" Leah shouted.

"If you behave, I wouldn't dream of it."

Leah's entire body, fraught with tension, shook uncontrollably. "Last night, during the blackout. There weren't any spare rooms. You don't know anyone here. You were in *her* room!"

Colin mock applauded the way Leah regularly did. "Very good!"

Putting her hands to either side of her head, Leah squeezed. "I can't take any more of this!"

"Just one more thing," Colin said. "I've been moving out of the house for months. Someone came in yesterday, soon after we left to come here, and removed the last of my clothing and personal effects. I won't be coming home with you ever again. And I will be serving you divorce papers."

"You cruel bastard! Why did you try to stop me from coming to this reunion? Clearly, you wanted to humiliate me in front of everyone. Why did you try to keep that from happening?"

"Believe it or not," Colin said, "I didn't want it to happen this way. And I feared you'd go after Clare, and I didn't want her being upset, especially as she's four months pregnant. I tried to stop Clare from holding this reunion. I knew this would happen. But she really wanted to see everyone … she has for years … and she knew it would be impossible for a while once the baby was born."

Clare looked at Leah. "As you see, I don't have the free time you thought I did."

Leah stood. "I despise each and every one of you horrid human beings." She turned to Colin. "Don't you dare destroy my uncle's image of me! Unlike you, he respects and admires me."

"I just told you, Leah … if you don't hurt anyone, I have no reason to say a word. It's not something I want to do. I'm not you. I don't hurt for the pleasure of it."

"I haven't hurt anyone," Leah said as she ran to the door. Gripping the doorknob, she turned to look at the group. "I'm the victim here. I am the only one who has been wronged. You're all a bunch of cruel, sadistic, shallow-minded, holier-than-thou, untalented fools." Opening the door, Leah took one last look at Colin, then slammed the door behind her.

For several moments, no one said a word. Colin was still fixated on the door. "And that's how you spell 'projection.'" Finally, Colin got up from his couch and took a seat next to Clare on hers. She sighed and leaned up against him as he put his arm around her and spoke: "I told you, love, it's all going to be okay. The rest of our lives belong to us and our children." Colin stroked her hair and kissed the top of her head. "My heart is yours forever and always."

Mesmerized, Dan watched the exchange, then whispered to Maggie, "They've waited so long. This is true love. They deserve every happiness."

Maggie started to speak, but stopped herself. She just smiled.

"Well, color me shocked, stunned, and blown the fuck away!" Larry said. "Day-am. What a story. I had no idea. Absolutely none. Clare, my sweet friend, why was it so difficult to accept that Colin loved you? You could have saved yourself so much heartache."

Clare looked up. "We're all vulnerable, Larry. We all have emotional scars. Some of us deal with them better than others. I've done a one-eighty since college. I'm stronger than I ever thought I could be. But I stupidly let something that happened in high school cloud my judgment and destroy my self-esteem."

"Can you tell us what that was?" Maggie asked.

Clare nodded. "In the eleventh grade, I had a boyfriend. His name was Nick. I was completely over-the-moon smitten with him. Ridiculously so. He used to talk about his dreams for our future, our world travels … romantic escapades we would have. I drank it all in. I felt invulnerable, and that was pretty amazing, because I'd never been exceptionally confident. But somehow, this teenage boy lifted me off the ground and taught me how to walk on clouds. And then, one day, this new girl came to our school. She was very wealthy, very pretty, and was, dare I say, not unlike Leah. And pardon my cliché, but he dropped me like a hot potato without a word. He never even said he was sorry and offered no explanation. He just left me to figure it out for myself. I remember one day the two of them were huddled together by her locker … looking at me and laughing. Everyone in school saw the way they taunted me. It was a gross humiliation.

"I thought I had gotten over it when I fell in love with Colin two years later. He was nothing like Nick. But my self-esteem had plummeted, and I was afraid of being hurt again … of being humiliated in front of my college classmates as I had been in high school. Yes, I was genuinely worried about people connecting our relationship to Colin getting published so frequently. But that was really just a lie I told myself … and then to Colin. Anyway, when Leah came along, and I could see how much she wanted Colin, well, I just refused to fight. I couldn't go through it again. I let the childish, hurtful actions of some silly teenage boy obscure my thinking. It wasn't until the day Colin showed up at my door, looking at our baby daughter and me with such love in his eyes, that I finally rid myself of sorrow I never should have nurtured and let grow. But such is life, and we are flawed human beings."

Bart looked at Clare with compassion. "When you told me your life had been complicated, I never imagined this. You are one strong woman, Clare."

"You are," Aimee said. "I hope you will forgive the things I said to you yesterday. I was being blackmailed, but that's no excuse."

"I figured as much," Clare said. "I just didn't know why."

"I'm going to say good night and leave six old friends to enjoy their last evening together," Aimee stood.

"Good night," Bart said. "I'm sure we'll talk soon."

Aimee stopped to shake off the icy chill that coated his words, then walked toward the door as everyone else said good night.

After she had closed the door behind her, Bart looked sadly at his friends. "I'll just say this much: I'm in shock. And I've had little time to figure out what I want to do. Right now, I just want to enjoy my time with all of you. There's so precious little of it left."

"That's so true," Maggie said. "I hope you figure it out, Bart. Did you mean it when you said all is good with your new film? Or was that just for Leah's benefit?"

"No, I meant it. The film will be fine. My marriage ... I'm not so sure."

"Good. I'm glad to hear that. About the film, of course." She turned to Colin. "One thing I don't understand despite Leah's paltry explanation. Why has she been so obsessed with Clare being a virgin, and why is she consumed with so much hate? It's positively chilling."

Clare handed Colin his drink. He took a sip, then put the glass down. "Despite being married to Leah for two decades too long, I'm not an expert on what makes her tick. Leah has a sister named Julia, who I've never met. They've been estranged for twenty-two years. Leah's father was a tough guy, overly strict and overly critical, but he passed away before she was out of high school. Leah's mother is alive, but they don't speak. The only family she has is Bob Kasper, her father's brother. And as cruel as Leah's been ... as Leah is ... I didn't tell her what I learned from Bob Kasper. He doesn't like her either. He finds her harsh, 'off-putting, and condescending,' to be exact, and said the only reason he shows any kindness to her at all is because his late brother was not a good father. Leah doesn't know this, but Bob is very close with his other niece, Julia. Leah's sister. He said she's like a daughter to him. But he doesn't care if he ever sees Leah again. He's all she thinks she has, and I didn't want to take that from her. Not unless she does something to hurt any of you." Colin paused to mull over his words. "I don't think she'll do that. The loss, as she perceives it, would be too great."

"Whoa," Larry said. "What a lonely life. So back to Maggie's question: what's with Leah's twisted obsession with Clare?"

"She hates that Clare was so well respected in college. Hates that she won the award Leah coveted despite not deserving. Leah has done very little with her life. You heard her: she never even tried to write plays on her own. Because, quite frankly, she knows she's not very good at it. She started a fundraising business but treated her employees so horribly that people kept quitting." Colin paused to snigger. "Something I'm sure none of you have any trouble imagining at all."

"Sadly not," Dan said.

"Her fundraising business is down to one large client who she handles on her own. Basically, her life is comprised of attending board meetings where people are nice to her because she has money ... and because she's Bob Kasper's niece. The only thing Leah ever does to make herself feel good is to compare her life to others she deems less fortunate than her. I haven't touched her in nearly two decades. How does she make herself feel better about that? She imagines that Clare is some pathetic virgin with less than she has. That vaunted mindset exalts her to some golden pinnacle only she can see.

"Yesterday she told you she had a friend who dropped her after she went back to her cheating husband. But her friend Laurel's husband never cheated on her. Leah saw him in a restaurant one day rubbing the hand of another woman. Yes, it did look suspicious. But her husband, Mario, was comforting his secretary, who burst into tears at lunch because she had recently had a miscarriage. Leah filled Laurel's head with so many doubts that she and Mario almost broke up. Leah knew deep down that I didn't love her, and she didn't want her friend to have the loving husband she didn't have. Laurel eventually figured that out and ended the friendship. The only people Leah ever socializes with, ever, are the ones she meets on vacation."

"I would feel sorry for her if she didn't go to such lengths to hurt others," Maggie said. "I'm just sorry you were trapped with her for so many years."

"I told her," Colin said, "that she should go find someone who could love her. But she didn't want to face reality or the embarrassment of being divorced. I tried reasoning with her, but our conversations never got anywhere, because Leah only knows one way to respond: with threats. She refused to hear what I was saying."

"He did try," Clare said. "So many times. But we both agreed we had to wait until Colin had tenure. We couldn't let Leah wreak havoc in our children's lives or their education. Our family, despite not being together every day, has been whole, loving, and healthy."

"A wise decision," Dan said. "If Leah knew you didn't love her, why did you need to make up the erectile dysfunction story?"

"That's easy," Larry said before Colin could answer. "Because if he didn't, she might suspect him of cheating. But, hey, the man can't get it up, where's he gonna go?"

"Ah!" Dan said. "Silly me. Of course."

"On the money, Larry," Colin said. "And may I add that she

never ceased to try and humiliate me for it."

"I wish you both every happiness going forward," Dan said. "I can't explain it, but you both look 'lighter.' You do."

"I feel light enough to fly away," Clare said. "And I'm pregnant!"

"I'm still absorbing what happened," Colin said. "As Clare said earlier, we've both rehearsed speeches we never thought we'd have the chance to give. It's almost surreal. But I do feel lighter. About 120 pounds lighter, to be exact!"

"I think everyone in this room has undergone a life-changing event in two days," Bart said. "Well, maybe not Maggie and Dan."

Dan laughed nervously. "Don't be so sure."

"Well," Clare said. "Now that Leah is behind us, let's turn this night together into the party it was meant to be!"

"Maggie wants to hear funny stories."

"I've got one," Larry said, looking at Maggie. "I don't think any of you know the one about Wally Decker trying to steal Madeleine from Henry."

"Oh, no!" Maggie exclaimed. "As if he had a chance!"

"He thought he did," Larry said. "Refresh your drinks, sit back, and get ready to laugh. This one is a doozy."

Chapter SIXTEEN

May 18, 1986 – 2:44 a.m.

Bart opened the door quietly so as to not wake Aimee. But as the hallway light lit the otherwise dark hotel room, he saw the bed had not been touched, and that an envelope lay atop the burgundy bedspread. As a wave of sadness crashed over him, then receded, he switched on the bedside lamp and sat down. Opening the envelope, he found two sheets of hotel stationery, with a letter written in Aimee's handwriting, front and back.

> *Bart,*
> *My chickens have come home to roost. For years, I worried that one day you would discover I was the driving force behind your first reunion film dying an unnatural death. My actions were never out of malicious intent, but rather out of fear and jealousy. I am not trying to make excuses. Nothing changes the damage I have done or the mistrust in me I have no doubt instilled in you.*
>
> *However despicable my actions, I have clung to the dim hope that after you made* Garden, *and it was the huge success I know it is going to be, that I would come to you, confess my*

sins, and beg for your forgiveness. But something in me
snapped, jealousy reared its ugly head once more, and I did the
same inexcusable thing all over again. I'm sure it was karma
that got me, as I had no clue Leah was nearby listening to my
every horrible word as I threatened Ken from a lobby phone.
And then she threatened me. I don't know how you found out,
but it doesn't matter. I'm glad you did. You may not believe
me, but I'm happy the film is a go. I don't have to carry around
my terrible secret anymore; I don't have to wait for the ax to
fall; and most importantly, you will not be denied what is
rightfully yours.

And yes, I will apologize to Ken and Sylvia.

I don't know if you want to talk about any of this. My
deception may be a blessing in disguise for you. It may be the
out you've always wanted, even if you didn't know it until this
weekend. Or maybe you did.

By the way, I lied (no surprise now) about seeing Windswept. *I*
watched it once when you were filming in Chicago. You may
have been acting when you made love to Holly, but I don't
think you were. All I know is that you never, ever made love to
me that way. I know in my heart that whatever is between the
two of you still remains, and that when you see one another
again, sparks are going to fly: onscreen and off. While it takes a
lot more than sparks to make a marriage, I still feel threatened
… and doomed. And I hate myself for that. I'm a fighter. I just
don't want to be a clueless idiot. Learning tonight how Leah
stayed in denial for decades, punishing the man she claims to
love, made me realize I don't want to do the same. Karma got

her, too. Way worse than it got me. And I hate that my situation resembles hers even in the slightest. I refuse to claim any likeness to that horror. I want to be the woman you always thought I was, and even if you're no longer in love with me. I want you to know I really am a good person. I just lost my way. That's no excuse, but I'm going to do everything I can to find it again. No matter what happens between us, I want to like and respect myself the way I once did.

I may be wrong about the fate of our marriage. I hope I am, but I don't think so. Right now, I need time to think, and so do you. We both have things to figure out. I'll crash at my parents' place and will work out of the New York office. So, if you want to talk any time soon, you'll know where to find me. Or write to me.

I'm sorry for the pain I've caused you. You're the finest man I've ever known; you didn't deserve any of this.

With all my love,
Aimee

He tucked the letter carefully back into the envelope, then lay it on the table. He looked at the empty bed. "Oh, Aimee. I'm sorry, too. So very sorry."

ˈ✳ˈ✳ˈ✳ˈ

Larry almost tripped on the envelope as he stumbled into the dark room. As soon as he flipped on the light switch, he saw it, lying on the floor, only inches from where he stood.

"Oh, Cass," he mumbled. "Did you leave a message for me? Did you change your mind, baby?"

Picking up the envelope, Larry wobbled over to the bed. Sitting down, he missed the edge of the bed and moaned as his rear end kissed the floor and his head hit the footboard. "Oh, shit! Damn, that hurts!" Holding one hand to his head, Larry took a moment to nurse his throbbing head, then opened the envelope. He pulled out the lone sheet of hotel stationery and read:

> *Larry,*
>
> *I am sorry that we met under such stressful circumstances, but I don't know how I would have persevered without you. You're a good man. By the time you read this, I'll probably be back in New York, where I've decided to stay for the foreseeable future. I haven't spoken to Bart, and I can't know anything for sure, but I feel certain my marriage is over. If I sound calm, it's because I don't quite believe the words I am writing. I'm devastated.*
>
> *I regret not having the chance to say good-bye to you. If you're still in need of a friend, because I know I am, give me a call at either one of the numbers below.*
>
> *In the meantime, take good care and be good to yourself. I hope everything works out as it is meant to be … for both of us.*
> *Aimee*

"I sure as hell do need a friend," Larry muttered. "But right now, I need to find the ice machine and chill my noggin. Damn, we all had way too much to drink tonight, but I don't want to be the fool who shows up for brunch with a lump on his head."

` ✶ ` ✶ ` ✶ `

Angry and intoxicated, Leah stumbled down the eighth-floor hallway. She stopped at the room she had twice burst into before, then slapped the palm of her hand against the wall to keep from falling. "I didn't get a chance to say good-bye to you sorry hypocrites, and I sure as hell am not depriving myself of that pleasure."

Pressing her ear to the door, she lit up when she heard the loud moans and groans emanating from the room. "Ha, ha! Gotcha now, you worthless blond turncoat and you adulterous piece of sanctimonious newspaper shit. Gotcha good. Time for some real humiliation."

Taking her hand off the wall, misjudging her ability to stand upright, she began to slide downward. On her way to the floor, she grabbed the doorknob to break her fall. To her great surprise, it turned. "Ha, ha. You're every bit as careless as you are hypocritical."

Licking her lips in anticipation and using the doorknob for support, she pulled herself up and opened the door. Bursting into the dark room, she took care to lock the door behind her and to ensure the safety chain was latched. She could barely make out the up-and-down thrusting of human bodies beneath the white sheet, but the moans and groans, now audible at full volume, delighted her.

"Sorry to break up the party, people, but Leah's here!"

Hearing a female voice scream out, only the dark of night could see Leah's smile, radiating euphoria. "Not getting rid of me that easily! Not this time, fuckers!"

Before she could say another word, an arm reached out from under the sheet and turned on the bedside lamp. "Well, hallelujah, Susie, our hooker has arrived for a threesome." Jumping out of bed, Pappy Cutter, his massive stomach flapping in sync with his manhood, ran over to Leah, and threw his arms around her. Within seconds, he began thrusting himself against her and kissing her neck, while the woman in the bed stood up and threw her hands in the air. "Let the party begin! Let me taste the forbidden fruit."

Screaming and cursing, Leah fought him, but that only made him grab onto her tighter, ripping her blouse open, pulling the right strap of her bra down, and exposing her breast. Dragging her to the bed, he placed her on it, then straddled himself on top of her, while his naked companion began fondling herself as she cried out in pleasure.

"Get off of me! Let me up, you disgusting pig!! You shouldn't even be in here. This isn't your room."

"It's my room since my wife kicked me outta our room. And now it's your room, too! Leah did ya say ya name was? The whore dispatch never gave me a name. They just said they'd send someone over."

"I'm not your hooker, you fat fool! I didn't come here to see you. Someone else was supposed to be staying in this room. Let me up now before I call the police and have you thrown into jail for molesting me ... if you'll even fit into a cell."

Pappy had barely lifted himself up when Leah squirmed out from underneath him, falling onto the floor with a thud.

"Aw, now that's a downer! You might have to fluff me up again."

Gripping the edge of the nightstand to right herself, Leah screamed and ran to the door as Pappy followed after her. As she fumbled with the locks she had so carefully put into place, Pappy, still oblivious to the fact she was not the prostitute he hired, began swishing his hips from side to side as if performing his personal version of an ancient mating ritual. "Okay, Lady Leah, we'll play it your way. You like to be chased. Susie and I can chase you if you want. Why the hell not?"

Finally, with great effort, Leah managed to unlock the door and lift the safety chain. Opening it, she ran into the hallway, her breast fully exposed as her shirt barely clung on. Only paces behind her, Pappy and Susie ran naked, whooping and screaming.

As Leah turned the corner, the twosome still behind her, she nearly crashed into Larry, woozy and carrying an ice bucket back to his room.

Staring, his mouth agape, Larry watched as a screaming, disheveled Leah led the raucous nude partiers to the stairwell.

"Day-am," Larry said, blinking in disbelief. "I hit my head waaay harder than I thought."

'✳'✳'✳'

As they lay in bed facing one another, Colin gently lifted Clare's chin. "Are you crying, baby?"

"Not crying. Maybe letting a few tears of joy and relief find their way into the world. I'm sure there are way more to come, but at the moment, everything is still phantasmagorical."

"For me, too. But a clear notch up from Kafkaesque, wouldn't you say?"

Clare smiled. "Without a doubt."

"Tell me, in the back of your mind, in the front of it ... did you hold this reunion hoping that this weekend would force the long-overdue revelation it did?"

Clare put her hand on his shoulder, then stroked his cheek. "Is that what you believe? Is that why you didn't want me to do this? Why you weren't even going to come?"

"I always wanted to come, Clare. I just didn't want to give Leah the opportunity to do what she does so well: make everyone else miserable." Colin sighed. "I couldn't predict what would happen, but I knew it wouldn't be pretty. With Leah in the equation, amicability and cordiality are always mathematical impossibilities. I just wanted to see everyone without the veil of ugly draped over us. Nor did I want to give credence to the pretense that I felt anything for her. The thought of our cherished friends wondering how and why I stayed married to that woman all these years consumed me. That and the idea that she and I are anything alike." He shivered. "Then there was the dilemma of how to sleep in your room, and not ours. I think that's one of the reasons she wanted to come, quite frankly. The blackout solved that problem, but if a power outage had never happened, trust me, I had alternate scenarios ready to go."

"You told me you'd work that part out." Clare looked up. "Never imagined we'd have divine intervention."

"Me, either." Colin smiled as he stroked her face. "But mostly, the biggest reason I was loath to come is because I didn't want to hide my love for you. And I wanted to boast about our children … the way Dan does about his. You know this, honey. There's nothing I've just said that I haven't told you before."

"I know." Clare looked into his eyes.

"So, is it too much for me to ask if you had any thoughts of the truth making a not-so-surprise appearance?"

"Earlier, you told everyone I decided to have this reunion now because it won't be feasible for a while after the baby is born."

"I did, and it won't be. But I'm still wondering if a part of you wanted to invite the truth to join us … baby matters aside."

"Do you really need to know?"

"I'd like to know. For the sake of closure … curiosity."

Clare closed her eyes for a moment, as if to search her thoughts, then looked at Colin. "I can't say for sure, but the more I think about it, the closer I come to a realization I never allowed myself to acknowledge before. Yes. A part of me probably did." Clare took hold of his hand. "Honey, you know that if I'd thought about *her* too much, had I imagined all of the what-ifs too profoundly, I might have chickened out completely. That's why I banished any possible scenarios to the back of my mind. It had been twenty years since we'd seen everyone. I kept thinking: how often do people wait for the perfect moment only to have it never come? You know as well as I do: things happen. Remember how we waited to see Dora and Donnelly again? It was just never a convenient time. We were all too busy. Yet, we all really wanted to see one another. 'Next month,' we all kept saying. And we meant it."

Colin frowned. "We did. But 'next month' never came. Donnelly died suddenly of an aneurysm, and Dora packed up her grief and moved back to Spain."

"She did. I'm still grief stricken over it." She took a moment to catch her breath. "I really wanted to see the Barrie Hillers. I didn't want anyone or anything to stop that from happening. Not even Leah."

Colin looked at Clare with great affection. "And you didn't."

"No, and when we meet next time, I hope Henry and Madeleine will be able to join us."

"And then we'll be complete, and emptied … as we should be."

"Yes. We will be. And while we're being totally honest with one another," Clare winked, "you never told me you were going to have the last of your things moved out while we were here. Did *you* envision this happening?"

Smiling sheepishly, Colin twisted his mouth. "Um, let's just say that when Leah insisted on coming, it seemed like a distinct possibility. But even if she had behaved, which was virtually an impossibility, I saw no reason to wait a moment longer. I have my tenure, Michael is out of high school, Leah drives me stark raving mad, and I'm desperate to be with my family every day. It was time."

"It was," Clare said. "The kids will be ecstatic. I'm ecstatic."

"Me, too. I can't wait to tell them."

"Do you think she'll fight you on the divorce?"

"Hmm. I've thought about that. I don't think she will, *only* because she'll want to tell her vast circle of casual acquaintances that she left *me*. And, knowing I've now got the ear of her beloved uncle, it's even more doubtful that she'd risk tarnishing the sparkling image she believes he has of her. But if she does prolong the inevitable, we'll handle it. We're together now, and that's what matters most."

"It is."

Colin smiled and put his hand on Clare's stomach. "How's our little tie-breaker? Boy or girl?"

"Could be both. I think we're having twins."

Stunned, Colin's jaw dropped. "Are you kidding?"

"Yes, sweetie pie. I am."

As Colin and Clare laughed, he turned away and reached into the drawer of the nightstand closest to him, pulled a small object from it, then wrapped his hand around it.

"You're hiding something," Clare said, beaming.

"I am." Colin looked at Clare, whose tears had reappeared in greater number. "Joy or relief?" Colin asked as he opened his closed hand to reveal a diamond engagement ring.

"Oh my," Clare said. "Joy. Pure joy."

Colin hopped off the bed and got down on one knee. "Clare Elisabeth Dreyser, love of my life, mother of my children, will you do me the honor of becoming my wife?" He laughed. "Oh, bloody hell, I didn't mean for that to rhyme. I mean if the rhyming had been intentional, it would have actually been clever."

"I know that." Clare laughed. "Are you going to get off the floor and put that gorgeous ring on my finger?"

Within seconds, back in bed, Colin slipped the ring on Clare's finger as he gazed lovingly at her. "That *was* a yes, right?"

Clare hugged his neck and kissed him. "Yes, a thousand times yes."

"So, have we exhausted all of the questions we had for each other?"

"Actually, I just have one more." Clare wiped the tears from her eyes. "How long have you had this gorgeous ring?"

Colin bit his lip and looked up at the ceiling, then at Clare. "Do you really want to know?"

"No. I'm not the least bit curious. It doesn't interest me at all. Forget I even asked."

Colin chuckled. "Sarcasm duly noted." He took a deep breath. "I bought it the day after I saw you again. The day after I met Colleen."

"Seriously?" Clare put her hand to her heart. "You've had this ring nearly twenty years?"

Colin nodded. "I have. And I bought it with a savings account I started at the age of fifteen." He reached over and stroked her hair. "I wanted to give you this so many times. But doing so while I still lived in that house of doom, while she still believed I would be with her forever, I couldn't do it. I couldn't cheat you like that. I couldn't cheat *us* like that." Colin paused. "And there's one more thing I couldn't do."

"And that is?"

"Wait even a minute longer to give you this ring," Colin said. "I hope you don't mind me proposing in the altogether, in the middle of the night, after a very long day. Not exactly what I had planned. I've had this hidden in a jacket pocket for all these years. I grabbed it right before Leah and I left to come here."

Clare held out her hand and admired the sparkling diamonds. "I'm so glad you gave it to me now. I feel whole; I really do. And it is very special that I'll be able to share it with our friends at brunch."

"You know," Colin said with a crooked smile, "I'm thinking

twins wouldn't be so bad after all."

"No way," Clare said, trying not to laugh. "You don't even joke about that! Now, please … make love to the happiest woman in the world, will you?"

Colin looked around the room. "Sure. Where is she?" They both laughed as Colin pulled Clare close. "I love you, baby. You know, this has been a long day, but from where I lie right now, it's just getting started."

MAY 18, 1986 — 5:54 A.M.

Naked, Maggie walked from the bathroom back to the bed and slipped in quietly next to Dan. Rousing from sleep, Dan pulled her close, softly caressing her hair.

"Oh, Danny, this is heaven. I have to keep reminding myself this is real."

"Not as often as I remind myself. I could stay here forever like this … with you. I've been so hungry for you ever since we first met."

Maggie sighed as she reached down to touch him. She stroked him briefly before taking her hand away. "I want to do this over and over before we go, but we must talk, my darling."

Reluctantly, Dan stopped what he was about to do and lightly kissed her breasts instead. "I know. I just can't get enough of you."

"Nor me of you," she said softly.

Dan smiled as he gazed into her eyes. "Perhaps we should sit up. I don't think we'll do too much conversing as we are now."

"No, we definitely won't." Maggie lifted herself up and rested against the soft headboard. "I'm very glad Clare was able to change breakfast to brunch. I don't think any of us got much sleep last night."

"Every second of those extra hours will be golden to us," Dan said, righting himself as well. "What time is it?"

"Almost six." Maggie glanced at the clock on the nightstand. "I think we've slept for all of forty-five minutes."

"We made love for over three hours. That much I know."

"We did." Maggie smiled as she recalled her bliss. "I wish we could freeze time. I love being with you."

"We don't have to stop. This can be our life, if you want it to be. I don't mean just the lovemaking, but having a real life together."

"But, Danny … you have a family."

"I do. Please believe me when I say that I'm not forgetting about them for a second. But the kids are so immersed in their own lives, and it seems that everything I do, even my conversations with Sally, are done by rote. I'm like a mechanical mate who talks with her about the children, what needs to be done in the house, where our next social engagement will be, and whatever is in the headlines. Sally is an exceptional woman; I've told you that. But I'm bereft of life and purpose with her. I've been so numb all of these years that I didn't feel the pain of my unremarkable existence until I saw you again. You brought me back to life."

"Oh, Danny!" Maggie stroked his forehead and let her hand cascade down his face like a gentle waterfall. "To hear you say it that way, I think it's been very much the same for me. We have a very different set of characters in our lives, but what we've been taking away—or not taking away—has been extraordinarily similar. And I have very good people in my life … I do … but I'm so alone in so many ways. I feel guilty saying that, knowing that I do have such loving friends. They would be horrified to hear me say that."

"I understand, love. We also have a fine social circle, but for the most part, our mutual friends aren't people who stimulate me intellectually. Not like the Barrie Hillers … minus Leah, of course. Nor are they like some of the intriguing people I work with."

Maggie made a half-hearted attempt to smile. "Well, when the Barrie Hillers get together again in two years, Leah won't be among us. And hopefully Colin and Clare will be married by then. They've waited so long."

"They have. But as long as their wait has been, they've had a happy life, despite the fact that their life … their family … has been a secret they've had to keep from so many."

"If I had not seen that fishwife in action again this weekend, I might not have understood why they made the decisions they did. But that evil woman is sociopathic. She is, Danny. She has no empathy for anyone. Clare and Colin did what they needed to do to protect their family. I don't even understand why that rotting pile of fish scales wanted to stay with a man who didn't love her. Much less respect her."

"Because she has no one at all in her life. Colin has been a mere possession, someone to exact control over. Someone to help her keep up a pretense, an illusion, to herself and to the world … that she is loved. I would imagine she hasn't tried to forge any lasting relationships with other people so she would never have to suffer the humiliation of rejection. But no more talk of Leah. She's taken enough from all of us this weekend. Can we talk about us, Maggie? About our future?"

"I do love you, Danny. And I'll tell you again. It is because I have always loved you that I never allowed us to be involved this way."

"But that was decades ago." Dan's face dropped. "Aren't things different now?"

Maggie reached under the sheets to touch him. "I'd say they are very different."

Dan closed his eyes as he vocalized his pleasure without restraint. "You thrill me. Even with the slightest touch."

Taking her hand out from under the sheets, she ran her

fingers across his lips. "You truly are my sunshine. I'm still the same person, except the wild oats I once yearned to sow have blown away. They've scattered in the wind to faraway places that no longer exist for me." Maggie paused to replay her words. "Well ... most of them, anyway."

His eyes filling with hope, Dan took Maggie's hand in his. "Does this mean you would consider us ... as a couple ... beyond this magical time together? As partners for life?"

Maggie contemplated her thoughts before speaking them. "Yes, Danny, I would. But right now is not our time. Not in the immediate future."

"Is that because you're worried about your health? About the scare you're undergoing?"

"This scare ... God please let it be no more than that ...would not keep me away from you. Yes, of course, I would want to be healthy, but that's not it."

Dan sighed as he tried to hide the frown that followed. "What, then, Maggie?"

Taking hold of his left hand, Maggie held it up. "This, Danny. This ring on your finger. The family you have, the woman you married. They're not something you just walk away from. That's not who you are."

"No, Maggie. That's not who I am. And that's why I've lived the life I have for all these years." Dan paused to reflect. "About a month ago, my younger daughter, Amanda, was in a musical at school. She's fifteen, going on eighteen." He smiled as he thought about her. "There was an afterschool rehearsal, and it ran late, until after eight. Sally was busy so I came home earlier than usual so I could pick her up.

"I waited outside in the car. When Amanda got in, she had this silly grin on her face that I'd never seen before. And then I realized: it must be a boy."

"Oh, how sweet. Young love."

"A bit scary for a dad, but sweet … I think." He sighed. "Anyway, before we drove away, I asked her how the rehearsal went. She was overly enthusiastic about the production, and then she mentioned a boy named Luke. I asked her if Luke was the reason for her smile."

"And? Did she tell you?"

"After she turned a deep crimson, yes."

"I hope she wasn't too embarrassed."

"Only at first. Actually, she was very happy that I had picked up on her happiness. She really wanted to talk about him. Though still a bit red-faced, she said he's the first boy she could have a real conversation with … 'and was hot, too.' The last part scared me a bit, but I was really impressed with her insight and the way she was able to assess the connection they had."

Maggie touched Dan's hand. "You seem upset. Is there more?"

"I suppose so. I have mixed emotions. It was a poignant conversation because my little girl is growing up before my eyes … but it was also a conversation that stunned me, and not because of her affection for Luke."

"How so?"

"Well, Amanda told me that she wasn't ready for a boyfriend, in spite of being fond of Luke, because when she had one, she wanted it to be true love, not like the 'friendship kind of love' that Sally and I have."

"Oh, my!"

"Yes. I was taken aback. And I was upset. I thought I had completely shielded my children from knowing about the platonic relationship their mother and I share, and here my little girl … just ever so nonchalantly … calls it for what it is. When she saw I was upset, she looked worried and mumbled something about how she thought Sally and I knew that the kids knew. 'Dad, it's so obvious,' she said. Then she got flustered, but soon pulled herself back together and went back to telling me how Luke has a new guitar and that he was going to give her lessons on his old one. I started the engine, and we drove home."

Maggie looked sympathetically at Dan before she spoke. "Did you tell Sally?"

"Absolutely not," Dan answered quickly.

"Because?"

"Because Sally is the only one in the family who is content with things as they are. I didn't want to tell her that the kids and I see things differently. I told you yesterday about all of the times I've tried to talk to her … to rekindle our romance. She's not interested, and I've long ceased to be. So you see, my dear, I wouldn't be walking out on someone who is in love with me."

Maggie shook her head and looked down. "Danny, I understand that. But even if she's not in love with you, I've no doubt she loves you … deeply … and as you've said, she loves the life you have together. I can't help you tear that apart."

Dan looked down, his face distorted by pain. A few seconds later, he looked into Maggie's eyes. "Don't I deserve to be happy? You know, on the way home that night, Amanda told me about the play she was in and how she enjoyed playing the character, but she was happy she could step back into her real life. And all I could think about is how I continue to play a character, and I don't have the luxury of stepping into the life I really want … with you. And I've always felt that, long before I saw you again this weekend."

"Oh my love, if it were right, I'd have you move in with me tomorrow. I would love you for the rest of my life. You're special to me in a way that no man has ever been. I have so much love in my heart for you; it's overflowing. But as much as your children may understand the friendship their parents have, they seem okay with that. If you left the family, it would be a very different thing, Danny. Just think: you wouldn't have been around to have that special talk with Amanda. Believe me, it will always matter to her that you were there that night when she wanted to talk about Luke." Maggie let out a long sigh. "They would all be devastated if you left. I don't know your children, but I know they would be. And you know it, too."

Dan covered his face with his hands to hide his agony. After a moment, he took them away and looked at Maggie. "But I have no intention of deserting my children. They're my pride and joy … my heart. They'd still be in my life on an everyday basis. And I'd see them as much as possible. Believe me, they're busier on nights and weekends than I am."

"But Danny, the point is that you're there when they need you. They feel secure as part of a family … a whole family. It would be so painful if you were to leave. My parents divorced when I was ten. I don't wish that on any child, although the larger problem for me was not the divorce as much as it was my parents being more interested in exploiting their respective freedoms than in raising me. Why do you think I was such a wild child?"

"Divorce is not what I ever envisioned for my family. But I'm so in love with you, and at home I'm just existing … in mediocrity."

"You're worlds away from that," Maggie's fingertips delicately stroked the inside of his wrist, then circled the palm of his hand.

Dan stopped to feel the pleasure. "I never knew this part of me to be an erogenous zone."

Maggie smiled. "When I was twenty-three, a ballet dancer I knew from Carnegie Recital Hall, Crane, told me this was one of the most erogenous parts of the body."

"Who knew?" Dan smiled, then turned serious again. "Maggie, are you saying that we can never be together? That I am doomed to live in a loveless marriage forever? And even more importantly ... without you."

"No. And it's not for me to make decisions about your life. But if it comes to be that one day you do leave to be with me, I think, perhaps, you should wait until your youngest child is out of school. Just the way Clare and Colin did."

"But they were still together—nights, weekends, vacations, holidays ..."

"I know. But Sally is nothing like Leah. She deserves more. I don't expect you to stay forever, my love. But let your children grow up in a family that is whole ... even if your marriage is only superficial. Your relationship with your children is not."

"No. My children are everything to me. You know that."

"I do. That's why you must be there for them ... at home ... when they need you. Don't let them worry about their parents splitting up before they graduate high school, even if they know it's not a great love affair. After Kevin graduates from high school, well, then we can reassess. That day is a long way from today. As much as we feel such boundless love, we need to get to know one another in ways we never have before."

"We do. But what happens in the meantime? Before we are truly together?"

Maggie smiled, then reached over and softly kissed his lips. "In the meantime, we'll talk. And we'll have our moments. I don't know how often they'll be. But we'll have them."

"Just moments?"

"My love, there are people lucky enough to live happily throughout each and every day. But for many of us, especially those in my circle, happiness is not a steady companion. It is a friend who visits only in moments, moments that we wait for with unbridled anticipation. And when we wade through difficult waters, we cling to the memories of our joyful moments to calm us, to bring us whatever strength we need to survive. These moments, like the magnificent one we are sharing this weekend, keep us going. Even if we can only smile internally, it sustains us." Maggie paused to fortify herself. "We will always have moments to look back on and moments to look forward to. I can promise that much."

Dan smiled, nodding as he took Maggie's hands in his. "I wish I didn't understand so well, but I do. I've been thinking of it a lot."

"You have? Any particular reason?"

"Believe it or not, it's because of a film I saw a couple years ago with my kids. Not a cheery subject; it was about an apocalypse."

"Oh."

"It's not a film I would have chosen, but Daniel and Kevin wanted to go, and the girls were eager to see it as well. It took place in an unnamed city that had been destroyed beyond recognition. People had died en masse, and the few who survived were going to colossal lengths to remain alive—battling those who threatened them, fighting beasts that rose from the ruins, and going to extraordinary efforts to save their loved ones—only to exist in a heap of rubble where they would continue to struggle for every moment they lived.

"I could see that my children were intrigued by the explosive action in the story, but that part didn't faze me. I just sat there wondering why the people kept going. What was left to fight for? Then I thought about you. If the world ended, and you were out there somewhere, I would never stop looking. I would look for my family, for my parents, and for everyone I love. My point is, although my gut reaction to the film told me that enduring in a dystopian world seemed futile, it occurred to me that the human spirit has a way of soaring past the rational … or, in some cases, the irrational human mind."

"Exactly," Maggie said. "Because as long as those people had life, they had hope. They had moments. Maybe beyond the rubble of that metropolis lay a field where the land was still fertile, where a future was possible. Hope isn't confined to boundaries; it is eternal. It drives us when all feels lost."

"Yes. It does. I remember thinking that there was always something to keep those people going. But I think their greatest impetus to survive was for the joy of being together. Having one another, they could survive anything."

"Absolutely," Maggie said with a poignant smile. "And I pray we never have to go through an apocalypse to prove your hypothesis."

Dan smiled. "I'd like to think our weekend with Leah was the closest we'll ever get to that."

Maggie laughed, then tenderly ran her fingers down his face. "So, for now, Danny, until our fate becomes clear, and it will, let's revel in our moments. Truly, my darling, it's all any of us ever really has."

"And hope," Dan reminded her. "Always hope."

THE END

LISETTE BRODEY is a multi-genre author of seven novels: *Crooked Moon; Squalor, New Mexico; Molly Hacker Is Too Picky!;* The Desert Series*: Mystical High, Desert Star, Drawn Apart*, and *Barrie Hill Reunion.*

Additionally, the author edited and published a book of her mother's poetry (written 50 years earlier) called *My Way to Anywhere* by Dr. Jean Lisette Brodey.

She has also published two short stories in an anthology called *Triptychs (Mind's Eye Series Book 3).*

She is hard at work on her eighth book, a collection of short stories in the literary fiction genre.

She lives in Los Angeles.

* * *

Lisette Brodey can be reached by using the CONTACT button on her website at lisettebrodey.com.

If you enjoyed this book, please consider leaving a review on Amazon.com. It would be greatly appreciated.

facebook.com/BrodeyAuthor/
twitter.com/lisettebrodey

www.ingramcontent.com/pod-product-compliance
Lightning Source LLC
Chambersburg PA
CBHW070632260626
47161CB00007B/2669